Macmillan of Canada
A Division of Canada Publishing Corporation
Toronto, Ontario, Canada

RIDING ON
THE ROAR OF THE
CROWD

Hockey Anthology
mpiled by David Gowdey

Canadian Cataloguing in Publication Data

Main entry under title:
Riding on the roar of the crowd

ISBN 0–7715–9456–9

1. Hockey — Literary collections. 2. Hockey. 3. Canadian literature (English).*
I. Gowdey, David, 1951–

PS8237.H6R53 1989   C810'.8'0355   C89–094503–9
PR9194.52.H6R53 1989

Text and cover design:
David Erland/The Richmond Studio

Macmillan of Canada
A Division of Canada Publishing Corporation
Toronto, Ontario, Canada

Printed in Canada

Sport, as a popular art form, is not just self-expression, but is deeply and necessarily a means of interplay within an entire culture. Rocket Richard, the Canadian hockey player, used to comment on the poor acoustics of some arenas. He felt that the puck off his stick rode on the roar of the crowd.

—**Marshall McLuhan**

Contents

Foreword

ORIGINS

IN THE ARENA

MOVING IN ALONE

Credits

Foreword

When hockey took to the ice in the seventeenth century, hundreds of players at a time joined in, skating all day and into the night, sticking torches into the snowbanks for light. The game was played almost without rules until about 1870, when clubs in Halifax, Kingston and Montreal decided to try to tame it. We can argue about how well they succeeded.

Although it seems transparently simple on the surface, hockey is as intricate as jazz, or a classical fugue. Ten players improvise more or less continuously, acting, reacting, accenting each other, turning mistakes to advantage. They glide down the ice in combinations, soar and collide, then break up and re-form into new patterns, like water or wind-swept snow. The moments of beauty change and vanish quickly but our impressions of the game and of those who play it stay with us all our lives.

The hockey figures in this book — Jean Beliveau, Max Bentley, Wayne Gretzky, Ken Dryden, Vladislav Tretiak, Fred Shero, Eddie Shore, Eric Nesterenko, among others — are not exactly heroes. They are more like images of possibility, representing an assortment of styles and attitudes, different ways of using the skills at hand that reflect different approaches to life. Other voices — Hugh Hood, Brian Fawcett, Jack Batten, Ken Brown, Roy McGregor, Hugh MacLennan — speak here too, each delving into the mystery of the game and the hold that it has on us.

It's easy to over-romanticize sports, to give them a significance they can't contain, yet they offer us more than excitement or empty metaphor. In early societies sport originated during ritual festivals. Contests were added to the ceremonial rites, and were designed to evoke peak experiences within common boundaries through a shared series of events. By focussing attention on these events, and then giving free, or nearly free, access to everyone, sports roused communal emotion and involvement to levels seldom reached before. In classical Greece, drama and sport both originated in the festivals at Mount Olympus. The first plays were an outgrowth of the festival games and were always highly competitive, with spectators backing their favourite dramatist the same way they backed a hometown sports champion.

Today, in societies swamped with formulaic narratives and gloomy reportage, sports provide us with immediate, often unpredictable, drama. They offer passage into another reality, a parallel world, where life-long loyalties still abide and emotions are still worn on the sleeve. Beyond that, they offer visual pleasures rarely found in day-to-day life. C. L. R. James, in a classic study of cricket, wrote that people are attracted to sports because participants display "significant form", in the manner of other fine arts. He quotes Ernest Haas, the photographer, who believed that "Motion, the perfection of motion, is what the people come to see", and adds,

> That flow . . . men since they have been men have always sought and always will. It is an unspeakable impertinence to arrogate the term 'fine art' to one small section of this quest and declare it to be culture. Luckily, the people refuse to be bothered.

Hockey is the one truly Canadian art form, despite its three-thousand-year history. As an art, its range is limited, and there is much that it cannot express, but its constant themes — movement, flair, courage — are the underlying material of all art. The painter Joan Miro discovered the game while living in New York City; he loved it, and I don't think it's too fanciful to suggest that some of its lines turned up in his paintings. There's a moment of harmony in a pretty play that makes it seem both inevitable and effortless — the stride into the open, the neat sidestep, the pass to the breaking man, the shot ringing in off the post.

I once tried to design a board game based on hockey, but a friend said it couldn't be done. You can't plan to score a goal, he said: "On the ice you don't know what you'll do until you start to do it." He was right, and the instinctual side of the game is its greatest appeal — it's the opposite of the way we normally act.

Spontaneity is blunted by ordinary life, particularly in northern countries, where people live indoors together for months at a time and passions must be held in check. Northerners are more polite, more reserved, more skeptical; we need to think everything through before we commit ourselves. But there's no time for that in a hockey game. When plays develop at thirty miles an hour there's only an instant to make your move, and if it works it's truly satisfying. Through the long winter nights hockey brings blood back to the surface, dramatizes and intensifies ways of being, releases speed and anger and grace, reminds us how much we can care.

As I collected the material I was struck by how many of my own memories returned, memories not only of the game but of seemingly unconnected events. When we experience something in the course of events, we may or may not be able to recall it later; but if the event is accompanied by a charge of emotion it will sear itself into the brain. Hockey runs on emotion, and can be a way back into our past. We remember not only what happened on the ice but what was happening at the same time in our lives. I hope the book works that way for you — I know it does for me.

David Gowdey
May 1989

Part 1

ORIGINS

Hockey captures the essence of the Canadian experience in the New World. In a land so inescapably and inhospitably cold, hockey is the dance of life, an affirmation that despite the deadly chill of winter we are alive.
— **Bruce Kidd**

A nation's character and soul is typified by its dances.
— **Boris Volkoff**

Never mind the damn puck — let's start the game.
— **Red Dutton**

HUGH MACLENNAN

Fury on Ice

HOCKEY NIGHT IN MONTREAL. The crowds on their way to the Forum from buses, trams and cars walk bowed against the winter wind — but who cares how cold it is? The colder the better, for hockey is a game that goes with frosty breaths, fur caps and overshoes, thick gloves that you beat together when the swirling players produce emotion so intense you couldn't stand it in July.

Inside the Forum the air is clear and cold — much colder than in most American arenas, but warm compared to Canadian rinks before the days of artificial ice. Overhead lights are blazing and the remaining empty seats show banks of gray, blue or orange according to price and location. Talk swells and echoes as the seats fill up — eight thousand, now ten, now fourteen thousand — until you look up and see that even the catwalks above the lights and the television cameras are black with people. Smooth, clean and white, the ice spreads out between the waist-high boards, drawing everyone's eyes, for the ice itself is a part of the drama of this game and the coloured lines beneath the frozen water make its expanse seem larger than it is. There are three lines across the rink. A broad red one transversely bisects the ice and runs between the giant C's of the home-club's insignia in the exact centre of the rink. Between the red line and each of the two goals runs a line of deep blue. Besides being decorative, these three lines determine the offsides, red marking the limit for a forward pass by the defenders, blue for the attackers. The two goals at either end of the rink and a few feet out from the boards look very empty. Even a child could bat a puck into them now.

There is a stir in the crowd, a spatter of handclaps, then a rising thunder. From the players' benches in the centre on opposite sides of the rink the two teams debouch onto the ice. *Les Canadiens* of Montreal, once known as the Flying Frenchmen, are receiving the Red Wings of Detroit.

Gerry McNeil of Montreal and Terry Sawchuk of Detroit, bulky in their goalies' pads and swaying as they move, skate slowly to their cages, turn about and face down the ice. From now until the game ends those nets will seem to shrink in size, because two men with nerves of steel and the reflexes of leopards — two men who have calculated shot angles to a fraction of an inch — crouch before them to keep the puck from getting past.

Now begins the invariable ritual that precedes every hockey game. We have seen it countless times but it always looks fresh. The warm-up begins and the players stream round and round their own halves of the rink, shooting at their own goalies, a pouring of red jerseys at the Detroit end, of white ones at the end defended by Montreal. With the warm-up come the familiar sounds — the ring and snick of skate blades and the special noises made by the puck. Against the goalies' pads the puck hits with a heavy thud: in close stickhandling it clucks: when it strikes the crossbar of the goal it gives out a loud clang; it makes a flat crack against the broad blade of the goalie's stick, and when it misses the goal and hits the boards it sends a reverberating bang through the whole arena. These puck and skate noises excite the crowd like a bugle before a horse race and thousands of men can almost feel their hands closing over a hockey stick as their recollections range back ten, twenty, perhaps even fifty years to a time when hockey was never played in a forum like this with red and blue lines, with artificial ice and comfortable seats and television, with French and English radio announcers reporting the game in frenetic voices to a listening nation and to hundreds of thousands of Americans.

A few minutes before 8:30 the referee and the offside judges glide onto the ice looking neat and small in their white jerseys and dark blue trousers. The teams line up, each on its own blueline facing toward centre ice, sticks held downward on the ice before them. The audience rises for the national anthem. The players look enormous because of their bulky pads and the added height given by skates. Their colored jerseys and long colored stockings are bright against the shining ice.

On the last note of music a roar bursts from the crowd, the alternate players skate off to the benches behind the boards, the goalies hunch forward, the centres bend for the face-off, the two wings and two defensemen on each side tense themselves, the referee gives a last look around to make sure there are no more than twelve men on the ice. Then, as he drops the puck, the black sweep hand of the huge clock at the end of the amphitheatre begins to revolve.

From now until the game ends that clock will share the drama. It will measure out sixty minutes of playing time, it will stop whenever there is a goal made, an offside, a penalty or one of those outbursts of wrath or enthusiasm in the crowd vented by throwing rubbers and overshoes onto the ice. It will rest for ten minutes after the first period and for ten minutes after the second, but compared to the time clock of a football game, it will move fast. There are few delays in ice hockey, and such long ones as do occur are exciting, for they are generally caused by a donnybrook.

The fact that there may be a donnybrook tonight adds to the excitement of this rabid Montreal crowd. For these two clubs, Canadiens and Red Wings, are not only the best in the world this season: there is so little to choose between them that the smallest kind of break — a glancing puck, a screened shot, a penalty at a bad moment — will probably decide the outcome. It is said these teams hate each other. They don't really. They merely behave as the Dodgers and Giants would if they carried sticks and could crash into each other at a combined speed of forty miles an hour.

There is Ted Lindsay of Detroit, finest left wing in the game, truculent and jaunty; merely looking at him makes some people mad. His mate on right wing is big Gordie Howe, top point-getter in the league, his superb skating legs built like tree trunks. Once he was even-tempered and smiling, but since his nearly fatal accident a few years ago he has become one of the bad men in the league. On defense for Detroit are Red Kelly and Marcel Pronovost. Names like Pronovost, once found almost exclusively in the line-up of the Canadiens, are now dotted through American-based clubs. They are good names in hockey, for this game suits the Gallic *élan*. Kelly also has a good name for hockey and at present is the finest defenseman alive. This is one Irishman who would rather play than fight, for Kelly more than once has won the Lady Byng Trophy for gentlemanly play.

But this a Montreal crowd and it worships its own heroes extravagantly. Ahead of them all is Maurice Richard, the Rocket, who breaks the league's all-time scoring record (his own) every time he drives a puck through the goal posts. He too was once amiable, but ten years of being close-checked and nagged by lesser men have given him a trigger temper, and in the matter of collecting penalties, the Rocket is right up front with Lindsay and Howe. Richard is the Babe Ruth of hockey, as powerful and as unpredictable. Smoldering darkly, he glides in and out, often playing two or three nights without showing a spark of brilliance, but on the fourth night he will explode — and nobody ever forgets the sight. There never was a hockey player with the Rocket's power to focus a crowd's emotion and jerk their hearts out. I have seen him — what follower of the Canadiens has not? — go careening in on a single skate with one enemy wrapped around his neck and another dogging his elbows, his eyes blazing yet so cool for all his heat that he will draw the goalie a few inches away from the spot he has picked and blast the puck into it. No man ever lived who could get a shot away faster than the Rocket. And when he breaks through, he seems to do so by sheer force of passion.

On defense for the Canadiens are two happy warriors, huge Butch Bouchard and smooth Doug Harvey. Butch is the team's policeman, amiable as most French-Canadians are if unprovoked, but when slashed so dangerous that the clinic prepares to receive his provoker. Among those on the bench who will shortly appear are Jean-Marc Beliveau, *le gros Bill*, mourned by the whole of Quebec City when he left his home town to play in the National Hockey League. Also on the bench is Boom-Boom Geoffrion whom I once saw score a goal while unconscious. Releasing a terrific shot from the blue line just as a checker crashed into him, he was knocked out an instant before the puck struck the net.

As for the two men who guard the goals, they seem miraculous to me. Other hockey players work in hot blood, but the goalie crouches and waits for pucks that flash at him at ninety miles an hour from point-blank range. I have seen a goalie led off the ice with nine teeth knocked out — and return ten minutes later to shut out the opposition. In 1936 I once saw two goalies, Normie Smith of the Red Wings and Lorne Chabot of the old Montreal Maroons, hold their forts intact from 8:30 on the Tuesday evening when the game began until about 2:25 the following Wednesday morning, when Modere Bruneteau won the game for Detroit with a screened shot. That Stanley Cup playoff — a Stanley Cup game can never end in a draw and if the teams are tied at the end of regulation play they continue until a goal is scored — lasted so long that we saw nearly three full matches for the price of one.

Now the charging lines sweep down on the defenses. They crash in, the pattern of the attack is shattered, the puck shoots off into a corner. There is a scramble, then out of chaos a new pattern forms and the red jerseys of Detroit pour down into the white jerseys of the Canadiens, the puck darts from stick to stick, a shot at the goal, a deflection to the side of the net, another counterattack and the puck is held in the Detroit end. A whistle blows, the first lines skate off and the second lines replace them. The puck is dropped again and the game goes on at the same furious pace; the goals are defended so expertly it seems impossible to score, and everyone knows that this is a game that can be decided in a single second. Somebody elbows someone into the boards, the referee signals the timekeeper and the little red light comes on beside the penalty clock.

Penalties are the climactic moments of a hockey game, for when one team plays for two or five minutes with a man short, the other throws in its first line for a power play. For the next two minutes the crowd utters a steady thunder of yells and jeers to ease its tension. The pace is frantic as the defenders work to keep the puck at the other end of the ice and the attackers battle for a goal. The shouting, gasping crowd shares all the passion of the wild struggle, feeling a part of its fury. Hockey is like that — it makes those who love it feel bigger, bolder, stronger, faster and more reckless than they really are. A shot, a rebound, another shot, still another save, another scramble, a razzle-dazzle of rapid passes and another shot misses the goal and crashes into the boards. The defense breaks loose and lofts the puck down the ice and the attackers have to go back for it. In the brief moment it takes them to re-group and send another attacking pattern down the ice, the crowd glances up to the scoreboard to see how much longer the penalty has to run. Eighteen seconds more. High in the rafters announcers as excited as anyone in the arena are screaming in French and English the progress of the game. "He's going in there on the left side — a pass out — there's a scramble in front of the goal — Richard has it — he SHOOTS — *HE SCORES!!!*"

And when he does so, like an instantaneous *panache* of triumph, a red light blazes on behind the goal. Sawchuk digs the puck nonchalantly out of the corner of his net and bats it down to the referee at center ice. He looks up at the clock and sees there are about forty-eight minutes left. Then he bends forward and faces down-ice again. The puck is dropped almost instantly and the game is under way again.

Natives of Spain and Mexico find incomprehensible the initial reaction of most foreigners to the bullfight. Canadians feel the same way when strangers express horror at the violence of ice hockey. They even query the novitiate's assumption that the chief attraction is speed.

If you rave to a hockey player about the speed of the game, he is likely to inform you that speed is secondary to the ability to stickhandle, swerve, break your pace, and to stay on your feet after the shock of a body check; speed is by no means as important as all-round skating ability. No Canadian has won a world's speed-skating championship in the last quarter century, but hockey players like Aurel Joliat and Toe Blake, who were never particularly fast, were nonetheless incomparably finer skaters than the men who race, just as cowboys are better all-round horsemen than jockeys. Speed-skating is only a kind of running on skates, but in hockey the skates of the player are so integrated with his body and brain that they become a part of his personality. The good hockey player never lurches, strains or runs. Watch him closely and see how he glides.

During one of the relatively rare delays that hold up the progress of a hockey game, I watched Maurice Richard skating around in that restless way he has. For what must have been a half minute, his blades never once left the ice. This kind of skating enables a hockey player to last for years despite the game's violence. Men like Elmer Lach and Milt Schmidt, in early middle age, could glide through a maze of hard-driving youngsters and appear the swiftest men on the ice when in fact they were taking their time. They moved from the hips rather than from the thighs and calves, and they drove hard only when putting on that extra burst of speed that took them through the defense. Even the huge Ching Johnson was this kind of skater, otherwise he could never have played NHL hockey in his fortieth year. Skating ability of this sort must be learned in childhood, and that is why men from this land of long winters dominate the hockey world. Of the great hockey players only Eddie Shore and the late Lionel Conacher developed skating technique after the age of fourteen.

The violence of hockey is another matter, for though some of it is encouraged by rink owners for its shock value, most of it is a part of the game itself.

Next to the Swedes and Swiss, Canadians in their daily lives are probably as self-restrained as any people in the world. By comparison, Americans often seem as volatile as Latins. Yet the favorite sports of Americans are neat, precise games like baseball and college football. Baseball I dearly love, but after growing up with hockey, I find American college football as slow as an American finds a week-long cricket match; even its violence seems cold to me. But the violence of hockey is hot, and the game at its best is played by passionate men. To spectator and player alike, hockey gives the release that strong liquor gives to a repressed man. It is the counterpoint of the Canadian self-restraint, it takes us back to the fiery blood of Gallic and Celtic ancestors who found themselves minorities in a cold, new environment and had to discipline themselves as all minorities must. But Canadians take the ferocity of their national game so much for granted that when an American visitor makes polite mention of it, they look at him in astonishment. Hockey — violent? Well, perhaps it is a little. But hockey was always like that and it doesn't mean that we're a violent people.

We are, though — underneath the surface. And our national game breeds heroes who are worshipped as frantically as Babe Ruth and Joe DiMaggio ever were. Nor do any athletes earn their hero worship in a harder field.

At the start of each season, a professional hockey player knows that he faces almost certain injury of a pretty spectacular kind. By the time he retires he has lost count of the stitches taken in various parts of his anatomy. Stick and skate gashes, broken jaws, cheekbones, teeth, collarbones, ribs, ankles, and legs; shoulder separations, sprains and dislocations are so common in hockey that teams seldom take the ice at full strength. Any difference in ability between the best teams in the National Hockey League is so slight that the Stanley Cup is usually won by the club which enters the playoffs with the fewest injuries. Yet in the entire history of the NHL, only one player has died as the result of a rink accident, and only one other has come close to death.

The one who died was Howie Morenz, the greatest all-round forward and the most beloved hockey player the game has known. Morenz has been compared to Babe Ruth, but he was much more like Walter Johnson; he had Johnson's rare combination of speed, power and gentleness, and there was something in his style that made everyone love him. I was in the Forum that January night in 1937 when his career ended. He had been playing marvelously that evening and the little smile on his lips showed that he was having a wonderful time. But once too often he charged into the corner relying on his ability to turn on a dime and come out with the puck. The point of one of his skates impaled itself in the boards. A defenseman, big Earl Seibert, accidentally crashed over the extended leg and broke it. Howie's head hit the ice with a sickening crack and he was carried out. Six weeks later, as a result of the brain injury, he died.

The all-but-fatal accident involved Ace Bailey and the great Eddie Shore, and Shore was almost as much a victim as the man he nearly killed. Yet, in spite of the censure Shore received, this was surely an accident. It was Shore's reputation for violence that made everyone assume that he had assaulted Bailey deliberately. And indeed, what the crowd saw that December night in Boston looked like a brutal, unprovoked attack. They saw Shore charge into Bailey at full speed and smash him to the ice. They saw big Red Horner, the Leafs' defenseman, drop his stick and slug Shore unconscious with his fist. But the crowd did not hear Shore murmur in anguish afterward that he had never even seen Ace Bailey, that he had been stunned by a body check and did not know he had crashed into him. Shore would have been held for manslaughter if Bailey had died, but fortunately Bailey recovered, and when he was well enough to talk he exonerated Shore. He himself had no idea what hit him.

There have been other donnybrooks far worse than the Ace Bailey affair. The worst of them involved that legendary character, Sprague Cleghorn, who played defense with his brother Odie for the Canadiens in the early 1920s. In 1923, in a playoff with the old Ottawa Senators, Sprague crosschecked Lionel Hitchman across the face and seriously injured him. And a few minutes before this event it was a miracle that Cy Denneny was not killed by another Canadien. This is how the staid Montreal *Gazette* described what happened to Denneny:

"Denneny scored from the boards on the south side of the rink and after the puck had lodged behind Vezina, the Ottawa wing started to coast around behind the net. Couture followed in behind and with his stick struck him over the back of the head, sending him rolling over and over on the ice to come finally to a stop twenty feet away."

Several riots interrupted this game. At one time twenty Montreal cops were fighting for their lives with the mob. Those who claim that modern hockey is rougher than it used to be are extremely forgetful.

But not even the old-time hockey player was a stumble bum. Two famous veterans of the hockey wars, Lionel Conacher and Bucko Mcdonald, have been members of Canada's Federal Parliament. (Bucko still is, but last spring in the annual softball game between the M.P.'s and the Press Gallery, Conacher dropped dead of a heart attack.) A good many more have won prominence in business and the professions, and once their blood has cooled, they look back on their old hockey-playing selves in wonder. Kenny Reardon in his day was one of the most fearsome men in the league — he was once forced to post a thousand-dollar bond to keep the peace for the rest of the season. Not long ago he confessed with wry amusement that he could not understand how he had ever been like that.

It was the hot excitement of hockey that made him like that. A natural aristocrat like Lester Patrick, who did more to develop the game than any other single individual, contrived to manage a hockey team without losing either his temper or his sense of proportion and his sons Lynn and Murray, now coaches, share a little of their father's detachment. But they are exceptions.

Far more typical among the coaches is Dick Irvin of the Canadiens, who feels about a losing team the way John Knox felt about sin. And of course there is Connie Smythe of the Leafs who coined the phrase, "If you can't lick them outside in the alley, you can't lick them inside in the rink." Smythe was arrested for punching a fan in Boston the night Ace Bailey was injured. Smythe can be heard screaming at his team over the roar of fourteen thousand people in Maple Leaf Gardens, and if he had had the size and ability he would have been a terror on the iceways, for he never asked his boys to do anything he wouldn't have tried to do himself.

If the men who play hockey professionally are a projection of the emotions of millions of their countrymen, it is because all Canadian boys put on skates and begin to knock a pseudo-puck around as soon as they can hold a stick. Inevitably they grow up projecting themselves into the jerseys of big-league giants.

In any small Canadian town — like Chicoutimi up the Saguenay River, Owen Sound on the windy shore of Georgian Bay, a tank village on the C.P.R. tracks west of Lake Superior, or a collection of raw frame houses under a towering grain elevator on the prairies — the kids coming home from school are stick handling along the streets. Years ago there wasn't much traffic and the snow was shiny-smooth from sleigh runners. Twenty years ago even an average player in the NHL was superior as a stick handler to any but a handful of the men in the league today.

The first Canadian teams to play for American cities in the NHL circuit — Boston, New York, Chicago and Detroit — contained superb stickhandlers and passers, and because of them hockey became a popular spectacle in the United States. There were the Cook brothers and Frankie Boucher of the New York Rangers who swirled through a defense in a razzle-dazzle of elliptical curves. There was that glorious Canadien line led by Howie Morenz with Aurel Joliat on left wing and Billy Boucher on right. There was that powerhouse of a line that played for Toronto — Primeau, Conacher and Jackson. A little later Detroit won the Stanley Cup with one of the lightest lines in hockey — Aurie, Barry and Lewis — whose stickhandling and passing made them lethal. Even some of the old defensemen were rare puck-jugglers, men like Babe Siebert, King Clancy and Hap Day.

In the little towns from which so many of those puck artists came, the kids were on the ponds or makeshift rinks as soon as school was out. Nobody skated without a stick in his hands, and if frostbitten feet had been a deterrent there would have been no hockey players. The boards of the rink were slapped together by the local carpenter, goals and scrapers made by the blacksmith, and the rink cleared of snow by the kids themselves. On clear afternoons when frigid air pinched the nostrils and made noses run, when the sky changed from deep blue through pale blue to aquamarine and rose, those rinks were a focus for the yells of all the kids in town. You could see their bright-colored jerseys weaving in and out, toques or peaked caps on their heads, and always there were one or two who would hold your eye. They were the ones who made their shoulders swerve one way while their feet went the other, who sliced through a melee with their heads up and the puck controlled as if their sticks were extensions of their arms.

Often there was a shack nearby where skates could be changed and hands warmed beside a hot stove. The stove was tended by a bad-tempered old man in galoshes who sold chocolate bars and soft drinks. The air was hot and foul, and the old man's perpetual refrain was, "Shut the door — and keep it shut!" To this day there are millions of Canadians who can't see a potbellied, rusty old stove without feeling nostalgia for a happy youth. It reminds a man of ice in the hair of his temples, of rime in his eyebrows, and of the lovely swollen feeling of throbbing feet after supper when he pretended to do his lessons.

As the maturity of a growing sport is reckoned, ice hockey is now in the adolescent stage reached by baseball in the era of John McGraw, which may be one explanation for the delicacy with which team managers and coaches refer to one another in public. Nearly a hundred years have passed since those legendary British officers of the Kingston or Halifax garrison (nobody knows which for sure) first began to bat ground-hockey balls about on frozen ponds while skating. Like so many games played the world over, ice hockey was an English invention.

But it took the climate and the nature of Canada to make it the game it is today. As early as 1893 there were enough representative Canadian teams playing hockey in regular leagues for Lord Stanley, then Governor-General, to buy himself immortality with the fifty-dollar piece of ugly silverware which still stands for the hockey championship of the world. A loosely formed hockey league was established in 1903 or 1904: oddly enough, in Michigan, though its stars were Canadians like Hod Stuart and Cyclone Taylor. The professional ice-hockey league that became the real forerunner of today's NHL began operations in 1909. Thirty years have passed since the Boston Bruins became the first American-based club in the NHL. About the same time, Canadian students made the game popular in Europe, and during the depression several hundred jobless men of mediocre hockey ability worked their way over from Canada on freighters and eked out a living by playing hockey in London, Paris, Prague, Vienna and Milan. Since the last war even Russia has taken up the game, and early in 1954 a team of MVD men called the Moscow Dynamos beat a fourth-rate Canadian outfit for the so-called amateur championship of the world.

This defeat at the hands of the Soviets caused some guilty self-questioning across Canada, for never before had a Canadian team, not even a fourth-rate one, been handled like this in international competition. Connie Smythe offered to take his Leafs to Moscow to show the Russians what real hockey was like. The Russians stalled by saying they lacked a suitable rink, and Frankie Boucher remarked that even if the Russians did accept, Connie should be restrained by the government because the Leafs are the roughest team in the NHL. "What's he trying to do," Boucher said, "start the third world war?" Just the same, it should surprise no one if the Russians accept a similar offer in a few years. Those state-supported Soviet teams are learning to play the kind of hockey we used to play twenty years ago. Regardless of what rink owners and coaches say, that was better than the kind of hockey in vogue now.

Another change which has altered the appearance of hockey was the introduction of the red line across center ice. The original purpose of the red line was laudable. Before it was introduced, a concentrated power play could hold the puck inside the defenders' blue line for minutes at a time, frequently until a goal was scored out of a scramble around the net. With eleven players jammed together in that small space, checking and smashing at each other, it was extremely difficult for the defense to work the puck clear into center ice, for a forward pass across their own blue line was offside and the play was recalled. But unhappily this change of rule was introduced at a time when coaches and club owners had begun to practice far more substitutions than had been common before.

With the game opened up by the long forward pass, it was now speeded up beyond the point of maximum beauty and skill. Coaches now use four different forward lines and sometimes add a few specialty players for good measure. Often a forward stays on the ice for less than a minute at a time. During that minute he skates frantically, harrying the star he is sent out to check. It is like sending a relay team of sprinters out to defeat Roger Bannister in a mile run. In this hurry-scurry hockey, stick handling no longer seems as essential as it once was, and the pace can be stepped up so fast that a true passing pattern cannot be developed. The NHL authorities insist that the modern game is so fast that the old-timers couldn't compete with it. So it is. But that argument proves only that two second-raters in any sport can beat a single first-rater. The real reason for the speedup has been the conviction that it carries more crowd appeal. Perhaps it does — to those who don't understand the fine points of hockey. But few who grew up with the game have been convinced that this new style is as satisfactory as the old one in which patterned rushes swept the rink from end to end.

Little of the box-office cynicism found in the modern game is innate in the players. In spite of their big salaries, the men you see on the rinks are there because they love the game. They play in the largest cities of America, but most of them are small-town boys at heart and carry with them the small-town spirit.

In any Canadian small town there used to be three public buildings that were always recognizable. One was the railway station, another the post office and the third was the skating rink. Modern methods of freezing ice, as well as preference for watching sport from the living room instead of from ringside seats, have closed most of the old skating rinks. But there are still a few around and they all look the same: big brown barns with sway-backed roofs. They were called hippodromes, coliseums, forums, arenas or simply "the rink." Their roofs were intended only to keep snow off the ice and the rough benches on which spectators sat. Except on hockey nights, the doors and windows were kept wide open, the interior temperature being considered ideal if no higher than ten above zero. Hockey was designed to be played on fast, hard ice; it slows down when the puck is sloshed about on a wet or sticky surface.

Of course, the spectators in the days of those old rinks were almost as crazy as the players. They arrived wearing furs or heavy ulsters, stocking caps, two pairs of socks and often carrying Hudson Bay blankets. Even with this protection they were in danger of frostbite, for in prairie towns like Brandon or Prince Albert the night temperatures could easily fall to forty below. So the crowds stomped their feet and their breath steamed out in clouds to mingle with the fumes of the boiling coffee they swallowed between periods. And the players got more fun out of it than they do these days because there were few substitutions. They would have caught pneumonia if they had sat waiting on the benches for ten minutes at a time as some do now.

Players and spectators were close in body and spirit then because every spectator was a player himself. That is why hockey these last fifty years has taken such a grip on the imagination of Canadians that it seems a part of their lives. That is also why the small towns which have kept their rinks in repair still supply the best hockey players.

Look at their faces as they pour off the bench and melt into the game without stopping the play. Intense, strong, tough and cocky — but also guileless and still amateurs at heart, carrying on the tradition of old-timers like Newsy Lalonde, who didn't so much play hockey for money as he accepted money to enable him to continue playing. In all its violent history, there has never been the slightest hint of a hockey game being fixed.

In the spring of 1954 when the Canadiens lost the final match of the Stanley Cup play-offs in overtime to Detroit, Elmer Lach (too old to be on the ice and knowing it) said, as he hung up his skates for good, that he would gladly give five years of his life to have scored just one more goal. Nobody thought he was insincere. Hockey breeds that sort of passion in those who love the game.

DOUG BEARDSLEY

The Sheer Joy of Shinny

SHINNY WAS THE FIRST DELIGHT of the first people. Among the native Wichita, the first man, whose name was Darkness, was guided to the Light by the flight of a shinny ball.

The game was played on a hard level of beach laid bare by the spring ebb tides. A Clackamas Chinook tale begins: "People lived there. . . . They played shinny all day long. When it became evening the children were still playing. The villagers told them in vain, 'Quit now. It is night now.' They did not listen. They played only the more. They said to them, 'It might happen that you scare out something there if you don't go inside at dusk.'"

Another myth tells how everyone in the village played together "at shinny ball, its name is shinny stick. The stick is bent. Once it goes to the goal each period, the wooden shinny ball. On each side are ten men, and so twenty men, young men, played shinny. And that was very dangerous, long ago it was a bad game. If he was hit by a shinny stick, he would split open, his hand would be broken open. He might be struck by the wooden shinny ball in the head or face, he would be split open on his chest. If he got hit he would be bruised. And too, some men hit each other, they fought. It was bad to play shinny ball." Obviously shinny had a reputation not unlike hockey had in the 1970s. In a later West Coast tale, the face of Wildcat is smashed into its present shape by a shinny stick.

We need no anthropologists to tell us that the shinny stick may have been analogous to the club of the war gods or that it was often seen as the male artifact. Animals often joined the game and played with their tails. You were not allowed to hit your opponent over the head but you were allowed to upset your fellow players by running against them and checking them to the ground.

The shinny ball was not the dirty grey tennis ball we use on the street today. In fact in some native societies the shinny ball of shining wood represented the sun. It was often made of a wood-knot of cedar bark or of buckskin decorated with elaborate bead work. It could not be touched with the hand but could be struck or kicked with the stick or foot. The shinny stick was invariably curved and expanded at the shooting end (one thinks of a lacrosse stick or the machine-made curve of our modern blade) and was sometimes painted or carved. Up until the 1860s the game was played with a ball much like a lacrosse ball.

From this mythic beginning it is easy to see shinny as a symbolic play of life, a realized ancient ritual *and* a carefree improvised game, taking us back to an unknown ancestral past. It was — and is — played in all northern countries, even in Scotland where the word originated from Scottish dialect to depict the whack of the stick against the shin, though our own Iroquois and Algonquin lay equal claim to this hypothesis.

In his book *Hockey Night in Canada*, Foster Hewitt traces shinny's first home back to the Greeks of 500 B.C. Certainly ancient Danes and twelfth-century Anglo-Saxons attached bones to their feet and skated. It is not improbable that they took field hockey sticks out on that same ice. In *Open Net*, George Plimpton pays homage to the patron saint of skaters, Saint Sydarina of Schieden, shown wearing skates in an early fifteenth-century Dutch illustration. The woodcut shows her falling to the ice; the caption tells us she broke a rib. She could have used a hockey stick for support. And early eighteenth-century Dutch have artistic evidence of "Figures a la mode" with bone skates and wooden sticks.

It would seem the games of ball hockey, bandy, hurley, and shinty have been around a long time. Private papers, letters, and legends tell us that English troops played the game in Canada as far back as 1783. In his book, Hewitt quotes a nineteenth-century historian: "Most of the soldier boys were quite at home on skates. They could cut the figure eight and other fancy figures, but shinny was their first delight." Not long ago Allen Abel reported from Siberia of Russian boys who batted "an orange ball about the frozen taiga...using splintered sticks." This "outdoor progenitor of Soviet hockey (is) played by teams of eleven tireless men on enormous expanses of ice." The wide-open shinny that results from such free-flowing contests develops the skills of controlling the puck, stickhandling, and pinpoint passing seldom seen in the NHL these days. The huge ice surface also lends itself to the backtracking, criss-crossing, and weaving that Russian national teams excel in. Abel reports that the Soviet Union has even held international bandy tournaments, hosting teams from the U.S. and Europe, but Canada, where shinny and floor hockey are played by millions, young and old, has never entered a team.

Everyone who ever played hockey has memories of shinny called pond hockey, street hockey, or boot hockey, depending on what part of the country you grew up in. A friend of mine remembers how he used to go to senior hockey games and "hang around the players' benches to collect the broken hockey sticks for road hockey or 'horse apples' as it used to be called. With some shellac and tape we'd fix those sticks up for shinny. In those days a stick cost $1.75, which was a day's pay. It was very expensive. A CCM bicycle was $48.00 (we're speaking of the mid-thirties) and the minimum wage prior to the war was that much per month. So you took good care of those discarded hockey sticks."

They always came at midnight. It was as mysterious to us as Santa Claus. As kids, and later as teenagers, we'd wait with rising anticipation and increasing tension as November drew near. Each day it grew colder. We'd walk our regular route to school, then suddenly detour the necessary few blocks to see if the municipal employees we called "park workies" had put up the boards and strung the lights. Each night, on the pretense of phoning one another to discuss a problem in our algebra homework, a two-word message, indecipherable to parents, was whispered as a sign-off: "Not yet."

The freezing days of early winter were welcomed with a conviction that could only come from winter people. How many mornings did our skates and sticks become an army of makeshift shovels scraping and flaying the protective snow to reveal the mirror-like surface beneath? At one time Montreal had over 250 outdoor hockey rinks scattered throughout the city. Most of these were in parks; a few were parking lots that would remain icy all winter.

One grew into shinny; it was a coming out of the house and a coming of age on the street. Now one had to perform. The fact that we were out on the street and not yet on the ice didn't matter. We were on stage, performing the epistle according to Foster Hewitt. Shinny is sheer fun, the comedy of ice hockey. The attraction of shinny is the comradeship. Yet even in shinny there is the sense of preparing for battle, putting on the equipment and reaching for the tools of the gladiator. Perhaps the comradeship is there because of the sense of preparing for battle. Other sports, such as football, operate out of lockers; in those early days hockey meant open space.

Shinny begins in the street. David Moore, a friend of mine from Montreal, recalls: "For us it was Wicksteed Avenue. It was a residential street, close enough to the group of us that usually got together. The major hockey rink was just down the street; while our game of shinny was in progress, we could see the lights of the hockey rink and that added something to the magic of the night.

"I played with Trevor Sevigny — who we called Sevenaxe — and David Chown, who had one brother who hit the big time with the football Alouettes. Sometimes the younger Chowns would come along but usually it was Sevigny, Chown, Leslie Arter, John Stafford, who came all the way from Balfour Avenue several blocks away, and Doug Stafford, Doug Lawson, and me. Within that group there were subgroups who would often band together, or sometimes, as in the game of Risk, make alliances to rule the world and then, in midstream, stab their neighbour in the back. And so it is with shinny. That's why it was so important to have one's friendships solid before the game began. In the midst of a play — in mid-stride — you could unexpectedly lose a trusted ally.

"If you had a good friend, as I had in Doug Lawson — the two of us were loners — well, we had a friendship that survived shinny and survived many changes of life. Each time we showed up at one of these shinny games I knew that he would cover my back and that I would cover his. When he got the ball he'd look around for me to whack it to. We always played with a tennis ball, of course, a frozen, ugly, unforgiving, little tennis ball. If it hit you in a place where you were unprotected it could really sting.

"But what I remember lovingly about the game of shinny was the galloping and the sound of the boots on the snow. I never could afford a pair of aviator boots that most kids wore. All my friends had them, but Doug Lawson and I came from more straight-laced homes where aviator boots were not seen to be a necessity of life. We couldn't afford the ones with the flaps that came down that had such authority and looked so casual.

"Lawson was nicknamed Rat, a name which has followed him through life among the people who knew him back then. He would stand close to the goal and deflect others' shots into the net. He got to be quite good at that; it was his speciality. As soon as he saw that the play was coming toward the other goal he would run and stand beside it. The goalie would, of course, venture out to cut down the angle, risking much more than a goalie would in hockey. The game of shinny was all about risk, and taking phenomenal chances. The goalie would venture too far out and Rat would tip it in.

"Rat and I would go to these games with a feeling that we would be co-operating in some way, helping each other through. This was never spoken of, just a sense that was there. He was my friend, therefore he would pass it to me and I would pass it to him. And we would be more aware of one another. In the tumult of a shinny game — especially one in which there wasn't much room to manoeuvre — you had to be especially aware of certain people for there to be any kind of co-operation. There were no uniforms; everyone was dressed roughly the same. It was very confusing. In mid-play you might forget who was on your team. Often, it didn't matter.

"It was really a very egotistical game. There was very little room for skillful team play; there was a lot of digging for the ball. Shinny is a lot like rugger as opposed to football. You dug for the ball and once you got it you had a breakaway. And if someone was in the right position you passed it to them.

"It was so comic because there was so little manoeuverability. Shinny is comedy; flopping down to block a shot, stampeding down the ice, breakaways, lunging after the person with the ball and knocking him down rather than really going for the ball sometimes.

"We considered it a manly game. You had to like physical contact. You couldn't complain if you were knocked off your feet. There were no rules. You could trip a guy; it was considered a little gauche but it was okay at the same time. If you had to you had to.

"As for equipment, well, you were certainly not expected to turn up at a shinny game with a new stick. In fact it was probably better to turn up with the stub of a stick. A new stick spoke of high seriousness which the game did not have. There was a violation if the game was approached in that manner. It just wasn't shinny. It was the same attitude that was reflected in the boot flaps being left down. You had a studied indifference to form. An indifference to rule, order; chaos itself.

"When I think of shinny I especially remember playing at night. The streetlights were higher than they are now. It was very dark. It was a still night and yet there were some flakes that appeared from some-where and were illuminated by the light before they fell to the ground. In this serene environment we charged up and down on this short patch of slippery, snowy street, every now and then pausing to allow the occasional car through, as if we were a roadblock. We were surrounded by silence and darkness except for the lights of the houses on both sides of the street and the odd pedestrian. We felt quite alone. And there we were, seven or eight of us.

"Teams were seldom even. This is very Canadian. Trevor Sevigny is on one side and on the other, to make up for him, there were two guys to even things out. There was a balance of ability. We could gauge to a fine point who was able to do what and their relative merits in the game. We often had five against seven and were still equal.

"There was very little you could do about changing your status in terms of how you were valued in the minds of the other players. I remember at times feeling on the verge of shinny greatness, having a good night and popping in many goals, but I knew for a fact that this was not going to continue, that this was just a flash in the pan. And the actions and the approaches of the other players to me, in my moment of success, was 'Oh, you got lucky' or 'Ah, what's the matter with you? How come you're this way tonight?' I felt a controlling mechanism was at work, a kind of balance that controlled the subtle status quo of who was worth what in the game of shinny. In life, I've seen that same balance at work in myself and in others.

"There were often people falling over, people hitting the street. We became quite intimate with the street. Sticks were used for balance but they were also used as much to trip and slash. There was a great deal of slashing. We used to flip or flick the ball from person to person, not the sort of play you would make on ice. You could count on there being a rut or a frozen ball of sand or some salt in the way to inhibit a smooth clean pass. You were always hampered by the physical conditions.

"And so the best thing you could do would be to golf or slash-swing at the ball with a great big wind-up. This wonderful wind-up was considered a major part of the sheer joy of shinny. You would wind up and whack the ball back from halfway down the ice, the snowflakes flying. Then there would be a pile-up of bodies as people dove after you to try and deflect your aim. Very seldom did we ever try anything in the way of subtle plays. It was grab the ball and try and get it in any way you can. If you hit it with your hand that was all right, kicking, slashing, digging.

"From the chaos in the corners in shinny you learned how to be aggressive, how to keep digging, how to be constantly alert, how to take advantage of an opportunity. We knew that whatever happened it wouldn't last for more than a second or two before the others were on us. You'd dig out the ball and start up, start running but instead of blades on your feet you had these slippery rubber boots. The comic element was that once you did get control — for that one brief second — of that slippery little ball it would not last for long; all the others would recoup and come after you before you got up a head of steam.

"Once you did get up a head of steam you were a force to be reckoned with and your momentum would keep you going.

"If the rink or road area were already occupied by skaters and hockey players, we shinny players would loom up over the horizon of the snowbank like Cossacks prior to attack and plop on the ice. It was the chaotic aspect of the aviator boots. We were like Huns. We would just stand there. It was the force of our presence, plus our numbers. We had won the ice. Usually, after a few minutes, the skaters took off their skates and joined us. Even the best hockey players were always more than willing to play shinny. And some of the great shinny players like John Atkinson never played hockey because they had weak ankles. John's ankles would flop over and get tired and so he could never skate well. The hierarchy of shinny was such that you could play the game well and never play hockey and still be honoured as a hockey player. It was the business about not taking yourself seriously, not taking the game seriously. It really didn't matter and yet we all knew it did. It's like being in school and doing well according to school rules and being accepted by the teachers as opposed to doing well in what's important to your peer group.

"After surviving a shinny match, hockey players felt that anything that happened to them in a hockey game was routine. This gave the hockey player a far better attitude toward bodychecking when he played the game on ice. It gave him a healthy disposition toward checking virtually absent in hockey today. He became accustomed to it and in a strange way looked forward to it. Handing out a good check is a wonderful feeling. There's nothing quite so clean and satisfying as knocking someone entirely off their feet with a good check when they least expect it. And it would soon be your turn. But that didn't matter. People are prepared to be just in shinny."

"Victoria schoolteacher Winston Jackson recalls: "We played spring, summer, and fall on roller skates in the street. These skates had heavy metal wheels, unlike the wooden or high-density rubber ones now. They sounded great. If you were in goal it was like an express train coming at you.

"We played with hockey sticks, a tennis ball, and orange juice tins as goals (whereas kids on the Prairies used scrap wood and grain sacks). In our milder climate here on the West Coast we were trying to emulate what it was like under 'real' conditions. If we were feeling professional and wanted to play a wide sweeping game we'd go to a Safeway parking lot with a big wall behind so one didn't have to be concerned about having to fetch a missed shot. Safeway stores did their parking lots very, very smoothly. On the road you took your chances. Cars didn't matter. But there were some rough surfaces, especially those with pea-gravel in the tar. This slowed the game down. The city tarred the street and sprinkled pea-gravel on and rolled it in with a steamroller. That was 'slow ice.' And if we got an outdoor lacrosse court they were really smooth, smoother than even the Safeway lots.

"One guy had a goalie stick and we took turns in nets. We'd all borrow the one cup and strap it on to the outside of our jeans. It made us feel big. We had something to protect. It made us like men."

"By the time we were between twelve and fourteen years old and in junior high the early morning trips to the arena for ice time before classes was beginning to kill many of us. But we loved doing it because it was seen as such a neat thing to do; to arrive at school, sweaty and red-faced, and to be seen putting your skates and stick in your locker. Being seen was everything."

Shinny is now played year-round, the result of our increasing drift away from a sense of the natural seasons and rhythms of life. The game of winter still contains some icy features though, in spite of its recent adaptation. Summer tennis balls are kept in mother's freezer to give the ball a better spin and make it dip. And summer shinny still has the sting of the winter game. It hurts. Some feel that summer shinny is even rougher than hockey or winter shinny because it is played with no equipment at all on a concrete or paved surface. In this respect summer shinny is closer to lacrosse than hockey. My nephews and their friends have the best of all possible worlds. They set up deliberately in the parking lot between the municipal swimming pool and the hockey arena. They can freeze the tennis balls in the ice-pile left by the Zamboni and play the game, with their girlfriends in the pool as spectators.

Wherever and whenever shinny is played there are never any referees; players are always on their own honour and various unwritten codes of conduct prevail. It is left to the players themselves to work out things between them. Perhaps this is why hockey players of an earlier era had a greater sense of sportsmanship than young players today.

Now there are organized winter shinny leagues in many parts of the country, the result of our compulsion to organize everything in our lives. Organized shinny in a contradiction in terms; it takes away the very spontaneity that is the chief attraction of the game. In Winnipeg bars I heard stories of the times when Bobby Hull, known as "The Golden Jet," would drive by an open-air rink after a WHA game, and park his car so that the headlights shone on the icy surface. After a few minutes of practising his famous slapshot, kids from the neighbourhood would materialize out of the darkness, sticks in hand, and Hull would play shinny with them.

Kids now play with a plastic orange puck on outdoor ice, if the latter can be found. There is no more impulsive phone call from the first kid who is struck by the sudden urge to be out on the ice with his friends battling the cold and a frozen tennis ball for the sheer joy of shinny. And there is no chain reaction of phone calls that, at an appointed time, suddenly brings twenty kids from all directions leaping from snowbanks onto the ice to take it over for two hours on a bright, icy Sunday afternoon to play a game without rules, referees, and time limit, in fact few limitations of any kind.

In this country where hockey is both hell and a holy thing, shinny is different. Shinny is where you can loiter on defence, or giggle at the outrageous moves of your opponents. You are taking the game too seriously if you keep score. A team is always one-up or four-up — the margin of three or four grunted out in a single syllable immediately after a goal is scored as the triumphant goal-scorer and his teammates turn up ice. If some god was keeping score he would need a pair of calculators. The nonchalance of shinny is one of its greatest attractions. You appear to be nonchalant but you're trying like hell. You always took it seriously, but were instantly able to stand back and look at yourself in a self-deprecating manner. The happy-go-lucky approach was never far beneath the surface. The paradox is obvious but true: it doesn't matter but it matters a great deal.

Playing only shinny, the game was particularly important to John Atkinson. It was his one chance to excel. One day he appeared at the rink a few minutes after we'd begun playing. He sat on the edge of the boards, feigning nonchalance until a break in the action made it possible for him to join us. I was in nets. He came back to me, a wry smile on his face I couldn't figure out, then went to centre to play for the opposing team. He got the draw. Suddenly I heard a strange sound. It was as if the ice were being cut open. I saw Atkinson weaving in on me, going around our centreman and the defence like they weren't there. He was putting moves on them I'd never seen before, moves that were impossible to make wearing rubber boots. As he bore in on me the sound of crunched ice grew louder. Atkinson put four or five moves on me before depositing his shot in the back of the net. There was a stunned silence. All of us stared at the ice. It had been cut up into squares as if some prehistoric animal dying of thirst had attempted to eat the ice. Atkinson's trail from centre could easily be traced. Several of us jumped him, holding him down while we examined his upturned boots. Four metal clips were attached to each sole. There may well have been no rules in shinny, but this was going too far. I can't remember when we laughed so long and so hard. John joined in the laughter, then changed into his shoes to finish the game. It was a great moment in shinny history.

Each moment is played for the particular moment; each moment of improvised action that results in a goal or a great save is held, savoured, suspended in time, and celebrated with a warming rush of adrenalin until the next great play is made. The only boundaries are personal to each player: degree of interest, ability, intensity, and physical stamina. The joy we feel when we make a great move comes from the unconscious sense that we are at the fullest extension of our natural abilities, our human powers. We are as at one with nature and each other as we will ever be, self-worth and personal dignity in the unconscious core of each one of us playing the game, for we know our chance to excel will come and we will take our place in the confraternity created by this universal game. In the meantime, between these high moments, the combined arts of stickhandling, controlling the ball, receiving a pass, avoiding a bodycheck, dishing one out, manoeuvering to get into the clear, learning how to rag the puck, and developing one's defensive skills — as well as the offensive skills of slashing, hooking, holding, and tripping — these are all practised, polished and occasionally perfected in a game that dishes out fun and friendship in equal doses.

ERIC WHITEHEAD

The Greatest Game
Ever Played

IN EARLY 1906 Frank was yet to earn his spurs as a full-time player in senior hockey, but even while a collegian he managed to stay close to the action at the top. During the previous season, while holidaying from Stanstead College, he had been called out of the stands early in a game between the Wanderers and the Ottawa Victorias to take over for a referee who had been injured in a collision. He did such a good job that when he was due in town again on a subsequent weekend he was asked to handle a crucial contest between Montreal and Cornwall, two teams that were in the thick of a bitter fight for the championship of the Federal League.

"That," said Frank, many years later, "was my most trying experience in hockey, as a referee, player, or coach. That particular game was a grudge match it ever there was one. The Cornwall players had taken a terrible physical beating in the Montreal rink this week before, and they had sworn to get even in their own bailiwick.

"Cornwall, Ontario, was a factory town, and the people there took their hockey very seriously. On the day of the game there must have been nearly 3,000 people jammed into a rink built to hold a little more than half that total. Walking onto the ice just before game time was like walking into a bear pit. I knew that I had a nasty job on my hands, and it didn't help to know that I would be the youngest and least-experienced person on the ice.

"The Cornwall players wasted no time laying on the wood, and I immediately began assessing penalties against them in an attempt to control the contest. This didn't sit too well with the fans, and when I sent one of the home-town boys off for opening a Montreal player's skull with his stick and the Wanderers scored a minute later, they all but tore the place apart.

"That one-goal I led held up, and when the game was over the crowd stormed down onto the ice and came after me. They had my route to the exit blocked and I was all but surrounded. I don't believe I would have gotten out of there alive had it not been for one of the Cornwall players, Reddy McMillan, who came to my rescue, flailing at the mob with his stick and screaming at them to get off the ice.

"He rushed over and backed me against the boards and stood in front of me while he tried to reason with the mob. He told them that to get me they'd have to get him first, and they finally backed off. Reddy saved my hide. The whole game was a terrible ordeal, but that finish was the most frightening part.

"However, the very undesirable custom then in vogue was to have the referee dress in the home-team's room, and I had some pretty anxious moments before I got out of the Cornwall quarters. I think it was during this experience when the idea was born in me for the rule requiring separate rooms for players and officials. This eventually became law. It might even have saved a life or two."

In a follow-up to that episode, the Cornwall team officials asked Frank to return the following weekend to referee another grudge match scheduled for the home rink against the Ottawa Victorias. It wasn't quite clear as to whether this invitation was a tribute to the coolness and the courage of the nineteen-year-old collegian, or whether the Cornwall folks just wanted another crack at him, but Frank didn't bother to find out.

"I declined. Fortunately. A far worse riot broke out in that game. One of the Cornwall players, Bud McCourt, was killed. Ottawa's Charlie Masson was charged with assault, accused of having clubbed McCourt over the head with his stick. He was acquitted in a court trial."

With Frank playing his hockey at McGill, Lester was getting his own baptism of hockey violence, vintage 1905–6, as the bright new star of the Wanderers.

Two other new Wanderers that year were Ernie Russell and Ernie Johnson, a pair of fine young forwards already established as stars of the game. For Johnson, later labeled "Moose," this was to be the first of twenty years' association with Lester, many of these as a magnificent and tremendously popular defenseman in the Patricks' Pacific Coast hockey empire.

The partnership got off to an auspicious start in the first game of the season, an 11–5 rout of the Victorias. Lester, on one wing, scored three goals for the Redbands, and Johnson, on the other, scored one. Unhappily for the big, good-natured Moose, his goal was against his own team. In attempting to clear in front of the goal, he had swept the puck more or less smartly into the netting. Despite this, he was hailed in the newspaper accounts as one of the game's outstanding performers, second only to Lester.

That was a relatively docile game, the Victorias having been definitely outclassed, but things began warming up a few weeks later in a contest against the one-time Cup holders, Montreal. Tied with the defending champion Ottawa team in the battle for the Cup, the Wanderers went into the Montreal game in great shape for a run at the Silver Seven, but came out in trouble, despite a 6–2 victory.

Early in the game, Lester was cut over the eye with a stick swung by one of his old Westmount buddies, Walter Smaill. He had to retire to the infirmary for mending, came back a few minutes later with a dozen stitches just over the eyebrow, but had to leave again because the wound was still bleeding and he was blind on one side. Teammate Billy Strachan was knocked to the ice during a melee, run over by a skate and departed with a severely gashed foot. Ernie Johnson squared off in a dispute with Montreal's Art Coulson and both went off for repairs, Coulson with a cut eye and Johnson with a broken nose.

But the next week all players were in the lineup as the Wanderers once again swamped the hapless Vics, 9–4.

The foregoing notation of these fairly average examples of exuberance in those early days is made merely because that second game set up one of the most remarkable confrontations in Stanley Cup history. And it starred the twenty-two-year-old from Westmount who had become the leader of the Wanderers in their quest for their first Cup Championship.

Having effortlessly brushed off the Cup challengers of Queen's University, the collegiate champions, and of Smith Falls, champions of the rival Federal League, the Ottawa Silver Seven faced the Wanderers in the real showdown. These teams had finished tied at the top of the newly formed Eastern Canada Hockey League, with identical 9–1 records, and a two-game total-goals series was scheduled to settle the issue. To the winner would go both the league title and the Stanley Cup.

For the first meeting in Monteal on March 15, 1906, the defending champions were 2–1 betting favorites, but the Wanderers obviously weren't listening to the neighbourhood bookies. Their fans went wild as Ernie Russell got four goals, Pud Glass go three and Moose Johnson shared a pair with Patrick in the home-town 9–1 victory.

The next game was booked for Ottawa on March 17, St. Patrick's Day, and the holiday date looked like a good augury for the Wanderers' rover of the same name. But the team appeared to need precious little in the way of favorable omens. Eight goals down for the round following their shock defeat in Montreal, the Silver Seven appeared to be headed for little more than an exercise in futility, but you couldn't tell that to their fans.

There was tremendous interest in the game, and Dey's Arena on Gladstone Avenue was sold out to its normal capacity long before game day, and that was just the beginning. When rush tickets were placed on sale at Allen & Cochrane's Store on Friday morning, the plate-glass window was smashed in the crush of the huge crowd, many of whom had been waiting in line all night. The local gendarmes were called to restore order, and three fans who objected to this intervention were tapped gently on the skull and hauled off in a paddy wagon.

The inside of the rink had been practically gutted in order to squeeze in as many bodies as possible without suffocation. Temporary standing platforms were erected at one end and doubledeck bleachers hoisted at the other. The grandstand press box had been torn out and a new one suspended from the rafters, a fact that brought howls of dismay if not downright fear from the reporters. Loose boards had been laid across the bottom of the press box, and a careless step could send a scribe hurtling between the two-by-fours and down onto the heads of the vice-regal party, who were seated directly below. In addition to the reporters' misgivings, the Governor General himself, Earl Grey, was reported to be a little apprehensive.

Despite the fact that just 200 tickets had been allotted to the Montreal fans, more than 1,000 had made the journey up the Ottawa Valley in special trains, jamming the Ottawa hotels and providing a land-office business for scalpers. The top $2.00 tickets were going for $10, with no guarantee that they were genuine. The visitors were also hungry for betting action, but despite their big goals' edge and their high hopes, they were no fools. Mindful of the Silver Seven's awesome unbeaten record on home ice, Wanderers' fans were offering no better than even money. At that, $12,000 was covered in one pooled bet in the lobby of the Russell Hotel, with most of the Ottawa backing said to be New York money.

Controversy rose to fever pitch when it was rumoured that the Silver Seven had "borrowed" the brilliant young Smith Falls goalie, Percy

Leseur, and would play him regardless of any protest against the illegality of this late addition to the roster. Another report had it that another "ringer," Kenora's Tom Phillips, one of the best forwards in hockey, was locked in a room at the Russell Hotel and would also start for the Silver Seven. Only the first rumour turned out to be correct.

At game time on Saturday, the rink was jammed with humanity, with clusters of intrepid youngsters all but literally hanging from the rafters. In an arena built to hold 3,000, more than 5,400 were shoe-horned inside. Another 2,000 were hammering on the doors to get in.

It was against this setting that developed what the *Sporting News* several years later in sober retrospect described as "The Greatest Hockey Game in History." Now, if all the Greatest Hockey Games in History were laid end to end, they would stretch from here to any far-flung fan of your choice, but there can be little doubt that this one was at least a contender for the title.

A deafening roar greeted the home-town team as it skated onto the ice for the two thirty-minute halves that would decide the championship. The Silver Seven were plainly fired up and a mile high and ready to slash into that eight-goal deficit. Twelve minutes after the puck had been dropped, Lester Patrick came cruising down the ice behind Moose Johnson, took a pass from his buddy, tucked the puck deftly behind ringer Leseur, and the deficit had grown to nine.

The Ottawas had just forty-eight minutes left in which to salvage some measure of respectabiltiy, and five of those minutes were gone before the first faint glimmer of hope surfaced. At that point, Ottawa's Frank McGee, the marvelous one-eyed forward who had scored four-teen times against Dawson City in that foredoomed Yukon outpost's incredible Cup challenge in 1904, made it 1-1 on the game, 10-2 on the round. Then Harry Smith narrowed the gap with another goal, and McGee struck again just before half time.

As the teams went to their dressing rooms the round stood at 10-4 for Montreal. The faint hopes of the Ottawa fans stirred to such an extent that midway in the intermission one of them fell off the back of the double-tiered bleachers. Miraculously, he was uninjured, having quite apparently been well fortified against such mishap, and thus suitably numbed.

The fellow had barely scrambled back to his perch when the puck was dropped to start the second half, Harry Smith got the draw, and raced in alone to beat the Wanderers' goalie. The building was still shaking when "Rat" Westwick took a pass from Harvey Pulford, and suddenly Ottawa was just four goals down.

Thirty seconds later the magic number was three as Westwick scored again.

The din was such that it could have been heard throughout the entire Ottawa Valley, and there was no doubt about it, the Wanderers were on panic street. Right after the last Westwick goal, Lester Patrick bent over his skate and was taking an inordinately long time fiddling with a shoelace while the referee waited to drop the puck. It was just time enough for his teammates to cluster around and formulate a strategy to stop the flood of goals.

The strategy was simple enough. Whenever the Silver Seven came down with the puck, the Wanderers would sag back and form a barricade in front of their goal, and as soon as one of them got possession he would flip it over the boards and into the crowd. The ploy incensed the Ottawa fans and baffled the Ottawa players, but just temporarily. After eight minutes of uproar, Harry Smith scored, and repeated two minutes later.

It was now 10–9 on the round, with ten minutes to play. Then it was 10–10 as Harry Smith swept around Patrick, was cross-checked by Billy Strachan at the goal mouth and then tumbled into the back of the net with the puck. The roar that went up from those Ottawa fans has perhaps not been matched in decibels before or since. Reported the *Sporting News*:

> The madness was such that Govenor General Earl Grey, quite an elderly man and not known to be athletic, was said to have leapt four feet in the air, and one fan who had not spoken to his wife in years rushed up and kissed her.

The place was bedlam. The ice was littered with everything the fans could tear loose, and hundreds of them poured onto the ice, stopping play as the bemused Wanderers huddled behind their own goal net. During the lull Earl Grey fought his way to the boards to lean over and shake Harry Smith's hand and smack him on the back with somewhat less than lordly grace.

This was the light side of what swiftly evolved into a small tragedy for the fans and their team that had come so far against seemingly incredible odds.

With both teams suffering from extreme fatigue, it was Lester

Patrick who sensed the kill as the Ottawa forwards laboured deep in the Montreal zone, drawing their defensemen with them. He got the puck, flipped it to Moose Johnson on a break, and a moment later beat Leseur with the goal that burst the Ottawa bubble. There were then just ninety seconds to play, and just before the whistle, Patrick, now plainly the coolest man in the arena, scored again to end this *Sporting News* pick as The Greatest Hockey Game in History.

The Wanderers had won the round by a goal count of 12–10 and with it the Stanley Cup. It was to be the first of five Cup championships for Lester Patrick as player, coach, and manager, in three different leagues.

Ernie Johnson, Lester's sidekick in three of those victories, fashioned his own little trophy in that frenetic win over the Silver Seven. Late in the game, some time after His Lordship had leaned over to congratulate the hero of the moment, Harry Smith, there was a scuffle along the boards during which Ernie, with one swipe of his stick, neatly dislodged the Governor General's stovepipe hat. A fan, presumably of the Wanderers, had picked up the topper and scooted off with it amid the confusion. After the game he came to the dressing-room door, asked for Ernie, and presented it to him as a token of his esteem. There is no record of Ernie having worn the chapeau into the shower, or indeed if there was a shower. But it had to be conceded that he had scored a unique and soul-satisfying hat trick.

Building the Gardens

FROM WHEN I WAS A BOY going to the track with my father to run his stories back downtown, I'd been interested in the races. I had been interested in other forms of gambling as well, including poker, which some of us started to play in high school. One time in 1915 after I joined the Army I left Irene one night saying I had to get some sleep, had to get up early the next day. Somehow on my way home my need for sleep evaporated and I checked in to a poker game that I knew was going on above a Yonge Street store. The game was operated by a bugler from Dufferin race track, who would take a dollar out of the pot every so often as the house cut. It was worth about $25 a night to him. Among the players that night was a jockey named Watts who had a mount in the King's Plate and said his horse, Tartarean, was going to win it. We were raided a little later by the police and I remember thinking this might be a little difficult to explain to Irene if I was arrested as a found-in, but they let me go, perhaps because I was in uniform. A few weeks later I was in Ottawa, in the Army, when the Plate was run. I laid a bet on Tartarean with a bookie and won. I was so dumb then that I didn't know all jockeys always said their horses were going to win, but that worked out all right and later I'd make a little money from time to time, especially on long shots.

In the late 1920s I owned a horse or two, and thought it was a big deal to have the hockey team's blue and white and maple leaf crest on my racing silks. But I'd never won a race, or even owned a good horse. Then one day at Woodbine there was this horse owner named Mrs. L. A. Livingston, a big woman who always wore big hats and flowing gowns. She came from around Cobourg and in race that day had entered a horse called The Monkey. In those days they called through the stands when a horse was scratched. I hear away down at one end the cry, "Scratch ... Mrs. ... Livingston's ... MONKEY!" And it comes nearer and nearer, as other criers picked it up. "SCRATCH ... MRS. ... LIVINGSTON'S ... MONKEY!" Then I saw her sailing along in her big hat, looking embarrassed as hell, everybody laughing, while the yell goes right down the length of the stands, "SCRATCH MRS. LIVINGSTON'S ... MONKEY!" She never came back. Sold all her horses, and I bought a filly from her called Rare Jewel for $250.

Just about that time, the Ottawa club in the NHL was in financial trouble, due to lack of support at the box office. They needed money so badly that they decided to sell their best player, King Clancy, then twenty-seven years old. He was not only one of the best defencemen in the league but one of the most colourful, lots of guts. The previous season he'd had seventeen goals and twenty-three assists, almost unheard of for a defenceman at that time. Ottawa hated to let him go but let it be known he'd be available for the right offer of players and cash. I had the players but we were still playing in the Mutual Street Arena, and even though we filled it about half the time there weren't enough seats to give us much ready cash. With the Depression, the $35,000 Ottawa wanted was, it seemed, the one insuperable drawback. There was another, however. Among all the feuds Clancy had going around the league, helping to fill rinks everywhere but in Ottawa, one of the big ones was with Hap Day. We'd been assured that the last place Clancy wanted to play was Toronto. James Strachan and the Montreal Maroons were said to have the inside track. If we could come up with the cash, I was willing to take a chance that Clancy would play for us, but $20,000 or $25,000 was as high as our directors were prepared to pay. It was going to take a miracle to get the other $10,000. Which brings us back to Rare Jewel, in the autumn of 1930, just a few weeks before the hockey season.

Rare Jewel didn't look like much. She kept on running last. I'd given her to Bill Campbell to train. He had never saddled a winner at Woodbine, and didn't think Rare Jewel was going to change that for him. We sent her to Montreal where the competition wasn't supposed to be as tough. She ran dead last, so we brought her back. Before birth she had been nominated for one of the best two-year-old races, the Coronation Futurity, but Campbell and his partner, a gambling friend of mine named Dave Garrity, didn't want to enter her. I didn't know anything. Like a lot of people who own horses, I was full of blind hope. Dude Foden had been exercising her. After her last blowout that week he came back and told me he thought she was coming around. "It's worth a chance to enter her, Mr. Smythe," he said, and against Campbell's advice I went down and laid down the cash to get her into the race.

What I didn't know then, and they both denied it forever after, was something that happened just before the race. Campbell and Garrity didn't trust one another very much. Garrity waited until Campbell was away from the barn that day and then dashed into her stall and fed her half a flask of brandy. He didn't tell Campbell. But Campbell came back, saw Garrity leaving, and then went into the stall, where he also gave Rare Jewel half a flask of brandy. That was one horse who didn't have to fly on one wing.

Well, all this time I'm over at the grandstand, laying a few bets. I already had bet downtown at the King Edward Hotel a day earlier when I ran into a bookmaker friend. He figured if I was entering Rare Jewel I'd want to bet. I told him I wouldn't bet with him because bookies usually set their own limits on payoffs. "Ah, I'll give you track odds," he said. I guess he thought I was just contributing — making a token donation out of loyalty to my horse. I think it was $40 I bet with him. But as it got near race time I started worrying. R. W. R. Cowie's colt Frothblower was the favourite, carrying about 127 pounds to Rare Jewel's 112. I thought maybe I should put $60 across the board on Frothblower just to protect myself. I was lined up at the pari-mutuel window when Smirle Lawson came along. I'd fired him as Leafs' club doctor the previous spring because he'd told a good game guy with a broken leg that the leg wasn't broken, go out and play. When the guy couldn't skate on it I sent him for an X-ray. It was broken, all right. I told Lawson, "You might be all right as a coroner, Smirle, but for the living you're a dead loss. You're fired." There was still animosity between us as he clapped me on the back at the wicket and said, "Frothblower all the way, eh, Connie?"

I slapped down the money I'd been going to bet on Frothblower and said, "Sixty across on Rare Jewel!" I don't know how much that meant I had bet on her, but she was still the longest shot on the board. I used to watch races from the top of the old grandstand. I was running along the deck there as fast as Rare Jewel was when she came down the stretch. Dude later got fined and suspended three days for rough riding at the top of the stretch, but he got her home in front, though it turned out he'd told his wife, even, to bet $10 on Frothblower.

In those days they put up the numbers of the payoff by hand. In the win column they put up $14.40 and stopped. I thought somebody must have bet a bundle on Rare Jewel just before the windows closed, so that it hadn't showed in the final odds. Then the guy casually put up a 2 in front of the $14.40, making the payoff $214.40 straight, $46.75 place, and $19.95 show! I won between ten and eleven thousand dollars, besides the purse of $3,570. It was quite a day — the first time my colours had ever come down in front anywhere, the first time Bill Campbell had ever saddled a winner at Woodbine, and the longest mutuels price paid in Canada that year. When I went down to the King Edward to see my friend the bookie he could only pay me half of the $4,000 and change he owed me. I had to wait about two or three days before he could gather enough to give me the rest.

But most important of all, when I was telling the Jockey Club to give me a cheque for my bets instead of the cash, I was thinking *now, we can buy Clancy. Now, we are going to win the Stanley Cup.*

A day or so later, Frank Ahearn, one of the Ottawa partners, told me they'd already made a deal with Maroons for Clancy; but they hadn't. I asked Clancy about his prejudice against playing for Toronto. He said, "No, I would love to play in Toronto."

"You've got yourself a deal," I said. "What do you want to be paid?"

"Anything you say," he said. Anything you say! I never had any trouble with Clancy about money in my life. He was the most *amateur* athlete I ever had. Just loved to play. And that's what Rare Jewel did for me. Somebody once said to me, "But you had the confidence to bet on her." I said, "I had the *ignorance*!" In those days I was like so many horse owners now or anytime; I felt that because I owned a horse, it was going to win.

I didn't have the whole $15,000 or so (the bet and the purse) by the time I made the deal. I gave the whole purse to the trainer and the rider, so more than Conn Symthe and Toronto Maple Leafs benefited from the fanastic win. But I paid my $10,000 down and five cheques for $5,000 each, post-dated a week apart starting the following week. The price, $35,000 and two players, a young defenceman named Art Smith worth about $10,000 in the hockey market, and a forward named Eric Pettinger worth about $5,000, made it a total of about $50,000 for Clancy, the most paid for a hockey player to that time. Around the league, people wanted to buy tickets to see what kind of a hockey player was worth $50,000. Most people think of 1930 as the first year of the Depression, the year after the stock market crashed, unemployed, hard times. I always think of it as the year Leafs got King Clancy. I must have felt good about it all year, because early in December that

year I went to V and S Motors on Sheppard Street, distributors for Stutz
and Franklin cars, and ordered a Franklin Transcontinent Sedan to be
delivered to our house on Christmas Eve, from me to Irene. Not that I
had the money — I had to sign a couple of notes for $500 each due in
March and May — but just because I felt so good about the future of the
Leafs and of another plan that was to be another major event in my life.

A few months earlier I had started to talk up the idea that we needed
a bigger and better arena to play in. I must have been pretty persuasive,
at first mainly among people who didn't have any money to put in. We
were in Montreal one day for a game with the Maroons. Greg Clark of
the *Toronto Star* was in our room at the Mount Royal when I was
expounding on what was becoming my pet theme, next to the hockey
team itself. With the Mutual Street Arena seating less than 8,000, about
half the time we were packing in 9,000 counting standees, but still
weren't grossing enough to pay our players what they could have been
getting with the richer teams in the U.S. "Also," I said, "as a place to go
all dressed up, we don't compete with the comfort of theatres and
other places where people can spend their money. We need a place
where people can go in evening clothes, if they want to come there
from a party or dinner. We need at least twelve thousand seats,
everything new and clean, a place that people can be proud to take
their wives or girlfriends to."

Clark got so excited that he took up my theme where I left off. He got
on the back of a chair, then onto the table, then stood on the bed,
telling us we had to do it, we had to get people convinced that we
needed a new arena. Somebody else there, I think a car salesman, said
we had to come up with a slogan. "That's the way you get things done
today — get them saying, 'We have to have a new arena! We have to
have a new arena!' To anyone who'll listen."

Money was very tight. From my own engineering and construction
experience I knew that we were going to need a million, a million and a
half, maybe more. But the more I thought about it, the more I was
determined to do it. I got a few people together to see what kind of
support we had; four Leaf directors, in the King Edward at lunch. My
old-time pal from the racetracks, Larkin Maloney, who was the general
manager at Canada Building Materials, was completely sold, on my
side. But Ed Bickle, partner in a stockbroking firm, was against it, a
handicap right from the start. He was supposed to have political

connections, as a bagman, but I don't remember him ever helping in anything much. Bill MacBrien, an insurance man, was sort of on the fence. Maloney and I were the only enthusiasts, so we decided to see what we could do.

A big firm of Montreal architects, Ross and MacDonald, had built the Royal York Hotel and other projects in Toronto. Architects in those days seemed to be more powerful among financiers than they are now. Ross and MacDonald had a lot of money at their command because of big jobs they'd done. Maloney and I went to Montreal to see them and tell them what we had in mind: an arena called Maple Leaf Gardens that would handle hockey and a lot of other events, from conventions to wrestling. The listened and proposed the project to Sun Life as a good investment. We were told that Sun Life would back us for about half a million. Then I made a big mistake. I was so excited at the good news that I phoned back to Toronto and told Ed Bickle what we had done. A few days later we were up at Lake Simcoe when someone mentioned to me, wasn't it good news about Bickle arranging the financing from Sun Life!

I said, "Maloney and I did that!"

He said, "Well, Ed Bickle is saying he did it."

After opposing the whole deal! But that was in character for Ed Bickle. Maloney was so angry with me for telling Bickle about it instead of announcing it ourselves that I thought he was going to punch me in the face.

Anyway, by then I was too busy raising money to coach full-time, so I named Art Duncan as co-coach to handle the team when I couldn't. We went to Sir John Aird, president of the Bank of Commerce, to tell him about Sun Life's support, and ask his. He said go ahead. We formed a company, Maple Leaf Gardens Limited, incorporated on February 24, 1931. Our directorate was like an honour roll of successful business-men. We worked out details of a stock prospectus, 100,000 preference shares at $10 par value, plus 50,000 common shares, no par value. A bonus of one common share would go to anyone who bought five of the preferred. All winter we'd been hunting for a site. The first one we looked at was on the Toronto waterfront, on land owned by the Toronto Harbour Commission. One of the people involved wanted $100,000 on the side to get the sale okayed. I refused to have anything to do with that, which turned out to be lucky. We looked at a site on

Spadina just above College, but some of the local landowners were against it. And then we hit on the right one.

The T. Eaton Company owned a lot of land around Carlton and Church. They said they would sell us a property one block north of Carlton, just above Wood Street — not much more than one hundred yards from where I was born. But I thought right on Carlton would be better. There were street cars on Yonge, a block away, another line on Carlton, another on Church. Eaton's not long before had opened their big new store at College and Yonge. I went to see the head man, J. J. Vaughan, and said, "Mr. Vaughan, we are going to draw hundreds of thousands of people to this new Gardens. If we build on Carlton, they'll have to go past your store, or a least see it, on the way to and from games. It would be better for you if we're on Carlton." He thought it over and said okay. We took an option on the corner for $350,000 — and Eaton's also said they'd take some of the stock.

I even sent Frank Selke, whom I'd hired a couple of years earlier as my assistant, and Ace Bailey, one of our best players, to make a few calls. Some of the richest men and companies around came in for an average of around $10,000, with lots of smaller commitments and some bigger ones. One day when the federal government had just made a big addition to the money supply, hundreds of millions of dollars, Jack Bickell called Alf Rogers, president of Elias Rogers Co. Ltd. and St. Mary's Cement Co. Ltd., and told him, "Alf, we've got to have a new arena! We're putting you in for $25,000."

I could hear Rogers' voice roaring back, "Don't you know there's a Depression on?"

Bickell argued that there were millions more dollars around that day than the day before, and that we'd never be able to buy materials and labour as cheaply again. In the end Rogers came in for his $25,000.

However, as the Depression deepened, some people who had committed themselves couldn't come up with the money. When Sun Life tried to back out, things got a little desperate. I went to see Sir Edward Beatty, president of Canadian Pacific and a director of Sun Life. I guess he was impressed because he called a few other Sun Life directors. A group of them told the company that if it backed out, they'd resign their directorships. Sun Life stayed in.

By then we were levelling the site. We knocked down all the old buildings, starting with the tobacco store right on the corner. Everything came down until there was nothing there but a pile of old bricks.

Some people laughed at me for hiring a watchman, but I had a kid just down from the west who was going to play a year of amateur hockey with the Senior Marlboros, a good prospect name Buzz Boll. He needed a job. We got him a little shack, a stove, and a fifteen-cent baseball bat. I can't remember myself exactly what I had in mind. Maybe that somebody would steal the corner we were going to build the Gardens on, I don't know.

By then the drawings were finished, a really inspired design that would allow every customer an unobstructed view of the ice, and make the Gardens the most up-to-date sports arena in North America — maybe in the world — if we could just get it built. Contractors had been asked for sealed bids. Sir John Aird, one of the Maple Leaf Gardens Limited directors, called a meeting in his office to open the bids. That was one of the worst, and best, days of my life. We seemed so near to getting the job done. But when the bids were opened and read, and the amount of money we had in hand or promised or even hoped for, was totalled up, we were — as I recollect — a few hundred thousand dollars short. That wouldn't be much today. Early in 1931 it was a mountain. We had tapped everybody who had any money, not once but two or three times. There was no going back to them and nowhere else to go, either. Sir John and some of the directors thought we should postpone the whole deal until things got better. I left the meeting to take a rest, trying to think what rabbit I could pull out of the hat now. Outside on a bench was Frank Selke.

I told him things didn't look too good. It was a depressing moment, to think that the project was all but being down the drain. Selke had mortgaged his house to buy stock, $4,500 of it. As we talked, an idea began to take shape between us. Suppose we could cut direct labour costs by paying the men partly in stock? Could we convince the unions that it would be to their benefit, keep about 1,300 of their members employed, if they'd agree to take 20 per cent of their pay in Gardens' shares?

It happened that day was the weekly meeting of the many unions in the Toronto Labour Council. Selke was a long-time member of the electrician's union. He has said since that he ran all the way to the Labour Temple to make his pitch. The business managers of all the unions listened. At first they were reluctant. If it was such a good deal, why were the rich guys trying to pawn off stock on the workers? Selke mentioned his own mortgage, as evidence of his faith. That helped and in the end, although they said each union membership would have to be approached separately for ratification, the response was favourable enough that Selke ran back down to the Bank of Commerce building to let me know.

The meeting in Sir John's office was still dragging along, going nowhere. I came out to talk to Selke. When I went back in and announced that the men who would build the Gardens seemed willing to take part of their pay in shares, Sir John Aird said quietly, "In that case, our bank will pick up the rest." I have always been given the main credit for building Maple Leaf Gardens in the depths of the Depression. Well, I didn't even know what a Depression was, so I just kept pushing. But to my mind the final decision, the final laying to rest of the feeling among some people that it was a crazy idea, came when the union men came in and Sir John Aird said, for the Bank of Commerce, "We'll pick up the rest."

In the end, the contractors who had submitted the low bid with a price shaved to the bone, Thomson Brothers, lost money on the deal. Allan Thomson and I dealt at the same Dominion Bank branch at Queen and Ossington. Even though they were losing money they were still doing the job. A lot of contractors would have come back to us and tried to renegotiate. I certainly admired Allan Thomson a lot more than one of our Gardens directors right then: Allan Ross, President of Canadian William Wrigley Junior Company Limited, and also a director of the Dominion Bank. He had wanted to be first president of the Maple Leafs. I'd made sure he wasn't. Anyway, when he found that the Thomsons were losing money at the Gardens, he recommended that the Dominion Bank call three of their notes the bank held. To call those notes would have bankrupted the company and Ross knew it. When I heard about it, I was furious. Fortunately, we had money right then. I called the bank the same day I heard about it and said "We're buying those notes, right now." Then I told Ross what I thought of him.

On June 1, steam shovels moved in to excavate. I don't know how you would build Maple Leaf Gardens today in five months, but partly it was accomplished because the men who built it believed in what they were doing. After all, they were going to be shareholders in it, weren't they? There was just one dissident that I ever heard of, a member of the electrical union that Selke had helped run for so long. The paid business agent, Cecil Shaw, also was connected with amateur hockey around town. Shaw argued with the man and got nowhere. Eventually they continued the argument with their fists. I've always thought maybe it was the best fight ever staged in Maple Leaf Gardens, and at the end Shaw was on his feet while the other guy was on his back looking up at the sky. The Gardens didn't even have a roof at the time.

We hustled stock all that spring and summer. I knew how bad the times were, not just from how tough the stock was to sell. Earlier, on May 1, at my sand pit I had to announce a pay cut for May 15, ranging form 10 to 20 per cent. Hap Day and I, as management, went down to a straight $25 a week. In August the long-time tenant in a house I owned on Willard Avenue wrote to say she couldn't pay the five months' back rent she owed and would I take a chattel mortgage on her furniture for it. All over town people were having mortgages foreclosed, or having to move because they couldn't pay the rent. As a minor footnote, Charlie Conacher came to me in some sort of a personal crisis that summer, needing $500 fast. His IOU dated July 14, 1931, I still hold. I owed money myself, but part of that was because by then I had bought 3,880 shares of Gardens' stock.

I realize now that getting the Gardens up and clean, painted, well-lighted, with ice and the bands marching out on the ice before a cheering crowd, all done between June 1 and November 12, was amazing. I didn't stop to think about it much that summer. Day and night, practically, I was down there, sometimes with MacDonald, the architectural expediter, sometimes with Allan Thomson, making decisions that would keep things moving. I supplied very little of the builiding material myself. I didn't want anybody to say I was feathering my own nest that way. Anyway, everything went too slowly to suit me. Because of the design, with no supporting pillars to get in the way of people watching hockey, some of the girders were so huge and heavy that they couldn't be carried in from elsewhere on the equipment of that time, and had to be fabricated on the spot. When Chicago Black Hawks came to town a day before the grand opening, there were still some finishing touches being done. But on the night of November 12, 1931, when the bands of the 48th Highlanders and the Royal Grenadiers marched out on the ice and played "Happy Days Are Here Again," the scene was pretty much as I had imagined it in my rosiest dreams. A lot of the people were in evening dress, including our twenty-two Gardens directors representing presidencies and directorships and sometimes sole ownership of some of the greatest firms in Canada (as well as one of the smaller ones, C. Smythe Ltd.). But up in the capacity crowd of

13,542 among the people who tried to drown out Gardens' President Jack Bickell's speech from centre ice with cries of "Play hockey!" were hundreds of the men who had built the place, and owned shares, and others who sold, or had to sell, their common stock at $1 a share in the early 1930's kicked themselves over the years. Counting share splits, those original $1 items became worth a hundred times that. But anyway, that night the dream had come true. Something had been built that became famous across Canada. Years later the first place some visitors to Toronto headed was to Carlton and Church just to stand there and look at the place they imagined around their radios every winter Saturday night after Foster Hewitt had called out his excitement filled, "Hello Canada!" into the farthest corners of the land, doing more than any other one man to make the Leafs and the Gardens as famous as anything in Canada.

FOSTER HEWITT *from* *the* DETROIT OLYMPIA

Game 6, Stanley Cup Finals, April 16, 1942

. . . We're at the eleven minute mark of the third period
Maple Leafs one, Detroit Red Wings no score
the face-off will be in the Leafs' zone at this end
the crowd urging on the Red Wings
you can hear them
Grosso, Wares, Abel
playing inside the Leafs' zone
Apps and Nick Metz and Don Metz
clear it back of their own net

Apps rolled a pass that Abel stopped
Abel falls and grabs the puck for a further face-off
Kampmann starts shoving with Stewart and the play is stopped
Stewart and Kampmann —
somebody throws, somebody throws a fish
onto the ice
well that is one for the books
from here it looked like a herring
it's a herring all right
Wares gets the fish
takes it over to the press box
face-off is at centre

and from the face-off Apps failed to knock it away
Detroit shoot it in again
and it's Stanowski into the corner

being bottled up by Wares
Wares is checked by Nick Metz
Nick Metz back of Broda
rolled one that Abel stopped
Abel is checked and Kampmann from the corner
waits, goes back of the net
failed a pass to Apps
Detroit in possession
shoot it back of the net again
here's from the corner
Detroit center out to the blueline!
Stewart's pass! and Apps blocked it
Apps starts out to center ice
is knocked down!
and failed to get away

the Leafs roll it up, over the Detroit line
and it's Abel going into the corner
Abel goes back of Mowers
watched by Nick Metz
Nick Metz covers him, he still has him there
and it comes back to Stanowski
he shoots it against the boards
it's into the corner for Nick Metz, he's stopped
and the Red Wings start out
three of them down the ice
coming at center
Grosso laid over a long pass and Wares...
missed it
Wares then shot it Stanowski stopped it
puck is loose and Detroit coming in again
here's a shot!
right on!
Broda!
kicked that to the side
and Stanowski on the left wing
rolled it out over the line
Nick Metz has lost his stick after being bowled over
Detroit coming in again

the puck bounced off the side of the boards
Broda held it and Nick Metz
was knocked rather goofy on that check.

One-nothing for the Maple Leafs
nearing the twelve minute mark in the third period
the crowd urging on their favorites
they're lining up in the Leafs' zone
here's a loose puck, it's knocked to the right wing
the puck is still loose
McCreedy failed to clear
Detroit fail to get a shot and it rolls out to center
here's a drive
it's stopped by Goldham!
a race for it
and Stewart and Goldham race after it
and Stewart beat him to it

Stewart back of the Detroit net
clears out to the blueline
Detroit coming up again four of them!
up over the line
a pass and the puck goes loose
it's Liscombe being checked again
it's loose again
Liscombe tried — here's a shot!
a scramble, and the Leafs
knock it off to the wing

Langelle shoots it down the ice
McCreedy is knocked down by McKay
and Detroit are beginning to rough it up
Detroit crashing into their checks every move now
as the crowd work them into fever pitch
One-nothing for the Maple Leafs

Brown is going to center-ice
Jerry Brown for Detroit
and lining up Taylor, Schriner and Carr

from the face-off it goes to the blueline
here's a shot!
Broda kicked that one out
Schriner rolled it but not out
Schriner then rolled it back to center ice
and Detroit shoot it back in
Schriner gets it
shoots it ahead
here's a breakaway!
Goldham!
going right in
he's right in
HE SHOOTS HE SCORES!
Goldham!
scores for the Maple Leafs!
going right down on Schriner's pass
to draw Mowers right out of his net and bang it home
to make it two-nothing for the Maple Leafs
Goldham, from Schriner
was the Maple Leaf scoring play
on a breakaway
Schriner fed him the pass
Goldham went in there like a veteran
and drew Mowers out of the net
and flipped it back behind him
time of that goal is thirteen . . . thirty-eight
as far as we can tell

now Detroit shoot it in the Leaf zone
it's shot back to center ice
two-nothing for the Leafs
and Dickens gets hold of it
flips it out to center
it's again Detroit coming in
here's Carveth cutting in on the right side
his shot! goes wide and Brown
goes into the corner
it's centered to Orlando
Schriner — and Taylor

get a breakaway!
one man back
they're going in
Taylor right in front of the net!
he's right in! HE SCORES!
Taylor!
from Schriner —
and that makes it three to nothing for the Maple Leafs

Billy Taylor
did the same act —
getting a breakaway with Schriner feeding it again
making a perfect play of it
and now the Maple Leafs lead three to nothing!
that was. . . fourteen-oh-seven.
you could tell someone was going to crack
and in this case, up to this point
it's been the Detroit Red Wings
they played great hockey
right up until the Leafs
finally took this lead
far from over yet of course
but that gives the Maple Leafs quite a substantial margin
to work on, the way they've been playing. . .

MORLEY CALLAGHAN

The Game That Makes a Nation

On the way to the Gardens one night when the old year like the snow on the ground was melting into the past, I was touched by that pleasantly nostalgic feeling for the lost hopes that had gone with the lost year. In the hockey world there were certainly a few minor frustrations: no tragic disappointments to be sure, but on a night with the snow falling across the street lamps the dear dead hopes one had put upon the Montreal Canadiens became one of those minor disappointments that made the world seem a little more cock-eyed. Canadiens ought to be always one of the great and powerful hockey teams, a team mentioned wherever the game is known. Why? I don't know, unless it is that from the time I was a kid they always seemed to be a team that stood for hockey, and when you grow up dreaming of players like the old-timers, Lalonde and Pitre and Vezina, well, I suppose it's just like running into an American doughboy somewhere in the Solomon Islands and asking him to give you a rational explanation for believing that the Yanks would always be one of the great teams in baseball.

One of the old year's hopes was that Drillon would flower in Montreal. But there is one thing about Drillon that was overlooked. If the company he keeps is inert, Gordon will be inert too. And a man is known by the company he keeps. But this wasn't to be an obituary notice for the Canadiens. Just a mournful regret. As I say, the light, soft-falling snow gets a man in a dreamy mood. Then at the corner we saw a gang of kids out on the middle of the road playing shinny. They were without skates and each kid was on his own, scrambling for the puck and trying to get in a little fancy stickhandling. They were all neighbourhood kids, and when a wet shiny face was lifted to the light, it was apt to be round or high cheekboned, or lean and blue-eyed: they were Anglo-Saxon faces and Scandinavian faces and Italian and Slavic faces. On the street that night, though, they were all one, they were just a collection of Canadian kids playing shinny. The game held them all together. Well then, I asked myself, wasn't that an intimation of the cause of the popularity of the old Canadiens of Montreal? In the main it was a French club, and in the daytime you read in the newspapers speeches politicians made about the failure of the English-speaking and French-speaking peoples to bridge the gap between them, but at nighttime when you saw Canadiens on the ice against the Leafs, they became just a lot of Canadian boys joined in something as Canadian as a beaver: they were joined in our great northern ballet, the hockey game. And it belonged to the French just as much as it did to those who speak English.

And come to think of it, hockey does more for the racial unity of this country than all the speeches of all the politicians who ever pointed with pride at Ottawa. Hockey is a game that belongs to no one racial group. Hockey is the stuff that is brewed in the melting pot of our nation. It sweeps away all champions of racial groups; it laughs at the supremacy of any racial faction. I sometimes wonder if those maidenly souls who write proper pieces on the undesirability of certain racial groups in the plan for post-war migrations to this country have ever let their eyes wander down a score sheet for a Saturday night in the National Hockey League. It would break their hearts. Look at the names they would read: Broda, Stanowski, Grosso, Orlando, Benoit, O'Connor, Grabowski, Pratt, Schmidt, Apps, Stewart, Shewchuck, Bouchard. You might get funny ideas reading such score sheets. You might begin to think that there were a lot of people in Canada who didn't come from your favorite neighbourhood in Toronto or even the older settlements in Ontario.

The kids went on playing shinny. They hooted and slashed with their sticks, and I suppose that right there on the street in the dawn of the new year with me on my way to the Gardens, hockey players were being born, and the soft snow was running down the back of my neck. It was the time of year when a man starts tossing wishes around. All kinds of best wishes for the new year. So there was one wish a man could toss off about hockey and be pretty fervent about it too. May the kids always play shinny on the corner. May they learn to stickhandle there and dream of the big league. They are not out there for exercise, they are not even out there because some gent in a big hat has told them that hockey builds character and a sense of precision team play. They are out there because they like it, and so far our game of hockey is just a game and it isn't being used as a cog in the totalitarian scheme to turn us into robots.

So I went on my way thinking how important it was that in the coming year with the nation geared up a little tighter for total war, that hockey should not die. If we get around to the point where we decided that it wasn't useful, it would mean that we have got around to the point of looking at all of life from Nazi eyes. Hockey is our winter ballet and in many ways our only national drama. When the Germans were at the gates of Moscow the Russians were still listening to the plays of their classic dramatists, weren't they?

. . . I know an elderly woman over seventy who never saw a game of hockey in her life who gets so excited just listening that she has to retire to her bedroom for a rest at the end of each period. That certainly means that for a lot of people hockey has become something more than a sport; it has taken on the role of a national folk play, a folk play that combines the brilliant solo work of a Russian Ballet dancer, the intrepid hero storming the redoubt against the bruising shock of the guards, the massed precision attack of the forward sweep and the crowd's rising crescendo like a great orchestral tone poem and the solitary undaunted figure of the goalkeeper as the classic figure of the man standing against fate.

And it all started there on the street corners and then on the ponds with the snow falling softly and the kids scrambling around, each man on his own, and that fact forcing him to learn to stickhandle. And then came the great teams, the great names, and the big gates, and when a boy was good at the game no one asked whether he was a new Canadian, a Frenchman or an Anglo Saxon; he just put his nose up, and any boy who is a national hockey star is a pure-bred Canadian and no one can tell him or the world otherwise.

The Siberia of Hockey

WITH EVERY MONTH IN HERSHEY, the feeling increased that my chances of ever returning to the Bruins were remote. This didn't bother Rose. She thought it was just wonderful living — and me playing — in her home town, and she got the mistaken notion that I would spend the rest of my life on defence for the Hershey Bears.

I didn't find the thought of being a lifetime Hershey Bear very distressing. I had acclimatized myself to life in the American League and found it not bad at all, albeit tough. The NHL was still a six team league in those days so the AHL was jammed full of solid hockey players dying to make it to the bigs but willing to fight it out in our league in the meantime.

When people talk about rough hockey today, they are referring to a brand of sport that is child's play compared to what it was in the AHL during the late 1950's. We didn't wear helmets. We didn't use mouth guards and most of us didn't have our own teeth. Those who ran afoul of my partner, Larry Zeidel, certainly didn't have their own teeth. Needless to say, Zeidel, The Rock, didn't have too many of his own molars either.

Once, when we were playing the Buffalo Bisons, Zeidel sliced Gordie Hannigan so badly that the blood was flowing out of his head to the beat of his heart. Hannigan was so bent on vengeance that he refused to go to the medical room for repairs until he had belted Zeidel. His teammates had to convince him to get stitched up first — he needed 30 stitches to seal the cut — and *then* come back and get Zeidel.

In those days there was hardly a raised eyebrow over such battles. Another time, we were playing Rochester and Zeidel got into a duel with big Eddie (Spider) Mazur of the Americans. The two of them looked like a pair of gladiators hacking away at each other. They were finally separated and thrown out of the game. As Mazur walked down the corridor to the dressing room, Zeidel plastered him with a punch and the brawl erupted again. Only this time the police came with guns drawn and sent the two fighters on their separate ways.

I was always learning. Watching Zeidel in action, I should have been more aware of the sucker punch but, naturally, I had to learn the hard way. Until my confrontation with Bob Baun of the Rochester Americans, I had always fought my battles fair and square. If someone bothered me or started in with one of our smaller players, I battled by The Marquis of Queensbury rules. No dirty stuff for Don Cherry. Then Bob Baun came along and altered my hockey philosophy.

A fight had erupted between one of my Hershey teammates and someone on the Rochester team. The rest of us just stood around to watch. I was on the perimeter of the action, minding my own business, when — Pow! — Baun skated up alongside me and punched me in the face so hard I was knocked to the ice. But that wasn't enough, he jumped me and put what seemed like a death grip around my neck. Every time I tried to get loose he'd squeeze even tighter, figuring that I was trying to get away. Actually, I couldn't breathe and was simply trying to keep from dying.

By now there was a pile of players around and I was practically hidden from view. I recall saying to myself, "So this is how it is to die." I figure that I was about one second away from croaking when Baun finally loosened his determined grip and I began breathing again.

After that episode nobody every suckered me. *I* was the one who did the sucker punching. I reached a point where I became so proficient at it I could sucker a guy sleeping on a bed. (In those days you learned early.)

At the end of the 1956–57 season, two things happened. One was great and the other terrible. The great event was the birth of my daughter Cindy, and the terrible event was a trade that sent me to Eddie Shore's Springfield Indians. That name sent shivers up a player's spine.

Normally, a player expects to be traded at any time and, though most of us don't like to move, we learn to accept it. But in the professional hockey world of the 1950s there was one exception — the Springfield Indians. Nobody, but *nobody*, wanted to be traded to Springfield if he could help it. There was one compelling reason for this: Eddie Shore, the Darth Vader of hockey.

The idea of being traded to Springfield was so scary that when the players signed contracts (with other teams) they made sure the contract had a clause stating *that they could not, under any circumstances, be traded to Springfield.*

To understand why, you have to know about Shore himself. Eddie was born on a wheat farm in Saskatchewan and toughened himself as a kid by hauling harvested grain to town and riding wild horses. When he made it to the NHL he had become one the most fearless athletes in history. He was an eight-time All Star and four-time Most Valuable Player. Most important, in terms of Shore's machismo, he had accumulated more than 900 stitches in his body as well as fractures of his back, hip and collarbone. His nose had been broken fourteen times and his jaw had been smashed five times. The man played with all the care of a souped–up Ford in a demolition derby. Which is well and good, but Eddie, when he became an owner, wanted all his players to behave the same way.

After Shore retired from pro hockey he bought the Springfield hockey club in the American League and ran it in a manner that would have made Jack Benny seem like a big spender. When Eddie first got the franchise in 1940 he used to park cars outside the arena until about ten minutes before game time. Then he'd go in, suit up, and play defense for the Indians.

Eddie didn't believe that hockey players should waste money taping their sockings so he would have his men take old tire innertubes, cut them into rubber bands and put them around the stockings instead of tape. When the Ice Follies came to Springfield Arena, Shore would be up near the rafters, operating a spotlight, just to save a few more bucks.

If there was a way of saving a penny, Shore found it and heaven help the man who tried to take it away from him. Once, he gave a demonstration of the uses of solar energy before anyone had even heard the expression. The Springfield rink was a barnlike structure with rows of windows near the ceiling on either side of the ice. Late in the morning, the sun would shine through the windows giving the rink its only natural light and warmth. That is, *if* the sun came out.

Well, on this day, the Cincinnati Mohawks were in town to play and asked Shore if they could have the ice for a morning practice. Eddie said sure, fine, nine o'clock the ice would be ready. So at nine sharp, Emile Francis, the Mohawks' goalie, stepped on the ice but there wasn't a light on in the arena; the place was pitch-black. Shore walked in and Francis asked him to turn the lights on so they could start the workout.

Eddie looked at Francis as if he were stupid and said, "Wait a half-hour till the sun rises and comes through the windows. Then you'll have plenty of light."

The Mohawks had no choice but to wait, but they got the last laugh on Shore. At the game the next night their coach, King Clancy, climbed over the boards before the opening face-off and presented Shore with a lantern.

Another way Shore would stick it to his players was with contract clauses. He had guys on the Indians who would have it written in their contracts that if they scored 30 goals or more a season, they'd get a big bonus from Eddie. But Shore had a way of getting out of that; as soon as the player in question reached 29 goals, Eddie would bench him for the rest of the season.

Those who played for Shore had to contend with more than his frugality. Eddie considered himself the Albert Einstein of professional hockey, and if you didn't believe it, all you had to do was ask him. He had more theories than there are pucks in the world and he was determined to pass these ideas along to his players whether they liked it or not. Usually they didn't, but they really didn't have a choice in the matter.

One of Eddie's theories was that there was an intimate connection between dancing and hockey, so one year he opened training camp by having his players tap dance in the hotel lobby and then execute ballet steps on the ice.

Shore once had a rather low-key defenceman named Don Johns. Donnie had spent a couple of years in the NHL with the Rangers but couldn't quite cut the mustard and now he was back in the minors with Shore who was determined to make a better hockey player out of him.

After a practice one day, Shore called Johns over to the side of the rink. Eddie never called a player by his first name; it was always *Mister* This and *Mister* That. "Mister Johns," he said, "you could be a better hockey player if you made some adjustments in your style."

"Okay," said Johns, "what am I doing wrong?"

"Mister Johns," Shore explained, *"you are not combing your hair right."*

Shore meant every word of it, *that* was the scary part. He told Donnie to part his hair on the other side. This would help him because "he would have something to think about."

A couple of months under Shore was enough to send some players back to their farms in Manitoba and Saskatchewan; especially when he would inflict one of his special techniques on them. Once, at a practice, Eddie had his players churning up and down the ice taking shots on goal. Suddenly Eddie blew his whistle and called a rookie over to him.

"Young man," he said, "don't you know you should be skating with your legs closer together?" And without waiting for an answer Shore pulled a piece of rope from his pocket, tied the kid's legs together, and then ordered him to skate. Can you imagine what it was like skating with your legs tied?

Since Shore himself was virtually immune to pain he assumed that everyone else reacted the same way. After one game, when Donnie Johns had been cut for forty stitches in his leg and was immobilized in a hospital bed, Shore visited him and said, "You ought to be ready to play soon."

"But Eddie," snapped Johns, "I can't even turn my leg..."

Shore would have none of that back talk. "Listen, Mister Johns, when I played hockey I once had a hundred stitches in my leg, and I was out only three — no, two-and-a-half — days."

Many who survived the Springfield Siberia look back on the experience with a mixture of horror and humour, and strange as it may seem, from one of Shore's championship teams fourteen players became professional coaches. . . .

There was something funny about the sight of Shore tying a goalkeeper to the net during a practice session. Eddie did this because he wanted to get the message across to the goalie that goaltenders should never fall to the ice.

Goalie Don Simmons was the victim of many a Shore theory. When the goalie was suffering through a particularly long slump, Eddie was convinced that Simmons had developed a mental block about goaltending. Shore insisted that Simmons return to his home in Port Colborne, Ontario, for a rest. "Go home to your mother," Shore suggested. "Help her around the house. Wash the dishes and do the chores for her. That'll take your mind off hockey. While you're at it, find a studio and take some dancing lessons."

The closest a goalie ever came to suffering a nervous breakdown on the ice happened in Springfield because of Shore. The Indians were playing the Cleveland Barons and referee Frank Udvari had called a penalty against Springfield that Shore felt his team didn't deserve. Eddie went bananas and when it became apparent that Udvari would not change his mind — when does a referee *ever* change his mind — Shore called all of his skaters to the bench. All, that is, with the exception of goalie Don Simmons.

When Udvari realized what was happening, he skated over to Shore and said: "I'm giving you ten seconds to put a team on the ice and then I'm dropping the puck."

Udvari watched the ten seconds click off and then moved into the face-off circle where the five Cleveland players were awaiting the start of play. The referee handed the puck to the linesman and he dropped it in front of Bo Elik of Cleveland. As soon as the puck hit the ice Bo pushed it ahead with his stick and along with his four teammates charged in on poor Donny Simmons.

The Barons were so stunned by the no-defence situation that they fought among themselves over who was going to take the shot. Elik finally let the puck go and missed the net completely. The Barons retrieved the puck and fired again...and again...and again with all their shots going wild. Simmons finally dove on top of the loose puck, stopping play. By this time Shore must have felt some compassion for the goalie because he ordered his other five skaters back on the ice.

Anyone who crossed Shore became a "Black Ace," one of the many extras he kept on the squad — but wouldn't dress — for punitive purposes. The Black Aces had to work extra hard in practice and were always available to play should any of the regulars enrage Eddie even more. In addition to scrimmaging with the team, the Black Aces were required to do odd jobs around the arena such as painting seats, selling programs, making popcorn and blowing up hundreds of balloons before the ice shows. When Kenny Schinkel was a Black Ace, he was helping Shore change a light bulb in the Coliseum's high ceiling. To do so, Eddie had to climb on a platform which the players pushed from bulb to bulb. At one point Shore was hanging onto an overhead cable with one hand and screwing in a bulb with his other hand when Schinkel "accidentally" pushed the tower from underneath him. Eddie was just hanging there from the cabels like a trapeze artist. Kenny finally thought he would see The Old Man afraid and screaming; but he hung by one hand and calmly looked down and said "Mr. Schinkel, would you please return the platform to its rightful place?" (You just couldn't beat him.) Schinkel finally got around to pushing the platform back so he could get down.

Few who crossed Shore escaped without some form of retribution. He had been known to lock a referee in his dressing room if he thought the ref had handled a game poorly or he would grab the loudspeaker microphone and denounce a referee (or an opposing player) for everyone in the arena to hear.

One night, during a game against Cleveland, he went berserk after referee Lou Farelli disallowed a Springfield goal even though the goal judge, Bill Tebone, had flashed the red light signifying the point. Eddie ordered Tebone to leave his post behind the net. He said that if the referee could overrule the goal judge there was no point in having one. When Farelli ordered Shore to get the goal judge back on the job, Eddie just ignored him and the game finally resumed without one important official.

Many of us who played in Springfield learned a lot of hockey from Shore. He was a masterful teacher and would spend as much time on the ice as any player would require, but he had so many quirks it was difficult to determine whether you suffered more from his idiosyncracies or benefited more from his teachings.

Schinkel, who played for Eddie more than most guys, was a classic example. Eddie would pay closer attention to him because he regarded Kenny as a son. If Schinkel didn't feel well Eddie would worry about him and prescribe one of his many instant cures.

One night Shore noticed that Schinkel was sniffling. It was the common cold that has baffled medical science. Eddie suggested that Kenny take twelve drops of iodine. Schinkel took the advice and it worked!

Another time, Schinkel was complaining of feeling lethargic. Eddie looked him over and suggested that Kenny was suffering from yellow jaundice. The Old Man prescribed his special "Marlet Treatment." This was one of Shore's favourites and he used it on several players. It was a laxative made up of a number of oils.

Schinkel tried half the prescription and almost instantly lost twelve pounds. He stopped the Marlet Treatment then and there. "If I had taken the whole thing," Kenny said, "I would have been dead!"

I give Shore credit, though. Some people are nuts and never realize it, at least Eddie had an inkling. He once said, "Most of us are a little crazy in some form or other. The thing is some of us admit it."

This was the man who would be my boss for four seasons. I was upset because I realized that my hopes for a big-league career were sinking fast. Poor Rose took it even harder. She had thought we were going to stay in Hershey for the rest of our lives. Now she learned differently. We packed the car, bundled up our daughter Cindy, put her in a crib in the back of the car, and headed for Springfield. We hadn't driven ten miles when the canvas ripped off the bags we had tied down on top of the car. Then it started raining and everything was ruined.

I wondered: could anything that happened with Eddie Shore be worse than this? It didn't take me long to discover the answer — in the affirmative!

Having heard so much about Eddie Shore before actually meeting him, I had pictured someone large and ominous. That, however, was not the Eddie Shore who shook my hand and welcomed me to the Springfield Indians. Eddie Shore, in living colour, was surprisingly small and bald, but obviously tough. He had many scars on his face and even though he was in his 60's he appeared to be in mint condition.

In no time at all I learned what Shore thought of me. He gave me a nickname — The Madagascar Kid. I think that's where he would have sent me, given the opportunity. One of the things he disliked about my style was my skating. By his standards it was lousy. "Mr. Cherry," he would say, "if you could visualize that in reality your manoeuverability is nil."

For all his idiosyncracies, Shore did have a magnetic quality. While we rebelled against him, we also listened to him, if not all the time then most of the time. But we were always trying to go one up on Eddie whenever possible. I succeeded once during training camp. It was an exceptionally warm day and a dense fog hung over the ice. Every so often the players would skate around holding towels in an attempt to dispel the fog, but it always came back.

During the workout, Shore became displeased with my skating (as usual) and called me over for a private meeting. I skated to the boards, listened to his harangue for about a minute and, even though he hadn't finished, I began to slowly back away while the fog enveloped me. In two seconds I had become thoroughly lost in the fog, but I could hear Shore roaring: *"I know you're there Cherry. You're goin' to pay for this once the fog lifts."*

Of course, the fog lifted and I paid for it. I became one of Shore's favourite targets, but I was in good company. There were always guys on the team who were willing to collaborate in an attempt to get even with The Old Man. Once, he had us on the ice practising two-on-ones — two forwards skating in on one defenseman. Eddie was berating me as usual about my hockey ability or lack thereof, with his back to the drill while I was facing the drill. The defenceman, backing up at full speed, didn't see Eddie. Naturally, Eddie couldn't see what was happening either. I could have warned Eddie, because I was facing the play, but I thought, "What the hell!" I stepped aside just as the big defenceman hit Eddie in the back. Eddie flew six feet in the air and so did the defenseman. Nobody laughed, because it would have meant their lives, but it was a great feeling. As usual, I paid for it later.

One day he had me and another defenceman named Duane Rupp — with whom he had a separate beef — stay on the ice after practice. He had us skate around and around the ice *for four hours and twenty minutes*. Torturous as it was, Rupp and I never gave in. Then Shore had the arena lights turned off and we skated in the dark. By this time, the only way we could keep going was with some sustenance. Fortunately, some of our teammates brought us some tea with honey; without it, we certainly would have collapsed. I asked Eddie the next day why the punishment, and he answered, "When I was instructing you yesterday, you glanced at the clock behind my head. When I talk to you, you look me in the eye."

Even though Pat Egan was the coach, Shore was on the ice most of the time, giving instruction. He loved to trade shoves with the players. He would hit a guy on the shoulder and send him flying backwards. Then he'd say, "Hit me in the shoulder." The player would hit The Old Man, but Eddie would be ready. He would bend his knees in his favourite stance and could always handle the blow. "You see," he would gloat, "I don't move. I have my skates planted right."

We used to let Eddie get away with this little game because if we didn't, we would all pay; until the day Kent Douglas joined us. Kent was that rare kind of individual who stands up for his rights no matter what. He was tough as nails and wouldn't take anything from anybody. When I saw The Old Man hit him on the shoulder I said to the guys, "Uh oh, watch this. This is going to be fun." After Shore hit Kent, Douglas said, "Don't do that Eddie." Eddie said, "Oh yeah? Now you hit me." Before I could get to Kent he had knocked Shore ass over teakettle. Kent would never play "the game" with Shore.

The Old Man and Douglas loved to argue over hockey points. Whenever we wanted to kill time we'd tell Kent to ask Eddie a question. Then we'd stand around for an hour and a half while the two argued about it.

Shore would argue with anybody. Cal Gardner was another. He had been in the NHL for a number of years with the Rangers, Maple Leafs and Bruins. Now he was winding down his career in Springfield. At this point in time it would have been foolish for anyone to start tampering with Gardner's skating style, but that didn't stop Shore. He bawled out Gardner for not using the Shore technique. Gardner was fuming.

Cal said to Eddie one day, "Eddie, how many years did you play in the NHL?" Eddie said, "Eight." Cal said, "Yeah Eddie? Well I played twelve." I thought somebody finally had Eddie, but Eddie shot back, "Yes, Mr. Gardner, but if you'd played my way, you'd have lasted sixteen years!" You couldn't top the Old Man.

The way Shore figured it, there was always a better way of doing things — *his*. Our goalie, Claude Evans, once came up with a shut-out in a 5–0 win. After the game Shore walked into the dressing room and fined Evans $50 *because he didn't bend his knees.*

I didn't bend my knees very well either. They were always stiff, like tree stumps, and there was nothing I — or Shore — could do to make them more supple. Once, when my knees were particularly stiff, he set a club record by calling me over for a bawling out five times in two minutes.

There were a few rare players who could do no wrong. Bill Sweeney was one of them. He was a smallish centre, who was Rangers' property, but never could seem to make it in the NHL. He had the "rep" of being too slow. With us, he was the number one scorer, the number one dart player, the number one golfer and not a bad drinker at that.

Sweeney had a bulbous red nose and, in his own youthful way, bore a striking resemblance to the great comic W. C. Fields. For five years I called Sweeney "W.C." and he had no idea why I had tagged him with the nickname. One day we were walking down the street and passed a theatre. There was a big billboard in front with a picture of W. C. Fields, his nose redder than ever.

I noticed that Sweeney was looking at the billboard in a funny way, not quite sure what was bothering him. He looked at Fields, then he looked at me, then he stared back at the billboard and it finally hit him. "You sonofabitch," he shouted. "All these years you've been making fun of me and I never knew it."

Sweeney was one of those gifted players who, in the era of the six-team NHL, was buried in the AHL for life. Another like him — who got a reprieve late in his playing career — was Barclay Plager, a hard-nosed defenceman. Barclay was the victim of one of the great fix-the-back capers.

Anyone who played for Shore was liable to be given treatment for a number of ailments and back problems were one of his specialties. The trouble was that Shore's treatments were often worse than the ailment itself, a fact of which we were all well aware.

One day we were sitting in the dressing room, kibitizing around, when Shore came walking down the hall. After a practice, the dressing room door would be left open. There was a mirror on it enabling someone in the dressing room to see who was walking down the corridor. On this day, Brian Kilrea, one of our better forwards who was given to pranks, noticed Shore coming. When the Old Man was within hearing range, Brian spoke loud enough for Shore to hear, "Gee Barclay, is that right — *is your back really hurting you?*"

That's all Plager had to hear. He knew that the Indians had had a defenceman named Bob McCord who had complained about a bad back. Shore got him on the table and ruined his back so badly that he couldn't play. Shore sent him to Three Rivers. If you were smart, you didn't let Shore hear about your bad back.

The Old Man walked over to Plager. "Your back bothering you?" he asked.

"No, no," said Barclay, "my back's okay."

"Get on the table Mister Plager."

"No, honestly, Eddie. My back's all right."

"GET ON THE TABLE, MISTER PLAGER."

Barclay had no choice. He climbed on the table and Shore went to work on him, pulling and jerking until poor Plager was a mess.

By this time Kilrea and the rest of us had executed an orderly retreat to a nearby bar and were downing a few when one of the boys walked in. "Did you hear what happened to Barclay?" the guy asked. "They put him in an ambulance and took him to the hospital. His back was so bad he couldn't straighten up. You better look out, Brian. The last thing we heard while they were putting him in the ambulance was Barclay screaming, 'I'm going to kill Kilrea!' "

Shore was always trying to straighten us out in one way or another; sometimes in the most unlikely manner. There was the time when he sent out invitations to the wives of all the players. They were asked to report to our dressing room at 7:30 p.m. Naturally, the women figured that The Old Man was throwing a party for the team. They put on their fanciest dresses, assuming that, for once, Shore would give us a good time.

One by one the women filtered into the smelly, liniment-filled room, jock straps hanging on pegs, smelly underwear (brown from never being washed) on the benches and nothing but ugliness around. At last, The Old Man walked in. He looked around at the women. "The club is not doing too well and there's a very good reason for this state of affairs. *You ladies are giving your husbands too much sex!* To prove my point, I'm going to ask Floyd Smith, who is newly married, to send his wife home." That was the end of the "party." Smitty's wife Audrey was devastated. She turned to Rose and said, "It wouldn't be so bad if it were true but it's not. I wish it was."

Those of us who played for Shore always wondered whether there was anybody in this world capable of trimming The Old Man's sails. We got our answer in the fall of 1957. The Bruins, who had operated Hershey as their American League farm team, decided to link up with Springfield. Shore would still own the club but the Bruins would operate it and a little, bald guy named George (Punch) Imlach was named the manager of the Indians, and later the coach.

If you didn't know better you wouldn't figure that Imlach could handle The Old Man, but Punch had been around a long time and owned an inner toughness that comes from working the minors for many years. Right from the start I liked Punch. He had a very positive attitude about life in general and hockey in particular. He knew that I had just about given up on making the NHL but he encouraged me nonetheless. "You should try for the big league," he said. "Mark my words — someday *I'll* be in the National Hockey League." I laughed to myself when he said that. Punch Imlach in the NHL. What a joke! But, by gosh, he did it, in spades.

What he couldn't do was take enough wind out of Shore's sails to last very long in Springfield. The problem with Punch was that he'd come to the Indians from Quebec, where he had had a free hand running the Aces. Even though the Bruins ran the Indians, Imlach still had to deal with Shore at the arena and that meant trouble.

Before the season was even half over Shore had tried to get the Bruins to fire Imlach at least three times. But the Bruins — who were still operated by Lynn Patrick — would have none of that. By the middle of November, Imlach and Shore weren't even talking to each other, and they both occupied offices in the same building.

A major cause of the friction was the dual operation of the team. Shore owned some of the players on the team and the Bruins owned the rest. Naturally, Shore wanted his skaters played a certain way and when Imlach disobeyed there was hell to pay.

The actual split between the two occurred over the issue of goaltenders. The Indians carried two goalies, Claude Evans, a pudgy goaltender who rarely left his feet, and Al Millar, who was less fat and less orthodox. Shore owned Evans and the Bruins owned Millar.

Imlach was partial to Millar. Al had played for him in Quebec and the Aces had won the Edinburgh Trophy, emblematic of the senior championship of Canada. He was also the best goalie in the Quebec Senior Hockey League, Millar's credentials were a hell of a lot better than Evans'. But Evans had one thing in his favour — Shore liked him, in his way.

We usually played our home games on Saturday night at the Eastern States Coliseum in West Springfield and normally made our goaltending plans a day or two in advance. Since Imlach was both G.M. and coach of the team, it was his job to decide which goaltender to use.

Shore didn't buy that kind of thinking. The Old Man summoned Punch into his office and demanded to know who would be in the nets on Saturday. Imlach told him it would be Millar.

The Old Man said nix to that. He would play Evans and that was all there was to it. Imlach started to give him an argument but Shore wouldn't budge. "Are you giving me an ultimatum?" Punch asked.

Shore didn't answer. He just stared at Punch, hoping that sooner or later Imlach would crack, agree to play Evans and the dispute would be ended then and there. But Imlach returned Shore's stare. Finally, after what seemed like an eternity, The Old Man said, "Yes, it is an ultimatum." With that, Punch thanked him and left the room.

On Saturday night Al Millar, Punch's man, was in the net. He had told Shore that *he* Imlach, was running the show, and if Eddie didn't like it, he knew what he could do.

The rest of us were horrified because we had been around Shore long enough to know that even if you win a battle with The Old Man, as Punch had done, you're apt to lose the war in the long run. Imlach knew that as well as anyone, including Millar.

Sure enough, Shore sought retribution — and got it. In no time at all Millar was traded; not once but four times that season and I'm sure it was because he was Imlach's man in the battle of the wills. So, while Millar was bouncing around from Chicoutimi to Buffalo, Boston, (he even played a couple of games for the Bruins) and Quebec City, Evans was our goalie, and the damnedest thing was, he turned out to be good enough to get us into the finals.

Imlach didn't hurt either. He turned out to be one hell of a good leader; we respected him for his inspirational qualities as well as his knowledge of the game. I think even Shore would acknowledge that. In fact, after we had been eliminated in the Calder Cup finals Punch ran into Eddie in the corridor at Eastern States Coliseum.

The Old Man looked at his upstart manager. "I guess you had yourself a pretty good year, son," Shore said.

"I guess so," said Punch. Then, each went his separate way. Imlach got a job with the Toronto Maple Leafs the following season and turned a terrible club into a contender almost overnight. Within a few years he had won four Stanley Cup championships and was the toast of the hockey world.

Punch got to be a pretty big man but he never forgot the little guys with whom he had once worked. I remember him visiting Springfield long afterward and I happened to be standing in the corner of the rink. Shore had suspended me, and I was feeling mighty low. Punch was with his entourage, led by King Clancy, and he very easily could have ignored me in the crowd. But he stopped, walked over, shook my hand and immediately asked about Rose and the family. I was so touched, tears came to my eyes. To think that a man with four Stanley Cup championships would walk out of his way to come and talk to me. Everyone was watching him, with his fuzzy cream-coloured fedora, and as he talked to me, my heart swelled with pride. The whole episode picked me up when I was at another low point in my career. I was having a hard time even practising with the Black Aces. The little episode had a profound impact on me.

For some reason, I felt pretty secure about staying in Springfield. We had just moved to another apartment, had finished putting the stereo, the fish tank and the television in place, and then I left for a game with Providence. After the game I went out with the boys for the usual beers and got home at about two in the morning.

I couldn't find Rose. She wasn't in the living room and she wasn't in the kitchen, so I walked upstairs to the bedroom and there she was fully dressed, standing on the bed. "What in hell are you doin' up there?" I asked.

"You're a nice guy! I've been waiting here for two hours," she said. "There are mice all over the place. Take a look."

Sure enough, the mice were acting as if it was *their* apartment. I set up a mouse trap and we got into bed. *Snap!* The trap went off. I got out of bed, emptied the trap and put another piece of cheese in it. Got back into bed and began dozing when — *Snap!* It went off again. Within an hour there were ten more *Snaps!*

The next morning I went to see the landlady and she promised to bring the fumigator over in a day or two. But that was all academic, as it turned out. That day I showed up for practice and Egan walked into the dressing room and handed me a letter. "Here's a little present for you," he said with a smile on his face.

I opened the letter. "Please report by tomorrow afternoon to Three Rivers, Quebec." Egan must have thought that I would haul off and belt him. Nothing of the kind. I looked up, smiled and said: "Thanks a lot, Pat old boy, toodle-oo!"

Now it was time to say goodbye to The Old Man. I shook his hand and said, "By the way, Eddie, how *do* I get to Three Rivers from here?"

"Nothing to it, Madagascar. You go up through New Hampshire, then over to Vermont and when you hit the Canadian border, turn right."

"Thanks a lot Eddie, I'll see ya around someday."

As I drove home I thought, "Poor Rose. Wait 'til she hears where we are going now! Oh well, she'll be rid of the mice, anyway!"

AL PURDY

The Time of Your Life

Childhood — when toads and frogs rain down the sky,
and night is velvety as under the skirts
of a goddess, where it's always summer —
In winter water pours from gardenhose,
and turns to ice in town backyards;
coal shovels clear a hockey rink for boys
to play war, mothers watch anxiously:
King Arthur's court, with Eaton's catalogue
for breastplate, a hockey stick for lance —

The later legend has a big-league scout
sitting in smoky small-town rinks,
watching the local flash, signing him
to a contract for those fabulous arenas
where heroes remain boyish forever
and women they sleep with are always their wives,
while money grins green and freckles fade —

Begin before the beginning:
shortly after birth, even before school,
with ice luckily thick or drowning thin:
the painted backdrop of snow and dingy houses
fades, only the shouting children are real:
and sometimes on hard-crusted winter snow
I've seen the game escape its limits,
and leap the width and breadth of things,
become a mad chase going nowhere, out
past dangerous places where the current
nibbles cheese holes — out to the wide wide bay:
where iceboats leave their tracks to race with birds,
and fishing shanties are lost castles beyond the town,
and slow clouds loom ahead like giant goalies —

Miles out in the far country
of Quinte the child stands
— senses he is being watched,
glances down at his feet,
which seem supported
by black glass above nothing,
where shadows with eyes,
green shapes whisper
"We'll eat your liver and lights"

Motionless as a waterfall,
he stands in no-time,
where sequence is tangled in creation,
before possible things converge
to be trapped in the inevitable:
the boy's deep sub-self
becomes aware of what looks
like a small hockey player
reflected on the ice watching him —
or else a boy with raw cold nose
— or else a complete stranger,
standing in the high blue barn:
and yet this four-foot two-thirds
man-sized carbon of himself is not
himself no matter what it looks like —
An order from somewhere makes one arm
lift up, holding the stick high;
the pinched face smiles grimly;
the body above ice mirror is instructed
to bend down in order that the owner's
eyes may permit a glimpse of the owner
himself, clothed in flesh but aloof
from flesh, remaining hidden:
                              politely
the boy's mouth opens, his lips slowly
carefully form the words:
                              "Thank you — "
After which a whoof
of expelled breath shrieks

a sudden "YEE — OUWW" at the sky,
and black ice with a mile-wide spasm
somewhere beyond the world's edge cracks —

He skates widly back to town
with long swooping twenty-foot strides,
batting an old tin can ahead of him:
a cold moon hangs above the town clock
tower that strikes hard iron of sky;
the blacksmith in his smoky cave
strokes a chestnut mare with one lame foot;
the elderly pumpmaker in his shop
crowded with pine scent, stops the lathe —
On either side the river lie
dark cubes of houses drowned in snow:
the boy dashes excitedly to one
of them, aching with news of an event
real or imagined, bursts the
door open, "Hey, mom (and forgets
whatever it was) — I'm hungry!"
Weather turns colder, the house
shudders and rocks, frost creeps
on blind white windows: and under
its patchwork quilt time moves
in a drift of birds a dream of horses,
and sticky buds breaking out of snow.
premeditations of flowers and lifting tides,
the sleep of men —

Even the shadow shapes inside their black
prison stay where they are, surviving the night,
and have been known occasionally to sleep —

DAVID GOWDEY

Tonight From
Make Believe Gardens

THE BEST DAYS WERE EARLY in the winter before the snow had fallen, when cold nights froze the lake below the dam and the open ice would stretch for miles. All day the sun was bright but distant, and there was no chance that the ice would melt. You could skate for half an hour in the same direction, the wind behind you, weaving back and forth but never having to turn around.

Later, when the winter had truly set in, we would set out for the river coves at the edge of town. Our shovels would reveal black ice beneath the snow, sometimes five or six inches thick. The ice had been warmed and rippled by the snow cover, but if a section had drifted clear the surface would be perfectly smooth and seemed as hard as granite.

One day my best friend Keith and I stayed long after the others had left, playing one-on-one on the pond near his house. As always, some part of us carried on an interior play-by-play which surfaced after a goal or a heavy check, to "rub it in" and extend the glory —

Keon fakes, cuts in, Young's underwear goes flying!
Keon moves in alone, he shoots he scores!

which would be countered within moments by,

Mahovlich was levelled by Gordie on that one — I think they're gonna dig a hole right there!

We each understood the other's remarks as coming from the same location, which we'd announce whenever we started from zero again:

Tonight from Make Believe Gardens in Chicago, the third game of the Stanley Cup Finals between the Detroit Red Wings and the

Toronto Maple Leafs, and now up to the gondola and Foster
Hewitt...

and here we'd pause while the voice started up, me the Red Wings,
Keith the Leafs, facing off again in Make Believe Gardens, the home
rink for both of our lives.

The sun went down but our game continued, until it was too dark to
see at all. I made a last rush, wound up to shoot, banked it in off the
boot which we used for a goal post. As we quit the game I realized that I
hadn't been able to feel toes or fingers for quite some time. This wasn't
surprising — it often happened — but I also realized as Keith waved
goodbye that he would be home as soon as he had walked over the
nearest hill, while I had a four mile trek ahead of me.

My fingers fumbled a long while with the laces, and my feet were
completely numb as I took off my skates. The rubber boots, the
goalposts, were likewise frozen stiff, and when I tried to put them on
they seemed to have shrunk. It was impossible. There was only one
thing to do. Gritting my teeth, a little panicky, I set off running through
the snow in my stocking feet, carrying my skates and stick but leaving
my boots and new Eaton's parka behind me in the snow. The parka I
could have put on, but I was warm in my hockey sweater and I felt that
the most important thing was not to waste any time.

I ran on through the darkness, startling small creatures, my mind
set on a single image, the fireplace in the front room. I dodged
brambles and branches in the path like defencemen, accelerated whenever an opening appeared.

Finally I saw the porch light; I reached the front door and banged
loudly. With my red cheeks I probably looked very healthy, and my
father was less dismayed by my condition than by my leaving the new
parka behind. But when he looked down and realized I wasn't wearing
shoes he went into action quickly. He built a fire and cautioned me
against getting too close, warning of "chilblains", a word which I
didn't know then and still can't define, but which sounded ominously
Victorian and permanently painful. He heated the stove, brought out a
bottle from the shelf beside the milk box. We sat in front of the fire
together, drinking cocoa laced with brandy.

After an hour we went back out into the darkness to look for
the parka. Snow was falling softly. I saw the coat and one boot right
away, but had to look high and low for the other. When I found it

it was already filled with snow. The puck from my last shot was sitting beside it.

Soon the snow was deep enough on the coves to warm and melt the ice underneath, which made it chip too easily. On his own time a teacher from the nearby school began a rink, freezing the pavement in the juniors' courtyard. After dark my father and I would cross the road and under a huge weeping willow tree play a spirited one-on-one, skating or sliding around on boots, using the upright bicycle stands for goals.

Sometimes in the early winter a freezing overnight rain would turn the schoolyard and its soccer fields into one vast sheet of ice. Ignoring the pebbles in the road we would skate to school the next morning, and on a weekend stay there all day. My brother learned to skate there on one of those afternoons, pushing a kitchen chair around in front of him, his snowsuit padding his frequent falls.

When the courtyard rink was discovered and became crowded we built a rink on our side lawn. I helped to shovel and tramp down the snow, and at night I'd look out the upstairs window and see my father watering it down again, giving it the extra coat.

One day he brought home two sweaters, Detroit and Chicago, from a fire sale at a nearby sports shop. They smelled wonderfully of smoke when I put them on, and I alternated them day to day on the various neighbourhood rinks. But though the Red Wings were my favorite team, and Glenn Hall of the Black Hawks my favorite goalie, I most admired a white Boston Bruins sweater I had seen in a window downtown, the only "away" sweater available.

The Bruins of the time regularly played the Canadiens in the Cup Final and were acknowledged to be the dirtiest team in the league. They were certainly rough and tough — Flaman, Boivin, Armstrong, Mohns, Toppazzini, Leo Labine, were all scrappers and hit men, and even their scorers — Stasiuk, Horvath, Mackell — were ready to mix it up any time. I had cheered them in the finals the year before, but it wasn't the team that was important to me. It was the beauty of the sweater itself.

One Christmas it arrived. The white wool was highlighted by gold and black trim and the black "B" stood out in the centre of the crest. The white was brighter than any wool I'd ever seen; I stared at it for a moment in its wrapping, dazzled, then put it on right away.

That night we set out for the grandparents' house and Christmas dinner. I was persuaded to wear a parka over the new sweater, though I insisted on keeping it unzipped. We arrived and unloaded our presents from the car, laid them under the tree. I carried the coats into a back room, spread them on the bed, took off my parka revealing the sweater, the sweater! re-entered to what I knew would be certain acclaim.

"BOOO BOSTON!" boomed an uncle, "BOOOO!" He was a Leafs fan. The Leafs were a clean team, had finished last, finished last every year — "BOOOO!" I was shaken up and disappeared for awhile until someone was sent to find me. Nothing has seemed as perfect as that sweater to me since.

As a very young boy I was in bed Saturdays before the broadcast began. The voices from my father's radio would float down the hallway to my room, Foster Hewitt, Imperial Oil and the Leafs of the middle fifties. My parents, like many other far-sighted families in those days, hadn't bought a television. If I thought to ask, a smaller radio was moved into my room, as long as the lights were out and my eyes were closed.

Although they contained the seeds of the champions of the sixties, the pre-Imlach Leafs were a sorry bunch, full of cogs, spare parts and Cullens. Their main play, the only one I remember, seemed to be George Armstrong or some other stalwart carrying the puck into the corner and centering to "no one there". This was repeated with such regularity that the other team soon tired of the charade, and after taking over control of the game they would sweep down the ice and score in a variety of ways, something the Leafs could have learned from.

The Hot Stove League between periods was at least as entertaining as the play, with Baldy Cotton, Bob Davidson and Elmer Ferguson swapping stories and opinions in a cozy way. Davidson seemed rather bland, and would fit in well on the networks today, but Cotton was funny and quick to name names, while Ferguson seemed slower and wise. I could picture the scene perfectly, see the stove burning, the room full of provisions, the cracker-barrel sages leaning into the warmth, away from the wind outside. I would hear the play begin again, then I slept.

At playoff time all of this changed. During the games from Montreal I would doze off listening to the intermission, but the sing-song voice of

Danny Gallivan would soon drift into my consciousness, rising and falling with the roar of the Forum crowd. The effect was totally different, warmer and more dynamic than the nasal, more linear Leaf broadcasts.

The other team perhaps would take a tentative lead, holding off the Canadiens while the pressure built up. The fury and unanimity of the Montreal crowd's reactions was a new world, and Gallivan's voice reached out with it. The voice swooped and soared, the high notes sometimes disappearing, and always when they needed it most — "Another shot! THEY SCORE! RICHARD!", the crescendo breaking from the crowd, Gallivan's voice seeming to bulge the microphone, followed by the inevitable ten-minute delay as the rubbers were cleared from the ice. I would usually hope for the other team, but when Canadiens won I was never disappointed. To cheer for them was to be on the side of an inevitable force; they could not have been stopped any more than one of us could stop history.

The next year Saturdays began to revolve around hockey. In the morning, snow or shine, there was the trip to the open-air rink where I'd stand with the other reserves behind the boards while my feet froze in their oversized skates. With running noses we watched the plays develop between those who knew how to skate, until the game was settled one way or another, when we'd be put out for our weekly shift.

Once, with an eye on seeing more ice time, I loudly mentioned my preference for playing defence in the coach's car on the way to the rink. Sure enough, once the first line scored I was sent out onto the ice. While I stood motionless at the blueline trying to get used to the new position, the puck carrier, thinking I would get out of the way, ran straight into me and fell. I tottered but didn't go down, and to the surprise of both of us was assessed a penalty.

This had never happened in a game before, and no one had ever said where the penalty box was. I skated in small circles for some time, until called back ingloriously to the team bench. The next week I didn't get on the ice.

Despite the downside, we were given a team sweater each week, unless too many players showed up, and were allowed to buy matching socks. Upon arriving back home my mother had always cooked my favorite meal, spareribs, which I would then down with gusto.

Saturday afternoon there was the trip for groceries, breakfast cereals and their prizes to ponder; Bee Hive syrup to buy. One cereal once

offered a flip book inside, illustrated tips for better play. My choice
when I arrived home turned out to be Gordie Howe deking Johnny
Bower on a breakaway; I couldn't have asked for more. Then the
groceries were shelved, the meat and ice cream stored away, the snow
on my father's gloves melting, the smell of powered doughnuts and
celery and wet paper grocery bags.

That year Punch Imlach took over the Leafs. A television appeared in
the house, prophetically in the dining room. I'd never had to share my
room, but for some reason my parents bought me a rather rickety bunk
bed. I would lie in the lower bunk before the Saturday game began,
thumbing through hockey cards or the *Weekend* magazine, with its full
colour Jock Carroll hockey portraits and Andy O'Brien's remarks. I
would stick the cards above me between the springs of the bunk above
me, fantasizing crisp passing plays in the middle of the air and wondering if the whole thing would come crashing down as soon as I closed
my eyes. I'd hear the beginning of the game on radio, then head
downstairs for the second period.

In the fifties the TV broadcast began about five minutes into the
second period, which added to the game's mystique. The viewer was
rushed right into the heart of the action and had to recreate his own
version of the first period. Foster Hewitt's brief descriptions of the
unseen goals were completely to the point, and the combination of
radio and television, the blend of imagination and presentation, was
better than either by itself.

On TV the dim figures raced across the screen. The lights in the
arena were kept low, and you never saw the crowd. More players
seemed to be in on the action than I had imagined — in my mind it had
often been only puck carrier against defender, with perhaps a teammate skating alongside. If the game was close I'd listen to the third
period back in my room, and sit up expectantly for the three star
selection.

The Leafs finally made the playoffs, and took on Boston in the semi-
finals. They lost the first two, and a gaggle of relatives gathered in the
dining room for the overtime of the crucial third game. The Boston
goalie was Harry Lumley, a veteran whose glory had faded. But he was
remarkable still, in that no matter how heated the action in front of
him became, every hair on his head stayed in place. Perhaps out of
deference to Lumley I'd smeared Brylcreem on my cowlick and spread
it around with a comb.

As the third period of the game had developed my ears began to turn completely red, burning with excitement and hair tonic. The prospect of sudden death overtime was too much — they blazed, and the heat was more than I could stand.

A cold washcloth was the only answer. Guffaws filled the room. With every face-off I tore to the kitchen to run fresh water over the cloth, then back again before the puck was dropped, the cloth held tight to my ears. Ehman finally scored against the wretched Lumley, bringing my torment to an end.

My brother and I were devoted players of what we used to call knob hockey and what others probably know as table hockey. Table boards have recently surfaced in bars and arcades, with plastic bubble domes fitted over the ice to stop spills and angry losers from causing any damage.

The new games come complete with automatic face-offs and scoreboards, and a crowd-like sound effect that cheers each goal. Players can control the crowd and start a rousing chorus of boos if an opponent gets chippy or holds the puck out of reach. Most of these boards feature the USA against the Soviets, huge plastic players with ultra-long sticks.

My own memories of the game revolve around the metal "original six", each goalie, and many players, with a different face and character. As a child each November I eagerly anticipated the arrival of the Christmas catalogues from Eaton's and Simpson's, turning at once to the new hockey boards. On Christmas Day, 1959 the first board arrived, complete with all six teams, red lights that flashed after every goal and a replica of the Stanley Cup. All presents for years afterward were inevitably anticlimactic. In the years that followed we removed barriers to allow passing behind the net, reworked the controls so the goalies could wander, gave Jacques Plante a mask. We wore out three boards over fifteen years of play.

As my younger brother's coordination improved, competition between us grew fiercer. We continued to play into our teens, while he turned out to be a fine athlete. At last it was the only sport where I could prevail over him, at least part of the time. Our physical skills at the game had become so similar that wins usually came only through cunning or luck and total abandon while flipping the knobs.

Our final playoff series was played on two separate home-and-home boards after a month-long regular season. It turned into a contest of wills, both of us doctoring our home board between games, bending player's sticks, practising ricochets, switching chairs to gain any kind of advantage. With the series tied at two games apiece we agreed to abandon the series deadlocked, the best result possible under the circumstances.

Two doors down along the crescent lived Ted, a chubby eccentric who later played goal for us through a decade of pick-up hockey. Ted had been to hockey camp one summer and for years afterward was easily persuaded to describe how he felt facing Eddie Shack's slapshot. He had a heavy build and his weight seemed to fluctuate; he would lose some of his bulk in the summer but it always reappeared when the weather grew cold. He had an understandable fondness for Turk Broda, the plump Leaf goalie of the late forties whom none of us had actually seen play but who stood as a beacon for all fat athletes.

He was compulsive about many things, which I guess is natural for an apprentice netminder. Eventually he spent a long career in college as a straight "A" student, earning several degrees in different subjects before finally finding work in experimental physics, but in those days his winters revolved around the Leafs and Johnny Bower, their great and ageless goalie. He had very fast hands and a quick mind, and made an excellent opponent in ping-pong and chess. Unfortunately, he also had very poor eyesight, which didn't help him at all as a goalie. His strengths never made up for this glaring weakness, though they did make for some spectacularly uneven play around the net.

Ted was also a table hockey player, with a methodical style of play. Here at the board, his obsessions took hold and wouldn't let him go. Any game played on his home turf was broken down into three one-minute periods, the time kept with a stopwatch in case the puck left the ice. As a goalie, Ted appreciated low scoring games and this was his way of keeping the score down, though I later wondered why he didn't make the nets a little smaller. The ebb and flow of the game, marked normally by yelling and a rising glow of excitement, was broken up into an endless series of stops and starts; the watch was continually checked and the score of each period dutifully noted on a pad in Ted's slow, box-like script.

After the game ("Another shut-out! That's five in eight games for Johnny Bower!") goalie averages would be worked out and the next game on the forty-four game schedule begun. The low emotional pitch was maintained throughout the day, and afterward the visitor left in the same state of mind as when he'd arrived, though with perhaps an edge of irritation. With the stops and starts and the standing by, possibilities were held firmly in check, but the process was still somehow absorbing. The clock — and real life — seemed to stop as we sat in the room waiting while Ted prepared a haven of shut-outs and statistics to balance the fast pace and goalscorers of the world outside.

Consciously or unconsciously he loosened up "on the road", two doors down. Here he could be tempted into playing a straight ten-minute game although he always seemed to enjoy looking for the puck while the clock ran on as much as he enjoyed scoring a goal. One Christmas a small tape recorder appeared on the scene, and when Ted arrived later in the day it was put to use as the instant replay unit, playing back the yelps and fragmentary play-by-play that led up to every goal. The effect was to condense a series of intermittent goals into a veritable orgy of scoring. Ted's senses took over and rebelled against their tethers. Within half an hour he had challenged my sister to a game to one hundred, tying up the board for hours. My sister later described seeing his face alight through the entire game, grinning wildly at each goal on both ends.

We were put to the test the next season when a friend, Glenn, organized a table hockey tournament. Glenn was no athlete, but he'd show up at weekend pick-up hockey, keeping reams of statistics that we'd pore over afterward. Before the tournament he insisted we name our players as well as our teams, so he could tabulate the scoring leaders. Ted dropped out of the running after a 1–0 loss to the hapless Bay Crimes, but Glenn and I went undefeated, and in the last game tied each other. As the playoffs began, one unlucky contender brought his girlfriend along to watch him play. Of course he was annihilated, his game stiffening under her intense incomprehension.

Glenn was a veteran of many chess tournaments and revelled in psychologically jockeying for position. His favourite ploy was allowing an opponent the first musical selection, then falling back on his own choice for the second half. This was announced with great fanfare, and was invariably the latest Animals' opus, the dreaded "House of the Rising Sun". As the first inexorable chords rang out, cranked up a few notches if Glenn was behind, the game of many a brave opponent began to crumble. It was strong medicine, and the playoffs were close, but when the final smoke cleared my team had prevailed, Jacques LePuc knocking in a rebound in the last seconds of regulation. My winnings were a frothy Mr. Pibb and the possession of the prized game board. I forgot to take the board with me that night, and it mysteriously had been spirited away the next morning when Glenn went on vacation.

Unfazed by the disappearance of the hard-won board I gloated for several weeks afterward, but Glenn was slow to accept defeat. Soon after his family returned in the fall I found him on our doorstep demanding a rematch, a new board under his arm. My brother was eager to hear about Glenn's summer, but we all knew the real reason he'd come, and after impatiently downing a Bee Hive sandwich his long awaited rematch began.

It was a lazy fall day and a haze had settled over the field outside. In the corner on the tube a Jimmy Cagney movie played silently. As play began I noticed it was "Public Enemy", one of Cagney's greatest roles; when I fell behind I thought maybe we should turn up the sound; and as the score mounted higher against me the movie seemed to demand more and more attention. By the end of the game my allegiance was split. Glenn fired a final salvo and Cagney was hit. He staggered endlessly down the street, finally collapsing on the stairs of a church, where a crowd of gawkers gathered. "He used to be a bigshot", declared a cop. I started to laugh and abandoned the board. For a moment livid anger flashed across Glenn's face, then he relaxed, totally spent, and accepted a glass of juice. He stayed another hour, then I never saw him again.

Hockey fans, because of the nature of their game, are less likely to be absolutists when it comes to sin. The basis of the referee's art is to make snap judgements on when the play has truly been affected, to recognize the act when someone takes a dive. Basketball, football, most of all baseball, are either/or games: either there was an obvious foul or not, either the runner was safe or he was out. Hockey rules demand finer judgments about the degree and intent of contact. This can lead to ridiculous oversights, particularly in the playoffs, but the sequence of continuous decisions tends to humanize the game. There is no such thing as perfection.

One playoff night in April, 1959 my parents went out, leaving us with my grandmother. Their party would be late, and my grandmother was well known as a soft touch when it came to staying up. The game was from Chicago, the upstart Black Hawks against the powerhouse Canadiens, and it didn't start until 9:30.

I'd never seen Chicago, even in pictures; we'd situated Make Believe Gardens there because "Chicago" had the right rhythm to round out the phrase. After a year and a half of Hockey Night in Canada this would be my first real view of a game from the USA. The week before, while saying goodnight, I'd caught glimpses from the dimly lit Boston Garden. As I'd watched, a small bomb had been thrown out of the stands — it exploded with a tremendous percussion and left a huge black smear on the ice. I was ready for anything.

I soon outlasted my grandmother, who went up to bed during the second period, making sure I was in my pajamas. I guess she expected me to go to sleep. The game was splendid, wide open and fast. Red Storey, always my favourite referee, usually had a great knack for knowing how far to let the play go, reining it back in before it got out of hand. This night, however, he would lose control. Perhaps he hadn't reckoned on the Chicago fans, who'd seen only five playoff games since 1946.

Canadiens went ahead in the third period on a goal by Dickie Moore. Just before the goal, Eddie Litzenberger of Chicago had fallen while being checked. When Storey let the play continue, the Canadiens swept down the ice and scored. Twenty thousand voices booed mightily. After a delay to clear the ice play began again. Bobby Hull flew over the blueline, was checked by Junior Langlois, and took a fully extended dive. Again Storey let it go. Claude Provost took the puck for Montreal and scored, putting the game and the series out of reach with only a minute to play.

Chaos reigned. The incensed crowd began to throw shoes, bottles, everything that wasn't nailed down. Storey retreated to centre ice under the rain of debris. I'd never seen anything lke it; the anarchic possibilities of the scene were intoxicating and I eagerly drank it all in. Suddenly a fan clambered over the boards, reached Storey at center ice and poured beer over his head. Storey jerked around, enraged. Beside him Doug Harvey clubbed the fan to the ice. A full-scale donnybrook erupted as twenty thousand people roared.

I'd never been so wide awake that late at night. I was appalled but totally engaged at the same time; my head felt like it was going to explode. Years later I was reminded of the scene, again on TV, by the street fighting at the 1968 Democratic Convention. Chicago, Chicago. There were fewer cops at the hockey game, but that might have been a good thing.

It was after one in the morning when the game finally ended, and another hour before I fell asleep, my brain still buzzing. I know it seems odd to write about the power of a sports event that happened six hundred miles away. We grow so accustomed to being bored by TV that we're almost immune to any emotional effects. But it doesn't always work that way. To a boy from a quiet Ontario city, raised on a regimen of school, the Queen and the Maple Leafs the box that night offered a glimpse of delirium.

Soon afterward I stopped going to church, and headed for the ice instead.

Part 2

IN THE ARENA

When I'm on the ice I look for openings.
That's what the game is all about.
— **Bobby Orr**

If you work in an office you never tell people personal
things that will let them know you. We all want to, but
we're afraid someone might laugh or walk away, so we
keep it inside. But once you get on the ice, things happen
so fast you can't keep anything inside. You don't have
time to present a facade. A man can find out what he's
got inside him, whether he's a bad guy, a coward, a good
guy . . . Hockey gives a guy a chance to be himself.
— **Jim Dorey**

What I get paid for are the practices.
I would play the games for nothing.
— **Tim Horton**

HUGH HOOD

The Style is the Man

ON A SUNDAY MORNING IN JUNE we arranged for some uninterrupted ice time at the Town of Mount Royal Arena. The idea was that I would watch Jean closely as he worked through the different phases of skating and playmaking, from the vantage point of the ice. Gerry Patterson, Jean's business advisor, came along too, and refereed for us. You don't get the same view of Jean, even from a seat at rinkside, that you do when you're playing with him — it's a totally different impression.

We weren't wearing uniforms or equipment, just shirt and trousers, so it didn't take much time to dress. I usually wear a pair of heavy woolen sweat socks over a second, lighter pair, when I'm skating, and I asked Jean what he uses.

"Just one pair, a light cotton sock. You've got the uniform socks too, remember. They don't have a whole foot in them, but they do have the strip that goes under the arch of your foot, so you've got a certain amount of bulk in your skate. I like to have my skates fit me like any other good-quality shoe — they've got to be flexible and comfortable, and I don't want my feet all muffled up in thick wool."

He finished lacing his skates and stood up. I noticed that he had to duck his head going through the dressing room door. Jean is six-three, and the skates add about two inches to his height. I was profoundly impressed by his height and speed when I got out on the ice beside him, and he didn't have game equipment on. With the shoulder and elbow pads and the rest of it, he must be a pretty overwhelming sight when he's coming at you and really putting out.

I pulled my skate laces tight, wondering if I should try to get along without those extra socks and then remembering that I'd likely have to buy another pair of skates, a half-size smaller. Jean will use three or four pair a year sometimes, but I keep a pair of skates almost indefinitely (I'm apparently not giving them the same amount of wear). I decided to stay with the ones I've got, but I can see that he's right about the way the boot should fit, because he moves in skates as though they were attached to his feet by nature. When I came out to the ice, Jean was already skating around in the style of a pleasure-skater, somebody whom you might see at any city park on a winter afternoon skating for fun. It was plain how much he enjoys skating from the way he moved — everybody has seen a man like this at a neighbourhood park, who simply loves skating for its own sake because he's good at it and because it's a tremendously pleasurable activity in itself. That's an element that even a keen analyst of hockey might miss — the sheer physical pleasure of the basic activity involved. Some other sports require such intense, painful, concentrated effort (often because the physical movements involved aren't natural to the human body) that whatever pleasure results comes mainly from the competition. But hockey is built on a physical action that is a delight in itself, and you could tell this by watching Jean that morning in the TMR Arena. He skates in a way that tells you at once that he just damn well *loves* to skate, enjoys it, would do it as much and as often as he could, even after twenty years of amateur and professional hockey. It was a treat to watch.

At first he wasn't making the hockey player's moves. He was turning from back to front, stretching his legs out far, relaxing and pleasing himself and looking more like a figure-skater than I'd ever seen him. I realized, watching him in those first minutes, that if he hadn't been a hockey player he might have been the greatest of classical figure-skaters. The whole rhythm and line of skating changes when you take away the hockey stick; plenty of hockey players lose their grace and balance without it. Jean simply looked, if anything, more stylish and graceful without the stick than with it. But the thing that really caught my eye was his joy in being out there, just skating.

I hadn't been on skates since the first week in April, so I proposed some warm-up skating — to give me a chance to calm down a bit, but also because I really needed to see what Jean does. If you come into the Montreal Forum at seven-thirty on the night of a game to watch the teams take their warm-up, even if you're in a box seat, you might be misled into thinking that the boys aren't moving too fast or putting out very much. They just seem to laze along, working out the kinks perhaps, loosening up the knees and thighs and hips, but not going very fast.

It would be a mistake to think that. I'm a reasonably good skater for a man of forty who has never been a professional hockey player and

who is in moderately good physical shape. If I work out for forty
minutes or so, I get to the point where I can get over the ice relatively
fast. *Relatively fast*, that is.

I would say from close, direct observation that Jean can skate much
much faster backwards, without apparent effort, than I can skate
forwards at top speed. Make no mistake about it, a skater like me and a
skater like Béliveau — we aren't skaters in the same sense. I asked Jean
to begin by taking those slow warm-up strides, going from right to left
(counter-clockwise, which is his best turn and my bad one) and we
skated along beside each other and talked. He was skating pretty
upright, standing almost erect.

I said, "I thought you bent over a bit more, quite a lot more in fact."

"Not at the beginning of my warm-up. Watch, here's how you
begin."

He was taking rather short strides, kinking the legs slightly at the
knee and moving from both the knee and the thigh, quite loosely,
almost as if he were walking.

"If you come onto the ice," he said, "and start moving your fastest
immediately, you're taking the risk of a muscle pull, in the groin or the
calf. And you don't want to put too much strain on your knees at the
start of a workout. Knee trouble has hurt more good hockey players
than almost anything else. I like to move around slowly, and pretty
upright, at the beginning. As a matter of fact, during the first three or
four days of training camp, I'm likely to get soreness in the lower part
of my back, over the kidney region, from the bending forward that you
have to do when you're going full out."

I said, "I think of your skating stride as one that keeps you bent well
over, with your head and shoulders out in front of your torso."

"Oh yes, I'll bend. But you have to remember not to get over too far
forward because it can begin to cut off your breathing. A skater who's
in a tight crouch will get winded much quicker than somebody who's
more erect. So your first few minutes are like this, easy, not pushing
too hard."

"Where does the power in your stride come from, from those big
muscle groups up the back of the leg?"

"The push comes from there, but there's another element of your
stride, a kicking or stepping action, from the knee. I think the power
comes from your push, and the quickness from the knees and the
muscles above the knees in front of the leg. I told you about the big

muscle development on Yvan Cournoyer's legs, just above the knees. I think that's where he gets his quickness. The speed with which you can flex and unflex those knees, with that kicking action, is even more important than the strength of your push."

He began to skate a little faster, and I began to feel myself struggling and sweating. "O.K., Jean," I said, "let's see you let it out a bit."

He was gone. Like that!

I was now skating as fast as I can, and the gap between us widened and widened until Jean was moving at least twice as fast as I was. It was as though he'd pressed a switch or turned a key. He just moved his whole rib cage slightly forward and down, leaned a bit, and left me. What this change reminded me of most was the shifting action in an automatic transmission — there's a faint whir and bump and then you're in a new speed range. As Jean moved from the relaxed warm-up skating into something approximating game speed (approximating it, that is, at no time was he extending himself) there was a *qualitative* change in his motion — the difference between the professional and the amateur of modest ability. This is a real difference, not just one of degree; if what Jean does is skating, then what I do is not.

We'd started off counter-clockwise — Jean's good turn, and my awkward one, and I'd noticed that he was able to lean much further over as he turned, thus cutting a much sharper curve, than I could. It took me four or five extra strides to make the turn around the end of the rink. When we began to skate to my good side, clockwise, I could get a little further down towards Jean's turning angle, but not enough to save a single stride. I was still moving my legs in a flurry of waste motion, while he glided into and out of those big rink-wide turns in three to four strides. He got much more distance on each stride than I did; he could go much deeper into the corner areas than I could because of his sharper turns, and he was so wholly in control of his balance and his whole body, and so unconscious of the difficulty of skating that fast, that he could pay full attention to anything happening at any point on the ice surface.

An ordinary skater like me must always have in the back of his mind that, after all, he is positioned on a slippery surface and can easily fall. That obviously never crosses Jean's mind as he skates; he is so completely habituated to it that the possibility of losing his balance doesn't exist for him.

This is true of his skating backwards, just as much as the other way

round. When we'd done about five minutes of warm-up, he began to
show me some of the other aspects of his skating style. He swung
around to skating backwards, then to the front again, then backwards.
I noticed that whenever he turned around he did it with his weight on
his left foot, and I pointed it out.

"Do you always do that?"

"I do it instinctively when I'm not in a game. And I think that I'd
turn from forward to backward on the left foot in a game. But to move
from backward to forward in a game — you've got to be able to do that
on either foot. Just think about it! If you're trying to forecheck in front
of the net, and the puck-carrier comes out to your right, you've got to
be able to turn to that side, instinct or no instinct. I imagine that
everybody feels more comfortable to one side or other. I'm not giving
away any secrets when I tell you that I swing around easier with my
weight to the left."

"Would that make any difference in actual play?"

"I think it may make some difference. It's easier to pick some
players' weaknesses than it is others, and naturally you'll try to exploit
them where you can. But you can't keep a 'book' on the players in
hockey to the same extent you can in baseball, where the pitcher and
catcher can confer and set up a whole sequence of pitches to try to take
advantage of a batter's faults. Sometimes when I'm coming in on a
defenceman I'll remember that he's weak to the outside and try to go
there; but that might be impossible because of the position of my
wings."

"That turnaround to skating backwards is pretty important, right?"

"Yes, a defenceman has to be able to do it without thinking about it.
He'll find himself in a game skating backwards as fast as he can move,
without remembering how he got into that position or when."

"Let's see you do it," I said.

Jean began to move backwards, crossing one foot behind the other
in a rapid turn, and then switching to the defenceman's style, moving
the hips from side to side in a crouch, and this was when I found out
how much superior his backward skating was to my forward movement. He seemed to be aware of the precise dimensions of the rink, and
to feel no need to look behind him to see where he was going.

He said, "I know where I am from what's in front of me. You get a
sense after a while of how much space you've got to move in. And you

know where the other players are supposed to be. You can move backwards pretty freely in a game."

"And you do that when you're forechecking?"

"Only occasionally. But a defenceman will skate backward almost as much as forward in a game, and it's much more important to him than to a centre or a wing."

Watching him move like that, going around back to front at high speed and talking to me at the same time, began to make me feel slightly dizzy. "Why don't we pause for a minute?" I said. "You can show me the right way to stop, and I can use a stop right now."

He sent up a shower of ice with his skates, doing something I'd never noticed before, probably because I'd never seen him skate at this distance. Most ordinary skaters, braking while moving forward, will turn their knees to right or left, and brake with the blades of their skates parallel, so that their skates exert an equal braking force. The natural result of this is a dead stop, and a second motion is required to begin skating again. Jean doesn't do this. When he stops, the rear foot, almost always the left foot, exerts the braking force. He rocks the blade from toe to heel, almost like a dance stop, with the forward foot barely scraping on the ice. Doing it this way, he finishes up as though he were still in motion — poised with his weight in balance ready to swing off onto a new course. He doesn't seem to try to jam on his brakes, but rather to swing to a stop, such that the stop is only a minute pause before a new action begins. The rocking action of the rear skate lifts his weight, as though he were making an almost invisible jump from a springboard, at the end of the manoeuvre. This is because the actual game is played in that way — no time should elapse between a stop and a new start; they should flow right into each other.

"It all comes from that rear foot," Jean says, "and the forward foot is like a rudder or a wing, a guide more than anything else. Often you don't come to a full stop between whistles."

"I've been doing it wrong all my life," I said.

"No, what you're doing is correct if you want to stop dead. It's just that most of the time you have to go in a new direction at once. So you move right through your stop and push up and off."

He did it again and I watched carefully; the swinging, lifting motion was very evident and extremely graceful.

Jean said, "Doing what you do is a good exercise, stopping completely and starting up again. I don't do it during the pre-game warm-up, but in practice, I'll do plenty of stops and starts for my wind; they really take it out of you. Another exercise that I use all the time is to skate around the rink at the warm-up pace, then when I come to the blueline I'll go as hard as I can to the next blueline, then slow down and make my turn, then go hard from blueline to blueline. That simulates game conditions very closely. You're changing speeds without thinking about it during a game, and you need to be able to shift gears, so to speak, without having to think about it. Any change in speed should come as a surprise to your check, so you have to be able to change without giving any sign that you're going to do it. Watch me."

He skated around the rink a couple of times, changing pace at the bluelines, and again the fluidity of his style was striking. Approaching the blueline, he'd be moving easily, and suddenly as he crossed it his whole body would blur into the new speed without any warning.

"That's an excellent exercise," he said, skating back over to me. "I think the Rocket had the best change of pace I've ever seen. You'd think he'd be going all out, when all at once he'd burst over that blueline so fast you wouldn't believe it was the same man. It's something you simply have to be able to do without having to think about it."

That's perhaps the really remarkable thing about Jean's style; it's completely natural and apparently unconscious; he'll make adjustments in his pace and balance, and the way he holds his body, constantly as the demands of the situation dictate, without strain or effort. And he can do things that you have to see close up to believe, amazing feats of dexterity. Watching from the stands, you might think taking a face-off a pretty simple operation, where even a mediocre player might have an almost equal chance against Jean. It isn't so.

We took eight or ten face-offs together, with Gerry Patterson dropping the puck. As the centres come up to the point of the face-off, their sticks are about at the centre of the red spot on the ice, with the tip of the stick as close to the edge of the spot as possible. You can't put the blade of the stick into the red area till the puck drops. A top centre moves that stick blade in there like a knife blade — snick, snick, in, out — and it's hard to believe how fast Jean's stick moves. When that puck hits the ice, his blade comes in, zip, zip, and the puck is twenty feet away, just where he wants it. Taking these face-offs with him, I was astounded — it's the only word — at the speed of this movement, and I could understand how Yvan Cournoyer could score a crucial goal against the Rangers *six seconds* after a face-off outside the New York blueline.

Jean's stick action at the face-off is difficult to describe. When I watched it happen the comparison that immediately occurred to me was the motion of a small snake's tongue. Those little snakes are often seen around summer cottages, and they catch insects on the end of their tongues, with the tongue sliding in and out so fast that you can barely see it. That's the way Jean moves his stick; he must have wrists of incredible strength and sensitivity because he doesn't just get the puck, he can put it precisely where he wants it. On several of the face-offs we tried he sent it back to the point to his left, and for the life of me I still can't see how he directed the puck in that direction. I watched as hard as I could, trying to win one face-off, and I could not see any movement in his stick blade that would move the puck behind him. But that's where it went; the aiming motion was too fast for me to see it. And I didn't win any face-offs either.

The movement of his wrists and the blade of the stick is simply too fast to see. We took one after another, and Jean would call his shot, "Left wing. To the point. In front of the net. Shot on net." And he put the puck exactly where he called it every time. Not within a foot of where he intended; *exactly* where he intended, just like a billiards champion. The delicacy of the wrist and arm motion must be quite a lot like that used in handling a cue, infinitely accurate. I think this particular revelation was the thing that impressed me the most about our workout. Jean has been taking face-offs for twenty-five years, and I figured he'd be a master at it, but I hadn't expected that what he does would be such a different kind of thing from the very best, most concentrated attention I could bring to the play.

We would move into position and I'd be concentrating just as hard as I could on moving my stick as the puck fell, and I'd listen to Gerry Patterson's voice, only half hearing it.

"You guys ready?"

The puck would drop and I'd move my stick as fast as I could, really flicking my wrists, and it wouldn't be any use. The puck would be at the blueline where the point man would pick it up. Gerry and Jean would be grinning at me, and I'd come out of my fit of concentration and say, "I can't see how you did that."

It was the same with the passing game. A little exercise that players will use in a practice or before a house-league or minor-league game is to stand maybe ten feet apart and start passing the puck back and forth from one to another, gradually moving back so that the distance increases; the object is to make the pass as flat along the ice and as crisp, sharp, as possible. You try to get that good wrist action going for you so that the puck has some zap on it, and you try to put it right on the other guy's blade. You can practice receiving the puck as it comes back to you, cradling it carefully by inclining your stick blade over it as it comes in. The trick is to ease that puck back onto your blade with no hops or ricochets which might cause you to lose control. Standing more or less still like that, you can pass pretty precisely — better than you might in a game. It's fun to do and it's very good for the wrists.

When Jean and I tried this exercise, I had a little better luck than with those face-offs. The arena staff had given us beautiful ice — not a scratch on it when we arrived — and the puck wasn't flipping over deep cuts or chips on the ice. It slid smoothly, which meant I could propel the puck better than I usually do. So that was fine; but it didn't put me in Jean's league, or remotely near it, even on this simple exercise. His passes were beautiful — it's the only word — in their precision and their extraordinary force.

It was their force that really got me. Ordinarily when you get one of these warm-up passes from one of your friends, it'll come quickly all right, but you don't feel it all the way up the handle of your stick and right up your arms into your shoulders. With Béliveau passes, you do. He'd be standing there, twenty feet away, plenty of light in the building, nobody getting in our way, and nevertheless I couldn't spot what he was doing that was so different from what I'm used to. He was doing something, though, because the puck was coming to me with the same minute accuracy as the face-offs. I never had to move my blade; it was as though the puck was attached to it the way a yo-yo is attached to your finger, or as if it were magnetized by my blade. Once or twice I'd swear that I moved my stick after Jean put the puck in motion and — I don't understand how exactly — the puck *still* landed right where it should on the stick blade, a little towards the tip. It felt extraordinarily comfortable, just right, and then I had a sudden wave of understanding. Just like he's done with so many real hockey players, he was *making me look and feel good*. I suddenly understood why Dick Duff says that everybody wants to play with Jean. As a hockey player I am not good, but Jean was making it possible for me to execute this simple play properly. I wasn't losing the puck; it wasn't nipping over the top of my stick; it was just right. And yet it came with great force. I felt my blade moved backwards by the force of the impact, and I could sense the shock in my fingers, in the muscles of my forearms, even in my shoulders; as they say in baseball, he was really putting something on it.

The same thing happened when we tried making pass plays while we were in motion. I'm a right-hand shot, so I asked Jean to feed me some passes as I was breaking up the right side. He positioned himself just outside the defensive zone on the left side, and I took a wind-up, then skated as hard as I could down the right side, trying to keep my stick well out in front of me on the ice as a target. Skating hard like that I tend to forget everything except trying for speed, and I wasn't anticipating the arrival of the puck the way a good player would. But every time we tried the play, it would come out of nowhere on a sharp angle, and lay itself on my stick blade, or where the blade would be if I hadn't gone off balance and lifted it, or hadn't veered slightly because of my uncertainty on skates at that speed.

When Yvan Cournoyer is executing this play, Jean knows that he'll have his stick where it's supposed to be, that he won't suddenly jerk his head to one side to keep his balance, or change course slightly. He can therefore lay that pass in there exactly. With an amateur of no particular skill taking the pass, he can't be sure that his wing will be in the right spot. And yet the puck was always well within my reach, in a spot where I could have completed the play if I'd been properly co-ordinated.

We tried this play four times. On the first try, I got so absorbed in trying to move my feet with decent speed that I didn't look for the pass, just concentrated on trying to hold my skating together. The puck passed in front of me and bounced off the right boards. Even at that, I was able to get my stick on it after it had taken a bounce.

"Pretty good," Jean hollered at me. "But you've got to look for the pass. Let's try it again."

I huffed and puffed for a minute, got my breath back, and gasped, "Yeah, nearly had it." I came back down the ice, turned and started down the boards again. This time the pass came in very tight, almost on my skates. Cournoyer would kick it ahead; I just let it bounce away from me.

"You're skating a little faster now," Jean said. "Again?"

"Wait till I get my breath. O.K., let's have that again."

Back around, wind-up for a good run at it — this time I was in the groove enough to be able to look for the puck and when I saw it come I made the mistake of sweeping my stick back to pick it up behind me. Instead it passed well out of reach and banged into the corner.

"You don't need to reach back for it," Jean said. "If you've got your head twisted around as you stab at the puck, you're going to get knocked down, because you won't be looking for the defenceman. You have to trust the man who's making the pass to get it well up there, so the puck is where you can see it and the defence at the same time. Now we'll do it again."

"O.K." Wind-up, rush, go go go . . . this time I completed the play, not perfectly but acceptably, taking the puck on the face of the stick blade just in the right place to get off a forehand wrist shot. "I'll quit while I'm ahead," I said to Jean. "I didn't think you could get me to make that play. I've never taken a pass right in my life."

"Well, it isn't an easy play," he said. "When it's done right it looks easy; the winger seems to put his stick on the puck without breaking stride and without changing the design of the play. He and the puck are moving very fast, and they've got to come together just exactly right. In the NHL you can't be close with your passes; you've got to be dead on. The first time you tried it, the puck was in front of you, and you picked it up off the boards. In a game, you couldn't do that, because it wouldn't be there; the defenceman would have moved it out to his centre. Unless the pass is accurate, and the wing knows how to receive it, it'll turn into a loose puck and possession will change hands."

I was feeling winded, so I said, "Let's take a break, and then I'll play defence on you, is that O.K.?"

We ran through one-on-one defensive play next. (During this work-out, Jean managed to cover every aspect of the game except goal-tending.) I got into position, first at left, then at right defence, and he rushed the puck on me. I think that, next to those bewildering face-offs, the chance to watch Jean rush the puck was the most enlightening thing we did. I keep coming back to this idea that we might think a face-off was a face-off, or a fake a fake, no matter whether it was Béliveau doing it or an untalented amateur. Ha!

I used to think of fakes as a recognizable distinct series of moves — a drop of the shoulder, a feint in one direction or another, a look to right or left, a deke with the stick — separate and distinguishable movements. When Jean makes a series of fakes, they come so fast that they blur together, and you just don't know where the puck is. The whole series is so smooth it's incredible. I'd heard of defencemen "getting tangled in their skates" but never thought it was more than a metaphor. It isn't a metaphor; it's exactly what happened to me every time he rushed the puck on me. Just like during the face-offs, I'd be watching him come towards me as keenly as I could and then the funny business would start. As nearly as I can figure it, he'd do six or eight different things in *under two seconds*, and then he'd be behind me.

It seems to me that I'd have time to think one thing — go left, say, or go right — and by the time I'd started to do it I'd know that I was going the wrong way, try to reverse myself, and find one leg going left and the other right. That's when I began to get the feeling of getting tangled in my skates.

The first time it happened, I said to myself, "I should have tried a pokecheck." So the next time I held my stick in the left hand and shoved it way out to my left, at the same time getting down as low as I could, trying to cover as wide an area as possible. He put the puck between my legs that time.

"If you do that with your stick," he said, "there's nothing to prevent me from moving the puck through there. And I know you're not going to hit me."

"You can count on that," I said, laughing.

"Another thing," he said. "You're backing much too far in. You're screening your goalie. What you want to try to do is make the play as close to the defensive blueline as possible. Everybody knows that, I think, but sometimes it's hard to do."

"There's one other thing I'd like to try on defence," I said. "You know that play where you lean on the defenceman, and control the puck with your right hand as you go around him? Let's try that."

"You want me to lean on you?"

"Not exactly. I don't think you'll have to, but I want to see what that play looks like from here."

"All right," he said, a little doubtfully, I thought, and he went back to centre-ice to start his rush.

The photographs of this particular play are famous; they always show Jean leaning over at an angle to his left, with his left arm crooked by his chest, with the other arm stretched way out so that the puck is out of the defenceman's area altogether. When you see the photograph, the action is still. I'd always wondered what it looked like to the defenceman in the middle of the play.

He started to come at me, and I got hypnotized. I knew what he was going to do, and considered making a move. But on skates Jean stands six-five, and seeing somebody that tall and heavy bearing down on you and preparing to lean on you is disconcerting. I suddenly remembered I had a wife and children, and thought to myself, "You'd better get out of the way before you get killed." He came by me just as he does in the pictures, down low to his left, and you can bet I wasn't doing anything to get in his way. I couldn't have got near that puck with a bulldozer. The idea of that much weight at that speed was the thing that persuaded me. Anyway, I got a good look as he went by in that familiar attitude, which looked just the way it does in the pictures except for the motion and its intimidating quality.

"I can see how you'd have a lot of success with that one," I said.

Jean said, "It's my best move," and chuckled.

After that it seemed to me safer to pack up the riskier parts of the session, so we finished with some shooting exercises, working in turn on each of the three fundamental shots; the slapshot from a distance, the wrist shot from closer in, and the backhand.

Jean began with his slapshot and I kept a close eye on him. Of the different shots, the slapshot is probably the most misunderstood by young players, who usually try for power at the expense of accuracy.

"It's no good at all if you can't put it on the net," Jean kept saying, underlining the point. "Plenty of players will get the blade up above their heads on the backswing, and then move it through the puck as hard as they can, like driving a golf ball or swinging for home runs. Now, even in golf or baseball a shorter and more controlled swing will give you greater accuracy, and you aren't on skates. It stands to reason that if you're moving fast on ice when you swing you'll need all the accuracy you can get. Otherwise your shot will be banging off the boards, ten feet from the net — which just means a loose puck and possession for the defending team. What you want to do with a slapshot is to combine power and accuracy. Here, I'll show you."

He shot several times with pinpoint accuracy, calling the target each time. "Upper left corner, upper right corner, left side low, right side low." He could put it anywhere he liked, and his backswing was very short. The blade of the stick was coming back maybe three feet, just about even with his hips, no higher. I spotted something else that was very interesting which you wouldn't be able to see from a seat in the arena. The blade of his stick wasn't sweeping through the puck completely uncontrolled. As the blade came down to the ice, the lower edge right on the ice surface, just before the point of impact Jean made a slight adjustment to the angle of the blade, like a golfer who is trying to get under the ball in a trap. There was the slightest little wiggle in there, just enough to put some additional control on the puck. This movement didn't slow up the stick's motion at all, but it was perceptible — getting the face of the stick blade more "open."

I mentioned this.

"Right, Jean said. "Maybe I'm taking something off the power of the shot when I do that; but you have to remember that I'm not taking slapshots from the blueline or beyond it. I'm usually shooting from thirty feet away or less. The defenceman who's blasting away from the point may be hoping for a deflection more than anything else. He just wants to be around the net, hoping that the man in front will get his stick on it. Plenty of goals are scored like that. But when I shoot, I'm usually in pretty good scoring position, and I'm shooting to score, not looking for a deflection. Not many people have noticed that little adjustment I put in there. I do it instinctively, I think, in an attempt to put a little hook on the puck — to make the shot a bit lively, not just a dead straight line."

"Do you do that on all the different shots?"

"With the wrist shot everybody does it, I believe. There isn't the same blasting action on the wrist motion, and you're much more conscious of the way the puck lies on your blade. When I take a slapshot, that stick waggle has to come unconsciously or not at all. But with the wrists moving, I can feel a much greater degree of control over the puck. The wrist shot is the most important shot, I think, and the one young players should concentrate on."

"That's funny," I said. "When I go out to the rink on winter afternoons all I see is kids banging slapshots off the boards."

"It's an impressive sound," Jean said, " and I guess it shows off your strength, but you won't score with it as much as with the wrists. That banging noise tells the story. When the puck goes in the net, you don't hear any banging."

He started flicking wrist shots from around twenty-five feet out, and he was getting plenty of power into them. When I remembered the face-offs, and the way he moved the puck on passes, I wasn't surprised to see how much zing there was in the movement on the puck. Actually I shouldn't say he was flicking his wrists, because he doesn't use a flipping, lifting motion; that would put too much loft on the puck and reduce its speed and liveliness. Like a good golfer or baseball player he seems to roll his wrists to impart power. The flicking action is too jerky and hesitant to result in either accuracy or smooth power.

"For a left-hand shot like me," he said, "the left hand, the hand further down the stick, is the power hand, and the right is the control hand. When you roll your wrists, you shouldn't jerk the stick and lift the blade, or you may top the shot. And if you dig too far under the puck it may simply flip into the air. It's a pretty delicate adjustment, and you only learn to make it after long practice. As far as shooting goes, the best advice I can give is to practice the smooth, even wrist shot more than anything else; it's the shot that will get more results than any other."

"It isn't a looping shot," Jean said, "and it has to come fast. The backhand, that's different. Most of the time when you're shooting from the backhand you'll be off balance and in a hurry, usually because you've gone to the backhand to evade somebody who's checking you closely. And the whole physical action of the shot is reversed. Instead of that lower-down power hand's *pushing* the stick, it's *pulling* it or sweeping it. It's practically impossible to get the same power on a backhand shot as on a forehand, and nobody uses it by choice. It's a strategic move, and it has to be more of a sweep or a flick than anything else. Even at that you can get something on it if you work at it. Just like the other ways to shoot, it needs as much control as you can manage. I think the most important thing with the backhand is not to lift it too much. A really fine backhand, like Red Berenson's, can look almost like a forehand, and it's usually a short sweep of the blade, not a flick."

Jean grinned, looking as though he remembered plenty of duels in the goal-mouth. "One special kind of backhand comes when you've had to come in very close to get the goalie to move and you've gone by him. If you've got the reach, you can go to your backhand and nudge the puck to the open side. There, of course, it's more like putting than anything else; you don't want to whack at the puck, a little tap will do it. Whack at it in a hurry and you may bounce it against the goal-post. I've had that happen, and I've felt foolish afterwards. In as close as that you want complete accuracy. You just show the goalie the puck on your forehand, and when he moves you draw it back to you, go to the backhand and go to the open side."

I've seen Jean do exactly that hundreds of times in games, when it looked so relaxed and easy that I figured that I could do it myself. After this Sunday morning session my eyes were opened, and I knew that he play as he described it required infinite precision and delicacy and I thought again of the snake's tongue, flicking in and out so fast that the eye couldn't follow it.

"I think that about covers things," I said, and we skated to the boards. Jean was warmed up. I could see that. But he wasn't taking any deep breaths, the way I was. It made me think of the referee and the linesmen in the NHL. They're out there for the whole game without substitutions, and they must do plenty of skating before the night is over.

"Are those officials pretty good athletes too?" I asked Jean.

"You bet they are. Some of those guys are wonderful skaters, and you know they're apt to be a bit older than the players. The officials in the NHL are hand-picked, and they can all stay right with the play. They have to.

"Now and then you'll find that one of the officials is having an off night, getting out of position and missing a call here and there," he said. "But for the most part they're right on top of the play, and they all skate very well. Sometimes I wonder how they can do it — stay out there right through the period, when the players are taking shifts."

I had one or two last questions to ask Jean while he was getting his skates off. I noticed that he used the same make of skates as I do, something that pleased me, perhaps irrationally, and I wanted to know whether he had any special comments on his equipment. There was, as it turned out, one very interesting thing about his skates.

"I wear a half-size larger on the left foot. Whenever I'm breaking in a new pair of skates, I always feel perfectly comfortable on the left foot as I've worn them for a bit. But I almost never get the right foot to feel exactly right, no matter how long I wear the skates, even though the boot is smaller than the left one. Look here!"

He held out his skates for me to examine. Sure enough, the left was a nine, and the right an eight-and-a-half. And the left boot looked — this is hard to describe — as though it had taken the individual shape of his foot more distinctly than the right. The left boot was a bit more worn and sliced up.

"Let's see your feet," I said, and I looked at them closely. The left foot wasn't so much bigger than the right as more developed muscularly — the difference between a part of your body that you use a lot and one that you use less.

"You know what?" I said. "I'll bet that's because your left foot is doing so much more work of the work in your skating. After all, you stop on the left foot, most of the time you take your shot off the left foot, and you turn around to that side much more than to the right. I'll bet you're putting the weight on the left foot eighty percent of the time."

There was no doubt of it; the difference in the muscle development was obvious.

Jean said, "I wouldn't be surprised if most people find it hard to fit both feet exactly with a standard pair of skates. After all, you can't walk into a store and ask the salesman to give you one size nine and one size eight-and-a-half. There's another thing. Two years ago the skate manufacturers changed the design of the toe cap on the skates I use; they switched from steel to a new plastic which is stronger and a bit lighter. And I can feel the difference still. The plastic leaves just that little bit of extra room in the toe. I found it quite hard to get used to, for a surprisingly long time. I don't exactly think about the fit of my skates when I'm playing, but I know when I'm not perfectly comfortable." He looked at his feet with a grin. "I guess there isn't much to be done about it."

"Do you wear the same skates all the time?"

"No. I usually use two pair at at time, switching them from game to game, sometimes even between periods if I'm not satisfied with the edge of the blades. Two pair will do me for half a season, then I'll work in two more. And no matter how carefully I break them in, one skate fits better than the other."

It seemed to me that a really enormous force must be exerted over a long time to make a significant difference in the size of the two feet; but the difference was there, visible to the eye. The twenty years of stopping, turning, putting weight into the shot, have left their mark physically after all.

That small discovery somehow seemed to me to mean something important about Jean and his career. Here's a man whose style in his life and his work is just about perfect, who does what he's meant to do with utter grace in a way that makes physical strain and the necessity of endurance seems invisible. And yet he too has paid for his style and grace; the twenty years of effort have left their mark on him, even on Béliveau.

That pleasant informal workout on the ice was one of the most unusual occasions of my life, because of the even decency and friendliness of its tone. Jean does things so well — it sounds extravagant to say this but it's true all the same — that other people do things well too. He makes you look good.

Saturday

"O body swayed to music, O brightening glance,
How can we know the dancer from the dance?"

— W. B. Yeats, "Among School Children"

THE TALK HAS LOCALIZED AND QUIETED. On our wide gray bench, on the floor, in identical white longjohns shrunk identically up our calves and forearms, we sit or lie and wait for Bowman. At 6:31 p.m. he enters. Instinctively we straighten, our heads turning as one, following him acorss the room. Short, with bull-like shoulders and neck, his head tipped back, his prominent jaw thrust ahead of him as both lance and shield, he strides purposefully to a small blue chalkboard. We wait quietly. With his back to us, he looks to one side of the board, then to the other, turns, turns again, and screams,

"Eddy! Pierre! Where's the chalk?"

We blink; the mood breaks. There is surprised laughter all around.

Bowman writes the Detroit Red Wings' line-up on the board, grouping defense pairs and forward lines together, adding three or four unconnected names at the bottom. Turning, he looks at us briefly, then throws out his jaw, his eyes jerked upward to a row of white cement blocks directly above our heads, where they remain. He's ready.

"We had a guy watch [the Wings] in Boston last week," he begins quietly, "and these are the lines they went with," reading off what he's just written. "But they've had a lot of guys in and out of the line-up, so there may be some changes."

His tone is calm and conversational, even subdued, and while he often begins this way, we're never quite prepared for it.

"What we gotta do is work on some of these guys," he continues slowly. "McCourt," he says, pointing to centre Dale McCourt's name, "this is a real key guy. He likes to hold onto the puck and make plays, a lot like Mikita." His voice picks up speed as if he is suddenly interested in what he's saying. "If ya give him the blueline, he can hurt ya." Then it slows and deepens to a rich baritone, in his eyes a look that wasn't there before. "We gotta get on this guy!" he blares, his right palm hammering the point into his open left hand. "Right on him!" Then, just as suddenly quiet again, "We gotta skate him," he says gently, still talking about McCourt. "This guy doesn't like to skate," and as that thought triggers another, his lips curl and tighten over his teeth. "We gotta *make* him skate!" he roars.

With only the slightest pause but with another change in tone, he discusses Vaclav Nedomansky, the former great Czechoslovak player ("He handles the puck well, but he'll give it up," Bowman says flatly, "specially in his own zone"), hard-shooting defenseman Reed Larson ("We gotta play him like Park or Potvin," he insists. "You left-wingers, play him tight"), Errol Thompson, Willie Huber, penalties and power plays, the Wings' defense, on and on like a never-ending sentence; and my attention span collapses. I look around and see bodies dancing on the benches from buttock to buttock, eyes ricocheting around walls, off ceiling and floor — Bowman's lost us. Then something he says reminds him of something else, and he gets us back again, ". . . and for crissake," he shrieks, his voice a sudden falsetto, "somebody do something about that squirt Polonich," referring to the Wings' pesky little goon Dennis Polonich. "I'm tired of him running around thinkin' he runs the show." Then more slowly again, his voice an angry baritone, *"Put that guy down!"* But before his last message can completely register, he quickly mentions Dan Labraaten's speed, interrupting himself to talk about Thompson's shot, then Jean Hamel and Nick Libett. He loses us again.

It's as if his mind is so fertile and alive that each thought acts as a probe, striking new parts of his brain, spilling out thoughts he is helpless to control, each with its own emotion. A transcript might read garbled, frustratingly short of uninterrupted thoughts, but his message is clear. It is attitude more than information. And though he drones on about the Wings, the message is about us. For the Wings, nearly a last-place team, are irrelevant if we play well, and Bowman won't pretend otherwise. So every few seconds, triggered by nothing in particular, he throws out a new thought, in an angry, insistent tone, and gets our attention back.

Some nights he talks only ten minutes; a few times, to our wound-up agony, twenty-five minutes or more. When he finishes, we mock what he says for most of an hour after he says it, until just before game time. Then as we panic to cram in all the last-minute thoughts and emotions we suddenly feel we need, we throw back at each other what he told us an hour before, this time in *his* tone.

Restless, bored out of our own private daydreams, we discover each other. Under cover of hanging clothes, we make jungle sounds, stick fingers up our noses, laughing wildly, silently, Bowman continuing as if unaware. Lapointe, his face loose and denture-free, stares at Lemaire innocently fingering the tape on his stick. Knowing what's coming next, we watch one, then the other: Lemaire looks up; Lapointe grins dementedly. Grabbing a towel, Lemaire buries his giggle and covers up. Then, like a slap in the face, Bowman interrupts himself and gets us back. "... and that Woods," he says, referring to Paul Woods, a small, quick center, who once played with the Voyageurs, "is there some reason we can't touch that guy?" he asks pleasantly. Then angrily, "Is there? For crissake, I see Lupien pattin' him on the ass," and before he can go on, we start to laugh. Startled, at first he seems not to understand the laughter; then, enjoying it, he begins to camp it up; "And Mondou," he continues, hunching over, wrinkling his nose, "sniffin' around him, 'Hiya Woodsie. How are ya, Woodsie?' and the guy's zippin' around havin' a helluva time." Unable to hold back, we scream with laughter. We're with him now. Then the look in his eyes changes. The joke's over. "You're not playin' *with* him!" he roars. "Hit him!"

He has been going nearly fifteen minutes. The periods of calm now longer, the emotional bursts more infrequent, he has just one left. Telling us to tighten up defensively, particularly the Lemaire line, he reminds himself of something very familiar: "And when we got the puck in their zone," he yells, "for crissake, don't just dump it out in front blind. That's the worst play in hockey." Mouthing the last few words with him, we look at each other and smile.

He pauses for a breath, and his tone changes one last time. Calm and conversational, as he was when he started, Bowman sums up: "Look, don't take this team lightly. They've had their problems, but they've had injuries and they're getting some of their guys back. And now they're comin' on a bit. They've only lost one of their last three, so we gotta be ready for a good game. We gotta think of our division first. This is a four-pointer, and we got 'em back in Detroit next week. Let's put 'em down now and we won't have to think about 'em the rest of the year."

His eyes leave the row of blocks above our heads and move to the floor in front of him, "Okay, that's all," he says quietly.

We leap up clapping and shouting. When he's out the door, the room goes quieter. Leaning back, Shutt carefully folds his arms. "Scott was very good tonight," he offers cheerily. Then, looking at the clock, "Cut in on my backgammon time though. That's gonna cost me some bucks." Standing, he looks over a room now busily in motion, "Okay, who's my pigeon?" he asks. Several heads pop up, then, seeing who it is, turn away, ignoring him. He tries again, "C'mon, who'll it be?" Seated beside him, as if tugging on his master's pant-leg, Lafleur mutters a half-hearted challenge. Though he beats him less often than he likes to admit, Shutt, a look of disdain on his face, turns and pleads, "Come on, Flower, give it a rest. Think what you do to my conscience," and looking around, he asks again. Nothing. His point now made, "All right, Flower," he sighs theatrically, "let's go," and with a grin and a board under his arm, he walks from the room, Lafleur shaking his head behind him.

With Robinson and Tremblay, I go to the weight room. Nearly as big as the dressing room, a few years ago when the Soviets showed they were good enough on the ice to make what they did off it seem important, the room was renovated and packed tight with weight equipment to encourage off-ice training. But since we have won so often without it ("don't change the luck"), the equipment has been forgotten or ignored by all but a few. Instead, we use the room in other ways: before games, it is a place to go when the game is far enough away it can still be escaped, when a roomful of players with nothing to do, anxious and uneasy, builds up the mood of a game before it wants to.

Lafleur and Shutt set their board on a bench. I lie on the carpeted floor near Risebrough, easing into some exercises. Across the room, eyes extruded, Engblom reddens from the weight of a bench press, Lambert reads a newspaper, Robinson glances at some mail, Chartraw here and there bangs at the heavy bag, Houle and Tremblay, half seated on a pop cooler, stir their coffee and talk. It is like a Sunday afternoon at the club — easy, unconcerned, the game still far away. Lying on my back and barely conscious, I stretch through old, well-worn routines, nothing new, nothing unexpected, counting holes in ceiling tiles until the holes and tiles disappear, nothing to jar me into remembering where I am and what I'm doing it for, moving only enough to blank my mind.

Some minutes later, aware of a sound, I stir. "Seven o'clock!" a voice cries again. "Everybody in the room." It is trainer Meilleur, and hearing him this time, I look up, and everyone is gone.

I walk back to the room, the game inescapable.

Shin pads, shoulder pads, socks, pants and sweaters cover the floor. The random movement in and out of the room has stopped. Voices that can't shut up rebound from its walls — the build-up has begun.

"Need this one, guys. Gotta have it."

"Yessir gang, gotta be ours."

"Big one out there. Big one."

But still twenty-two minutes until the warm-up, it's too serious, too soon, and, feeling uncomfortable, we back off. The mood changes.

"It's a four-pointer, gang," Houle reminds us, unaware of the change.

"You're right, Reggie," Savard says absently. "If they beat us they're only forty-seven points behind us."

"Yeah, then we gotta think about 'em the rest of the year," mocks Shutt, and there's loud laughter.

Risebrough looks across at Chartraw: "Hey Sharty, you think about 'em?" There's no answer. Chartraw, lying on the floor, a towel over his head, didn't hear the question. Risebrough asks again. The towel moves. "Who?" Chartraw asks.

"The Wings," he is told.

"The Wings," he repeats, and says nothing more.

Feeling the mood swing too far, something in all of us becomes panicky.

"Hey, c'mon guys, gotta be ready."

"Goddamn right, guys. These guys are playin' well."

"That's right, that's right. They only lost one of their last three."

But still too early, again it breaks.

"Yup, only one of their last three, only eleven of their last thirteen," chirps Shutt, and there's more laughter.

"I hope you were listening, Tremblay," Robinson shouts, thinking of something else. "Ya don't just dump it out in front blind. You heard him, 'It's the worst play in hockey.'"

Gainey looks at Lapointe. "Hey Pointu, what number we up to now?" he asks.

Lapointe, who knows such things, shrivels his eyes. "Uh, lemme see," he says, thinking aloud, "the worst play in hockey, number 117, I think," then, more sure of himself, "Yeah, 117."

"Hey, what was 116?" someone asks.

"Shootin' it in your own net," a voice shouts, and there's more laughter.

Every practice, every game, more than 150 times a year, every year, I put on my equipment the same way — inner jock first, then longjohns, sweat socks (the left ones first), outer jock, garter belt, hockey socks (the left one first), pants (left leg first), skates and pads (left ones first), arm vest, and finally sweater (left arm first). Dressing in layers as we do, the order can't vary much, but when it does, when I put on my right skate before my left, it doesn't feel right and I take it off again. It isn't superstition, it's simply habit and what feels right.

When I put on my equipment, it must go on at a steady, preoccupying pace: by 7:07, pants; 7:12, skates; 7:17, pads; 7:20, arm vest and sweater. After each is put on, as if reaching a checkpoint, I look back at the clock behind me: too fast, and with time and nothing to do I think about the game or whatever else crosses my mind; too slow, and I rush, and by rushing wonder if somehow I've affected how I will play. Not wanting to wonder, not wanting to think about the game or something other than the game, I keep rigidly to schedule. After a somnolent day of newspapers, naps, walks, TV, ceiling holes, and hypnotic exercises, I want to arrive at game time undistracted, my mind blank, my emotions under control. I know that if I can, the rest of me is ready.

It never quite happens, of course, and after this long I know that when a game begins, none of it matters anyway. Still, to keep worried, nagging voices under control, it is a routine I won't give up.

Suddenly remembering something he's heard, Shutt blurts, "Hey, ya hear Pit [Pete Mahovlich] got into a fight at a Penguins team party? Yeah, some guy knocked him down."

He gets murmurs of interest, but no surprise.

"Hell, doesn't take much to knock Pit down at a party," a voice mumbles.

"Or anywhere else."

"Poor old Pit," Robinson laughs, shaking his head, "no wins, eighty-four losses."

Waiting his chance, Tremblay jumps in before he is ready. "That's like you, Robinson," he growls, and, startled, we look up. Houle stifles a grin.

"Ooh Larry, that's a shot. You're not gonna take that, are ya?" Houle asks, doing his best to see that he doesn't. Before it can go any further, Lapointe steps in. "Hey, c'mon, let's be fair," he says, sounding suspiciously fair. "When has Bird *ever* had a fight?"

There is silence.

Happily back into something he started, Tremblay repeats the question, "When *has* Bird ever had a fight? Anybody remember?" We look blankly at each other. "Anybody?"

Robinson can't hold himself back any longer. "*Câlisse*, listen to that," he snaps with pretended outrage. "You guys're pretty brave startin' something, but ya sure disappear fast."

Suddenly contrite, Tremblay hangs his head. "Yeah, you're right, Bird. You *do* help us a lot," he says almost apologetically. "I mean, the way you stand up to 'em, threatenin' 'em, pointin' that finger of yours at 'em," and, standing up, hunching up his shoulders, he glowers at an imaginary face inches beneath him, his right index finger jabbing frighteningly at the air.

"'Hey, don't do that to my buddy,'" Tremblay warns in a not quite deep voice, "'don't *ever* do that. If I catch you breakin' his jaw again, *point point point*,'" he says, jabbing three more times. Pausing as if something further has happened, he goes on, this time more excited: 'Hey wait a minute. Wait a minute!' he shouts, his voice pitching higher. "'Ya did it again. I told ya not to do it, didn't I? Didn't I?'" he repeats, now really excited. "'Jesus, now ya got me mad. I can't believe how mad I am. Boy, am I mad,'" and finally pushed to the limit, anger exploding out of him, "'and if you *ever ever* do that again, *point point point*...'"

There is loud laughter.

Gradually, hearing each other laugh, we become scared and quickly stop. "C'mon, we're too loose. We got a game tonight," a voice shouts. Then another.

"That's right, that's right. Gotta pick it up, guys."

But with the slightest pause, the spasm breaks. Savard turns to Lambert. It happens at almost the same time each time we play the Wings. "Hey, Lambert," he taunts liltingly, "you should be mad, Lambert," and with that, and knowing the rest, Lambert begins to laugh. He had been drafted originally by the Wings, a year later left unprotected and claimed by the Canadiens. "They didn't want you,

Lambert," Savard needles with great delight. "They just shit on ya. Come on, Lambert. Get mad. Get mad."

And when Savard finishes, Robinson, Gainey, or one of several others starts in on him. "You too, Sarge," the voice will say, and with that we begin to laugh. Nine years ago, the Wings, already in the playoffs, eased through the final game of the season, losing 9–5 to the Rangers, putting the Rangers in a tie with the Canadiens, and, after the Canadiens lost to Chicago, into the playoffs on total goals; the Canadiens, Savard, Cournoyer, and Lemaire included, were eliminated. "Come on," the voice taunts, "they quit on ya. They made ya look like assholes, Sarge. You owe 'em something. Get mad, Sarge. Get mad." And with that, as abruptly as the subjects came up, they go away until the next Wings game.

Ten minutes. I strap on my right pad. Preoccupied with time and equipment and not yet the game, the room is quieter, if no more serious. Too quiet. Uneasy, thinking of Cournoyer, the team's captain, at home, his distinguished career probably over, Lapointe says, "Hey, let's win this one for Yvan," and instantly the room picks up. "Poor little guy," he continues, "his back all busted up, probably just lyin' at home..." and as he pauses as if to let his words sink in, Shutt and Houle jump in before anyone else can.

"...havin' a little wine..."

"...a little Caesar salad..."

"...poor little bastard," Lapointe muses sadly, and we all laugh.

I'm not sure what I thought the Canadiens' dressing room would be like before a game, though in me there was certainly a lingering image and a Marty Glickman-like voice that went with it:

"Here we are inside the dressing room of pro sports' greatest franchise, the Montreal Canadiens. See and hear the majestic Béliveau, the lion-hearted Richard, the enigmatic Mahovlich. Watch as a team of proud, aging veterans readies itself for one more crack at hockey's top prize, the coveted Stanley Cup."

The first time was almost eight years ago, in Pittsburgh before my first NHL game. I remember being surprised, even disappointed, that it seemed so like every other dressing room I had been in: players undressing, dressing, no special words spoken, no mood of a different quality, no solemn rituals that set it apart. Then about ten minutes before the warm-up, it changed. The powder sock appeared. An ordinary sweat sock filled with talcum powder and taped shut at its open end, though uncommon today, it was used by many at the time to turn tacky black stick-tape a more pleasing shade of gray. This time, it appeared for a different reason.

"Hey, nobody get Fergie's new suit," a voice shouted, and before the fractious Ferguson could move, the powder sock splattered against his dark blue jacket, leaving it a not-so-pleasing powder blue. Amid laughter, a sympathetic voice cried, "Oh Fergie, that's terrible. Here, lemme help." The helper rubbed at the powder with a large ball of cotton, plastering it over with a thick cotton mat. Furious, laughing, Ferguson grabbed the sock; others, their skate laces dragging, ran from the room with their clothes, the sock pinballing here and there after them. When it disappeared about five minutes later, five minutes before the warm-up to my first game, a heavy talcum cloud filled the room.

I can never sense the mood in the room before a game. Noisy, or quiet, each can be read a different way; both can mean the same. Some players use noise like exciting mood Muzak, riding it, building with it until game time; others need noise to blurt out the oppressive tension they feel, others to comfort themselves that all is well. I used to worry at the one-liners and frequent laughter before a game. Not my way, not a goalie's way, it seemed an incompatible distraction from what we were doing. But now I worry less. For a one-liner, a burst of encouraging chatter ("C'mon *this*" or "C'mon *that*"), an earnest gem of information, even a powder sock, can come from the same state of mind, depending on the way a player deals with pressure. Only for important regular-season and playoff games does the room sound different: a little more quiet, a little less laughter, as if noise is unneeded, laughter too easily misunderstood.

With only a few minutes left, Shutt suddenly remembers and looks across at Lupien. "Hey Loopie," he says with an unconcealed grin, "you and Mousse [Mondou] gonna get Woods?"

We begin to laugh, then laugh even harder thinking of what's coming next.

A chorus of mocking, adolescent-high voices fills the room.

" 'Hiya Woodsie. How are ya Woodsie?' "

" '. . . How're the wife and kids, Woodsie?' "

" '. . . Hey Woodsie, I got a new boat. It's a real beauty.' "

Laughing at first, Tremblay looks at Lupien. "Hey, Lupien," he snarls, "why don't ya give him a kiss?" Lupien sets his chin, then smiles. The routine is done.

"*Tabernac*," growls Robinson, breaking a skate lace. "Eddy, Eddy, I need a lace!" he shouts.

"Left or right?" a voice asks.

"Ri—," he starts, then stops angrily. "Eddy!" he tries again, "Boomer! Gaetan! Peter!" No one appears and he's run out of names.

"Oh, Ed-dy, Boo-mer, you can come out now." Nothing. A moment later, Lafleur appears. He's been at the Forum since 4:30 p.m., was fully dressed at 7 when I first noticed and probably long before that. He's been in the room at times, other places other times, and now he's back — his hair greased flat to the sides of his head, combed straight up in front, his teeth out, a toothbrush in his hand, brushing furiously at his gums. Lemaire sees him first.

"*Ta-berr-nac* . . ." he exclaims.

We look up; amid laughter, as if reading from a newspaper, a voice intones, "'. . . he waits as if in a trance, his only thought the game still four hours away. . . .'"

"*Câlisse*, you got *them* fooled, Flower," Savard laughs.

"Hey Shutty," Lapointe taunts, "there's your meal ticket."

Shutt, who has made a career feasting off his linemate's rebounds, is typically nonplussed. "Ah, that's the way I like to see him," he says, "ready, but not too ready. There'll be rebounds tonight."

Five minutes.

"Good warm-up, guys. Good warm-up."

Laces get tied, straps tightened, last-minute shoulder pads slapped into place. The clock eases forward with each anxious glance: two minutes, a minute, thirty seconds.

"Here we go, guys. Here we go."

Messages get shorter, louder, more urgent, and are unheard. Risebrough and Tremblay pace the room, then Mondou, Napier, Hughes, and one by one several more. Palchak hands me the game puck. Everyone's standing; we're ready.

Bowman enters.

"Okay, let's go," he says quiently, and with a shout we spring for the door.

The Forum is almost empty. A few hundred fans cheer as they see us in the corridor to the ice, but with no support from 16,000 vacant seats

around them, suddenly self-conscious, they go quiet. Grim-faced, my
eyes on a spot always a few feet in front of me, when I hear their fragile
sound I look up, and remembering this is the warm-up, I look down
again. The Wings are on the ice, I skate around, glancing back to look
for Vachon, but, out of sync, when I'm at centre he's a hundred feet
away circling his net. Skating faster, cutting each corner as I come to it,
a few laps later I pass him at centre, and we smile and nod as goalies do.
Gilles Gilbert winks, Tony Esposito and Chico Resch skate by as if
preoccupied with other things, Bernie Parent hovers near the centre-
line, reluctant to be anywhere else until the ritual is done. A few times,
eyeing each other up opposite sides of the ice and certain to pass at
centre, I looked suddenly away just to make him wait. But each time it
bothered me more than it did him, and a few laps later, smiling and
nodding I would play out my part.

I used to look for Joyce. A Forum usherette behind the visiting team's
bench, Joyce met me on the street one day, and we stopped to talk like
old friends. A few days later at the Forum, when I skated by in warm-
up, we smiled and nodded to each other. We won; and I played well.
From then on in each warm-up, skating counter-clockwise so I had the
width of the ice to get ready, I would smile and nod to Joyce. Then last
year, losing more often and playing poorly in the Forum, I stopped,
and haven't said hello to Joyce since.

I still have the puck that Palchak gave me. Free of the dressing room,
the team dances and cuts happily by me, but without a puck for nearly
a minute, they're getting impatient. When I was seven or eight years
old, the Toronto Marlboros, then a junior farm team of the Leafs, had a
goalie I liked named Johnny Albani. Small, with a short black crew-cut,
when Albani led his team onto the Gardens ice he would drop the puck
he held in his catching glove and shoot it off the protective glass to the
right of his net. *Clink*. It was a sound we heard only at the Gardens, for
at the time only the Gardens had protective glass, and a sound more
special because a goalie, using his awkward paddle-like stick, had
made it. So when I got home, grabbing my goalie stick and puck I
would go out to the backyard and try to emulate Albani. There, time
after time, I would draw the puck back, pivot, and power forward, at
the critical moment of release feeling my wrists roll over, my arms and
stick slam into slow motion, the puck slithering away in an arc, never
leaving the ground.

Years later, wrists firmed up, hours of practice behind me, Albani-

like I would lead my team onto the ice with a shot off the glass, but too often it was an unsatisfying shot off the boards, sometimes one that never left the ice. So, in time I tried something else. Turning joy and achievement to humourless superstition, *before each game, I must take the first shot; it must strike the boards to the right of my net between the protective glass and the ice. If it doesn't I will play poorly.* So, as the team waits anxiously, I look for an opening, fifteen to twenty feet of uncrowded space to take my important shot.

It's one of many superstitions I've come to burden myself with. I don't tell anyone about them, I'm not proud I have them, I know I should be strong enough to decide one morning, *any* morning, no longer to be prisoner to them. Yet I seem helpless to do anything about it.

Sports is fertile ground for superstition; crossed hockey sticks, lucky suits, magic stones, and things more bizarre, it comes from the mystery of athletic performance — the unskilled bat that goes 4-for-4, a goalpost, a bad hop, a *move*, brilliant and unconceived, that *happens*, and never happens again. *Luck*, we call it, and coming as it does without explanation, leaving the same way, when it comes we desperately try to hold onto it, isolating it, examining its parts and patterns, if never quite to understand them, at least to repeat them by rote. What did I do yesterday different from other days? What did I eat? What did I wear? Where did I go? Who did I talk to? and each answer becomes our clue, not a serious clue, of course (of course!), but still the best we have. So we use them — don't change the luck.

But I use superstition in another way. I don't want Joyce or the first shot to be the reason I play well. It may be "better to be lucky than good," as we're often reminded (for a loser can be good, but only a winner is lucky), but I want to feel connected to what I do, I want the feelings a game gives unshared, undiminished by something separate from me. So, instead I use it as a focus for the fear I feel. Afraid of a bad game each game I play, I use Joyce and the first shot to distract me from the fear of a bad game, which I can't control, to the supersitition, which I can. I have turned it into a straw game, one with no other opponent, with standards and requirements *I* set, which I know I can meet. So when I *do* meet them, when I successfully smile and nod to Joyce, when my first shot hits the boards to the right of the net, I give myself reason not to fear a bad game. If things change, if Joyce quits or turns away when I look at her, if my shooting deteriorates, I simply

change the game and set new, *achievable* standards. For me it's a way
of controlling the fear I can't eliminate, a way to blank my mind and
keep it blank when other ways fail. Off the ice, there are no lucky
horseshoes, no four-leaf clovers, I need no supersitions; on the ice,
older and more insecure, I need more each fearful year.

I see an opening, not as large as I would like, but cutting sharply for
it, I drop the puck. Eager skaters dart after it — I shoot. The puck
wobbles badly, but strikes where it must. Feeling a tiny surge of
pleasure, I skate around mindlessly.

Round and round, and each lap the clock is eighteen second closer
to zero. Over the glass, fans shout, reaching pens and programs toward
me, but looking down at the ice, readying myself to play, I pretend not
to hear. I glimpse usherettes, ushers, photographers; Eddie, behind the
penalty box, a small, shy, older man who once a year gives me a
wrinkled brown bag containing pajamas for Sarah and Michael that he
made at work; Lennie, in the same corner where Pete Mahovlich,
reaching his stick over the glass, would regularly sprinkle him with
snow, laughing, grateful, with hundreds of fans as his witness, a *friend*
of the team. Tonight Lennie stands in the exit talking, waiting.

Round and round we go. Gainey stops, the team stops and turns the
other way. Larocque goes in net. I keep skating, glancing at the clock,
aware of nothing else. At 15:00, I stop in front of the penalty box for
stretches; at 10:10, my mask is in place; at 10:00, I skate to the net.

Like skippers in a fast-turning rope, Larocque jumps out, I jump in,
the rhythm uninterrupted. But I am cold and unready, the pace is too
fast, and shot after shot goes in. Before I can worry, Robinson skates to
the middle of the ice, motioning everyone to the blueline. Facing only a
single shooter, gradually I gain control. At Cornell, I tried to stop every
shot in the warm-up; each one I didn't stop represented a goal I would
allow in the game. With faster, better shooters, I have no chance, so I
changed the game. Now I must stop only enough shots that the ones I
don't stop disturb neither me nor the team. Like every other part of my
game day, unworried, untired, uninjured, I want only that the warm-
up come and go without trace.

With about three minutes left, I begin to think about *it*. Since I was
young, a practice couldn't end until I had stopped *the last shot*. It was
someone else's ritual first, probably my brother Dave's, but for every
practice and warm-up since, as the proper end to something and the
base on which to build something else, it has been mine. But sometime

during twenty-five years, the ritual got complicated. It remains unchanged for practice, but for a warm-up *I must catch cleanly (no juggling or trapping) a shot from a player unaware his shot must be caught (no gratuitous flips). And then I must leave the net. If I don't, I will play poorly.* It is not so easy as it seems. Undefended shooters come in close and try to score, and I must stay in net long enough to get warmed up. Yet I have help, at least I think I do — Robinson. We have been teammates for more than four hundred games, and Robinson seems to understand. I have never told him, nor has he ever asked, nor have I told anyone. But as the clock flashes down, as I dance about my crease anxiously, he seems always to get the puck, and with it to take a shot I can catch.

With less than a minute remaining, as Robinson moves slowly into position, I catch Lapointe's shot and leave the net.

Tremblay rips off a skate, "Eddy! Eddy!" he yells. "*Câlisse*, I'm slidin' all over the place."

"Good warm-up, guys," says a voice coming through the door. "Good warm-up."

A few steps behind, another, "*Câlisse*, we gotta be sharper than that. We're dead out there!"

It's quieter than before. Ready or not, we have fifteen minutes. Nothing can be put off any longer. Skates, some sweaters, shoulder pads, and elbow pads come off, sticks are re-examined and taped, helmets adjusted, bodies slouch back against cool concrete block walls. An ice pack behind my head, now and then I sip at a Coke, looking at the program, putting Wings' names to numbers and faces I didn't recognize in the warm-up. Three seats away, Shutt does the same. Everything is slow, almost peaceful, each of us unconnected one from another, preparing in our own separate ways; as the game approaches, we reconnect. Against the Islanders or the Bruins, the room can be quiet or loud, it makes no difference. We know we are ready. Tonight, we aren't so sure, about each other, about ourselves. So sometimes we're quiet, and sometimes we make ourselves loud.

"C'mon , big gang," Houle exhorts, breaking the silence, "an early goal and they'll pack it in."

"Yessir, guys, they don't want any part of it." But again nothing.

"*Câlisse*, where's the life?" Robinson yells. "We're dead in here. C'mon, c'mon...."

Houle looks at Lapointe taping his wrists, turns and shouts in the direction of the toilets, "Hey Pointu, you in the shitter?" Then louder, "Can't hear ya, Pointu. Can't hear ya."

Lapointe looks up, then down again, saying nothing.

Lemaire, who, with Cournoyer injured, is the senior player on the team, tapes a stick, minding his own business. "C'mon, Co," Savard interrupts pleasantly, "this might be your last game. Never know, Co, at your age you might die out there."

Another routine begins. Lemaire giggles convulsively. Tremblay shrugs, "Who'd notice?" and there's loud laughter. But set to jump in, Shutt stops himself, then Robinson, and suddenly it ends.

"C'mon, c'mon, we're not ready!" a voice shouts. There is a pause, a change of tone, then another shout, more pleading this time.

"Hey, c'mon, let's be good homers, guys." Nothing. With a deep breath, Robinson tries something different.

"Hey, c'mon guys," he says casually, "gotta play it, might as well win it."

We know why we want to win. We know how a win can make us feel; we know how we feel when we lose. We know that we are better than the Wings, that we're expected to win, that we expect ourselves to win; that we *should* win. Still, before every game we worry that this isn't enough, that reasons unchanging from game to game have become wearied and clichéd, so we try others: seasonal reasons — "Let's start [finish] the season [the second half] off right, guys"; "Two points now is the same as two in April"; pride — "Need it for the division [Conference, overall], gang"; money — "Forecheck, back-check, paycheck, guys"; "C'mon, might mean fifteen Gs [two Gs]"; home reasons — "Let's be homers, guys"; road reasons — "Let's not be homers, guys"; "Let's start [finish] the trip off right"; practical reasons — "It's a four-pointer, guys"; "C'mon, they've been hot [cold] lately"; "Two points against these guys [Wings, Canucks, Capitals] is the same as two against the Islanders [Bruins, Flyers]"; "Let's not give 'em [Bowman/Ruel, the fans, the press] anything to give us shit about"; others — "Hey, let's win this one for ——[an injured player]."

The reasons interchangeable, the logic and emotion invariable, it is usually to no effect. Still, every so often, something is said that reminds us of something we believe in, that is important to us. At the start or end of a season, when I hear, "Let's start [finish] the season off right," it means something to me. Before a game on the way to the West Coast, already dreaming of the peace and freedom a win and the weather can give, when I hear, "Let's start the trip off right," it pumps me up a little. Others have different things they react to, and in filling quiet times this way, occasionally we say the right thing for someone who needs it.

The mood is beginning to change. Programs are down, ice packs, Cokes put away; equipment is taped up, snapped up, laced up; bodies are twitching, coming off walls, eyes narrowing, tightening; moods, still separate, are building, and coming together. It's like a scream about to happen. Suddenly, it all comes crashing down. *Whaack*. Lafleur is back. With heads down retying our skates, we didn't see him enter, slamming his stick on the table in the center of the room. Tape, gum, laces, ammonia sniffers, eighteen shocked and angry bodies bounce violently in the air.

"*Maudit tabernac*, Lafleur!"

"Wake up, *câlisse*," he laughs, and is gone again.

At 7:53, Palchak walks over to Lapointe, Lapointe looks at the clock, and a little upset tells him he's early and should come back in four minutes, when he's supposed to. Watching the clock another minute, at 7:54, Lapointe goes to the toilet. A minute later, he's back. Two minutes later Palchak arrives to stone first his right skate, then his left. Finished, he does the same to Robinson's and Engblom's skates. It began with Cournoyer a few years ago — "the magic stone."

Four minutes remain. All day, bodies and minds have been fighting for control, and now, finally, bodies have won. Metabolisms in slow idle scream louder, and higher. Words grunt from mouths unable to hold them, and crush up against each other.

"Need it! Need it, gang."

"On that McCourt, guys."

"Nedomansky too."

"Don't let Polonich get 'em goin'."

"Gotta have it! Gotta have it!"

"Who's got the first goal?"

"I got it!"

"I got it!"

"That's it! That's it!"

The buzzer sounds three times — three minutes to go.

"Wake-up call! Wake-up call!"

"Three minutes to post-time, gang."

Mondou gets up, walks around the room slowly, stopping in front of each of us, tapping both our leg pads with his stick.

"Gotta have it! Gotta have it!"

"They're hot, guys!"

"C'mon, put 'em down? Put 'em down!"

"Gotta watch Larson!"

"Good start! Good start!"

"Get on Woods, guys!"

"Skate 'em! Skate 'em!"

"Four-pointer, guys, Four-pointer!"

One by one, we're standing. Pacing, slapping pads, kicking kinks away, revving up.

Bowman enters. He starts to talk, but we've nothing left to hear. The buzzer sounds again, once. It's time.

"Okay, let's go," Bowman says, and with a shout we break for the door.

I go first, then Larocque, then Lapointe. Lafleur, to the right of the door, taps my left pad, then my right, with his stick, jabbing me lightly on the right shoulder with his gloved right hand. He does the same for Larocque and Lapointe, then squeezes into line, ahead of Robinson. One by one the tight-faced line continues, to Napier, second to last, and Lambert, last. As we come into view, the noise begins and builds.

"*Accueillons*," the announcer shouts, "let's welcome, *nos Canadiens*, our Canadiens!"

The organ rumbles, the crowd lets out a surging roar. I swivel past the players' bench; my padded legs shuffle in single file through the narrow open door — *don't fall*, I think to myself — and I jump onto the ice. The others burst past me. Round and round and round they go. Eyes down, staring at a series of imaginary spots always twenty feet in front, I glide to the net. I clutch the top bar with my bare left hand. I scrape away the near-frictionless glare ice of my crease. From goal-line to crease-line, my skates like plows, left to right, right to left, sideways eight to ten inches at a time, I clear the ice.

The clock blinks to zero; the horn sounds, the whistle blows, the players spasm faster.

. . .*gloves in front, stick to the side, watch for Lemaire, don't forget Robinson*. . . .

They file past.

"Let's go, Sharty, Bo, Mario," I roll-call the names as they go, my pads tapped, slapped in return. Lapointe approaches slowly, his stick in his right hand, tapping the left post, both my pads, then the right. Risebrough slashes hard at my left pad. At a distance Lemaire winks, then taps my blocker. Circling slowly, waiting for the others to go, Robinson, stick in his right hand, taps the left post, both my pads, then the right. *Don't change the luck.*

"*Mesdames et messieurs*, ladies and gentlemen, *les hymnes nationaux*, the national anthems."

A cherubic, silver-haired man steps onto the ice —Roger Doucet, his tuxedoed chest puffed like a pigeon's. I stiffen, then drift in and out as he sings; between anthems I shift my skates so as not to wear ridges in the ice. When he finishes, there is loud applause, the mood two anthems closer to the game.

I take a deep breath. My chin tucked to my chest, my eyebrows like awnings hooded over my eyes, I put on my mask. Referee Wally Harris, turning to his right, holds his right arm in the air, the goal judge to his right flipping on his red goal-light. Turning to his left, Harris does the same. I don't see him. Years ago, I decided that if I saw a red light before a game or before any period, I would see many more behind me during the game. So I look away, earlier, longer, than I need to, just to be sure. Then slowly I peek upwards — to the face-off circles, to Robinson's legs and Savard's, to Jarvis's, McCourt's, and Harris's legs at the centre-ice circle. They are bent, set in face-off position. I look up.

With a rhetorical nod, Harris asks Vachon if he's ready; Vachon nods back. Harris turns to me, and nods.

I've made it — through a purposely uneventful day, mostly unworried, unbothered, uninjured, undistracted by me or the game, ready to play. Others may sit in darkened rooms staring at an image — of opponents, of themselves — rehearsing movements or strategies, rehearsing hatreds; I keep moving, physically, intellectually, to keep moving emotionally. For if I let myself stop, I wonder, and if I wonder, I worry, and gradually grow afraid. But fear, like a landscape seen from a passing train, blurs with speed and proximity, becoming nonrepresentational, and unrecognized. So each year I move a little faster, until now, moving so fast for so long, I find that I can almost forget fear, unaware even of the ingrained superstitions, rituals, newspapers, naps, and walks that let me forget. Finally, they are just natural, unnoticed parts of my game-day routine.

I nod back.

Hockey Players

What they worry about most is injuries
              broken arms and legs and
fractured skulls opening so doctors
can see such bloody beautiful things
almost not quite happening in the bone rooms
              as they happen outside —

And the referee?
              He's right there on the ice
not out of sight among the roaring blue gods
of a game played for passionate businessmen
and a nation of television agnostics
who never agree with the referee and applaud
when he falls flat on his face —
              On a breakaway
the centreman carrying the puck
his wings trailing a little
              on both sides why
I've seen the aching glory of a resurrection
              in their eyes
              if they score
but crucifixion's agony to lose
  — the game?
              We sit up there in the blues
bored and sleepy and suddenly three men
break down the ice in roaring feverish speed and
we stand up in our seats with such a rapid pouring
of delight exploding out of self to join them why
theirs and our orgasm is the rocker stipend
for skating thru the smoky end boards out
of sight and climbing up the appalachian highlands
and racing breast to breast across the laurentian barrens

over hudson's diamond bay and down the treeless
                              tundra where
auroras are tubercular and awesome and
stopping isn't feasible or possible or lawful
but we have to and we have to
                              laugh because we must and
stop to look at self and one another but
                    our opponent's never geography
                              or distance why
                    it's men
                    — just men?

And how do the players feel about it
this combination of ballet and murder?
For years a Canadian specific
to salve the anguish of inferiority
by being good at something the Americans aren't —
And what the essence of a game like this
which takes a ten year fragment of a man's life
replaced with love that lodges in his brain
                    and takes the place of reason?
Besides the fear of injuries
is it the difficulty of ever really overtaking
a hard black rubber disk?
Is it the impatient coach who insists on winning?
Sportswriters friendly but sometimes treacherous?
 — And the worrying wives wanting you to quit and
your aching body stretched on the rubbing table
thinking of money in owner's pocket that might be in yours
the butt-slapping camaraderie and the self-indulgence
of allowing yourself to be a hero and knowing
everything ends in a pot-belly —

Out on the ice can all these things be forgotten
in swift and skilled delight of speed?
 — roaring out the endboards out the city
streets and high up where laconic winds
whisper litanies for a fevered hockey player —
Or racing breast to breast and never stopping

over rooftops of the world all together
sing the song of winning all together
sing the song of money all together . . .

        (and out in the suburbs
there's the six-year-old kid
whose reflexes were all wrong
who always fell down and hurt himself and cried
and never learned to skate
            with his friends) —

STAN DRAGLAND

Incognito at the London Gardens

Where are the days of Tobias
when one of the most-shining stood by the simple house-door
a little disguised for travelling and no longer frightening
(a youth to the youth when he looked out curiously)?
—Rilke

AN ATHLETIC EVENT itself
the best athlete in the audience tonight
ladies and gentlemen will you please welcome
some god passing through to leap like that
face not seen as it looks directly up, an impression of shaved jaw,
straining tendons in the neck, out of the white shirt open at the collar
under the overcoat unbuttoned in the warmth of the arena. At the
height of his leap, and he is always up there, the white shirt pulls out of
his jeans, a glimpse of muscled torso taut and slender. He is always
there at full stretch. So much explosion to be always caught! One arm
reaching high, high. Inside his shirt the arm is trying to pull out of its
socket.

This is physical magic pure as any miracle that happens on the ice,
the court or pitch, in the ballpark, on the turf grass or clay.

He is always up there. But comes down with the puck he catapulted
from his seat to catch. The upward leap so true he lands in a crouch
exactly where he took off. Now there is a boy beside him. There was no
boy on the way up, no boy burned into the picture of him always aloft.
When he lands there is a boy beside him, looking astonished into
excited grin as he gets the puck.

Or he lands on his seat which breaks on impact pitching his knees
into the back of the seat ahead, breaking both kneecaps. Or about to
land on the boy in the seat alongside he tries to catch a seatback with
his free hand, something else with his feet to arch himself protectively.
But comes down hard. The boy would suffer only a bump and a fright

but for ducking and twisting away so one of his arms is driven into the armrest of his seat and breaks. He howls in pain and the puck will not console him. The hands of people in neighbouring seats reach up to signal for attention, fingers point: first aid required here. The man lifts the boy in his arms. They meet the St. John's Ambulance crew halfway up the steps.

Before and after the event that burns into our brain the human being at full stretch there is no god, no myth, only a hockey game. So we are hardly present at the burning of the bush, the shooting of our silver bullet. There is only the murmur of the man next to me, 'Do you see who that *is*,' before the leap dissolves in the fracture and fuss. Now the referee has another puck and playoff tension swallows the boy's distress, the exit; face-off and the lady behind and three rows up directs her attention to the game. The puck had her name on it. She ducked into its path. If not intercepted it would have broken her jaw.

The Flyers' Bible

THE FIRST THING I'd like to say is, that as a coach, to emulate another coach is wrong. I think the first step for a coach is to motivate himself, that's the most important thing. He must constantly motivate himself. I feel, after every game, you can be lulled into self-pity. If you lose, you can find a million reasons for losing, you can say the referee was no good; you've got a couple of players who are overweight and can't do anything about it; you've got a couple of players who are not trying, or the other team is paying their players more money. You can think of a million reasons, but when you start doing that, then that's a sure route to failure. Win or lose, you've got to concentrate on what happened in the game, your good points and your bad points and mark them down. I usually spend about two hours after every game by myself, I try and remember everything that we did well, whether we won or lost; and everything we did poorly, so I can remember the next day and possibly go over it. The first thing to do is try to motivate yourself as coach, because you can't do anything with players until you motivate yourself.

Whether you're in athletics or in business, the manager or coach not only shapes the expectations and productivity of his subordinates, but also influences their attitudes towards their job and themselves. One person, by his effort and will alone, can transform another person. When we lose, it is my fault, I don't blame the players, and I don't blame the referees. I have a team and it's up to me to motivate them; and get as much as I possibly can out of them for their own good, for the good of their families, for the good of our fans, and for the good of hockey. . . .

I believe a coach must pour the totality of his being into his team, a coach must realize that success, greed or envy, is tied in with future vulnerability. This is what I mean: you see a lot of coaches, big-time coaches in sports — all of a sudden they've come to the conclusion that they know it all; they're the ones that are responsible and solely responsible for victory and they create this impression in the dressing room, around management and with the fans and the press, so finally, the coach rubs the right person the wrong way. I believe no one is indispensable, win or lose. I believe that if you win, everyone is responsible for winning, every player on the team, the coach, the manager, the trainer, the scouts, everyone; they're necessary before you can win; no one person is indispensable.

Everyday on the blackboard at our training camp rink and also at the Spectrum, I try to put up a new slogan, something that's meaningful. I think a great saying that has lasted thousands of years has lasted because it is great; it was great yesterday, great today and it's going to be great tomorrow. I call these statements 'Mind Vitamins'. We take vitamins for the body, why shouldn't we take vitamins for our minds. I'd like to give you an example of some of the things I might put on the board, every day or every second day. One is, "A leader is interested in finding the best way, not in having his own way". When I talk to my team I say, "we're not going to do it my way, we're going to do it our way and if you've got a better way, I want you to tell me immediately", and they do, because I want the best way, not my way. The next day I might put up a sign like this: "Failure is not fatal, but failure to change might be". Now, you say, why do I do this silly thing. I remember a couple of years ago when we lost with four seconds to go in Buffalo, I said, "Where did we go wrong?" I had a million reasons for losing, and finally I woke up, sometime around August, and realized where I had gone wrong. I had changed my style of coaching. I was in the minor leagues for 20 years, I had coached all these players, I had coached over 300 men who play in the big league, so I must know these guys; but being out of the big leagues for 20 years had frightened me a little bit. I had too much respect or too much awe of the players in the big league. I never reached them emotionally. I believe you can reach a person emotionally even if he's 50 years old and I remember this day in August when I was watching The Three Stooges and I almost became hysterical in front of my son; he thought I had lost my marbles. The next day I watched a movie, *Love Story,* a story about a hockey player; it was a very, very sad story and I had tears in my eyes and right there and then I realized that's the reason we lost. I wasn't reaching them in every way. You can reach a person emotionally whether he's 10 or 90 and I think this is what you've got to do and I think that's what I mean by 'mind vitamins', to stimulate the mind and make the person think.

Here is another one: "It is what you learn after you know it all, that counts", or another one: "Ability may get you to the top but it takes character to keep you there". Here are a few more: "Labour of the body frees you from the pains of the mind", and that makes us happy hockey players. The players laugh at this one, but it made them think. Another one: "A few weeks of hard work (this is before an important game), a lifetime to remember"; in other words, work like hell tonight and you'll remember it forever. The very first day of each year, I send them a letter and this letter is actually borrowed from John Wooden, the great basketball coach whom I consider one of the greatest coaches of all time in any sport — his record proves it — and they have to put this letter in their locker; it has to be there every day, right in their locker, and every two or three weeks, I read this to them again so they can understand completely how I coach and this is what it contains: "If you discipline yourself towards team effort, under the supervision of one who is in charge, even though you might not always agree with his decisions, much can and will be accomplished. You're allowed a certain failure without discipline. I am very interested in each of you as an individual, but I'm going to act in what I consider to be in the best interests of the team for either the moment or the future. Your race or religion will have no bearing on my judgements, but your ability and how it works to my philosophy of team play, very definitely will. Furthermore, your personal conduct and appearance will undoubtedly be taken into consideration, either consciously or unconsciously." And this is the last paragraph which is very important: "There may seem to be double standards at times, as I most certainly will not treat you all alike in every respect; however, I will attempt to give each individual the treatment he earns and deserves, according to my judgement. In keeping with what I consider to be the best interests of the team, you must accept this in the proper manner for you to be a positive and contributing member." Now what this really means, and every couple of weeks I bring it out, especially after a loss, is that I want them to understand how I coach.

We are not born coaches; it is said God created everyone equal, well, that's ridiculous, some are born smarter than others, some are born stronger than others, some are born into wealth and so on; all I know is that I don't treat Bobby Clarke the same as I treat everyone else. Sometimes I give him the odd day off, but there's a reason for it, because he does five times as much as anybody else. If a player's not playing regularly, he has to work twice has hard in practice. It's not my fault, it's really his fault because he's not as good as the next person and he has to take it in the right frame of mind. I've had teams where, if the player's an extra man, he wants to get off the ice after practice, the same as the regulars, but this is ridiculous, he has to work harder in practice to maintain his condition in case we need him in the future; and he has to learn to accept this and a lot of them don't want to accept their role. I think this letter explains it to them and I think it's very important.

I put this up on the board and I think this really defines our team, what our team is all about: "Self-discipline is far more valuable than authoritarian discipline, it is what the athlete has, who knows his goal and sets his own path to success." In other words, I want my players to discipline themselves. I can't be with them every day, I can't go to bed with them. Self-discipline is the best form of discipline. If they have to wait for me to discipline them, then we don't have a hockey team.

The next thing I'd like to talk to you about concerns the letters I send to my players, right to their homes. I think this is important, sometimes even their wives will see it. Here's a letter I sent to them last year, dated the 17th of March, just before the playoffs were starting and I wanted to bring out a point to them. The playoffs are a time when the game goes back to the coaches. You have more control of the team because you're not always running around trying to catch airplanes. You have more time to apply your theories; to scrutinize scouting reports more clearly, and intensify your preparation because you are free to concentrate on one team, but that is before the game starts. Once the whistle blows, the control reverts to the players. In our case, that means the players will have to force themselves, and this is important, to do the things they do not necessarily believe in, simply because I tell them that they are the right things to do. In other words, I've been telling them for maybe three weeks before the playoffs start that I've been studying films of the particular team we're going to play, myself and maybe my assistant coaches, maybe for two or three hours a day, and we know more about this team than they know about themselves right now, and there's going to be a given moment in the game when we may have to change strategies and I don't want to be questioned. I don't want them to question me, maybe they can question me during the course of the year, but in the playoffs things happen quickly and can change the whole direction of the playoffs. If I tell them to do one particular move, I don't want them to have any doubt, I want them to do it and that's the reason I send them that letter.

Here's one I sent to them on April 4th. "Society is so contrived that it is virtually impossible to combine power, position and privacy or even celebrities and privacy. Those willing to court fame or assume leadership are, by those very terms, forced to relinquish their seclusion. Yet as men, public stars glitter more brilliantly. They begin to covet more ardently their modes of attitude and the novelty."

What we really want is to be able to wrap ourselves in an invisible cloak from time to time and at times of our own choosing, but there is no invisible cloak outside of fairy tales, there is instead on old Spanish saying: "Take what you want, said God, and pay for it." What you take or are given in the way of influence or glory, you must pay for in constant exposure to public scrutiny, and the reason that I gave them that particular letter that particular time was because I know in the play-offs, everywhere you go, you are bothered constantly. You don't have a moment's rest. Just before you enter the arena, you might have to spend 20 or 30 minutes autographing; you're in a hurry, and you're upset and worried about the game and then after the game you're bothered by the press constantly and the public. I want to let them know, if you want to be a winner, you still have to pay a price. But I think it's a better price, it's better to be a winner, than a loser. If you're a loser, no one is going to talk to you; but I still think, if you're going to win, you'll have to accept this, that your life, at times, is going to be almost miserable. In other words, I expect my players to go everywhere they can, do everything they can, for the community . . . to go on TV, radio, go to kids' groups . . . everything, even during the course of the year, even during the playoffs. One player came to me the night before the biggest game of the year, and said: "Fred, I'm sorry, because you put out a directive that in the playoffs no one can go anywhere, on TV during the playoffs, because you've got to concentrate on the game." I said, " I didn't put that out, the management did that, and I don't like that idea." "Well," he said, "I made these arrangements a few months ago for a charity." So I said, "You make these arrangements, it's for charity, so what if it's the biggest game of the year, you go, don't worry about those management things because I'm not management."

On April 22nd, I sent them this letter: "The difference between the good and the great hockey players is their attitude. The good hockey players are happy to win the odd game, the great hockey players want to win every game." I tried to get it into their heads that we can't say to ourselves, "Well, we can afford to lose this game, we're two games up." We can't afford to lose any game, because you may never make that game up again. I don't want to take too much time on this, but I think this is important. On May 9th, while we were in the playoffs I sent this to the players; I was very upset at the time: "One in the series to date (and this is our team I'm speaking about), one man is working like hell and one man is doing all the fighting, and I'm sure you know who I'm talking about, Bobby Clarke is working like hell and he's also doing all the fighting." So I tried to get it across to everyone that we all have to contribute a little bit more in the way of checking, I don't mean fighting necessarily, but I do mean in working and using the body. "Two, last year everyone contributed with all their skills and all their courage. Three, every man must look in the mirror and ask himself these questions: (a) Did I hit when I could or did I let the man off the hook? (b) Did I honestly go in the corner or did I arrive late deliberately? (c) Did I hold my ground in front of the net according to our system, even though two men were pounding me like hell from behind, or did I hide at the side of the net or behind the net? (d) Did I overstay my shift, when I knew damn well I should be off? (e) Are we just seeing others' mistakes and not our own, and trying to blame others? and (f) How many cheap penalties have we taken during this series; is this showing discipline?

[W]hen this happened, I think it was because we were doing all these things wrong, but I don't believe in naming names, or in embarassing people, but everybody here I'm sure, if he played for the Flyers, knows what I'm talking about. When I said "Did I hit when I could?" everyone knows and thinks, well he probably means me; I probably had a chance to hit a man and I let him off the hook; I took the easy way out, I went for the puck and I missed the puck.

Did I honestly go into the corner? Well, that could apply to maybe 20 guys in the last couple of games, they went in but they arrived late or when they did get in there, they didn't fight that hard.

Did I overstay my shift? Maybe 10 or 15 guys did that, and as a result, I couldn't straighten my lines out when I wanted to. All these things could have meant the difference between victory and defeat.

Now I would like to go over the 16 rules that are commonly referred to as the Flyer's Bible. Breaking any one of these rules could be the difference between whether we win or lose. So after a game, I might go over the rules and require the players to write out the rule they broke, 5 times. I don't even mention their names, they know which rules they broke.

#1: Never go off-side on a 3-on-1 or a 2-on-1.

A useful exercise, the next time you watch any hockey game, is to count the number of good scoring opportunities that are ruined because a player goes off-side. I tell my players that going off-side is like back-checking for the other team. The Russians are very disciplined and very seldom go off-side. About eight years ago I watched a film of the Russians against a top Canadian amateur team. The Canadians were a top team because every one of them either made the big leagues in a few years or they could have made the big leagues but decided to stay in school. According to game statistics the Russians were only off-side once so I decided to watch the film again. I stopped it at this off-side. I found out the Russians weren't off-side, the referee was wrong. So discipline is a big part of their game; it's not necessarily a great system that they have, it's discipline.

#2: Never carry the puck backwards in your own end except on a power play.

The Russians go backwards, everybody else in hockey goes backwards, but I don't believe in it. Passing backwards in our own end to a teammate, to eliminate the opposition is okay. This is what I mean. We have the puck just inside the blueline and we're challenged. We know that we're going to get checked, so we start going backwards and end up getting checked deep in our zone. All we had to do was dump the puck two feet and we are out of the zone. I maintain it is better to dump the puck and gain the zone when you're going to get checked. We don't have a team that's as disciplined as the Russians and I don't have the time to train my players as long as the Russians have to train.

They can regroup and go back, but this is my system and this is what I want. However, if the puck carrier is being closely checked and doesn't have the opportunity to get the puck out, then it's okay to pass backwards to get away from the checker. In other words, you try to make room to pass it out again. But how many times do you see games lost because the man got checked in deep. He is trying to get out with no room and gets checked or he goes all the way back and he gets stopped in deep. In this case you are better off passing it back to a man that's free, if there's nobody back that's free, then just dump it forward and gain the zone.

#3: *Never throw a puck out blindly from behind your opponent's net.*
This happens at least five times in every big-league hockey game. Two men are in the slot being covered and the man in the corner with the puck is being checked, gets a little nervous and throws it out blindly. This happens four or five times a game. It could result in the loss of a game, or it not the loss of a game, more pressure on your goalie because they're breaking out when you should have control of the puck. If my player has the puck in the corner, and he is not sure he can make a good pass or is afraid or a little tired and figures he can't handle the defenceman coming at him. I instruct him to put it along the ice towards the post. It might go in because sometimes the goalie doesn't cover well, at least, you might get a rebound...You're better off freezing it or putting it at the side of the net. But don't throw it out blindly. When Canadian fans see this, they usually boo the man that didn't get the puck and yet he had no bloody chance of getting it!

#4: *Never pass diagonally in your own zone unless 100% certain.*
We lost a big playoff game two years ago because of this. A player threw it blindly from the corner up through the centre. It is ridiculous to pass diagonally unless you're 100% sure because it is so easily intercepted. You're better off holding on to it or dumping it forward and getting it over the line.

#5: *Wings on wings between blue lines except when better able to intercept a stray pass.*
This is one of the real big failures in pro hockey. Many games are won or lost between the blue lines. You will see it happen at least seven or eight times a game in professional hockey. The defence is standing up, ready to take care of the puck carrier; but then one winger leaves his wing and goes to check the centreman. He has no chance of getting the pass, but he's going to take the chance. Now he upsets his defenceman. His winger is free and they walk in and almost score a sure goal, or at least have possession deep in the zone. I always wonder why they

can't follow this simple rule. I remember once I had a player 38 years old who had been in the NHL for a long time. He was on his last legs, but he always left his wing. I know he was smart enough not to leave his wing so I finally brought him in and asked him why he was always doing this. He indicated he didn't know why, so I told him it was because he didn't have the courage to check and that he was afraid of his wing. To overcome this, I told him, he gambled, hoping and praying that he was going to get a loose puck. He was a small man so I told him that I wasn't asking him to fight his man, just stay with him. You don't even have to touch him physically, just stay with him so that our defence knows that the man is covered. I told him he was taking the easy way out, which was not the right way and not to continue to do it if he wanted to play for me. As I mentioned, this happens in every big league game, players leave their wing, resulting in a free man to get the pass.

#6: The second man must go all the way for the rebound.

I don't know how many times you'll see a man on a breakaway or a partial breakaway who doesn't score with a man who is trailing in the corner or behind the goal line. The second man gives up and just hopes and prays that the first man will score. He should really be hoping and praying that he doesn't score because *he* wants to score! If you are the second man coming in and there is a rebound, quite often the goalie is off balance or he's on his knees, and you're going to score an easy goal. I want the second man to come in directly in the middle of the net, about ten feet behind the man with the puck. Then when the rebound comes out your chances are equally as good at getting the puck regardless of which side it comes out on. Otherwise, if the puck comes out on the right, and if you are on the left side of the net, there is no way you can get to it. But if you come in lined up with the middle of the net, you're almost 100 % sure of getting it. It is important to make sure the second man prays the first man won't score! He should set his stick on the ice and keep ten feet behind the puck carrier. If he is in too close, the puck might come out hard and he will not get it. He has to be ten feet behind with his stick on the ice, and he has to concentrate.

#7: When the defence has the puck at opponent's blue line, they should look four places before shooting.

A player has no right to score from the blue line. If he can score from the blue line, it's because the guy in the other net is not capable, and shouldn't be in the league or the shooter is too good to be in the league. The only time you're going to score from the blue line is when the goalie is screened or isn't ready.

When we have the puck at the left point, in our system, the right defence must be even with the outside post. Then if the puck is shot around quickly, he can take one stride and get it before it goes over the blueline. If he is too far over, they can move it through the middle. We have our left wing at the hash mark, our centreman high in the circle. We never score from the slot; we haven't scored a goal in two years from the slot. If the puck is at the left point, we want our right winger in front of the net. He has got to have the courage to hold his ground, put his stick on the ice, bend his legs and feel confident that two men cannot knock him down. As long as he puts pressure on that stick, I don't care how small he is, he can stand his ground. Now, [the defenceman] looks 4 places (i.e., to see if any player is free.) If not, then I do not want him to shoot to score, but just to get it near the net. Actually I prefer that he move it to the left winger. Quite often the defenceman gets the puck and immediately shoots it. There is nobody around the net because they don't have time to get there. Also, from the face-off, when the puck comes back to the point, he shoots immediately, but the man who is supposed to go for it hasn't got time to get there. I say, if you're going to shoot, hold it a split second at least. You're under no pressure unless a man's right on you. If you're under no pressure, you've got to give the man who's lined up at the right of the face-off circle a chance to fight his way to the front. At least he has a chance for the rebound — but don't shoot immediately. If he shoots immediately and misses the net by eight feet, then all three men are caught.

#8: When waiting in front of the opponent's net, face the puck at all times and lean on the stick.

Quite often players will get a lot of tip-ins, and not even know it hit their stick. The reason is, they're facing the puck; they've got their stick on the ice, the puck comes along the ice and even though two men are trying to hit from behind and knock him down, he still has a chance to score a goal with his stick on the ice.

#9: When the puck carrier is over centre with no one to pass to, and no skating room, he must shoot it in.

Now the Russians would not shoot it in, they'll go backwards and open it up or do something else. However, if our centreman is coming over centre towards two defencemen with his two wings covered, he will shoot it in. Every centreman on my team is left-handed, and has no right to beat two men. If he can beat two men, he should get more money! So I want that puck not to be shot on the net. You never shoot on the net from the outside, it's got to be shot in the corner. In this case the right corner, and the right winger knows before the centre even releases it that the puck is going to his corner. The wings are covered, and our chances of getting control are just as good as theirs, or at least in freezing it in the corner. If a defenceman is carrying the puck, he is now the centreman as we believe in five to attack and five to defend. He will go in all the way. If he's left-handed he shoots it into the right corner; and if he's right-handed, he shoots it into the left corner. If he has to carry it in or make a play, he has licence to stay there until we lose control of the puck. You'll see a lot of teams in pro hockey that have their better defenceman shoot it in, and then stop, and come back. He has eliminated himself from the play. My men go in all the way! If he's in the middle or if he's on the wing, he still makes that same pass.

On a power play, it's so hard to think about that every once in a while I have to go over it again. Tommy Bladon is always on the power play on the right point. He will come over centre, the wings are covered, and since he is a right-hand shot he must shoot it into the left corner. He knows to the split second when he's going to shoot it in. If he hesitates and does not go after it, it ruins a scoring chance because in order to gain control of the puck, I want two men on the puck at all times, especially when the other team is short-handed. So as soon as he shoots it in, he knows that he should be in there too and that the winger is going to help him. But if he shoots it in and stops, we have only one man going in, and he might be arriving late. This happens quite often and you've got to get on his back as often as possible. As soon as he shoots it in, he knows that he's got to stay in there. He's the centreman! He might be the centreman for the next 30 to 40 seconds until we lose control of the puck. Our centre would now be the point man and he will remain there. But you see what usually happens. The defencemen will go in halfway, and double back, when they should have gotten control of the puck.

#10: No forward must ever turn his back to the puck at any time.
All players must know where the puck is at all times. Only defence-

men are allowed to turn their backs for a fraction of a second on a swing to the corner in our zone. In other words, you'll never see anyone on our team swing. The Russians swing, everyone in hockey swings, but we don't. With many teams, when the puck is shot in and the defenceman gets control, the winger will go into a swing and the defenceman cannot make the pass to him until he comes out of the turn. This is all wasted motion and wasted time. My man goes directly to the boards, facing the puck all the time because the puck might come immediately, and away we go. You'll see teams in pro hockey where this guy swings, that guy swings and nothing's going to happen until they come out of the swing. But in our system, it is only allowed in one particular case: a defenceman who swings in the corner. Many times you will see our forwards coming back and all of a sudden our defenceman checks their man and gets the puck. They will just turn sideways to the boards and be ready for a quick pass. All the players know what's happening at all times. A lot of players when they go into this turn, don't even know if the puck is in the net or not.

#11: No player is allowed to position himself more than two zones away from the puck.

It took me a long time to explain this to some of my players, some of whom have played professional hockey for ten years. They don't understand how they can be wrong! If we are inside our own blue line, and one of our men is over centre-ice, it is ridiculous. He can't make a pass to him. What's he doing up there? He's got to be inside centre. Quite often you'll see in pro hockey a player is standing up over centre. There's no way! He might as well go and sit on the bench.

#12: Never allow men in our defensive zone to be outnumbered.

This is very important. If we have two defencemen in our zone with the forwards around the blueline, then they probably have 3 forwards inside. If we don't make that pass through, we're in trouble, a three-on-two or two-on-one. I believe the only man who can leave our zone is, generally, the centreman. However, he could be the winger. But if the winger leaves, then the centreman has got to stay in; if they have two men in our zone, I want three. It doesn't matter which players are in the zone as long as we outnumber them. Defensively, I don't even want to be at even strength. We want to outnumber them. You see it quite

often, the defenceman gets the puck inside the blueline and three
forwards take off. They cross centre and can't even get the pass. If it's
passed to them, they are off-side. But they still persist in it. Only one man
is allowed to leave the zone in my system and it is usually the centreman.
We always outnumber our opponents in our defensive zone.

*#13: When delayed penalties occur, puck carrrier is to look for the
extra man at centre-ice. The extra man is responsible for covering the
opponent's goalie.*

Quite often on a delayed penalty, it happens maybe three or four
time a game, five players jump on the ice at the same time. They all
want to get on. They all want to be extra men. Quite often teams are
caught for having too many men on the ice. Nobody on my team is
allowed to stand up. We must see if there's a goalie coming off; and
nobody can jump on the ice until the goalie touches the boards. The
rule says he's got to be within ten feet...I don't want to take that
chance because we have a chance for a goal. Why can't we wait another
split second? There's no rush, so we wait 'till he touches the boards
with his stick. Then I touch the man who I want to go on the ice. I
might want a big goal scorer to go on or I might want a real tough guy;
but when he jumps on the ice he immediately goes to centre ice if the
puck is in our zone. As the goalie is leaving, he touches the first man
and they holler 'Delayed penalty, delayed penalty,' so everybody
knows that there's a delayed penalty.

Take your time, relax, don't rush, don't panic. A lot of teams say
nothing and play 30 or 40 seconds on a delayed penalty with the extra
man on and they don't even know it. Their own team doesn't even
know it because the goalie didn't alert everyone that a delayed penalty
has been called. So our goalie alerts the first man he passes. As soon as
they get the puck, they look for the man at centre. He might be free for
a quick goal. If not, they carry on in their usual way, the best way they
can. When they cross the blue line the extra man should go directly for
the net. Now I like to have a tough guy stay in the crease to bother the
goalie and bother the two defencemen.

Never leave the front of the net. But occasionally they have to; for
example, if the puck is fired from a bad angle. When we get set, we
know we have a man in front who could possibly screen the goalie or
tip it in.

#14: When the opponent's penalty is almost up, every player should know who is his responsibility.

This happens I'd say, in our league, about 30 times a year. The player gets out of the penalty box and he scores a goal and everyone blames everyone else. Well, we have a system for this and no one has scored a goal on us in two years in such situations, and no one will, if we keep working the system. It's the responsibility of my goalie to watch the penalty clock and, with 30 seconds to go, alert the defencemen about the time left. Once he does this, it then becomes the defencemen's repsonsibility. If we're facing off deep in their zone, with 15 seconds to go in the penalty, the key man is our off-side defenceman. He moves one foot outside the blueline because we found out that if you move out just one foot, that's enough. The man leaving the box can't break away without our defenceman getting him. But if you hang inside the blue line, you have very little chance of getting him. In fact, you have no chance whatever if you don't even know he's come out. So the important thing is to have your goalie instruct the defencemen how much time there is left in the penalty; and then when it gets close, whether we're facing off or not, we've got it in their zone. We want to keep it in there. The four men stay in that zone, only one pulls out.

#15: Back checking, 2-on-1 or 1-on-1, even on the power plays, your man must pick up the trailer; if there is no trailer, then he is to come in behind the defence.

Many times in a pro hockey game, a 2-on-2 develops and the backchecking forward skates leisurely back because he feels since it is a 2-on-2 everything is under control.

It's not under control! When he's coming back, he should look around for the trailer; if no one is coming, he's useless if he stays in the centre zone. I want him to start moving if no one is coming and immediately cut in half way behind the defence. In other words, I want him half way between the defenceman and the goal. Then our defencemen know that they can challenge. They don't have to worry because we have another line of retreat. But on most teams in pro hockey, you see the guy hanging around centre. He feels he has nothing to do because he has come back and there is no one to cover and he's not involved in the play yet. He should come down directly behind the defenceman, swing in behind him, and tell him that he is covering for him. Give him the encouragement or the courage he needs to stand up.

However, if one of their forwards is moving up quickly, then his job to pick up the man, leaving the two defencemen to their own resources.

#16: With two men in forechecking, specify the responsibilities of the third man.

When the puck is in the corner and we have two men forechecking, who are at liberty to do what they want and play as aggressively as they want, then the third man should be just outside the circle, even with the outside post. Now as soon as we get the puck, we know the man is usually free and in a good scoring position. A big problem in pro hockey occurs when the puck swings from one corner to the other. The man in front goes in immediately even though he has no chance. He just eliminates himself from the play. That is what I don't want. If you're sure of getting the puck, then go immediately. If there is any doubt, you go halfway, then take a look at your winger; if he's coming back, then you're at liberty to go in all the way. If your centre and winger are in the other corner and you go before one of them is coming out, there is a chance you could trap three men if you don't get the puck. The other winger and centre could get held or fall down and be trapped easily. Also, if you're going in with a two man system and a third man in the slot, as we call it in North America, it's ridiculous (this is what happens in pro hockey) if the wing is open on the same side. Many defencemen don't cover this wing, and a lot of them are afraid to. There is no sense going in with the two men because their wing is free. They simply move it around to the wing and away they go. If your defencemen don't have the courage to pinch in on the wingman, then there is no sense in sending two men in. You might as well send one in and have the second pick up their winger. But in our system, the defenceman pinches in. We know we can challenge aggressively with two men, and still know that the wingman is going to be covered. Also we know that our third man is outside the circle even with the outside post. If he is sure of getting the puck, he goes in immediately. If he's not sure, he goes in half way and looks to see if his other winger is coming back. If he's coming back then you don't have to worry, the most they can come up with is three men against three. If no one is coming out, then he swings and picks up his winger.

Well, gentlemen, those are the 16 rules. I know when you go over them quickly they don't seem important but I think they are very important during the course of a game, and will often determine its outcome.

JEFF GREENFIELD

Why the Rangers Will
Never Finish on Top

> *. . . Gave proof, through the night,*
that our flag was still there . . .
A stirring.
> *. . . Oh, say does tha-at star-spangled ba-a-nne-er ye-et wa-ave . . .*
The clapping and whistling start, faintly, somewhere in the far
reaches of the balcony.
> *. . . O'er the la-and of the free . . .*
It is spreading — cheers, claps, whistles, shrieks from Air Blast
horns and plastic trumpets, from every part of the arena.
> *. . . And the home . . .*
Forget it. When the New York Rangers are at Madison Square
Garden, you never hear the last words of the National Anthem. A
continuous roar explodes through the Garden; the skaters, lined up at
attention along the blue lines, break from their stances, wheel, and
skate by their nets, tapping the leg pads of the goalies for luck. The
referee hovers over the circle at centre ice, ready to drop the frozen
rubber puck between the sticks of the players and begin the game.

From her permanent seat in the first row of the balcony — it's called
the "mezzanine," for the same reason that the smallest tubes of tooth-
paste you can buy are called "large" — Wanda performs her face-off
ritual. As the last strains of the National Anthem are swallowed by the
crowd, she shuts her eyes, makes the sign of the cross, and clasps her
hands to the sky in prayer. This affirmation of faith completed, Wanda
leans over the railing, cups her hands to her mouth, and screams with
unbelievable power, "Come on, you sons of bitches — *kill 'em!*"

Wanda and the 17,000 others who filled Madison Square Garden for
every Ranger home game are not "enthusiasts" or "fans." Communicants, perhaps. More accurately, they are witnesses — witnesses to a
tragedy.

As everyone remembers, Aristotle taught that tragedy is a catharsis
of emotion through pity and terror; an exercise in which we learn

something of life by watching heroic mortals struggle in a web spun by Higher Forces. We do not watch *Oedipus Rex* or *Hamlet* to find out whether Rex will reign happily ever after, or because we hope Hamlet and Ophelia will settle down at Elsinore. We go to be moved by the spectacle of a man challenging his inexorable fate. For the followers of the New York Rangers, this winter marks the resumption of one of the longest-running tragedies in history.

The New York Rangers never win: such is the Eternal Verity that decrees their fate and imprisons their fans. Yes, they win games. Yes, they field respectable, even enviable teams. But when the final test comes, the Rangers never win. They have not won the Stanley Cup, symbol of major-league-hockey supremacy, [since 1940]; of the five other veteran clubs, only Detroit has gone as long as sixteen years without tasting ultimate victory. The Rangers until 1972 had not even been in the final round of Cup play for more than twenty years; another record of futility unmatched by the established clubs. Even in the regular season standings, a matter only of pride, the Rangers have not finished first in [forty-seven] years.

Losing is nothing new to the sports fans of New York City; indeed, they treat failure with the kind of wry affection offered by an eminently rich, respectable family to a black-sheep uncle whose catastrophes are international, explosive, and slightly risqué. New York is the Big Apple: failure is dealt with summarily and ruthlessly in the world of commerce, industry, finance, politics, and the arts. In forgiving the failure of our teams, we New Yorkers can offer the kind of compassion we are ourselves unlikely to receive.

What is different about Ranger fans, however, is that they are the only group of New York sports fans *never* to have tasted the big victory in more than thirty years. The Dodgers *did* win a World Series finally (beating the unbeatable Yankees in seven games in 1955). The Mets went from a ninth-place finish in 1968 to a 1969 World Series; so explosive was the celebration that bus drivers let passengers on for free, and Mayor Lindsay's re-election was demonstrably assisted by the good will that spread over the city. And the fans of every other New York team have the remembered taste of victory. Yankee rooters live with the memory of dynasty; the Jets have Joe Namath and a Super Bowl trophy; Giant football fans, reading their road maps to Hackensack, remember the Eastern Division championships of the late fifties and early sixties and a once-impregnable defense; the Knicks have a 1973 basketball championship and a still-powerful team.

But to be a Ranger fan is to hold to the term's original meaning: fanatic. Moreover, rooting for the Rangers has afflicted all of us — for I am one of them — with a nearly incurable schizophrenic rage that removes Ranger hockey from the realm of Sport. Ranger fans, for example, do not stand by their heroes; they are the ultimate summer soldiers of winter sports. A single missed check or bad pass can instantly erase a night or a week or a season of spectacular play. Indeed, there are those who make insult their chief obsession.

Take Wanda (I have changed her name for fear of physical reprisal), the girl who sends up a prayer at the start of each game. Wanda has the most recognizable, piercing voice in the Garden. She also seems to have learned her vocabulary by speed-reading men's-room walls: the breadth and imagery of her obscenities are breathtaking. Often, Wanda arrives forty-five minutes before game time, when the teams are practicing and the arena is empty and quiet. If Wanda is in good form endearments like these greet the Rangers:

"Rod Seiling, you stink. You're smelling up the ice, Seiling. Get cancer."

"Gilbert, you fairy! Drop dead! You're no superstar, Gilbert, you're a superfart!"

"You bum, Neilson, why don't you get hit by a truck, you c--------r!"

Throughout the game, Wanda questions — graphically — the manhood, ancestry, sanitary habits, patriotism, and sobriety of every Ranger player. But it is *her team* — she wants them to win. When a Ranger scores, it is Wanda who leaps to her feet, embracing whoever is next to her, suffused with ectasy. When the Rangers win a game, it is Wanda who is chief celebrant. Her joy at their triumphs and her anger at their failures are constantly at war with each other, and the sounds of combat fill the Garden every Wednesday and Sunday night.

Or consider Red: one of the authentic communicants. Red and his colleagues know everything about the Rangers. They know where the players live. They show up at practice sessions to roar encouragement and abuse. They study the yearbooks and the charts. They can remember — and will tell you, with very little urging — every mistake every player made in every game over the past four seasons.

Hard-core fans like Red hold a place of honour at the Garden; through him, the ordinary fan can test his judgement. There are two fifteen-minute rest periods in a hockey game, natural occasions for Instant Analysis and Querulous Commentary. At any given moment, clusters of communicants and acolytes are grouped around refreshment stands or in the aisles, reviewing the shortcomings of the Rangers.

Here, Red is in his element. Somewhere in his early twenties, Red has all the makings of a loser. He is very overweight; his face is round, chubby, topped with bright orange hair. He is perhaps a gas-station attendant, a shipping clerk. But here, lounging against the balcony guardrail, his back to the ice, Red is king. He knows everything you always wanted to know about the Rangers — and if you are afraid to ask, he will tell you.

When Red holds court, novices and apprentices group around him from neighboring sections, firing their tentative opinions at him two or three at at time, ready to change their minds immediately if Red should disagree. It sounds like children on a beach, imploring their slumbering parents to watch them, *really watch* them.

"Red! Red! Did you see Carr poke check — "

"Red! Hey, Red! That Gilbert stunk up the ice tonight, didn't — "

"Hey, Red! Pretty good checking by Tkaczuk — "

Like a chess master taking on twelve opponents at the same time, Red turns from one to the other, scornfully dismissing one, magnanimously assenting to another.

"Unbelievable," he says. "Unbe*liev*able! *Three* power plays and we get *four* shots on goal. *Four!* If that — Gilbert? How the hell can you blame Gilbert, didn't you see — get out of here with that crap. *Seiling.* Neilson and Seiling *together* can't — hitting? *Hitting?* Where did you see hitting? Damn right. I tell you . . ."

His audience is rapturous. It's so hard to get Red's attention that it is something of a privilege to be attacked as an idiot. At least he listened.

Driven by such passion, torn between joy and fury at the performance of his team, the Ranger fan cannot be expected to spare compassion on the foe. And he does not. In common with hockey fans across the continent, the Ranger rooter is one of the most unsportsmanlike sports buffs in existence.

In baseball or football, an opponent's injuries brings a hush to the most partisan crowd. The trainer rushes onto the field. After a few moments of ministrations, the enemy combatant struggles to his feet and gamely hobbles off the field to the cheers of the fans.

With Ranger fans . . . well, take the case of Ted Green, a former Boston Bruin defenseman now with the New England Whalers of the

WHA, a feared player who seemed to regard hockey as an unfortunate interruption between brawls. In the fall of 1969, in the midst of a fight, a stick crashed down on Green's skull and fractured it. After hanging between life and death for days, Green returned to hockey with a steel plate embedded in his head.

In any other sport, Green's courage would have earned him respectful cheers. But last season, at the Garden, Green was met by a chorus of jeers and boos.

"Come on, Green, get off the ice, you're all washed up," one fan yelled over and over. "Go home you has-been." And then, as a lull settled over the crowd and the steel-plated Green skated into position for a face-off, a voice came booming out of the balcony:

"Come on, Ironhead, get off the ice!"

This gleeful and absolute hatred of the enemy blossoms during a fight. There is, in hockey, no idiotic propaganda that violence is only incidental to the game. When you put strong men on skates and arm them with sticks, people will hit each other. Almost no one gets hurt in a fight — skates don't give much traction — so most fights start and end with arm-wrestling, pulling a jersey over a rival's head, and falling on the ice.

But when a real brawl erupts — with fists flying all over the ice — the fans forgive anything, including a losing game, to roar out the blood lust. (It is, indeed, something of a tradition for a losing hockey team to stage a wild fight in the last period of play to inspire its rooters.) During the Stanley Cup opening round a few years ago, the Rangers were losing to the Toronto Maple Leafs when an all-out Pier 6 brawl erupted. In the fracas Toronto goalie Bernie Parent left his net to join in, a severe breach of etiquette, which holds that goalies — valuable and vulnerable players — are neither aggressors nor victims in a fight.

Suddenly, to the astonished roars of the crowd, Ranger goalie Ed Giacomin skated the length of the ice and crashed into his opposite number. After fifteen minutes of mayhem, order was restored — and Toronto goalie Parent found himself without his $200 customized face mask. Ranger Vic Hadfield had yanked it from his head and thrown it into the crowd, when it mysteriously disappeared.

"Keep it! Keep it!" the fans started chanting when they realized what had happened. "Don't give it back! Don't give it back!" They didn't, and Toronto was forced to put in a new goalie. (Incredibly, another fight broke out thirty-four seconds later, and the substitute

Toronto goalie started throwing punches, and Ranger Giacomin *again* skated the length of the ice to crash into his rival. This time the face mask was securely anchored to the goalie's face.)

Given the willingness of Ranger fans to pour abuse on their heroes and villains, they are beyond hope when it comes to judging the fairness of referees. It is often hard to distinguish between legal and illegal moves in hockey because the game is so fast and so violent even when it is played according to Hoyle. But after thirty years of frustration, New York's hockey maniacs are convinced that *somebody* must be out to get them. And just as it is easier to persuade unemployed workers about powerful conspiracies of Eastern bankers than it is to convince affluent middle-class people, so the very record of futility is proof that the referees are in league against the Rangers. Learning this Truth — learning to yell, "Get the ref! Get the ref!"" whenever he calls a penalty against Us — is something like a rite of passage.

Here is an eight-year-old boy attending his first hockey game, far back in the second promenade, sitting with his father, who has paid a scalper $20 each for two $7.50 tickets. The father has the look of a perpetual victim, the kind of man who works for a combination of Scrooge and Mr. Dithers, the kind of man who is insulted by bus drivers and snubbed by Sabrett hot-dog vendors.

But tonight, the father is part of the Crowd. As the game begins, the referee is introduced.

"Boooo! Booo!" the father shouts. " You're a bum! Go home!" His son watches in fascination.

As the game progresses, the father's indignation mounts. Every time a Ranger player is penalized, he is out of his seat.

"Ref, you stink! You Communist!" His voice breaks, sweat pours down his face. He draws on an inexhaustible wellspring of rage: every syrup-voiced politician, every creditor, is down there on the ice, disguised as the referee.

The son learns quickly. By the time the first period ends, he is standing on his seat, hands cupped to his mouth, echoing his father's anger:

"You...rotten, lousy louse! You bum!" There is no generation gap at Madison Square Garden.

Father and son also possess another abiding characteristic of New York hockey fans: they love not wisely but too well. Unlike their Canadian counterparts, New Yorkers do not grow up with hockey; few of them play the game as children, or even watch it frequently. It is, unlike baseball, football, or basketball, an acquired taste. It is also, at first glance, a ridiculously simple game. Once a fan learns about off-sides (the puck must precede an attacking player across the blueline) and icing (you can't counter an attack by shooting the puck all the way down the ice) he knows enough to follow the play of the game. No self-respecting football fan would dare to offer advice without couching it in jargon: red dogs, crack-back, blitz, zig-out, passing planes, moving pockets, flares and loops. In the Garden, the advice tends to be simpler.

"Shoot!" the father yells as the Rangers set up a play. "Shoot!" he yells as they regroup behind their own goal. The arsenal of offensive weapons — swift passing, feints to draw defencemen out of position, faked shots — he has no truck with these. "Come on, shoot, shoot for Christ's sake, sho-o-o-ot!" It is rather like listening to Al Capp advise the National Guard on how to cope with student dissent.

At this most intense, the fervor of a Ranger communicant tran-scends normal modes of communication. Iris, the queen of section 320, has reached that height. She is an anomaly — a hard-core Ranger fan who is a black woman. Most hockey fans are men, largely drawn from the white working class. But Iris is more than a token. She comes to the games armed with a large wicker basket: in it is a portable radio, so she can listen to a broadcast of the game she is attending; binoculars; a Ranger yearbook; and score sheets on which she records every goal and every penalty of every game.

So completely is Iris taken with the sport that she no longer cheers in English; she speaks instead in the language of tongues.

"Yaaahhh, yaaaahhhh, c'moooonnnn!" she cries, as a Ranger flies down the ice.

"Whhaaat?" she screams as a Ranger power play is nullified by an offside call. "You — what — aaaaaggghhh!"

A Ranger trips an opponent, and a penalty is called.

"You cra — arrgh —faaaghhhh!"

For all of us — Wanda, Red, Iris, the father — the 1970–71 season was going to be Our Year. It was only logical: the Jets and Mets in 1969, the Knicks in 1970, and 1971 was the Rangers' turn. And after the Rangers won the first round for the first time in twenty years, it seemed indeed that this time the fates would be on our side. And so, in the sixth game of the semi-final round, we gathered to watch the Rangers battle the Chicago Black Hawks and their fate.

The Black Hawks were ahead in the series, three games to two. A loss would eliminate New York; a win would send the teams to Chicago for a decisive seventh game. When the Rangers fell behind 2-0, it seemed that the inevitable tragic end was in sight. But the fates were playing subtler games this time.

By the third period, the Rangers had tied the score at 2-2. By the end of the period, the score was the same. But there are no ties in Stanley Cup playoffs; the teams keep playing twenty-minute periods until somebody scores — and whoever scores first wins the game.

As the first overtime began, the tension became ridiculous. Even Mike the Usher, gray-haired, iron-faced, horn-rimmed, imperturbable, was perched on a stair, watching intensely.

The opening minute of play. Both the Rangers and the Black Hawks come within inches of scoring the decisive goal.

"Jeez," Mike says. "I haven't bitten my nails in thirty years."

"Keep bitin' 'em," a spectator growls. "That's the last time we won the goddamn Cup."

The first overtime period ends with the score still 2-2.

"I can't look," Mike the Usher moans. "The only way I can take a game like this is if I'm half in the bag."

The second overtime period begins, with Chicago attacking mercilessly. A shot hits the right post of the goal. Two inches over and it would have won the game and the series for the Black Hawks. Another Chicago shot — and this one hits the left post.

"They're tryin' to kill me," Mike yells. "The bastards are tryin' to kill me."

The second overtime period ends. Between the mass rush to the men's rooms, and the queue for frantic telephone calls to wives and babysitters, some of the exhausted fans doze in their seats.

The *third* overtime period begins. It's been forty years since the Rangers played a triple overtime game. The crowd is silent, half from tension, half from exhaustion. Then, two minutes into the period, a Ranger shot is blocked but rebounds out in front of the net. Peter Stemkowski slams the puck past the Chicago goalie. The red light flashes on. The Rangers have won.

For a full two seconds the bone-weary crowd, hypnotized by four hours of hockey, sits stunned. Then the roof gently lifts off and the Garden goes up for grabs. Mike stands up solemnly and begins shaking hands with the men and kissing the women. Iris is dancing, hugging everyone within reach.

"You know," Mike says, "I *know* we're gonna lose that seventh game, but at least I can die happy."

"Lose?" yells a bystander. *"Lose?* You're outta your mind. We're going all the way. All the way!" Three days later in Chicago the Rangers lost 4–2.

This winter the witnesses have returned. The scalpers shuffle back and forth in front of the Garden, surreptitiously hawking their wares in front of the uniformed police. "Who's selling?" "Who's buying?" "Who needs two?" "Who's got one?"

The fans pour abuse on the Rangers, they revile every official, they cheer every goal. By now, they are telling themselves, this year, this time, all the way. And by April or March, or perhaps by May, if the torture is extended, the Rangers will lose — gallantly or foolishly or heroically, but they will lose, and we will tell ourselves, well *next* year . . .

MARTIN O'MALLEY

The Enforcer

SOME MEN HAVE GROWN TO OLD AGE without ever having been in a fist fight. Others can remember three or four. Brian Spencer is only twenty-two but he has been in so many fights he really can't remember all of them. They are a blur of hot blood and sudden, rapid punches.

He finished a dish of chocolate ice cream in the coffee shop at the Westbury Hotel and, quite boyishly, tapped a false tooth in the lower left side of his mouth and said that was the only tooth he's ever had knocked out, and it wasn't even in a hockey game. It was knocked out in a bar in Calgary. Ha, ha; but he stops and does not go into much detail because it is not good for the image for players to be going around getting their teeth knocked out in bars when they are playing junior hockey. No, if his teeth are in good condition it is because he does not lose many fights, and because when boys his age in Ontario and Quebec were playing forty or fifty games a winter he was playing maybe seven or eight in northern British Columbia. And he played on outdoor rinks where the puck sometimes got lost in the snow and where you heard a tiny "ping!" when your ears froze.

It is hard to think of Spencer as a heavy in the National Hockey League. Big John Ferguson of Montreal is a heavy and he is strong and grey. Ted Green of Boston looks as hard and intractable as a fire hydrant. There is a heavy on the Philadelphia Flyers who is called Mad Dog Kelly. Spencer's nickname is Spinner and it is too exuberant and playful for a villain of the rink.

His face is delicately handsome, with dark blond hair curling behind his ears. His eyes are blue and a bit cold but they do show humour. Sometimes he seems actually shy and vulnerable. He is 5 foot 10 and weighs 180 pounds, not intimidating by NHL standards, and yet last winter he overpowered Green, bear-hugged him to the ice, and he smashed Mad Dog Kelly in the face. He played fifty games with Toronto Maple Leafs last season, scored nine goals and collected 115 minutes in penalties. Before coming to Toronto he played twenty-three games with Tulsa Oilers in Oklahoma, scored six goals and collected 103 minutes in penalties.

So explain the paradox.

People more familiar with hockey told me to look at Spencer when he is not wearing a shirt because he has the finest physique on the team. He is a fanatic about physical fitness, and when he played junior hockey in Saskatchewan and Alberta he did forty-five minutes of exercises every night, including one-hundred push-ups. He has a vicious temper. And they asked, "Have you seen his hands?"

His hands are thick and square, like two Harold Robbins' bestsellers. Patches of skin have been torn away and his knuckles have the size and protuberance of walnuts. We visited an electronics shop in Toronto and the proprietor, a man who said he was a German commando in the war, looked a Spencer's hands and assumed he took karate. It is easier to believe the stories when you see the hands.

When he is checked hard, even if it is a clean check, he retaliates instantly. In the third period of a game last December he was cross-checked behind the Toronto net by Gary Dornhoefer of Philadelphia. In one sweeping motion as instinctive as a cat twisting in the air Spencer fell, got up, shed his gloves, chased Dornhoefer to the boards and hit him so hard on the side of the jaw that Dornhoefer collapsed. Out cold.

His temper explodes off the ice, too. One night last winter he parked his car on a lot near the Sutton Place hotel and walked with his wife and two-month-old daughter to the attendant's hut. The attendant asked for his licence number and when Spencer couldn't remember it the attendant cursed and said he was stupid. Spencer grabbed him by the throat, slammed him against a car and threw him to the ground. A lady at the Westbury Hotel once chastised him for reading newspapers without paying for them and he hurled a fistful of coins at her face.

He does not apologize for these acts. He says he is from the bush and he is not yet accustomed to the casual surliness of the city where people insult others gratuitously. "Where I come from," he said, "if anybody talks to you like that, if they swear and call you a stupid ass, it means one thing — it's a fight." If he is driving a car and someone cuts too sharply in front of him he wants to get out and smash him in the face. "I'm not known as a pansy type of player. I get hit, I get hot. These things are natural to me, instinctive. I have a bad temper. I just hope these things go well for me."

So far, they have.

He is not a skilful player. He can skate well, and he can hit, but sometimes the puck will hit his stick at the crease and half the net will be open and he will flub the shot. Sometimes he seems too intense, too excited. You find yourself quietly rooting for him, hoping this time the puck will stay in place.

He has the right attitude, a word coaches and general managers like to use. During training camp last year he ran laps while wearing a cast for torn ligaments in the knee. He stays on the ice after scrimmages and practices puck control and shooting. After only three seasons of truly organized hockey, with Calgary, Swift Current and Tulsa, he made it to the NHL. John McLellan, the coach, says Spencer helped the team out of a slump last December, had a good January, but tailed off badly toward the end of the schedule. He will have a good season this year, he said, if he plays a rough, aggressive left wing and scores fifteen to eighteen goals.

Jim Gregory, general manager of the Maple Leafs, says for every man in the NHL there are others who have more talent but didn't make it because they didn't have the right attitude. "Spencer will be all right if he doesn't try to be too fancy."

Brian and Byron Spencer were raised on a 900-acre farm near Fort St. James in northern British Columbia. They were twins, though Brian's hair was blond and Byron's red. Their father logged and operated a gravel business and worked sixteen-hour days but he never made much money. The house had no indoor toilet, no electricity. Brian and Byron were his only children and he had plans for them.

He bought them skates when they were five and took them to nearby Stuart Lake, a peanut-shaped lake that freezes several feet thick in winters that get as cold as 30 and 40 below. Later, he built a rink at the farm, drove in the posts, nailed up the boards and installed lights, which he hooked to a generator at the gravel plant, so the boys could practice at night.

Roy Edward Spencer boxed and lifted weights when he was a soldier, but he was never a skilful athlete. Work was the key, he told the boys. If they could keep improving their skating speed, if they could skate faster at eight than at seven and faster at nine than at eight, they might become professionals some day. He bought a stopwatch and stood at the boards and timed them.

Brian had his father's irascible temperament and competitiveness and he eventually showed more promise than Byron.

On Saturday mornings when he was thirteen and fourteen his father got up at 3 o'clock, roused him from sleep, and the two of them got in the car and drove forty-five miles over the snow to Vanderhoof where the first hockey games started at six. Brian put on his equipment, got on the ice an hour before the game and skated while the sun came out and his father watched from the boards.

One day when Brian was on the rink in Fort St. James his father stepped on the ice in his shoes and walked to where the red line would be on a marked rink. He yelled at Brian to keep skating. Brian came up the ice at full speed and as he approached centre ice his father suddenly ran at him, checked him — and knocked him out.

He did not play that many games until he was seventeen. Before that, some days he practiced alone for up to twelve hours. When he was seventeen, however, he shifted from defence to forward and played for three teams in Kitimat: juvenile, senior and a local commercial team.

When he was seventeen he had also survived the worst temptations of life in the north. He had quit school when he was fifteen and drifted into a tough, hard-drinking crowd that did such mindless heroics as wreck houses and sink boats. He hitched rides on lumber trucks to play hockey in Vanderhoof and when he couldn't get rides back he slept in parked cars.

"I came close to just giving everything up. I had to do so much more than the other kids to get anywhere and wasn't doing very good. I wasn't getting enough rebate on the work I was putting in. I had no money and I wasn't eating and I broke out in a rash with welts the size of eggs on my stomach. The other kids could slough off and play on the same team and do just as good.

"Of course, now some of them are dope addicts, driving delivery vans. There's not one of that crowd of maybe thirty guys who left that town and made something of himself."

He met Red Berenson of St. Louis Blues at a hockey camp in Nelson in the summer of 1967. Berenson was impressed with his desire and rough style — he broke a man's arm arm-wrestling in a pool hall — and arranged for him to play with Regina Pats juniors in 1967–68. He spent a few weeks in Regina, then went to a new junior team in Alberta, the Calgary Centennials.

He returned to Saskatchewan and started the 1968–69 season with Estevan Bruins. He was learning to control the puck, he was heavier and more confident, then he got into an ugly skirmish with a team-mate, Greg Polis. The fight carried on into the dressing room and when it was finally broken up the coach suggested they cool it and shake hands. Spencer refused and the team decided it didn't want him. He was traded from Estevan, a first place team, to Swift Current Broncos, a last place team.

It is one of the ironies of the sport that the man who indirectly got Spencer into the NHL was none other than Greg Polis. Polis, playing for Pittsburgh Penguins, slammed Leafs' Guy Trottier into the boards and Trottier hurt his shoulder and the next day at noon Spencer got a call to come to Toronto.

Spencer was with Tulsa Oilers in the American midwest, smashing faces, slamming bodies and scoring the odd goal against teams in Dallas, Fort Worth, Oklahoma City and Omaha. Toronto needed some-one like that. The Leafs were in last place, tied with — horrors — Punch Imlach's Buffalo Sabres. The day before Spencer arrived, Rex McLeod wrote in *The Globe and Mail* that "a favourite recreation of most National Hockey League teams . . . is pushing around Toronto Maple Leafs."

After the call from Toronto, Spencer picked up his skates, took the next plane out of Tulsa and played that night at Maple Leaf Gardens against Montreal. Toronto won 4–0 and Spencer won two fights with Terry Harper.

Things were falling into place.

The next day, in Tulsa, Spencer's wife gave birth to a baby girl.

He had not told his father about Wednesday's game so he called him Friday, said he would be playing with the Leafs against Chicago the next night, that the game would be televised coast to coast and that he would be interviewed on television between periods. Toronto beat Chicago 2–1, and Spencer won another fight.

It is a big night at the Caledonia Inn in Fort St. James when a local boy is playing for Toronto Maple Leafs and Toronto Maple Leafs are playing on television on a Saturday night. When Spencer scored three goals and Toronto beat Pittsburgh 5–2 on a Saturday night last January there was much drinking and hollering at the Caledonia Inn. More than one-hundred regulars, Indians and whites, sent a telegram to the boy at Maple Leaf Gardens.

It was the kind of thrill Brian's father dreamed of, but never experienced.

The morning after the Chicago game Spencer was awakened in his room at the Westbury Hotel by a call from his mother in Fort St. James. She told him that his father did not see the game, he had been shot and killed at a television station in Prince George.

People in northern British Columbia complain of being "shat upon" by the south. They see the unpaved roads and hear promises and feel the disdain for people who live "in the bush." The day after Brian called him, Roy Edward Spencer, fifty-nine, already dying of uremic poisoning, heard that CKPG-TV in Prince George was not going to televise his son's game. He took a gun, drove eighty miles, and forced the station off the air.

When three RCMP arrived he shot at them and hit one in the foot. They returned the fire and a bullet ripped through his chest and killed him. Brian was being interviewed on television when his father was lying in the snow outside station CKPG-TV.

A Jesus freak outside the Westbury Hotel showed Spencer some booklets published by The Church of the Final Judgement. He selected one called Fear and took it to his room on the sixth floor. Some of the roughest men in professional sport — football, boxing, hockey — are fascinated by fear.

"The fear of failing was the biggest fear I've ever had," he said. "Failing in school, failing in human relationships, failing on the ice. The fear of being incompetent within your team, as a team. I think fear is a great help in an ambitious person."

Other books were scattered on one of two twin beds: Hitler, Patton, psychiatry. A pile of fan mail lay strewn on a chair. He picked up an orange from the night table, broke open the top with a ballpoint pen and sucked on it as he talked. I asked him about the tough players in the NHL and any theories he might have on fighting on skates.

"You're wearing maybe twenty-five pounds of equipment, so first you have to throw your gloves down, and you can only hit the guy in the face; you can't hit him anywhere else. I mean, what's the use? you might break your hand.

"You've got no footing so you try to anticipate what the other guy's going to do. Try to brace yourself and keep upright because if he puts you on the ice he has an advantage. Try to block him, stay on your feet, maybe throw him on his back and get a few in. It's mostly grabbing and giving the odd shot.

"The way I think is that I can't be beat. You use discretion, of course, but I can take all kinds of punches and I know I'm not going to get hurt. If he hits you with a stick, fine; you bleed a little, you get sewn up. This is what hockey is geared for now."

Anyone in the NHL is tough or they would not be there, he said, but some players are tougher than others, and not all tough players are good fighters. It takes a special attitude, a capacity for anger. John Ferguson is a good fighter but Spencer does not respect him because at times he suspects fighting is all Ferguson can do well. He respects Ted Green of Boston, Vic Hadfield of New York, Barry Gibbs and Ted Harris of Minnesota, Bob Kelly of Philadelphia, Marc Tardif of Montreal, Bob Plager of St. Louis and Rosaire Paiement of Vancouver. He respects them, but he will fight them anytime, anywhere.

During training camp, a coterie of Maple Leaf executives sits at the top of the blue seats on the east side of the rink and watches the daily scrimmages between "whites" and "blues." The men talk among themselves but when there is a bump or a splendid whack, if two players are spitting and clawing at each other, the men in the blue seats cackle.

It is curious.

We walked to a parking lot two blocks from Maple Leaf Gardens. Spencer's gold 1969 Cadillac was at the front of the lot and as we got in two players walked by, Brian Glennie and Guy Trottier, and one of them laughed and said, "Always go first class, eh Spinner?" Spencer sat at the wheel and looked sheepish.

He bought it last summer in Tulsa for $4,600 and he put the initials "B.R.S." on a plate in front of the grill. He drove it to Fort St. James with his wife and there, on the unpaved roads, acknowledging the old faces, he felt some of the elusive glamour. No bruises, lumps or torn cartilages, just the boy triumphant and a gold Cadillac. It was a good summer. He was honoured as Governor of New Caledonia and presented with a beaver skin from Ottawa. Men he played hockey with in Vanderhoof asked him about Keon and Ullman and one day he visited a reform school and talked with the boys and the guards. The farm hadn't changed much; his mother had planted a garden in the rink his father built. He kept it in shape by loading lumber into boxcars for two weeks, $15 a night, and when the summer was over he put his wife on a plane for Tulsa and drove back to Toronto in the Cadillac by himself.

And now we were sitting in the car with the soft seats, the automatic windows and locks and the brocade trim and Spencer was embarrassed. Glennie bumped over a curb in an old Cortina, waved, then scooted west on Maitland Street. Spencer stared at the steering wheel, expressionless, and said he was thinking of trading in the Cadillac.

"Why?"

"Because I don't want it to seem like I'm blowing off."

He is conscious of his image. When he has doubts about what to do, or what to say to the press, he usually turns to George Armstrong, the captain of the team and the man who helped Spencer through the worst of last December. He relates more with Armstrong and Bob Baun than with young players who learned to skate on artificial ice and were coddled on well-managed teams in well-managed leagues. He did some modelling for a men's clothing store last winter but he has no illusions of being a Joe Namath or a Derek Sanderson.

"I'm not a cool guy, a real on-the-ball type of guy. I like to laugh and joke but I can't tell a joke. It's just not in me. I'm too serious."

He met his wife in October 1969, one night when he wasn't playing for the Oilers. She was with friends two rows ahead of him and she did not know much about hockey, having seen only about five games in her life. He took her to a game later when he was playing.

"When I first saw him play he got into a fight and I was really frightened. I thought, 'Oh no, what have I got myself messed up with?'"

He won the fight, of course. She came to Toronto late last December and moved into a rented bungalow in Scarborough. She soon became accustomed to seeing her husband fighting. "It doesn't bother me now because I know he can handle himself. He's tough. The only time I worried about him was when the whole Philadelphia team jumped over the boards at him."

He knows his strengths, weaknesses and limitations but he believes some day he will be a great hockey player, as great as Keon, perhaps as great as Howe. He was told in British Columbia he could never play junior and when he played junior he was told he could never play professional. He stays on the ice after the scrimmages and practices puck control and shooting. When he has bad days he says maybe he will be only competent and not great.

Ten years? Fifteen years? There is not much time.

"If anything jeopardized my job I would eliminate it," he said, chewing on each syllable. "Hockey comes before anything, before my wife and kid. I owe a lot to my wife and kid and I think that for seventeen years I've been playing hockey with only one thought — making the National Hockey League. One year I've been married. So you take seventeen years and one year..."

Bonk! Clink! Ooomph! The sounds of hockey in an empty arena. The red, blue and green seats in the Gardens magnify the sounds and even from the greys you can hear the distinct, guttural curses of the players. It is still training camp and the players are fighting for positions, fighting for jobs.

Spencer pulled a groin muscle in a scrimmage yesterday but he is back on the ice. He skates after the puck in a corner and bumps against John Grisdale, a young, red-headed rookie defenceman who played the last four years at Michigan Tech. Grisdale retaliates this time and the two players are wrestling against the glass in the peculiar struggle of a hockey fight. "Mostly grabbing and giving the odd shot," Spencer said, and that is what he is doing in the corner. Then there is a quick, unexpected flip and Spencer is on his back and Grisdale is on top and you can hear the cackles from the blue seats. Grisdale and Spencer had collided in the morning scrimmage and it had sounded like a horse hitting a fence. Spencer smashed Grisdale with an elbow and the other players told Grisdale he didn't have to take that so in the afternoon he retaliated and fought with Spencer. And won.

A rookie must build a reputation quickly to make the NHL. When Spencer played nine games in Toronto at the end of the 1969–70 season he did not get any goals or assists but he was noticed because he flew around the rink and hit people and never backed away. When he came to Toronto last December the team was in last place but it won ten of its next eleven games and by the end of the month it was in fourth.

"Spencer may just be what we need to get us going," coach McLellan told the sportswriters in the dressing room after Toronto beat Chicago 2–1 for its second consecutive win. "He could be one of those guys who play better in the NHL than in the minor leagues."

He kept getting attention. His father was shot and killed, one morning in Chicago he missed the team bus and was fined — an astounding infraction for a rookie — he knocked out Gary Dornhoefer, he scored a hat trick in January. Even this year in the preseason exhibition games when he had not yet played a full season in the NHL, some fans at Maple Leaf Gardens would chant, "Go Spencer!" and "Get'm Spinner!"

To his own surprise, he has become a favourite.

After a scrimmage one morning, Spencer told me that Doug Acomb, one of Toronto's top draft choices, had "jumped camp" to go back to school. Acomb is the same age and was fighting for the same position as Spencer. In 1968–69, he was captain of Toronto Marlboros and got fifty-five goals and thirty-eight assists and looked like a sure thing. But he did not impress at training camp. In 1968–69 Spencer played in Saskatchewan and was traded to a last place team because he got in a fight with a teammate and wasn't wanted. Now he is Number 15 for the Maple Leafs.

He spoke about this the way a junior executive might speak of squeezing out a vice president. Spencer is boyish and likeable but he is ambitious and he can be ruthless.

"I've been put down too many times, but I've got over it. If you hurt me in some way I will step on your head and go over the top of you. And I won't feel bad about it. If you hurt me in any way, look out."

JEFFREY KLEIN AND KARL-ERIC REIF

"We Have Only One Person To Blame, and That's Each Other"

TO MOST AMERICANS, hockey is Canada's most identifiable cultural export. What's the first thing that just about any American will say when you ask one to name something Canadian? If it isn't "beer" or "Neil Young" or "cold Arctic air mass," it's "hockey." This doesn't mean that hockey and those other things are the most *significant* cultural artifacts Canada has given the world — far from it; rather, it is merely a reflection of how little most Americans know about Canada.

But for many of those few Americans who do know anything more substantial about The True North Strong and Free, there is another failure of understanding. "How can such a peaceful country as Canada have produced so violent a game as hockey?" they ask. They know that the crime rate in Canada is much lower than it is in the U.S., people don't go around with guns blowing other people's brains out nearly as much, the nation's foreign policy or economy isn't geared toward the ability to wage or discourage war through might of arms. And Canada has long been a haven for such escapees from violence as runaway slaves, draft dodgers, refugees....And so on. So, they wonder, how can a country with such a history of non-aggression, whose inhabitants are cheerful, have-another-beer-and-I'll-throw-another-log-on-the-fire-eh? types, have invented and propagated a game that has for so long reveled in bloodletting?

They're right about the game reveling in bloodletting, but they're wrong in their perception of Canada's history — its history has not all been the placid one they believe it to be. Although Canada's past has hardly been so chock-full of mayhem as that of its southern neighbour, it has been contentious and at times violent. And one of the most violent times in Canadian history just happens to have coincided with the era that saw the birth of hockey.

Ken Dryden has presented a superbly reasoned theory to explain the prevalence of violence in the game, one which we believe to be the best offered by anyone, by far. In a nutshell, he theorizes that in the early days of hockey, when there were seven and more men to a side playing a small ice surface, collision was inevitable and frequent. Tempers rose, and there were fights. From the very beginning, the people in charge of the game let the fights go, believing, as they still believe today, that fighting relieved the tensions of a contact game and prevented anything far more serious from breaking out. Dryden identifies that as the "drive-discharge" theory — which he notes is a Freudian concept — in which fighting is seen as a cathartic and thus useful activity.

But Dryden subscribes to a different notion. Citing the anthropologist Richard Sipes' theory that behaviour learned is behaviour repeated, he points out that once a fight is permitted, a player — and an entire sport — learns that it is always permitted and thus acceptable. Fighting in hockey, therefore, is not an outlet for aggression, it's a *learned response*, a chronic condition. Permitted and even encouraged from the very birth of the game, fighting and dirty play have become acceptable forms of conduct, and even, at times, of strategy.

Dryden's thesis makes perfect sense, but as airtight as it is, it lacks one particular element of historical perspective; that is, it doesn't take into account the effect contemporary events in the world outside hockey might have had upon the game. So as a corollary to Dryden's theory, we present the following.

Any social activity undertaken by a people is shaped by the era from which it springs. Like it or not, sport is no exception. (Some people, especially sportswriters, bristle at the mere suggestion that sports — "their" subject — can be looked at analytically in any other context beyond who won, who lost, and why. Until, of course, there's a drug scandal or something.) When baseball came into being in nineteenth-century America it was ridden with the same racism that was so much a part of life in the nation at large, and even today that racism rises to the surface in baseball more than it does in any other sport in America. In 1986 there were at least two occasions in which black players who accused their teams of discrimination were either suspended or released outright. It's also worth noting that the Boston Bruins had a black player in their uniform (Willie O'Ree in 1957–58) before the Boston Red Sox baseball team had a black player in theirs (1959). Minority groups excelled in basketball because that sport was conceived as an urban game, to be played in city gymnasiums, and it was in America's urban centres that minority groups lived. Today, basketball is still primarily an urban game; a higher percentage of players are black, as well as Jewish, in basketball than any other American sport. From its start, basketball has presented no colour bar to blacks, and today, with its tradition of free personal expression firmly entrenched, basketball players are the most richly creative practitioners of their sport among all the sports dominated by Americans.

American football, which came of age in the late nineteenth century, stressed from the very beginning the quasi-military mass movement of "squads" of players who seek to penetrate and occupy "enemy territory." The sport reached its highest crescendo of violence at the turn of the century, when there were several fatalities as a result of the juggernaut tactics, like the flying wedge, then in use. At the time, the American government was busy dispatching troops and naval squadrons to various points in the hemisphere and the Pacific; it was during this era that the U.S. conquered and/or occupied much of Central America, Cuba, Puerto Rico, Hawaii, the Philippines, and several Pacific islands. Today, football boils with tactical terms like "blitz," "end run," "long bomb," "flanker," "suicide squad," and, most ominously of all, "doomsday defense." Its teams bear nicknames like "Raiders," "Vikings," "Maulers," "Invaders," "Chargers," "Buccaneers" (their logo is a pirate *clenching a knife between his teeth*), "Bandits," "Gunslingers," "Outlaws" — a whole catalogue of brigands and pillagers — and that's just the professional teams. These are all birthmarks from football's childhood, spent during a time when mass military undertakings were the order of the day. (In Canada, where the military tradition is not as strong, the game never became as popular, and it retained more of the trappings of rugby, the sport's direct ancestor. Still, in nicknames like "Rough Riders" and the "Blue Bombers," football's military side shows through.) In Britain, rugby was a sport invented at an exclusive boarding school by the children of the ruling class, and it continues to this day to have an air of "the old boys" about it. Meanwhile, the ancient game of soccer has always been the game of the working class; so now, when unemployment, poverty, and frustration plague that class, there's rioting at soccer matches. There isn't any rioting at rugby games — even though rugby is a much more violent sport than soccer — because historically the people who watch it are well off and have nothing to riot about. These are all ultra-simplified, thumbnail examples — we're hardly the first people to say these things — but they remain accurate observations.

Hockey came into being in mid- to late nineteenth-century Canada. Here are some of the things that were happening in the country at that time:

As the American Civil War ended, some Union soldiers of Irish descent hit upon the idea of invading Canada, occupying part of it, and holding it hostage. In return, they would demand that Great Britain grant Ireland its independence. The U.S. government looked the other way as the Fenians, as they called themselves, prepared their invasion. In 1866, they attacked the Niagara Peninsula and took Fort Erie. They advanced to Ridgeway, where the local militia forced them to retreat to the U.S., but only after a bloody battle. In 1870 they tried again, this time in an attack from Vermont, but again they were forced to retreat. In 1871 they tried to attack Manitoba, but U.S. troops stopped the attack before it got started.

In 1870, the Métis of Manitoba (people of mixed Indian and European heritage) opposed the annexation of their territory into Confederation and set up a provisional government at Fort Garry led by Louis Riel. Federal troops were dispatched to quell the rebellion, but the U.S. government would not permit them to pass through the Soo Locks; that, and the Fenian threat, almost led to a Canada–U.S. confrontation. Meanwhile, an Ontario man was killed by the rebels. The Canadian troops eventually got to Fort Garry and put down the rebellion, forcing Riel to flee to the U.S. In 1885 Riel returned, this time to Saskatchewan, and led another rebellion. Some more Ontario men were killed and this caused rioting in Quebec between English and French Canadians. Troops were dispatched to Saskatchewan and the rebellion was again put down. Riel was captured and executed.

From 1898 through 1900, Canadians fought in the Boer War, but there was great debate over the extent to which Canada should be involved. French Canadians, who opposed the war, rioted when Prime Minister Laurier moved to send regular Canadian troops to fight alongside the British. In 1900 the British lifted the four-month siege at Ladysmith, and English Canadians in Montreal celebrated by forming a mob that attacked the offices of a French-language newspaper that wasn't flying a Union Jack to mark the victory. Lester Patrick and Art Ross were teenagers then, and they were involved in the rioting that ensued, as is described by Eric Whitehead in his book *The Patricks, Hockey's Royal Family:* The Messrs. Patrick and Ross, lured downtown by the smell of excitement, were on St. James Street a little later when the unruly mob came roaring by, preceded by a young man waving a Union Jack and several others waving hockey sticks. It was the hockey sticks that did it. To the young adventurers from Westmount, flags were no big deal, but hockey sticks they could understand. This had to be their kind of mob. They joined the group as it streamed off toward Laval University, the city's French-speaking citadel of higher learning....Finding no Relief of Ladysmith celebration in progress there, the mob swarmed onto the campus and raised two Union Jacks....The ensuing battle lasted for more than an hour, and it took a squad of fifty policemen to restore peace."

These are some of the things that were going on during hockey's embryonic period. The game was developed against a backdrop of violence, and so it is little wonder that the game itself is violent. Rioting, mobs, violent rebellions against authority, touchiness bred of a very real fear of invasion from the United States, deep and bitter resentment between the French and English and between the native culture and the transplanted European one — the residue of all this was implanted in hockey's mentality from the start. Since hockey's birth, it has exhibited the effect of its environment in the form of bench-clearing brawls, the striking of officials, fighting in the stands, the resolution of real or imagined slights on the ice through the use of sticks and fists, and often, just plain chaos.

All this actually sounds like great fun, and it does draw fans. Over the decades, hockey's presiding officials may have seemed powerless to stop the violence; in reality, they didn't *want* to stop it. In the early days, when the financial success of the game was a dicey thing for the owners, the endless vendettas players carried on among themselves and the rioting by fans directed against referees and opposing teams were great drawing cards. Why take away a drawing card? Why shoot yourself in the foot? The belief that many fans turned out to see bleeding and brawling persisted through the years. Later, as the notion that overt violence was an okay thing to sell began to seem a tad distasteful, owners, club officials, public relations men, coaches, writers, and broadcasters began to attach euphemisms like "robust," "lusty," "policeman," and "enforcer" to players who were out for blood. When a fan was told that Red Horner or Jimmy Orlando or John

Ferguson or Lou Fontinato or Reggie Fleming or Garry Howatt or Tiger Williams or Chris Nilan or Torrie Robertson was the hometown club's "policeman," it let the fan believe that the player wasn't *starting* fights, for God's sake, he's *showing the other team that he won't allow them to push out guys around.* He's *righting wrongs.* He's *not afraid to back away from the rough stuff.* That's it! . . . "back away." He didn't *start* the rough stuff. He's *responding* to it. He's a *policeman,* a *Defender of the Peace.* It's okay to root for him. I don't have to feel bad about hoping to see him bash the other guy's teeth in with his naked fist!

But don't say "naked fist"; say "fisticuffs," "fracas," "donny-brook," "altercation." Make it sound like *fun,* which we must do, because *people might get the wrong idea.*

And make no mistake about it, you youngsters out there who weren't around a few years ago, the folks in charge of hockey absolutely reveled in this stuff! They encouraged it! They *sold* it, like professional wrestling! Here are some excerpts from a poem by sports-writer John Kiernan, which ran in the program of the AHL Buffalo Bisons in 1968. It's called "I'll Take Hockey":

> . . . *the diamond sport is quiet to that reeling rousing riot, to a slashing game of hockey at its prime;*
> *It's a shindig wild and gay, it's a battle served frappé.*
> *Give me hockey, I'll take hockey any time!* . . .
> . . . *But for fighting, fast and free, grab your hat and come with me,*
> *Sure the thing that they call boxing is a crime. And for the ground and lofty whacking and enthusiastic smacking,*
> *Give me hockey, I'll take hockey every time!* . . .
> . . . *Yes, for speed and pep and action, there is only one attraction,*
> *When the bright steel blades are ringing and the shinny sticks are swinging,*
> *Give me hockey, I'll take hockey every time!*

This is a rousing poem for sure, and we like it. But we feel a little guilty for liking it, because frankly it reminds us just a bit of those Renaissance poems celebrating the joys of warfare. Like this one unearthed by the French historian Marc Bloch and quoted by Barbara Tuchman in *A*

Distant Mirror: the Calamitous 14th Century. It's by the thirteenth-century troubador Bertrand de Born:

> ... And when the battle is joined, let all men of good
> lineage
> Think of naught but the breaking of heads and arms. ...
> I tell you I have no such joy as when I hear the shout
> "On! On!" from both sides and the neighing of riderless
> steeds. ...
> Lords, mortgage your domains, castles, cities, But never
> give up war!

Tuchman points out that in *The Inferno,* Dante depicts Bertrand in hell, holding his severed head and using it as a lantern. Serves him right. By the same token, we might imagine that in some Other Realm, Kiernan is being repeatedly butt-ended by Sprague Cleghorn.

Over the past twelve years or so, however, there has been a backlash against violence in the game, spurred in large part by several government investigations and by the realization in society as a whole that violence of any kind is dangerous and anti-social. Not surprisingly, today you don't see any such rhapsodic poems as the one above in official publications — in fact, you can barely find any reference to fighting whatsoever in any program or league-produced publication. It's unfashionable to admit that you're appealing to people's baser instincts, so the owners have omitted any explicit reference to violence. Any mention of violence nowadays and the moguls get touchy. Even the ridiculous cartoon variety presented in the truly awful movie *Youngblood* drew such an outraged reaction from the NHL office that the league banned all advertisements for the movie in all league and club publications, as though the league was the Vatican, and *Youngblood* was Godard's *Hail Mary.*

Meanwhile, in the letters columns of sports pages and hockey magazines today you see more and more calls for "kicking out the goons" and "cleaning up the game." Most fans don't want to see fighting, say the letter-writers, and those five percent who do are only spoiling it for the rest of us. Oh yeah? Then why, when a fight breaks out today at a hockey game, do practically *all* spectators stand up to get a better view? And that ubiquitous cheer you always hear whenever the home-team player manages to wrestle his opponent to the ice — that's not just five per cent of the crowd cheering, it's more like seventy-five per cent. All of the fans and commentators who decry the violence are well intentioned, but they're talking through their hats when they say it's only a tiny minority who like to watch fighting. And we know for a fact that some of those who say they would abolish fighting themselves subscribe to the "policeman" myth: when their guy starts the fight, he's a goon; when our guy starts the fight, he's not backing down, he's standing up for his teammates. The notion that only a small, demented minority enjoys watching violent play and fighting is false. The owners and governors know this, and that's why there'll be no season-long suspensions for recidivist fighters and high-stickers in the near future, and clubs will continue, as they always have done, to pay the fines levied against players for brawling. They'll even continue to reward their players for brawling, as the Kings owner Jerry Buss did in 1981 when he gave John Gibson a color TV for sucker-punching Paul Holmgren. Hockey remains what it always has been, at least as it has been played in North America: a violent game.

It doesn't have to be. In the Soviet Union, Sweden, Czechoslovakia, Finland, and just about every place else, it isn't violent. Over the 1985–86 season, we were able to watch several Soviet elite league games at Columbia University's Harriman Institute, where they have a satellite dish that picks up the signals from the USSR's second TV channel. We saw plenty of instances in which players went into the boards heavily, grappled roughly in the corners, tripped one another in the circle prior to the face-off. Conditioned to see a fight begin, we watched and waited for the sticks to go down, the gloves to come off, the fists to come up. But not once did that happen. They players jawed at each other and at the referee, but they never even came close to going at it. Once, in a game between Khimik Voskresensk and Central Army, there was a collision along the boards and the two players glared at each other. The Khimik player gave a little shove to the CSKA player. Both linesmen were all over both players in an instant. There was no attitude on the officials' part of "if they're evenly matched, let them go at it"; even if the players had wanted to fight, the linesmen saw to it that there was no time to throw a punch. Both players were sent off with majors.

One game we saw pitted the arch-rivals CSKA (virtually no one, apparently, roots for the perennial-champion army team) against Spartak (the trade union team that just about everybody roots for.) The game was hotly contested; indeed, it was downright bitter. Most Soviet hockey games look more like basketball than North American hockey; there is very little body contact, all-out emphasis an offence, an endless parade of fast-breaking two-on-ones, poor defence, and awful goaltending. The CSKA-Spartak game was different! Plenty of heavy hitting (a lot of it gratuitous), good strong defence, and ill temper. At one point there was a pileup in the corner in the CSKA end and a Spartak player came flying in with a blindside elbow that caught a CSKA player up near the chin. The CSKA player crosschecked the offender in retaliation. Play came to a stop. The players cross-checked each other back and forth, without much force, but with escalating vigour. All the skaters paired off and grabbed each other, and although there was none of the sweater-pulling that in the the NHL serves as the prelude to a general rumble, clearly there was malevolence in the air. The linesmen tried to get between the principals, but too many players were in the way. This was it! Soviet fisticuffs! But it was not to be. The two main "combatants" stopped their shoving and simply stood staring at one another, complaining. Each held his stick down low, in hands that were still gloved. The linesmen finally arrived, the players separated, and several went to the bench to await the meting out of penalties. That was that; according to the post-doctoral fellow who had been monitoring Soviet sports all year long on the Institute's satellite hookup, it was the most fractious incident of the entire hockey season.

If Europeans can play hockey without undue mayhem, then maybe the game here isn't violent by nature but only by nurture. When we were in high school, during the heyday of the Broad Street Bullies, our gym class offered floor hockey for the first time, a decision the school administrators no doubt regretted. Where before, in basketball, wrestling, softball, we had played without incident, we now turned into raving lunatics. Every five minutes, somebody would be squaring off with somebody else — "You stepped on my fuckin' foot, you asshole!" "Yeah? You wanna go at it?!!!!" — and the gym teachers would have to run over and get between two hotheads. This was going on *in a school,* and in the fifty-five minutes between math and study hall, yet. And it was going on during the years in which the Flyers were deliberately pummeling everyone else into submission — a strategy most of the clubs in the league were beginning to mimic — and it was being shown on U.S. network television, beamed right into our homes along with whatever games we could pick up on the Canadian channels, with people like Ted Lindsay and Howie Meeker rhapsodizing about the laying on of lumber (sounds almost beatific, doesn't it?) and the importance of the fearless willingness, the *eagerness,* to "mix it up."

In another environment, it was different. Somebody we know went to a high school in the woods of western New Jersey at the same time we were attending high school in hockey-drugged Buffalo. They had just built a rink at the school and were icing a hockey team for the first time ever. All the soccer players decided to go out for the hockey team, including our friend, "because we thought it looked so cool gliding around on skates. We didn't know Jack Shit about hockey." The team was horrible, and in one game the netminder got involved in some goalmouth hostilities with two or three opponents who started whaling the tar out of him. "We all stood around and watched the poor guy getting beaten up, which we thought was terrible. We were all saying, 'Somebody should do something about that, you know?' All the players' fathers were sitting in the stands screaming for us to go over and do something, but hell, the guys on the other team were a lot bigger than us. We didn't want to get beat up! So finally all the fathers jumped over the boards, ran down the ice, and started beating up on the other team. That was it for hockey as far as we were concerned." These guys had no idea that hockey as it was played in North America, especially during the seventies, was not supposed to be an elegant game; it was a battle of intimidation. Like musicians who go into an audition intending to play intricate Bach cantatas, only to find the orchestra crashing into the most bombastic Wagnerian excesses, these hockey players were in the wrong place at the wrong time. They didn't know that you're supposed to "stick up for your goaler," much less that other teams will deliberately try to pick fights with your goaler. We should add that today our friend earns his living by making violins.

One of the incredible things about the violent side of North American hockey is that the fans *don't* get involved in the fighting. In the U.K., it's a different story. As everyone knows by now, the going gets awfully rough at an English football ground. But all this malignity is carried out in the name of a sport that is the most peaceful of all. There is virtually no fighting in soccer, practically no way for a player to get really badly hurt. In hockey, where the prospects for serious assault or injury on the ice are great, there is virtually no violence in the stands. Mind you, you don't want to be sitting in the wrong section at a Rangers-Islanders game, but on the whole there have been very few player-fan "incidents" over the past two decades, despite all the potential catalysts for it that exist in the way the game is played on the ice.

A major reason for the relative calm at hockey games is the relative wealth of the spectators. It's expensive to attend an NHL game, and you've really got to shell out the green — or, in Canada, the Queen — to buy a ticket. Most fans at the rinks have the bucks; they're the upper middle-class, not the kind of people to raise the banner of class struggle and storm the barricades, or cause any kind of trouble whatsoever. Today's hockey fans don't participate in fighting; rather, they get their vicarious kicks from watching it, which is why everyone stands up and starts yelling whenever a fight breaks out on the ice.

But that's today. It used to be different.

King Clancy told us about the twenties and thirties, when "it was a different kind of people who went to hockey games. In Boston, there were these women who'd line up on either side of the corridor that led from the visiting dressing room to the ice. We'd go down that corridor and these women would stand there and kick us and spit on us. Christ, we used to hate going in there."

Here's a wire service description of what happened in 1933, after Eddie Shore almost killed Ace Bailey during a game in Boston:

> . . . After Bailey was tripped at the Garden, Shore returned to his defense position in the Boston zone. Horner immediately rushed over and knocked him down with a heavy right the jaw. Shore's head was split open when it hit the ice, and Dr. Crotty used seven stitches to close the three-inch gash. Both players (Shore and Bailey) were carried off the ice, and while Connie Smythe, the Leafs' manager, was rushing to the side of his injured player, he became involved in a fist fight with several spectators outside the Toronto dressing room.
>
> One of them, Leonard Kenworthy of Everett, accused Smythe of delivering the blow that shattered his spectacles and injured his eye. Kenworthy, Boston Garden officials said, will apply for a warrant charging Smythe with assault tomorrow morning.

In *Checking Back,* Neil Issacs writes that after the game, Shore went to the Leafs' dressing room to apologize to Bailey. "I'm sorry, Ace,"

Shore is reported to have said. Bailey, whose brain was hemorrhaging, was barely conscious when he replied, "That's all right Eddie. It's all part of the game." *It's all part of the game.*

Going further back in the history of the game, one finds a much closer correlaton between the mayhem on the ice and the mayhem in the stands. And we find that both seem to have been much worse than anything the game had witnessed in recent decades. As Charles Coleman went through old newspaper accounts in his research for the first volume of *The Trail of The Stanley Cup,* he found an endless procession of absolute bloodthirstiness:

> There was alot of excitement when Montreal defeated Toronto 4–3 of February 27th. Bert Corbeau and Babe Seibert started a fight that eventually involved all the players, officials and a great many spectators. (1926)

> Referee Mike Rodden was threatened with a lawsuit for hitting a spectator in a game at the Mount Royal Arena. He was defending himself while trying to get to the dressing room.(1926)

> Cleghorn and Hitchman had been exchanging bumps all evening until near the end of the game Cleghorn cross-checked Hitchman in the face knocking him out. Cleghorn was banished for the match and a riot almost took place. The ice was showered with debris and referee Marsh was attacked.(1923)

> The game between Quebec and Toronto on February 3rd was terminated with two minutes to play, when the officials and police were unable to restore order. The Toronto players took the ice feeling aggressive, as their train being late, they did not have time for supper. During the game Joe Hall attacked Corbett Denneny and Reg Noble lost no time in retaliating. Finally Ken Randall became embroiled with a spectator which started a general fight in which bottles and chairs were thrown on the ice. The game was called and the Toronto team escorted to their dressing room by the police. The players were attacked on the way to the train and several of them mauled. President Robinson suspended Randall indefi-

nitely for his participation in the brawl, although referee
Smeaton reported that he had not seen the incident. However, Randall was only out for one week.(1917)

Canadiens defeated Quebec 4–3 in Montreal on February 26th after 15 seconds of overtime. At the end of the
game, Joe Hall hit Arbour and in short order players and
spectators were involved in a free-for-all.(1916)

A Donnybrook broke out at Montreal Feb. 25th when
the Bulldogs defeated Wanderers 3–2. Art Ross struck
Eddie Oatman over the head with his stick, knocking him
cold. The spectators joined in and the police had to inter-
vene to restore order.(1911)

Coleman's book begins with the 1893–94 season, and the first inci-
dence of fan hooliganism appears in 1894–95:

The game at Quebec was marked by a great deal of
rough play. Weldy Young and Dolly Swift indulged in an
exchange of pleasantries that provoked other battles. The
crowd became very demonstrative and hostile towards the
visitors. . . .

At the conclusion of the match, the crowd pursued referee Hamilton
and umpire Findlay. The officials were seized as they were about to
enter a rig for the station and dragged back to the arena where an
attempt was made to force them to declare the game a draw. Police
eventually broke up the demonstration and the officials retired with
what dignity they could master after a rough handling.

It's difficult to say how much of a role socio-political currents played
in bringing about the frequent fan violence of the early years; any solid
conclusions must await a detailed, scholarly study. But we're willing to
bet that the fairly stormy events sweeping Canada at the time had much
to do with it, just as we're willing to bet they had a lot to do with the
violence on the ice that still persists today.

That violence on the ice does seem to have been far worse then than
it has been for the past few years, and certainly far more vicious than
anything perpetrated by the Flyers during their reign of terror. Quite
often, players even attacked referees. We won't quote Coleman or
contemporary news accounts here, but we will say that for every

incident of violence in the stands Coleman mentions, there are at least three monstrous acts of violence on the ice. The worst came on March 6, 1907, when Bud McCourt was killed by blows received from a stick during a brawl in a Federal Amateur Hockey League game in Cornwall. Charges were brought against a player in that "incident," but they were dismissed for lack of conclusive evidence. It was one of dozens of cases in the first two decades of this century in which players were arrested for their roles in brawls. But police intervention ended in during the early twenties, for some reason, and did not recur until the early seventies, with the notorious Dave Forbes-Henry Boucha "incident"; the game, it was supposed, policed itself.

What is alarming is that the league presidents over the years did such an awful job of policing the game. They very rarely imposed anything more than a few games' suspensions, and quite often in the early years players and clubs simply ignored those suspensions. By the time the NHL had established itself as the only major league, the suspensions stuck, but they were mere wrist slaps in comparison to the enormity of many of the players' crimes, and they continued to be for decades. In 1975, when Forbes butt-ended a twenty-five stitch cut millimeters above Boucha's right eye, Clarence Campbell said it was "one of the most vicious (cases) I have ever been called upon to deal with." Stern words from a man whose stiff sentence in response to Rocket Richard's high-stick attack against Hal Laycoe and punch-out on linesman Cliff Thompson brought about the "Richard Riot," but Campbell's punishment of Forbes for this "vicious" attack? Ten games.

No hockey fan needs to be told that the same milquetoast sentences are meted out today by John Ziegler and Bryan O'Neill, but as Ken Dryden points out, they are only part of a pattern hockey authority set for itself many years ago, some time after the day in 1904 when OHA President John Ross Robertson said, "We must call a halt to slashing and slugging, and insist upon clean hockey in Ontario, before we have to call a coroner to visit our rinks."

It's not as bad now as it used to be in the old days. Furthermore, hockey is no longer the only sport that revels in violence. Brawling is on the upsurge in baseball and basketball, and the sight of dugout-emptying mêlées and seven-foot giants leveling jaw-shattering punches at each other is becoming more and more commonplace. There are relatively few slugfests in football, but the sport's programmed ultraviolence — and the slick promotion of it by the football leagues themselves — is also on the rise.

Of course, you don't hear commentators complaining about the spiking, beaning, elbowing, brawling, forearm-shivering, and deliberate "crunching" in those sports, and that may have something to do with the fact that those sports are *American* — part of the continent's dominant culture — while hockey is Canadian, *foreign,* and therefore fair game for reproach. It's no longer fair to criticize hockey alone for its violence when those other sports now have enough fighting and filthy play in some of their games to put plenty of hockey games to shame. So, despite everything we can say to decry the violence that persists in the game, we'll still take hockey, anytime.

DAVID GOWDEY

Cooler Heads: Suggestions For Cleaning Up The Game

BELIEVE IT OR NOT, there was a time in the National Hockey League when freezing the puck didn't invite a mêlée. Participants in a touchy situation after the whistle most often simply skated away from one another, while Foster Hewitt closed the matter for listeners with his reassuring, "Cooler heads prevail". It's a noble phrase; unfortunately, we seldom hear it anymore. The game that used to last two hours and twenty minutes in now nudging the three hour mark, and most of the difference is due to the parade of offsetting double penalties.

I'd better add before going any farther that I enjoy a genuine hockey fight as much as anyone — a spontaneous explosion in the heat of battle is pretty dramatic stuff. But the game today is demeaned and brought to a standstill by the endless post-whistle "confrontations", the dreary eyeballing and shoving on the boards, the long minutes spent untangling every goalmouth scramble. Many ways out of this dilemma have been proposed, but some of the most interesting haven't been tried yet.

Frank Boucher once wrote that a hockey referee has one of the hardest jobs in the world to do well. Boucher believed that if referees called every penalty by the book, and received the backing of the league, unnecessarily rough play would eventually die down. But the problem may go deeper than that.

The NHL has recently made efforts in this direction. Beginning in the 1987–88 season more penalties began to be called late in the game and in overtime, after the league had gone over four years without a power play in playoff overtime. Yet most referees, unconsciously or not, still remain unwilling to call substantially more penalties against one team than the other. Conventional wisdom states that a well-run game is one where the referee is invisible, and many feel that if they heavily penalize one team over the other they are playing too big a role in determining the outcome.

The reality may in fact be the opposite. In his book *The Violent Game* hockey columnist Gary Ronberg put forward the case that this tendency to "even out" penalties ultimately benefits the home team, and is the reason for the much higher rate of home team victories in hockey over all other major sports:

> A team generally plays with more assurance at home. It takes more chances. Instead of sitting on a lead it is more likely to try to break the game open....In terms of fouling, especially flagrant fouling intended to intimidate, the home team is expected to be more daring. It is much more likely to feel that it can afford an early penalty, or even an early score against it, if it can establish its physical superiority over the opposition.

In other words, it's more than cheering that builds up a home ice advantage. When a referee has a tendency to even out penalty calls, the more aggressive home team gains a distinct advantage, since in effect it is being penalized less for its aggression than the visitor.

> As of now, (visiting teams) have the unhappy choice of moving immediately to combat the threat of hometown intimidation or laying back and accepting the abuse. If they choose to be belligerent, they risk penalties that may lead to scores against them that they cannot afford. If they choose to be passive, the visitors rely on the vain hope that with the referee's help they can survive. The choice is to be penalized by the referee for protecting yourself or by the aggressors for failing to....Confronted with such a choice, most teams will opt for belligerence and challenge the referee to crack down.

Hockey has always been rough, but an intentional pattern of play based on cheap shots and breaking the rules is a recent development. Twenty-five years ago a great deal more respect existed among players for each other's skills. A new player's courage was always tested, but very few players were carried by a team solely for their toughness. The size of the rosters wouldn't permit it — a player had to be able to pass, skate and shoot at a certain level. In the fifties the most heavily penalized players were Ted Lindsay and Gordie Howe, both top scorers; among the enforcers of the sixties Howie Young was a tremendous skater with a great deal of potential before he wasted it on booze and brawling; Lou Fontinato was a better than average defenceman; Orland Kurtenbach was more than a fighter; Eddie Shack was Eddie Shack.

But there was one player in particular who helped to change the way the game is played. The success of the Canadiens of the middle sixties, an unheralded dynasty that won five Cups in seven years, was based in no small part upon their reliance on John Ferguson to create open ice for his flashier teammates. Ferguson, who also possessed reasonable hockey skills, was the most feared player of his time, willing and eager to run a goalie or plant a fist in an opponent's face. The peak of his success coincided with the 1967 expansion. As career minor leaguers were brought into the limelight and the average level of skills deteriorated, many borderline players strove to copy his successful formula in order to keep their NHL jobs.

The change in the expanded schedule added to the effect, notes Ronberg:

> In the old six-team league, most home teams didn't dare
> to take too many liberties with visitors because they knew
> that they would soon (often the next night) have to play
> in the visitor's rink. The teams had fourteen meetings in
> which they evolved a brutal but fairly stable balance of
> fouling. They were enemies but they were also
> neighbours who, in a sense, had to live in each other's
> homes. . . . Today a home team is virtually free of this
> restraint. By the time it pays a visit, months may have
> gone by, and the animosities (in some cases even the
> players) may have been dropped. The next confrontation
> is just too far in the future to be a deterrent.

The 1967 expansion ushered in this new era, but another dilution of talent in the early 1940's had similarly far-reaching effects. When most of the talent in the league was overseas fighting, NHL governors were faced with a perplexing problem. At that time there was no centre red line, and any pass over a blueline was illegal. The puck had to be carried out past the blueline to start an attack, and carried into the opposition's end to get close to the net. This meant plenty of stickhandling and combination passing, and plenty of crowd-pleasing collisions at the blueline when the defence reacted.

After 1942 most of the players who had the stickhandling and passing ability to be able to advance the puck were lost to the war. Teams were being caught in their own end for minutes at a time and play was slowing to a walk. The centre red line was introduced by Frank Boucher, with strong support from Jack Adams, in an attempt to open up the play. No pass could be made over two lines, but single-line passes were now legal. By allowing break-out passes as far as centre the rule change forced opposing defencemen back towards their own net, and gave forwards more open ice.

The new rule worked at first, until players discovered that they no longer needed to carry the puck into the offensive zone: they could throw it into the corner wihtout being called for icing and stand a fifty-fifty chance of getting it back again deep in scoring territory. The combination play previously needed to gain ground was suddenly no longer necessary; all that was needed was the speed to reach the corners and the willingness to duke it out once you got there.

Defencemen now had to be more mobile, but bodychecking in open ice began to be a thing of the past, since the opposition seldom had possession of the puck when play entered the zone. The skills required to time a clean bodycheck were no longer very valuable; what soon became much more important was the ability to keep the front of the net clear when the puck came out from the corner. With all the extra pushing and shoving tempers grew shorter, and play became less decorous. The game has followed this direction ever since.

There has certainly been great hockey played recently, particularly at the international level, but this is an exception that proves the point. The Soviets and most other international teams, indeed most skilled puck handlers from any country, don't believe in accepting merely a fifty-fifty chance of gaining territory when they have possession of the puck. The Soviet game has always been based on combination play, and their stickhandling and passing skills allow them to carry the puck into the offensive zone time and again. They are occasionally still met by a devastating check, which itself adds to the intensity of the game.

Boucher realized the monster he had created and later petitioned for the repeal of the rule, but the damage had been done. Hockey had shifted from a game played almost wholly in open ice to one played in large part on the boards, and at anything less than the very highest levels the game as a spectacle has suffered.

It's interesting to see that among the players we remember fondly from the fifties and sixties, the greatest stickhandlers — Bentley, Schmidt, Abel, Beliveau, Howe, Kelly, Bathgate — and the best body-checking defencemen — Horton, Pronovost, Boivin, Gadsby — all grew up as boys playing the game in the years before the red line was introduced. Their talents were formed under the rules that existed before World War II. Bobby Baun, Brian Glennie and the Plagers, perhaps the last of the great bodychecking breed, were to come along a few years later, but their main propensity was driving people into the boards, rather than meeting skaters in open ice.

Recently Bobby Clarke and others have taken up Boucher's cause, suggesting that the red line be abolished, the bluelines moved farther away from the goals, and passing be allowed up to the far blueline. Boucher also felt that the puck should once again have to be carried over the opposing blueline, and that a shot from outside the line behind the net should be whistled down as icing. These variations on the old rules would eliminate the dump-and-chase style and the frayed tempers that go with it, and at least in theory bring back true body-checking as well as stickhandling and intricate passing.

Hockey today is fast and often wide open, but the growing movement to temper the game's violence still has a long way to go. Players now begin pro careers very young, often before they learn the basics of playing defence, while at the same time the game has speeded up. Equipment and tactics have been refined — skates are faster and padding lighter; line changes are made at a dizzying rate.

The throng of fast, offensive-minded players has led to an increase in slashing and hooking, since the easiest way to slow down an escaping check is to bring the stick to play. The influx of players from Europe, where sticks are carried higher, has added to this tendency. In the old days highsticking often led to a fight, but helmets and face-shields tend to reduce fighting, and as a result, violent retarliatory stick-work has dramatically increased. The cycle is hard to break, but an intriguing suggestion for cutting down on rough play at an early age has recently been offered.

Sociologist Edmund Vaz believes that hockey violence could be reduced if youth teams were being rewarded in the standings for playing within the rules. He feels that the traditional approach, oriented towards controlling the individual, has failed, and says that a method should be introduced into the game to encourage teams to police themselves, rather than constantly be trying to get away with what they can to gain an intimidatory advantage.

> The desire for success in athletic competition is. . . congruent with the basic values of success-striving to get ahead in the larger society. . . . What is wrong is when winning the game is extolled so highly that little attention is given to how one achieves it.

Vaz rejects several of the alternatives that are commonly offered as ways to combat hockey violence. He feels that increasing the number of penalty calls tends to disrupt the flow of the game, while lengthening a penalty to three or four minutes, or forcing a player to sit out the whole time despite a goal against, would aid the power play team to such an extent that referees would be pressured into calling *fewer* penalties. In any case, trying to crack down by imposing stiffer penalties from above would be futile. Negative reinforcement doesn't work. Instead he suggests a kind of positive reinforcement:

> What is required is that players be taught to *want* to obey the normative rules of the game, that is, that conformity to normative rules be institutionalized and become a major value of the hockey sub-culture. . . . The task is to modify the game so that the values of success and of conformity to the rules of the game are both rewarded. And whenever rule violation is committed, both the offender and the team must be sanctioned.

The system he proposes would reward a team's obedience to the rules as well as its winning the game. An "ideal" number of penalty minutes per team per game would be established by the league, perhaps an average of the past season, or less than the average if the league wished to reduce penalties. A team that played a "clean game", that is, that didn't exceed the "ideal" number of penalty minutes, would be awarded bonus points in the standings regardless of who won the game. For example, the scoring system might award 6 points for a win, 3 for a tie, 0 for a loss, with a bonus of 2 points for having played a clean game. Thus, a "clean win" would be worth a total of 8 points, a "dirty win" (that is, winning while exceeding the ideal allotment of penalties) worth just 6 points, and a "clean loss" worth 2 points for the loser. Using this model, one team could lose slightly more games than another, but if it consistently played cleaner hockey it could still finish higher in the final league standings.

With this system in place the rules of the game would become a standard to be met, not avoided.

> Standards for the assessment of players will gradually change. Violent behaviour will become much less functional for winning games and achieving personal status in the league. . . . The application of group (team) pressure on offenders (players) is an established means of changing individual behaviour. . . . Since he wishes to remain in good standing in the eyes of teammates, a player is unlikely to resist team pressure on matters that the team considers important.

It is quite likely that this system would reduce the amount of chippy play; at worst, if teams exceed their totals, the situation would revert back to the present one. It seems worth a try, at least up to junior hockey.

Playing Against Orr

IN HOCKEY IT IS CALLED A "REP", short, of course, for "reputation". Mine grew out of North Bay: one game, one moment, the clock stopped, the game in suspension — and yet it was this, nothing to do with what took place while clocks ran in sixty-eight other games, that put me on the all-star team with more votes than Torchy. Half as many, however, as Bobby Orr. But still, it was Orr and Batterinski, the two defencemen, whom they talked most about in Ontario junior.

Bobby Orr would get the cover of *Maclean's*. I almost got the cover of *Police Gazette* after the Billings incident. My rep was made. The *North Bay Nugget's* nickname for me, Frankenstein, spread throughout the league. I had my own posters in Kitchener; there were threats in Kingston and spray-paint messages on our bus in Sault Ste. Marie; late, frantic calls at the Demers house from squeaky young things wanting to speak to the "monster."

They didn't know me. I didn't know myself. But I loved being talked about in the same conversations as the white brushcut from Parry Sound. Orr they spoke of as if he was the Second Coming — they sounded like Poppa praising the Madonna on the church in Warsaw; for me it was the same feeling for both Orr and the Madonna — I couldn't personally see it.

Orr had grown since I'd seen him first in Vernon, but he was still only sixteen in 1964 and seemed much too short to be compared to Harvey and Howe, as everyone was doing. He'd gone straight from bantam to junior, but Gus Demers still said he was just another in a long list of junior hockey's flashes-in-the-pan. Another Nesterenko, another Cullen.

We met Oshawa Generals in that year's playoffs, and the papers in Oshawa and Sudbury played up the Batterinski-Orr side of it. "Beauty and the Beast," the Oshawa *Times* had it. The *Star* countered with "Batterinski's Blockade," pointing out that the Hardrock's stategy was to have Batterinski make sure Orr never got near the net, though no one ever spoke to me about it. I presume it was understood.

On March 28 we met on their home ice, the advantage going to them by virtue of a better record throughout the season. I said not a single word on the bus ride down, refusing to join Torchy in his dumb-ass Beatle songs, refusing even to get up and wade back to the can, though I'd had to go since Orillia. My purpose was to exhibit strength and I could not afford the slightest opening. I had to appear superhuman to the rest of the team: not needing words, nor food, nor bodily functions.

If I could have ridden down in the equipment box I would have, letting the trainer unfold me and tighten my skates just before the warm-up, sitting silent as a puck, resilient as my shin pads, dangerous as the blades. The ultimate equipment: me.

I maintained silence through "the Queen" and allowed myself but one chop at Frog Larocque's goal pads, then set up. Orr and I were like reflections, he standing solid and staring up at the clock from one corner, me doing the same at the other, both looking at time, both thinking of each other. We were the only ones in the arena, the crowd's noise simply the casing in which we would move, the other players simply the setting to force the crowd's focus to us. Gus Demers had advised me to level Orr early, to establish myself. Coach Therrian wanted me to wait for Orr, keep him guessing. I ignored them all. They weren't involved. Just Orr and me.

His style had changed little since bantam. Where all the other players seemed bent over, concentrating on something taking place below them, Orr still seemed to be sitting at a table as he played, eyes as alert as a poker player, not interested in his own hands or feet or where the object of the game was. I was fascinated by him and studied him intently during the five minutes I sat in the penalty box for spearing some four-eyed whiner in the first period. What made Orr effective was that he had somehow shifted the main matter of the game from the puck to him. By anticipating, he had our centres looking for him, not their wingers, and passes were directed *away* from him, not *to* someone on our team. By doing this, and by knowing this himself, he had assumed control of the Hardrocks as well as the Generals.

I stood at the penalty box door yanking while the timekeeper held for the final seconds. I had seen how to deal with Orr. If the object of the game had become him, not the puck, I would simply put Orr through his own net.

We got a penalty advantage toward the end of the period and coach sent me out to set up the power play. I was to play centre point, ready to drop quickly in toward the net rather than remaining in the usual point position along the boards and waiting for a long shot and tip-in. Therrian had devised this play, I knew, from watching Orr, though he maintained it was his own invention. I never argued. I never even spoke. I was equipment, not player, and in that way I was dependable, predictable, certain.

Torchy's play, at centre, was to shoulder the Oshawa centre out of the face-off circle while Chancey, playing a drop-back left wing, fed the puck back to me, breaking in. A basketball play, really, with me fast-breaking and Torchy picking. The crowd was screaming but I couldn't hear. I was listening for Orr, hoping he might say something that would show me his flaw, hoping he might show involvement rather than disdain. But he said nothing. He stared up at the clock for escape, the numbers meaningless, the score irrelevant. He stood, stick over pads, parallel to the ice, back also parallel, eyes now staring through the scars of the ice for what might have been his own reflection. Just like me, once removed from the crowd's game, lost in his own contest.

The puck dropped and Torchy drove his shoulder so hard into the Generals' centre I heard the grunt from the blueline. Chancey was tripped as he went for the puck, but swept it as he fell. I took it on my left skate blade, kicking it forward to my stick, slowing it, timing it, raising back for a low, hard slapper from just between the circles. I could sense Orr. Not see him. I was concentrating on the puck. But I could sense him the way you know when someone is staring at you from behind. I raised the stick higher, determined to put the shot right through the bastard if necessary. I heard him go down, saw the blond brushcut spinning just outside the puck as he slid toward me, turning his pads to catch the shot. His eyes were wide open and his head passed the puck; he stared straight at it, though it could, if I shot now, rip his face right off the skull. He did not flinch; he did not even blink. He stared the way a poker player might while saying he'll hold. Orr knew precisely what my timing was before I myself knew. I saw him spin past, knew what he was doing, but could not stop; my shot crunched into his pads and away, harmlessly.

The centre Torchy had hit dove toward the puck and it bounced back at me, off my toe and up along the ankle, rolling like a ball in a magician's trick. I kicked but could not stop it. The puck trickled and suddenly was gone. I turned, practically falling. *It was Orr!* Somehow he'd regained his footing even faster than I and was racing off in that odd sitting motion toward our net.

I gave chase, now suddenly aware of the crowd. Their noise seemed to break through an outer, protective eardrum. There were no words, but I was suddenly filled with insult as the screams tore through me, ridiculing. It seemed instant, this change from silently raising the stick for the certain goal, the sense that I was gliding on air, suspended, controlling even the breath of this ignorant crowd. Now there was no sense of gliding or silence or control. I was flailing, chopping at a short sixteen-year-old who seemed completely oblivious to the fact that Batterinski was coming for him.

I felt my left blade slip and my legs stutter. I saw him slipping farther and farther out of reach, my strides choppy and ineffective, his brief, effortless and amazingly successful. I swung with my stick at his back, causing the noise to rise. I dug in but he was gone, a silent, blond brushcut out for a skate in an empty arena.

I dove, but it was no use. My swinging stick rattled off his ankle guards and I turned in my spill in time to see the referee's hand raise for a delayed penalty. I was already caught so I figured I might as well make it worthwhile. I regained my feet and rose just as Orr came in on Larocque, did something with his stick and shoulder that turned Frog into a lifesize cardboard poster of a goaltender, and neatly tucked the puck into the corner of the net.

The crowd roared, four thousand jack-in-the-boxes suddenly sprung, all of them laughing at me. Orr raised his hands in salute and turned, just as I hit him.

It was quiet again, quiet as quickly as the noise had first burst through. I felt him against me, shorter but probably as solid. I smelled him, not skunky the way I got myself, but the smell of Juicy Fruit chewing gum. I gathered him in my arms, both of us motionless but for the soar of our skates, and I aimed him carefully and deliberately straight through the boards at the goal judge.

Orr did not even bother to look at me. It was like the theory you read about car accidents, that the best thing you can do is relax. Orr rode in my arms contentedly, acceptingly, neither angry, nor afraid, nor surprised. We moved slowly, deliberately, together. I could see the goal judge leaping, open-mouthed, back from the boards, bouncing off his cage like a gorilla being attacked by another with a chain. I saw his coffee burst through the air as we hit, the gray-brown circles slowly rising up and away and straight into his khaki coat. The boards gave;

they seemed to give forever, folding back toward the goal judge, then groaning, then snapping us out and down in a heap as the referee's whistle shrieked in praise.

I landed happy, my knee rising into his leg as hard as I could manage, the soft grunt of expelled air telling me I had finally made contact with the only person in the building who would truly understand.

If it would stop there, the game would be perfect. But I knew, having taken my best shot, I would have to deal with the rebound. My hope was to clear it quickly. I pushed Orr and began to stand, only to be wrapped by the linesman trying to work a full nelson around my shoulders. I went to him gratefully, shifting with false anger, yanking hard but not too hard, according to the unwritten fighter–linesman agreement. He was talking in my ear the way one does to calm down a dog who has just smelled porcupine.

"Easy now, fella. Just take it easy now, okay?"

I said nothing. I pulled hard; he pulled back hard. He twisted me away; I went with him, scowling, delighted.

"Get the trainer!" I heard the referee shout to one of the Generals.

I twisted back. Orr was still down on the ice. The other linesman stood above, waiting to embrace him, but Orr just lay there, eyes shut, face expressionless.

"Chickenshit!" one of their larger players yelled at me and then looked away quickly, afraid to own up to his words. I lunged toward him, but gratefully let the linesman reel me in.

"Just easy now! Easy, easy, easy," he said in my ear. I felt like barking, just to throw him off.

The referee signalled to the linesman to get me into the box, and I let him wrestle me over with only a few stops and twists. Some of the crowd was hanging up over the glass and screens, throwing things, spitting, screaming. They looked like the muskrat Danny had once taken on a tip trap and failed to drown; we'd put it in a box and stabbed cattail stems through the cardboard at the little fucker until it ran at the screen we'd placed over the top, screeching and spitting at us as if it would have torn us to pieces if it hadn't been blocked from us. These rats seemed voluntarily caged. Unlike the muskrat, they welcomed their confinement. If they broke through and got to me they'd have trouble finding the courage to ask for my autograph.

Orr did not return to the game. We won 4–1 on Torchy's hat trick. I scored the fourth on a desperate empty-net attempt by Oshawa, and the slow slider from centre was booed all the way into the net, making

it sweet as if I had skated through the entire team and scooped it high
into a tight corner as the last man back slashed my feet out from under
me. I even asked the linesman for the puck, just to rub it in.

But such sweetness never seems to last. The X-rays went against us,
Orr returned for game three and after six we were out of it, retired for
the season. Orr scored or set up seventeen of the Generals' twenty-two
goals over this stretch. I scored twice, set up three and spent sixty-two
minutes in the penalty box, twelve of them for boarding him. But Orr
and I did not make contact again until May 19, 1974, when Eddie Van
Impe, Moose, the Watsons and I set up the defensive minefield that
even the Great Orr with perfect knees couldn't have penetrated. Philadelphia 1, Boston 0. The Flyers take their first Stanley Cup in six games.

Thinking back on it now, I don't know why I went home that summer.
I think I told Torchy and some others it was so I could get in shape,
work out, add some upper-body strength, but it was a lie. I think really
I had some vision of Batterinski returning as the conquering hero. But
how to do it? Could I walk up and down Black Donald Hill carrying my
scrapbook, wearing the three team jackets, pointing out the new teeth,
carrying the team trophy for top defenceman? I had no idea. I was just
going home for the first summer back since my first year in Vernon. No
more wrestling with the front-end loaders at the mine. No swelter in
the smelter. Just Poppa, Ig and me. . . .

At twelve noon on June 4 the Pembroke bus pulled in to the White
Rose at Pomerania. I checked on my new Timex with the date and "The
Hardrocks" where there should have been numbers. A gift from Gus to
the team. I wondered who would notice first.

Outside the air-conditioned Gray Coach the air was thick and
humid, a haze turning Black Donald Hill into a ghost where the church
began and the steeple vanished. I felt foolish not having a car. Torchy
and I had become so used to the white Valiant that we had come to
regard it as personal property, much like Lucille. I had a suitcase, a
duffle bag and that cursed two-mile walk ahead of me.

No thoughts of a glorious parade through town now, only that of
trying to slink home without being seen. The big jesus hockey hero,
carrying his own luggage, walking. Oshawa had given Bobby Orr his
own car so he could race back home to Mommy and Daddy in Parry
Sound. Gus had given me a watch, so I'd know how long it would take
to walk.

Hanging Together,
Falling Apart

IT WAS LATE AFTERNOON five weeks later, in a small meeting room on the convention floor of the Edmonton Plaza hotel. The bar was an ice-filled tub of beer, with a scattering of whisky, rum, gin and mixes from which the tiny press contingent poured their own. A few reporters were tapping typewriters. Others were moving the coffee machine so they could plug in an electric long-distance copier, which when hooked to a telephone sent typewritten stories to newspaper offices in the East.

Coach Billy Harris slipped in almost unnoticed. His thick hair was a prematurely silver grey in contrast to his summer tan and dark blue sweater. The afternoon workout had ended an hour earlier. This nightly visit by the coach and a few players to the press room was part of the Team '74 training camp style; instead of having reporters stand around the dressing room among the wet underwear and damp jockstraps to ask their questions. A few players arrived; Tardif, Rejean Houle, Backstrom, among them.

There, that afternoon, Harris made a statement of intention never to be forgotten, by public or press, throughout the series. "We were talking earlier about our style," Harris said. "I can tell you one thing, that when we start our exhibition series against the juniors in Medicine Hat tomorrow night, part of my pep talk will be to see if we can play the next sixteen games without a penalty." That would take in five tuneup exhibitions against the Western Canada Junior Hockey League all-stars, the first four games in Canada against the Soviets, exhibitions with Finland and Sweden, the last four in Moscow against the Soviets, and a final exhibition in Czechoslovakia. "I want this team to avoid retaliation," Harris said. "We don't want to hand the Russians any advantages they don't earn. . . .The thing is, I don't think they're dirty. So we shouldn't always be thinking about retaliation for anything that happens in the heat of the game — except we should be thinking: *don't* retaliate. Take the power plays away from them if we can. They're too good at power plays. They scored nine power play goals against Team Canada '72 . . .".

The reporters later questioned Harris about going through sixteen games without a penalty, drawing a confession that maybe it was an unattainable ideal, but still one worth shooting at.

Those were the happy carefree days of Team Canada '74, before the pressure was on. In some ways — the early ideological agreement to avoid retaliating, to shun penalties like the plague, to obey referees without argument — those days made a poignant contrast to what was to come. Team Canada '74's penalty-less record actually lasted only until the first game with the junior all-stars, but all through the exhibition series Harris kept hammering away at the ideal. After Team Canada had beaten the speedy, tireless juniors 7–2 in Medicine Hat, scored in the last minute to win 6–5 in Brandon, and lost 3–2 in Calgary in a game marred by stupid penalties, we were on the chartered Electra heading for Saskatoon. I slipped into a seat beside Harris.

"It's a little bit frightening when prior to the first period you tell them what you don't want to see happen, and within ten minutes it's happening," he said, referring to his talk with the team before the Calgary game. "I accept the fact that when a guy has been playing the game for a long time, and is burned up at something, it's hard not to do what you've been doing for ten years. But I told them if they can't control their reactions to situations in these exhibition games, how are they going to control them when we get into the real series? In Calgary we're losing to a lot of kids, okay, and it's got to be frustrating. But we've been using frustration for ten years as an excuse for the way we act against European teams. How long can you keep doing that?"

It is ten days later — nine p.m. in Quebec City, September 16, inside one of the conference rooms at the Château Frontenac hotel. There is a blackboard at one end of the room. The players are all present. Gordie Howe is wisecracking in one corner, Bobby Hull chuckling amiably in another. Tom Webster is wearing the dark shades that are his habit. Johnny McKenzie's bright, open countenance is a reproach to anyone who might think he played right wing in any manner other than the most honest, upright and true. Jim Harrison had been taking runs at Paul Schmyr, André Lacroix and McKenzie in the workout that day —

perhaps in exasperation over being among those due to sit out the first game. The two Howe sons are there, Marty and Mark, the youths of the team. (Although, as their father once said about Mark, "Once he learns that he's the *second* strongest man on our team....") And also quiet Pat Stapleton, Ley, Selwood, J.C Tremblay, unobtrusive Rick Smith, the buccaneer visage of Schmyr; Backstrom, MacGregor, Henderson, Mahovlich, Walton, Cheevers, McLeod, Gratton, Al Hamilton, Bernier, Houle, Tardif, and the man everyone insists on calling little André Lacroix, built like a short giant.

As a professional player Harris had come to regard most team meetings as unnecessary. During his years with Punch Imlach of the Toronto Maple Leafs, a team meeting was held every morning of every game day. Punch felt his job was to send players out of team meetings with a feeling of concentration that would persist until the final whistle nearly twelve hours later. Over the years, some players — Harris among them — heard these speeches hundreds of times. They became meaningless: a time for day dreaming. All the same, during the months of putting this team together Harris would sometimes lose track of words on a page he was reading or find his attention lapse during conversations, while his mind groped for what he would say in the team meeting on the night before the first game in Quebec.

Now in the Château Frontenac conference room Harris moved to the blackboard.

For the first half-hour or so there were no surprises. Occasionally using the blackboard, Harris reviewed the tactics they had been working on ever since training camp began. He summarized what the team had to do offensively and defensively to cope with what he knew of the Russians. He talked to the players about composure. "When we lose our composure it's a plus for them," he said. "Their game plan will be that they can upset us, get us reacting to the referees, get us running around forgetting the main purpose we're here for. So try not to lose your composure. Even when we score goals, don't get overly excited. Be a little bit like them...".

Then Harris moved away from the blackboard. There was no tape recorder in the room, no one was making notes. Those present remembered what followed as being spoken without histrionics.

What he said was that more than thirty years before, his father had had the opportunity to represent his country. "It was a little different situation," he said. "He left his wife and three young children, one of them me, to go and defend his country. He was killed over Germany in 1944.

"We're not involved in any war but I would appreciate it if everyone would co-operate in this situation with something of the same kind of dedication and self-discipline."

He told them that this was the most emotional he would get in the entire series. He had never said this to anyone before, but felt that there were some parallels between this team representing their country, and his father and tens of thousands of others representing their country in much more deadly competition. He said he was not a flag-waver, but in a quiet way was a very proud Canadian.

"The happiest occasion of the next twenty-one days," he said, "will be when we get on the plane to come home. If you don't appreciate your country yet, you certainly will when it comes the ninth of October. Let's not wait until the eighth of October and then sit down and think, 'Jeez, that's a pretty good country we live in,' when it's too late to do anything about it."

The players listened in silence. The total impact at the time could only have been ascertained by talking to them immediately afterwards, but no member of the press knew at the time that anything out of the ordinary had happened. The players, who sometimes reveal such things, kept silent on this one. It was mentioned only by Bill Hunter in an allusion he refused to expand upon, that at the team meeting on the eve of the first game something happened that had brought the players closer together.

In my notes headed September 17, Game One, Quebec, the first line reads: "Cheevers at centre ice for awhile, looking at the Russians." I can see it now. During the warm-up after a spell in goal blocking shots, Cheevers skates out to the centre red line. He pushes his mask up to the top of his head and stands motionless, staring at the other team. He'd played against some of these players before, and watched the 1972 Team Canada films in Edmonton. He can see that Tretiak in the Soviet goal is not extending himself to make stops. This is the Soviet style: to give pre-game shooters a warm psychological glow from seeing pucks go into the net. The Valeri Kharlamov, glancing at Cheevers and seeing that he is being watched, rounds the Soviet net with one of the dozens of pucks in their end. As he comes out of the corner he flicks his stick-blade at the puck to lift it two or three feet straight into the air. Before the puck can fall to the ice he catches it on his stick-blade and skates rapidly, turning at the blueline, juggling the puck so that it does not fall to the ice until the point has been clearly made for Cheevers that he can make the puck sit up and talk while twisting and turning at full speed.

Soon after, the siren sounds to end the warm-up. The Soviet players leave the ice quickly. The Canadians, who were on the ice first, do not leave at once. Then they straggle off in ones and twos. When the ice machine comes out for the pre-game flooding, J.C Tremblay is still there skating, shooting, loosening up, with Hull, Smith, Backstrom, Houle and Tardif.

None of this can be seen except in the Coliseum. Across the country millions of Canadians are hurrying through dinner in the East and the central prairies, or hurrying home in the far West, to be at their TV sets when the pre-game ceremonies begin. In Toronto, John F. Bassett, principal owner of the Toronto Toros, lands in the early evening from doing business in Schreveport, Louisiana. He goes immediately to a friend's home to watch the game. When the national anthem begins to play, he rushes to the bathroom to throw up. He vomits three times in the next two hours. The tension of what this game would do either for or against the WHA and his heavy financial and career commitment in it — including the fact that he had persuaded some of his friends, such as John Craig Eaton, to invest in it — put him through what he said later was one of the most tension-filled nights of his life.

In Quebec, Ben Hatskin of Winnipeg has not eaten lunch. He has not eaten dinner. He has not had anything to drink. He has never been so nervous in his life. Bill Hunter of Edmonton was so sick at 4:30 p.m. that he did not think he would be able to attend the game. He made plans for someone else to take over his duties as manager if he were not able to leave the hotel. Bobby Hull had never felt so tense. A few minutes before the game his arms felt like stone, he said, and he had no confidence that he could even take a pass, let alone shoot the puck.

All this was related in some way to every tension-filled moment before every game over the past 20 years when Canadian hockey teams had skated out against the Russians. But now it had this something extra — compounded of the Russians shattering the NHL all-stars in 1972's first game, how some hockey fans and writers had doubted loudly that Gordie Howe, at 46, could keep up with the Russians, and anyway how this bunch from the WHA could cope with the team that had outscored the best in the NHL two years before. Some of the last words spoken before Team Canada went to the ice that night in Quebec City came from Howe. "I only hope for the sake of everybody that we are not disgraced," he said.

I remember now the instant Joe Kompalla, the West German referee, dropped the puck. It fell between Ralph Backstrom and Vladimir Petrov. Suddenly an amazing thing was happening. There were Gordie Howe and Frank Mahovlich on the wings, moving into the Soviet zone — Howe holding off Valeri Kharlamov with one strong left forearm and handling the puck with stick gripped only in his right hand as he had often done against all kinds of opposition, almost forever. Mahovlich was roaming free ahead of Boris Mikhailov, the Soviet captain and heart of their team. Backstrom was getting his shoulders hunched and his legs pumping to break free from Petrov, who had 134 Soviet national team games behind him.

The Canadians were outplaying the line that was known as the best in Soviet hockey, and outplaying them effortlessly, reassuringly, as if the issue had never been in doubt. They held the play in the Soviet end. They got the first shots on Tretiak. In the big and beautiful rink, people were roaring with — well, a lot of it was relief.

The Lacroix-Hull- McKenzie line took over and did the same kind of job. The Bernier-Tardif-Houle line came out, with Houle outskating everybody. Then Walton, Henderson and MacGregor began a promising rush which was whistled down, offside. . . .

The first Canadian goal came on the third shift of the Lacroix line, their best. Lacroix and Hull broke out of their own end with only Aleksandr Gusev back. They swooped in on Tretiak. Gusev slapped away Hull's pass but it went in the corner, Lacroix after it. He got the puck and started for the side of the net at Tretiak's left and then cut behind and held the puck, stickhandling, defending his position at the side of the net, giving Johnny McKenzie enough time to steam in from right wing to the edge of the crease. When he got there the puck arrived simultaneously from Lacroix and McKenzie jammed it between the post and the goalie.

Goal! Bedlam! The goal-scoring song of the Quebec Nordiques fans roared in quick-time from all over the rink, led by their superb organist.

Yippee ay yippee ay yippee ay ay ay
Les Nordiques sont là pour compter
Yippee oh yippee oh yippee oh oh oh
Les Nordiques sont là pour gagner.

The score could have been higher for Canada in the first period. Frank Mahovlich, playing one of the great games of his life, got the puck to Backstrom in the goalmouth but it hopped over his stick. Lacroix put Hull in cold for a slapshot but defenceman Gennadi Tsygankov got his stick in front of the puck and it soared harmlessly into the crowd. Backstrom fought his way out of the corner with Mahovlich in the clear at the front of the net, but Backstrom could not get his pass away because he was being held flagrantly from behind. There was no penalty call. Joe Kompalla, the West German referee, was letting things go at that time — but weeks later Bill Harris could remember that particular play. It should have been a penalty. Without the holding, Backstrom would have been able to get a pass out to Mahovlich for a clear shot on goal.

Up to the end of the period it had been beautiful hockey. The crowd stood and cheered as the two teams left the ice. Across the land people were sighing, grinning, shaking their heads, their fears receding. And as he followed his players to the dressing room, Harris was remembering what Gordie Howe had said thoughtfully just before the game began: "I only hope that we are not disgraced."

There had been a falsity about the lack of penalties in the first period — in infractions had been there, but they weren't being called. After twenty-four seconds of the second period Joe Kompalla called a tripping penalty on Reggie Houle, who'd been checking Kharlamov. Then for the first time we saw a combination that was to be out there often over the next eight games in time of emergency: Pat Stapleton and J.C. Tremblay on defence, Bruce MacGregor and Paul Henderson up front. All fast, experienced, crafty, skilled in the arts of ragging and anticipating, all of them daring enough to seize any chance to turn the penalty-killing role into an attack on the other net. They went against one of the world's best power plays: the line of Petrov, Mikhailov and Kharlamov, with the steady, accurate Gusev on one point and the magnificent, big Yakushev up the other.

MacGregor and Henderson up front swirled in one at a time to pick up the Soviet puck carrier coming out of his own end, skate him off, harass him. They got the puck and passed it back to Tremblay, who put it over to Stapleton, who passed it up to MacGregor who skated in circles and then fed Henderson a pass.

In the Soviet system, and we began to see it now, the plan for 1974 had some differences. A man often would carry the puck in and drop a short pass back to a trailer for a shot from just inside the blueline. At times three men would zoom in one after another. The lead puck carrier would drop a pass. The next man would pick it up and take a stride before dropping another pass. The third man would take a shot through the underbrush of legs created by the first two men dashing for the net, taking defencemen and back-checkers with them. The Soviet defencemen were going to score many goals in the series from just inside the blueline. Their first came on such a play. Gennadi Tsygankov and Sergei Kapustin both handled the puck before it came back clear to Vladimir Lutchenko. Paul Schmyr made a good sliding stop on one shot but the puck went back to Lutchenko and he zipped it in to tie the game.

Still, Team Canada was dominating the play. Walton put Henderson in for a good try, but Tretiak made the save. Then Ralph Backstrom called on his experience way back in the exhibition series against the juniors when he had noted several times that European referees almost always reacted with a penalty call to a man with the puck trying to fight his way through two defencemen and falling when squeezed off. Legs pumping, Backstrom tried to jump between Lutchenko and Valeri Vasiliev, went down, and heard the whistle for a penalty to Vasiliev.

The Canadian power play now had the Walton line plus Hull and Howe. Howe went behind the net, was tied up, but held back the man who was checking him long enough for the puck to slide where Walton could get it. Hull was in the face-off circle to Tretiak's right. As the puck came to him from Walton he let go a wrist shot that broke Vladimir Shadrin's stick on the way by, and beat Tretiak. Canada was ahead again. The *Yippee-ay-ay-ays* rolled out again in the tumult.

Selwood was penalized for tripping soon after. Vasiliev got the puck to Kharlamov, who fled through the centre zone with Rejean Houle chasing him. Houle reached out with his stick as Kharlamov neared the Canadian blueline. But instead of impeding Kharlamov, the tip of Houle's stick seemed to shove him forward into an even faster break in on Stapleton and Tremblay. As Kharlamov curved and swept between them, Tremblay did manage to lift the Russians' stick high off the ice.

Cheevers came out a little. He didn't think Kharlamov had a play left. At the last instant Kharlamov's stick came back down and lifted the puck over Cheevers' shoulder into the top of the net. The score was tied again, 2–2.

Now, thirty-four seconds after Kharlamov had tied the score during the power play on the Selwood penalty, Schmyr took a tripping penalty. Team Canada killed that one safely but Schmyr had only been back twenty-four seconds when he was checked heavily along the boards. No penalty was called. Schmyr reacted as he probably has reacted in all his hockey-playing days — he set off to even the score on his own account. He was called for cross-checking. Eight seconds later Petrov scored from Gusev and Kharlamov. The Soviets were ahead for the first time, on two goals during Canadian penalties — the very factor Billy Harris had spent so much time warning his team against.

For the first few minutes of the third period, the Soviet team seemed to be taking command. Mikhailov was in clear on Cheevers when the puck stopped dead on sticky ice and he could make no further play. The Bernier line could not get out of its own end. The pressure was relieved only when Kapustin drew a penalty for holding Tremblay. The Lacroix line, plus Henderson and Schmyr, couldn't score but now the tide of the game was gradually turning again.

When the Bernier line returned to the ice, Canadian domination was complete. Just after Kapustin's penalty was over Houle carried the puck in from right wing, cut across the goal, and in trying to jam the puck home tripped over Tretiak and flew through the air to hit the ice and slide into the corner. Houle got up and had another chance that failed. He was in a third time, only to be beated by Tretiak — who within seconds robbed MacGregor on another shot.

Tretiak was under heavy pressure from Backstrom, Howe and Mahovlich at the ten minute switch-ends point of the period. Bernier was back on his next shift, in the clear, trying to fire the puck between Tretiak's legs, and failing. The crowd was in a steady uproar. But then at 14:18 Lacroix and McKenzie put Bobby Hull in close for a wrist shot. When the puck went in, Hull went into a joyous war dance. That made it 3–3.

In the last minute came the play that had the country talking for the next two days. The Backstrom-Mahovlich-Howe line maintained heavy pressure around Tretiak. In the corner to Tretiak's left, Howe held two defencemen off with one mighty arm and slid the puck out to

Mahovlich, steaming in from his wrong wing. It was Mahovlich against Tretiak, man on man. Mahovlich sped across the front of the net, made a big move on Tretiak, intending to shoot the puck into the open corner. Tretiak flung himself across the goal and eliminated all but the tiniest opening. Trying to hit that small space, Mahovlich missed by a fraction of an inch.

No one will ever estimate what that tie — even a tie — meant on that first night. "To win or tie was so important," Hatskin said later.

You could see that in Harris' face when he came across the ice to a room where the press gathered to hear what the coaches had to say. The coaches shook hands, the burly Boris Kulagin and his opponent, ten years younger. "Very nice," said Harris, and when it was translated Kulagin nodded and said that although the game was a draw, it was the spectators who had won.

He also mentioned the last try on goal by Frank Mahovlich, foiled by Tretiak's great move. The Soviet defenders, Kulagin said, had made a bad mistake in letting Howe and Backstrom spring the puck loose to Mahovlich. A few sombre words in Russian followed. The translation: "Usually Frank MacHallovich does not forgive such mistakes."

In Quebec City after the warm-up, with the focus of seventeen days' hard physical and psychological training right in the gunsights, Harris did not fire his team out of the dressing room yelling and cheering. He reviewed three or four important points and then said mildly, "Okay, let's go out and have a good time, just like a shinny game." The sytle was pure Harris. He never abandoned it, no matter what the provocation. That night in Quebec when Canada dissipated a 2–1 lead in the second peiord on Soviet power play goals after Canadian penalties, he did not rail at the players responsible.

"Maybe on some penalties I showed my feelings briefly but then I snapped myself out of it," he said later. "I've told my players not to react, yet I catch myself doing it, getting upset inside. I know I have to control it, because how can I expect them to control themselves if I can't?" But he had not gone into the dressing room and said, "Schmyr, that was a stupid thing you did." Harris just talked quietly to him, not so much on the play itself as on the principle — that kind of retaliation was what he was trying to avoid. (Schmyr didn't take another penalty for the next two games.)

There were also some bad calls that night by the Russian linesman,

Sergei Gushin, that would have sent many coaches leaping to the rail, screaming. Gushin was just not equal to the subtlety and precision that went into certain situations where a hair's-breadth stood between a good play and an off-side. Several times he called such plays wrongly, whistling them down. "So as not to show any anguish on two really bad calls, I just turned my head away," Harris said. He would stand with one foot up on the back of the bench, or leaning against the wall behind the bench, outwardly composed.

There was criticism of Harris sometimes through the series for not using his big guns enough, especially Bobby Hull. He didn't heed the criticism. He placed his big men to make them last. At the end of the Quebec game, where four lines had been used more or less equally in 45 to 60 second shifts, Ralph Backstrom asked Bobby Hull if he thought he could have gone out every third shift. For years, Hull had been used to playing 30 or 40 minutes of every game. Hull told Backstrom that night there was no way he could have gone out every third shift — as would have been the case if Harris had cut back to three forward lines, or had asked Hull to work on two lines. Backstrom said to Harris later, telling about this conversation, "If Bobby couldn't go every third shift, nobody can."

When the series moved to Toronto and some players were crowing, "Now we know we can take 'em," Harris was careful not to let this early vindication of his coaching methods, and the team he'd chosen, show as premature elation. "Nobody has lost sight of the fact that the Russians can beat you in one minute, if you let up," he said (prophetically), saying nothing Kulagin could use as a psychological aid for the second game.

Before that game, I sat with Harris high up in the Gardens seats. We talked about the Quebec game, and changes he planned for this one. There were two main reasons for switching his line-up. One was that he had made a commitment to all players that if they gave up the last part of their summer to work for Team Canada, they would all play in some of the games. The other had to do with Mark Howe, the youngest of Gordie's two sons. "I want to get Mark in the line-up," he said. "I think he's a super hockey player and he's a good defensive hockey player. I think our club will be a little stronger with him in there." Then, not exactly as an afterthought: "I think it'll make Gordie happy, too."

Gord Howe's pleasure in having his nineteen-year-old son Mark moved in with him and Backstrom paid off so quickly that it was almost uncanny. That line didn't start the Toronto game, so young Mark would not be put on the spot instantly against the Soviets' best, the Kharlamov-Petrov-Mikhailov line. Then, in killing a holding penalty to Rick Smith called at 1:44, André Lacroix and Bobby Hull were the first two penalty-killing forwards — they'd been out there with Johnny McKenzie when the penalty was called. Less than a minute into the penalty, they were replaced by Bruce MacGregor and Paul Henderson off the Mike Walton line. In another thirty or forty seconds Harris put Mark Howe and his father out to finish off the last few seconds of the penalty. Now when Smith returned to the ice, he could immediately be replaced by Ralph Backstrom and the line would be intact.

The teams had been at full strength again for about forty seconds when the Howes and Backstrom — three abreast in a loose array stretching almost from boards to boards — skated up the ice, with Gordie handling the puck, holding off his check, looking at the patterns being made by Soviet forwards coming back. He could have shot. He could have passed to the closest man, Backstrom. But with Tretiak over at Gord Howe's side of the net, his best play, if he could make it, would be to pass to Mark on the other wing, giving Mark a chance at a quick shot that would find Tretiak having to move the full width of the goal to cover the other corner. To those recalling the play, it seemed that Gord Howe's pass had a lot of legs and sticks to get through before it found Mark. Gord himself says there was only one player with a good chance to intercept. He shot the puck to the perfect spot for his son to accept it. As soon as the pass began, Tretiak made his big move to the other side to cover. He was still moving that way when Mark took the puck and in the same motion passed back so that Backstrom, in the centre, could drive the puck into the part of the net that Tretiak had just vacated.

It was one of the prettiest goals of the series. Gordie Howe told me later he would like to have it on film. "It would be nice to look at that play sometime later at home, when I'm old and grey," he said.

Canada got another goal. André Lacroix from McKenzie and Tremblay, later in the first period. Before this one Harris again fed the confidence of Mark Howe, the nineteen-year-old. This was done by putting him with Lacroix, McKenzie, Bobby Hull and J.C. on the power play after the Soviets' tough young twenty-one-year-old, Sergei Kapustin, drew an interference penalty. So when Lacroix scored, Mark had been on the ice for both Canadian goals. Before the first game in Quebec he had been unable to sleep, developed a migraine headache from worry and tension. This was the perfect therapy.

Cheevers had to make two exceptional saves, one out of a pile-up in front of his goal, and another point-blank from Aleksandr Yakushev at 19:55, to hold the 2–0 margin until the end of the first period. Hull scored to make it 3–0 early in the second. The play went alertly from Brad Selwood, breaking up a Russian rush, to McKenzie, who shoved it ahead to Lacroix, who pulled the defence wide to the right before putting a pass over to Hull.

Mike Walton was pulled down on a clean break and awarded a penalty shot. He tried to slap it high to Tretiak's right. Tretiak got his upper arm and shoulder in the way. Walton later second-guessed himself for using a big slapshot instead of what he called a "half-slap" that would not have telegraphed his aim so accurately. Yakushev scored finally for the Soviets after Brad Selwood made a good play to block one shot, but was down and out of the action when the puck came back to Yakushev for another shot. That made it 3–1.

By then Harris was having other worries (and not showing them) on the bench. Lacroix was playing chippy hockey. He took a swing at Petrov ("he speared me") and the two of them were shoving when Hull came between them and talked them out of it, without penalties. Lacroix did get a needless high-sticking penalty at 15:39 of the second. But then came a play that showed how deeply Harris' quiet way of talking to Paul Schmyr two nights earlier in Quebec had sunk in. This was at 18:59. The puck was being held against the back boards in a pile-up of three or four players behind the Canadian goal. After the whistle, from six feet away, Aleksandr Maltsev skated in and hit Schmyr with a hard crosscheck, knocking him down. At any time up to and including the Quebec game, Schmyr would have retaliated instantly. This time he fell hard to the ice, leaped to his feet, and didn't even look at Maltsev.

The Soviets kept up a passionate pressure that lasted until 16:24 of the third period when Maltsev was penalized for high-sticking Lacroix. Half a minute later Hull and Lacroix, battling for the puck deep in the Soviet zone, got it back to the point of J.C. Tremblay. His knee-high drive on the net was obscured by Lacroix and Johnny McKenzie mucking in there close to the crease keeping the defencemen and Tretiak off balance. Lacroix also made a big move as if to tip J.C.'s shot when it came by. He didn't touch it, and neither did Tretiak. Johnny McKenzie was so excited at that goal that, looking for someone to pat on the behind, he patted the Soviet defenceman Viktor Kuznetsov, who looked very surprised.

With only a minute to go and having played much of the last three minutes, J.C. Tremblay drew a high-sticking penalty. But the Canadians then were in control, 4–1. In that last minute they passed the puck, ragged it, kept it from the Russians, and the crowd began to rise. Three of the first up, in the seats behind the Canadian bench, were Johnny Bassett of the WHA, Ben Hatskin and league president Dennis Murphy. They had something special to cheer about. But the rest of the big crowd rose, too, applauding the team and the coach — whose stock right then, although he did not know it, had to be high because of the changes he was about to make for the third game in Winnipeg.

Harris was going to have to explain often, in the next few days, exactly why he removed five players from the line-up for the Winnipeg game — Mahovlich, Gordie Howe, Cheevers, Selwood, Ley — and put in five whom he had not thought strong enough for his successful line-up in Toronto.

"If it had worked," Gordie Howe told Harris later, "you would have been a genius." But even when it didn't work, Harris patiently explained to all questioners why he had made the changes. He said he would do exactly the same thing if he had to do it over again: "If I had played the Toronto line-up right back in Winnipeg, some of them were so tired that we might have had ten goals scored against us, instead of eight."

All the same, psychology is part of hockey. As the old Soviet coach Anatoli Tarasov once said, "To live in sports without victory is not much living." When the Russians looked down the ice and did not see Cheevers waiting to challenge them, their confidence was boosted. When they began to skate and did not find Mahovlich and Howe looming over them, they felt even better.

So the Winnipeg experiment failed, 8–5. But when the team headed for Vancouver with newspapers and broadcasters trumpeting, "We blew this one," Harris had learned something important — that he could not beat the Soviets with less than his best line-up, rested and playing its best. The players realized this too, a fact they might have forgotten in the euphoria after the Toronto game.

"I badly want to win this one in Vancouver," Harris said that

Sunday, flying out of the cold prairies toward the coast. "If we can do that and go to Russia leading the series, we should be all right. Remember in 1972, we lost in Montreal, won in Toronto, tied in Winnipeg, and lost badly in Vancouver. Then when we lost the first game in Moscow we were down 3–1 in games, and needed a miracle to win it." He didn't want to have to depend on any miracles.

He shouldn't have needed a miracle in Vancouver, but for an explanation of what did happen maybe it is necessary to go well beyond the boundaries of the game itself. To me, this was the first time one system was really up against another one. A remark by Coach Boris Kulagin may have some meaning here. It came late in the Winnipeg game. Russia had been leading 7–2 and suddenly Canada scored three to make it a 7–5 and looked capable of coming back all the way. Kulagin called his players to the bench area. Canadians being Canadians, he said, they tended to leave things to the end, "but just because we have a lead, nobody has a right to relax." They promptly scored another goal and put the game out of reach.

Until Vancouver, it had been one hockey team against another hockey team — all conditions equal.

In Vancouver, that changed. I stayed there in the same hotel as the Russians. It was the Century Plaza, a modest apartment hotel with kitchen-bedroom-living room units available by the day, week or month, and cheap. The lobby was about the size a motel office. There was no central air conditioning. The Vancouver temperature when we came in from the cold prairies at noon Sunday was in the mid-80s and sunny, the hotel breathless and hot. I had coffee in the Century Plaza's routine coffee shop off the lobby, then walked, sweating, a few blocks down the street to see how Team Canada was living.

When I walked into the vast, sumptuous air-conditioned lobby of the Hyatt Regency, I could see a throng of people. Some I recognized. They were the Team Canada wives — or in some cases mothers (Cheevers and McLeod both invited their mothers along, and the third goalie, Gilles Gratton, brought both his parents). Among them also were WHA owners and dozens of their guests, also Moscow-bound as part of the league's VIP charter. They are a wide range of women, the players' wives, from the quietly attractive to the girlishly suburban — lively, bright and pretty. Many were mothers of young children or even grown children and some were excellent managers not only of their homes but of some of their husbands' business affairs. They stood in a large area around the elevators, chatting, a group that needed only some glasses in their hands (which weren't there) to look like the so-called happy hour at a reception or dinner. That was the day Team Canada became a family affair. And whatever the other considerations, in hockey atmosphere the Hyatt Regency sure as hell was not the Century Plaza.

The truth is, I liked the Century Plaza. It was homey. The manager was obliging. When some of us, Russian and Canadian, couldn't get a cab to the rink the hotel's maintenance man drove us there. When I got back, a Vancouver secretary called Linda Tretiak, carrying with her the rather far-fetched idea that she must be Tretiak's cousin, came with her long silky black hair and bare brown midriff, to wait for him. In the Hyatt she would have been lost, wouldn't have had a chance. In the Century Plaza all she had to do was tell her story in the tiny lobby to a couple of curious onlookers. We made sure *something* came of it. We told Aggie Kukulowicz, the Russian-speaking Air Canada man. When the team arrived, Tretiak was first off the bus. "Slava!" Aggie called, and told the story. Tretiak looked exceedingly doubtful — but handed Linda a pin as a souvenir, then could not move fast enough as she moved warmly close to him and kissed his cheek while his teammates looked on, grinning.

Then and later I found I had the feeling there was a dimension to the series here in the Century Plaza that one could not see in the less personal atmosphere of the Hyatt. The team's air-conditioned bus was at the curb, engine running, from early morning until they were finished at night. Every time the players were going anywhere, they'd come down early and stand in the street by the bus, stroll up and down, lounge against posts, group around to read a newspaper. I have seen a lot of hockey teams in my life. These guys looked precisely like a hockey team, on the road, with nothing on their minds except the game.

The day of September 23 was beautiful, sunny. The game started at five, so TV coverage in the East could start at eight. The tension was as high as it had been in Quebec. The big men were back, but they could take over where they left off in Toronto? Or was that night gone forever?

This time the Canadians did not leave it all — or even anything, unfortunately — to the end. At the start, the customary opening fury of the Soviet attack pinned the line of Backstrom and the two Howes in its own end, somewhat in confusion. Then the old man, as the players called Gordie Howe, made a move that lifted the team. Mikhailov, Petrov and Kharlamov were buzzing around Cheevers. Mikhailov, left alone in the corner after taking the puck from J.C. Tremblay, skated along the back boards. When he neared the area behind the goal he suddenly made a move to cut in front. Howe saw the move an instant before it began. He shut off Mikhailov so hard that he hit the side of the goal himself, almost lifting it off its moorings. It was the first time in the game that a Russian had been knocked off the puck. Still, when Mike Walton missed checking Valeri Vasiliev at the point, a pass came out to Vasiliev from Kharlamov and he fired it back in low and screened for the first goal.

That was 3:34. Harris was switching lines rapidly. On the next change Backstrom and the two Howes came out for their second shift. Harris was remembering the inspirational move Gord Howe had made earlier. Somebody had to turn back the tide then running strongly for the Soviets. Howe was the man, as Harris had suspected. About forty seconds later Pat Stapleton had the puck in the Canadian end, then got it back to Backstrom. Backstrom was on the left side of the ice skating hard into Soviet territory. Mark Howe was inside of him, more toward centre. Then Backstrom saw Gord Howe. He was moving toward the net like a dreadnought, fending off blockers, unstoppable. Backstrom got the puck across to him. Howe took another stride through the slot in front of the goal and drove the puck waist high past Tretiak to tie the score.

But the Soviet momentum was still great in these descendants of the old night shift in Moscow. Johnny McKenzie took an elbowing penalty for retaliating after he'd been knicked on the face by a Soviet stick. Stapleton and Tremblay had already played much of the first five minutes. Harris sent them out again with MacGregor and Henderson to kill the penalty, but Mikhailov scored the power play goal on a corner passout from Petrov. The Soviets led again, 2–1. The action began to lean toward Canada on the next shift. MacGregor was skating in deep to forecheck and break up plays before they got started. The Bernier line, with Mahovlich and Houle, put on the heat. A few seconds later, Kharlamov and Gord Howe were levelling elbows and sticks at each other in heavy going. The crowd kept up a steady stream of roars, imprecations and groans. Bernier took Gusev heavily but cleanly into a corner and Gusev slashed at him, drawing a penalty. For a few seconds the Bernier line was out there for the power play with Stapleton and Rick Ley, then Harris took Stapleton and Ley off for Bobby Hull and Paul Schmyr, leaving the Bernier line. Mahovlich got the puck back to Hull at the point. He slapped it low and direct past Tretiak to tie the score again, at 2–2.

That goal began one of the finest five hockey minutes of all time. The Soviets were trying — they even outshot Canada in the period — but they were overpowered. Hull went in on a pass from Stapleton, made a shot from a bad angle that Tretiak stopped but could not control, and then moved in front to pick up the loose puck and score on a wrist shot to Tretiak's left, his glove side, at 15:11, to make it 3–2.

Just under two minutes later Rejean Houle took the puck in the corner from Bernier, defended it against Soviet checkers by masterful stickhandling, moved to the side of the goal and laid out a perfect pass to Mahovlich skating in, from left wing. Frank was being shadowed and impeded by a defenceman, but he had the puck on his long reach as he put a big move on Tretiak and backhanded the puck into the goal. That was at 17:10, and made it 4–2.

Seconds later, there was a face-off at the Soviet blueline. Lacroix fought for the puck, got it and skated in at an angle toward a corner. This drew the defence with him, and left Hull open for a pass. Hull's shot this time was to Tretiak's stick side, the third goal for Hull in the period, each from a different place, each aimed at a different part of the net. (That, no doubt, was in Tretiak's mind at the end of the game when he skated up to Hull, shaking his head, and then gripped Hull's hand).

In the interval with Canada leading 5–2 the rink buzzed with superlatives. Why, sure, this was what this Canadian team could do. Hull, Howe and Mahovlich were mentioned again and again. One man I talked to compared the sheer power and resolve of Howe's fight to get into position for that first tying goal, to the famous Landy–Bannister mile run at the British Commonwealth Games in Vancouver twenty years before. "You see a guy like that with determination written all over him, forging along, only one thing in mind — and God, I am glad I saw it," he said. "I'll remember that goal forever."

The strategy had been, from the beginning, that Team Canada had to play what Harris called "prevent" hockey against the Soviets. "You can't blow them out of the rink, you can't even open up on them, or they'll get to you,'' was a line he'd used many times. In the second period, Canada played careful hockey. Cheevers had to be good on a point-blank deflection from his old goal-crease sparring partner, Mikhailov. Mikhailov had speared Cheevers in the groin in the Quebec game, an injury that hurt Cheevers for the rest of the series. He thought about Mikhailov every day as he lay with an ice-bag high on his thigh to reduce the pain and swelling, and took particular care with Mikhailov always after that, although he could not prevent him scoring from time to time.

Paul Schmyr took a penalty, his first since the Quebec game. Canada killed it off. Sometimes, later, they ragged the puck even when they were at full strength. They were playing for a break and to prevent the Soviets from getting one. Puck control was what they wanted. They managed that, too, until 11:04 of the second when Yakushev took a pass just inside the blueline form Yuri Lebedev. His low shot from the blueline went in cleanly to make it 5–3.

The careful play of the Canadians persisted in the third period. They never made a move unless it was a safe one. They were in control with the 5–3 lead and less than four minutes to go when there was a whistle for a face-off in the Canadian end. Then consider what came next. (Century Plaza versus the Hyatt Regency?) The Canadian team had been dominant, had scored big, and held hard. The way it was going, in just a matter of time the final whistle would go and Team Canada would leave for Europe ahead in the series.

Some players later called what happened a moment of inattention. Others said that the puck was dropped too rapidly. Professional referees do tend to wait a few extra seconds until both teams are set for a puck to be dropped. International referees are less patient. For the face-off André Lacroix was standing where he should have been but was not ready. A conversation was going on among the Canadians about how to make the next play. They hadn't finished talking when suddenly the next play was upon them. Before Lacroix was set, the puck was dropped. The Soviet centre then did what had been rare through the entire series — he won the face-off from Lacroix and batted it back to Maltsev. Maltsev stopped it with his skate, kicked the puck up to his stick and shot from the edge of the face-off circle. Cheevers wasn't really ready, either. That made it 5–4.

That was 16:08 of the third period. Fifty-one seconds later the

Russians were back. The play this time was no error. It had worked often through the previous game. Gusev shot from just inside the blueline, with Russians and Canadians both milling in front of Cheevers. It was in. The score was tied, 5–5. The tennis court hockeyists from the old Commune Square days of long-gone summers, watching TV in Russia, must have smiled to remember how crude they had been then, and how polished and deadly now.

The Canadians had one more big chance. Tsygankov was penalized for tripping at 17:51, upsetting Mark Howe and he tried to take a pass from his father that would have meant a dangerous play on Tretiak. Canada had Bobby Hull on one point, Gord Howe on the other, plus Lacroix, McKenzie and Mahovlich — three of pro hockey's greatest all-time scorers, and two others who were no slouches either. Howe had two of the best chances, but could not score. In the Canadian dressing room, Johnny McKenzie said, "There's a lot of heads lowered in this room tonight. We lost a game we should have won."

Years earlier in Moscow, I'd been part of a group where a Russian was telling a Canadian something about the game, then halted apologetically. "But does the egg tell the chicken?" he asked. In Vancouver the answer to that seemed to be: yep.

The Man Tarasov

THERE WERE THREE GOALIES on the Central Red Army team in the summer of 1967; Victor Tolmachev, Nikolai Tolstikov and Vladimir Polupanov. Head coach Anatoly Tarasov wanted a fourth goalie to make the training more efficient. At the time I wouldn't even have dared to dream about playing on Tarasov's team. He had such great players as Konstantin Loktev, Alexander Almetov, Veniamin Alexandrov, Anatoly Firsov. How could a fifteen-year-old think of playing with them?

One day Tarasov said to the coach of our junior team, "Let this boy come to practise with the seniors." Then he pointed to me. I was stunned! Shortly after that I began my training with the famous Red Army team, who had been USSR champions many times, and who supplied the majority of players to the National Team.

I tried hard at every practice. During the games I tried to stop every shot, even the impossible. "OK, try harder," Tarasov would say, patting me on the shoulder approvingly. Coming from him, it seemed to be the highest of praise, especially since I already knew how little praise he gave. Often, however there was criticism mixed with the praise. He was probably afraid that I would become overconfident. "Don't listen to compliments," he reminded me. "When people praise you, they rob you! And if I criticize you, it likely means that I need you."

At the Red Army Sports Club training camp which is located in a suburb of Moscow called Arkhangelskoye, I shared a room with Vladimir Lutchenko and Nikolai Tolstikov. Probably because of my long neck and high voice, they gave me the nickname "Gosling." My mother asked the waitress at the Sports Club, Nina Bakumina, to look after me, and she certainly did. She always gave me the most delicious and plentiful meals.

It all seemed like a day dream at the time. Still a teenager, I was beside our country's most famous hockey players. The veteran Alexander Pavlovich Ragulin shared a room with Viktor Kuzkin. I remember that when I was on duty at the Sports Club I was too timid to even enter their room. And I was even worse with Tarasov. I was scared to come across him! But I wasn't the only one. The veterans were afraid of him too. Tarasov's demands never seemed unreasonable to me, however, because I understood, then as now, that Tarsov had only one goal: to make Soviet hockey the best in the world.

Anatoly Tarasov was a very well-organized person. He knew his purpose in life and didn't like lazy people. I owe very much to that man. Even what some people called Tarasov's 'moodiness' I consider to be the peculiarity of his fatherly talents.

Valery Kharlamov told a story about Tarasov's moods. Once during a practice, Valery's skatelace became untied. He stopped and knelt to tie it. When Tarasov saw him, his eyes grew wide and his face angry. He began to yell at Kharlamov. "You, young man, you just stole ten seconds of hockey from me, and you can never make it up to me!"

I recall once, after receiving new goal pads, sitting and sewing them with a large needle. Anatoly notice it. "Do you want to use them in the next game?" he asked. "Yes, I do," I said, standing quickly to attention. "Very well, Tretiak, tomorrow you will do your dry-land exercises wearing those pads." It was raining outside the next morning. Everybody was astonished to see me in running shoes and goal pads. But there was a simple explanation to it. Tarasov knew the rain would stretch and soften the rough skin of the pads, preparing them for the next game. Only he could have known that it was going to rain that day!

When Tarasov called a player by anything but his first name, or when he spoke very politely to him, everyone knew that it meant trouble. In the fall of 1969, after a playoff game for the Championship of the USSR, he called me into his office for the first time in my life. "I'd like to talk to you, young man." I was scared. I couldn't think of anything I'd done wrong. "Do you know why I called you here?" "No, I don't." Then go out and try to think about why!" Confused, I closed the door and left. In an hour I was called again to stand before his frightening stare. "So, did you think about it?" In complete bewilderment now, I shrugged my shoulders. "OK," he said, suddenly changing his anger to friendliness. "Take a chair and sit down. Don't be afraid, sit over here. Yesterday you let in two goals under your right foot. Why? Let's think about it."

Tarasov insisted that I always think. He wanted me to analyze every mistake, every failure. "Vladik, have you ever thought of yourself as a crab? Think about this. A hundred legs and a hundred arms! Look." He stood in the middle of the room and demonstrated what, in his opinion, a crab-goalkeeper would look like. His idea hit home. That is how we worked. I can honestly say that there wasn't one practice to which Tarasov came without new ideas. He amazed all of us every day. One day he had a new exercise, the next an innovative idea, and the next a stunning combination to remove the effectiveness of our opponents.

"Do you think playing hockey is difficult?" asked Tarasov in the early days of my career. "Of course," I answered, "especially if you play with the best." "You are mistaken!" he said. "Remember, it is easy to play. To practise is difficult! Vladik, can you practise 1350 hours per year?" His voice was rising. "Can you practise to such extent that you may end up physically sick? If you can, then you will achieve something!" "1350 hours?" I couldn't believe it. "Yes," said Tarasov sharply.

During the practices he could get us into a mood that made it easy to overcome his monstrous workloads. "Practise until you drop," Anatoly would demand, laughing. The severity of our practices could be judged by the response of hockey players from different teams who practised with us. They would leave after the first day, massaging their hearts. We laughed at them. Once we were joined by a famous Swedish hockey player, Svedberg, but he didn't last long either. On the third day after dinner, noticeably pale, he started to say goodbye to everybody. "We Swedes don't grow up to practise like this. I don't want to die," explained our guest before his premature departure.

I will never forget Tarasov's lessons. Now, looking back after many years, I clearly understand that he was not only teaching us hockey, he was teaching us life.

I remember Anatoly suddenly quizzing young Valery Kharlamov in the middle of a practice. "Tell me, please, when you have the puck, who is in charge?" "Of course," answered the talented Kharlamov, "I am in charge." "Wrong!" said Tarasov angrily. "You are a servant of your teammates. You play on this Soviet team to benefit your comrades. Be happy for their achievements. Don't put yourself first."

He taught us to be noble and proud of how hard we worked. He had a saying; "To work like a miner," which in real life meant to practise his way.

Anatoly was constantly reminding me that I alone was worth nothing, and that my success was the success of the whole team. I believed in that without any doubt. If I hadn't, I don't honestly think anything worthwhile would have become of me.

Let me pass along a couple more examples that show the essence of Tarasov's coaching abilities. Anatoly believed that the worse the weather was, the better it was for us to forge our abilities. One day, when we were supposed to play our traditionally strong rival Dynamo, the temperature was thirty degrees below zero. We were leery about going outside for our dry-land exercises. We could easily have all caught colds. Standing in the crowded hall of our Sports Club waiting for Tarasov, we hoped that he would cancel the outdoor workout. Finally Tarasov appeared. Pretending that he didn't see anybody else, he approached me, the youngest. "Why are you here, young fellow?" he asked. "But everybody is here," I replied. "That is of no concern to you. You were supposed to be outside a long time ago, working with the tennis ball." Everybody left the hall, as if they had been swept out by a storm.

Tarasov trained me always to carry a tennis ball with me and never to leave it, even for a moment. Wherever I went, I had to throw and catch it all the time. I remember once we were swimming in the sea and Tarasov asked, "Where is your tennis ball, young fellow? You have to carry it in the water, too." And he wasn't kidding! Not at all. Nikolai Tolstikov and I were forced to make pockets in our swimming trunks for our tennis balls. Now you might get the impression that that was too much. But, who knows what would have happened to my life without that tennis ball, which undoubtedly sharpened my reaction speed and my hand-eye coordination?

Once my teammates used tennis balls for a practical joke. Mishakov and Firsov were studying at the Institute of Sports, and were preparing to take an anatomy exam. The professor asked them "Are you ready to take your exam?" They weren't sure about how ready they were. "The exam is important — you must be prepared," said the professor. He pointed at a skeleton in the corner of the classroom and told them to study it thoroughly.

"Can we take it to training camp?" asked Mishakov. "We will study it bone by bone in our free time." They loaded the skeleton into their car and brought it to Arkhangelskoye. I was at a movie at the time. When I returned to my room, I saw a pile of bones on my bed. The skull had my toque on it, and the skeleton's hands were each holding a tennis ball. It was their way of telling me that Tarasov's demands were going to kill me! It may not have been the best joke, but I laughed along with the rest of the team. Mishakov was an expert at practical jokes. It wasn't a coincidence that the Red Army team became quieter when he left us.

Inspiration was always one of Tarasov's main motives, and his training procedures were based on solid principles developed over a long period of time. He had an excellent idea of what the perfect goaltender should look like. I once heard Anatoly himself telling a story about the perfect goaltender:

"The first time in my life that I met a world class goalkeeper was in 1948. He was a Czechoslovakian named Bogumil Modry. Not long before, Modry had been named the best goalkeeper at the World Championships in St. Moritz, Switzerland.

"At that time, our best Russian goalkeepers were not tall, and probably because of that there was a false impression that goalies had to be short. Modry presented a different picture. He was a six-foot giant with hands like shovels. He amazed me. Everytime I met him, I shook hands with him, just to see the size of those unbelievable hands.

"He appeared to be a friendly guy, and he spoke Russian fluently. Bogumil offered me technical advice without any hesitation, introducing me to his on-ice workout ond his dry-land exercises. They were very interesting, but I repeat, the size of his body and his hands impressed me the most. 'What form of practice helped you to become such a great goalkeeper? I asked. 'I play soccer, tennis, and, of course hockey,' smiled the kind Modry. 'What about weightlifting or gymnastics?' I asked. 'No, I just play . . . .'

"Modry had developed his hockey skills simply by playing the game itself, and, combined with his natural talent, had made his way to the top. At that time you could develop naturally. But we Russians, we had to catch and surpass the Czechs, Swedes, and Canadians. There was no other task before, so what did it mean to us? It meant that Modry's way was not for us. Time was not on our side.

"I studied with attention all of the remarkable goaltenders whom I met," continued Tarasov. "For example, Harry Mellups, the native of Riga, demonstrated to me his inner seriousness, his ability to critically analyze his own game. Grigory Mkrtchan distinguished himself by his constant aspiration to search for new methods, to experiment. Nikolai Puchkov was possessed with exceptional fearlessness and had very high self-esteem. He would clench his teeth and defy anyone to attempt

to score on him. It was a pleasure to work with Viktor Konovalenko. He
was the epitome of absolute tranquility. Konovalenko was always cou-
rageous, reliable, and respectful of his rivals. I don't ever remember
him complaining of unfairness. After letting the puck into the net, he
would only say, 'Outwitted, outwitted. . . .'

"Later I met Jacques Plante. The legendary Canadian goaltender
proved that the efficiency of the goalkeeper could be higher if he chose
not to play close to his net, but to cover a large area. I remember in
1967 the National Team of the USSR played a game with the Montreal
Canadiens Juniors. On four occasions our forwards went one on one
with the Montreal goaltender, and those were great forwards. Alexandrov, Krutov, Almetov, Mayorov! But all their best attempts went for
nothing, because standing in the net for the Juniors was Plante.
Because of him we lost 2-1. Four times — one on one! We became
believers in Plante. He won our entire team over. After the game the
Juniors carried him away on their shoulders.

"I studied Plante and noticed that he was using the technique of
recoil. He would skate away from his net to meet the puck carrier, thus
decreasing the angle of the shot, and then would recoil back to his net
as the player approached. Aha, I thought, we can use this technique. I
was also stunned by his faultless ability to study his rivals. His intelligence was obvious. He knew how to play each forward that he faced
from our team."

Anatoly continued his story. "Gradually in my consciousness, I was
developing a concept of the ideal goalkeeper. I moulded it slowly,
avoiding borrowing automatically the traits of other outstanding goalkeepers. I tried to study and improve every aspect of the game,
critically looking at the old established teachings of goalkeeping
school, and questioning them.

"I thought more about Jacques Plante. His method of skating out to
meet the opponent was undoubtedly a formidable weapon. But what
would happen if, tomorrow, the rival became a little more innovative
himself? What if he chose not to shoot the puck, but to pass it to a
teammate in a better position? Would Plante be caught flat-footed? I
came to the conclusion that it was necessary to make the goalie more
manoeuverable, and ready for all surprises. He would have to be an
acrobat! He would have to have the ability to skate in the open ice along
with our forwards!

"Although Modry was a good goaltender, God be my witness, the

Czechoslovakian player was neglecting his athletic training for no good reason. Craftsmanship will shine in its fullest only when it has a strong base. Speed, endurance, strength, and dexterity are needed in every hockey player, but the goalkeeper has to develop these qualities in a different way than the forwards. He must do so in relation to the specifications of his position."

Tarasov concluded, "I decided that it was absolutely necessary to upgrade the overall level of play of our goalkeepers in order for them to gain more respect on our team. It became important for them to develop a high sense of intelligence and the ability to analyze our rivals quickly. The goalkeeper had to become a major figure on the team. Just as I was coming to all these conclusions, I saw a tall boy by the name of Vladislav Tretiak. I liked his outward appearance; I immediately recalled Bogumil Modry. They looked alike, with the same mighty stature, the same huge hands. Tretiak was the person I was looking for. I started to work with him immediately. It was like he had been sent to me."

Once, Anatoly puzzled me with two questions: "What is the speed of the puck when shot, for example, by Firsov?" "A hundred kilometers per hour? I am not sure," I answered. "A hundred and twenty," Tarasov corrected me. "And do you know," he said, "that it is not humanly possible to react to a puck flying with such speed when shot from near the net? Even if you practise very hard it is impossible! Yet Jacques Plante catches pucks like that, and so does Konovalenko. The answer is not in their reaction abilities." "Perhaps it is their experience," I guessed, still not knowing what Anatoly was getting at. "Experience — that's too general. Think!" said my coach. Frankly, I was confused. What was going on? Why should one bother to perfect his reaction skills if they wouldn't be successful against the best forwards anyhow? I thought. It seemed like the goalkeeper was doomed, practice or no practice. Tarasov was enjoying my state of confusion. "The only thing that will help you to get your mind out of the vicious circle it's in is your intelligence! You are going to have to learn to read people's minds. Yes, yes! Before your opponent shoots the puck, you are going to have to learn where it's going!

"You have to know beforehand how the game will develop, who the forward will pass to, when there will be a shot at the net. You have to know everything about forwards! Everything about defencemen! Everything about hockey! More than any other hockey player!" said Tarasov.

I hope that you can see what Anatoly was getting at. If it sometimes appeared that the pucks were merely flying into my trapper, it was actually because I anticipated the shooter. I developed and used for many years that same feeling which Tarasov was talking about at the beginning of my career. When a forward started to shoot, my left hand was already moving spontaneously to intercept the puck.

Before my time, as far as I know, when teammates discussed the strategy of the game or when the coach gave directions, the goaltenders didn't participate. Nobody asked their opinion, and no one would have cared if they offered it. Tarasov changed this philosophy. Early in my career with the Red Army team, I started to participate actively in all the affairs of the team. When Anatoly Tarasov invited each line to talk with him before the game, I was present at every meeting. I listened to my teammates with attention and wasn't shy about speaking out. The players didn't hesitate to ask my opinion. Sometimes the forwards, having invented a new on-ice tactic to use, would ask, "What do you think — will it work?" "Yes, it's good," I would answer, "no goaltender would be able to defend against that." Or, conversely, I sometimes criticized the idea. I enjoyed having the glorified old-timers, to whom I was like a son, listen respectfully to their boy-goaltender. This attitude of togetherness clearly shows the spirit of our team.

I was growing up, avidly absorbing not only hockey wisdom, but more importantly, perceiving the essence of such things as team work, responsibility, and courage. From the very beginning my coach trained me to think creatively of my role as a goaltender. He wanted me to put my mind to work first, and then my arms and legs. In the evenings at our base in Arkhangelskoye, Anatoly often invited me to his room.

"Come, sit down," Tarasov would say. "Don't you think, Vladik, that you have started to let pucks into your net more often than you're supposed to? Let't think about what's happening." And we would sit down and talk. The next morning at practice, Anatoly wouldn't forget to ask me, "Did you think up any new exercises? What are they? Show me."

In August of 1969 I went to Sweden for the first time with the Red Army team. We participated in several exhibition games, then Anatoly took me to a little town named Vesteros, where the Swedes had a goaltending camp. We practiced from early morning to late in the evening. I wanted to prove that I was equal to the other talents there, but frankly speaking, it was a little bit hard to vie with them. For example, William Holmquist could run twice as fast as I could. I watched with great interest their exercises on on-ice drills and tried to remember all of them.

As a result of my attending that camp, the Swedes now say jokingly that it was they who gave me a ticket to the big time. Of course they are exaggerating about the ticket, but I really did bring back some good fundamental drills from Scandinavia, and my first successes in the international arena were related to having been at that goaltenders' school.

While I was at that camp I received a T-shirt, given to me as a gift by the Swedish star Holmquist. I considered that T-shirt to be lucky for me and I wore it until there were more holes than T-shirt. My mother got tired of fixing it all the time, but I couldn't throw it away. Eventually I had to throw it out, but of course the experience that I gained from training with the best Swedish goaltender stayed with me forever.

When we returned to Moscow, our team played in a Soviet sports tournament sponsored by a large newspaper. In the first game, we played the Traktor Team. We played well and won 3-2. In the next game we played the Champions of the country, Spartak. I was sure that our starting goalie would be Nikolai Tolstikov. But a couple of hours before the game started Tarasov announced, "Tretiak will play." My knees started to shake. My teammates, noticing my nervousness, tried to calm me down. I was quick to notice, however, that they weren't so calm themselves about having a boy play goal for them in such an important game.

The game started with Spartak storming to the offence. Luck was with me, and all of their shots were aimed directly at me. Spectators applauded and cheered loudly every time I deflected even the weakest shot. They were obviously sympathetic to the young boy who was defending the Red Army's net. We won 5-0 and I had been the luckiest person on earth.

Following that game there were very hard practices and then more games. I tried to prove to everyone possible that my success in the game with Spartak wasn't an accident — that I was a real goalie! It wasn't an easy thing to prove. Many people were surprised by my age. There had never been a seventeen-year-old goalie in international hockey.

Before the beginning of the traditional Izvestia tournament in Moscow, a tournament that gathers the best amateur national teams in the world, Tarasov recommended to the council of coaches of the Soviet

Hockey Federation that they include me on the National Team. Anatoly didn't get much support. Tretiak is too young, they thought. Can you rely on such a youngster? But Tarasov insisted, and when he insisted, they listened.

Thus, I ended up on the National team in the fall of 1969. I have in my possession a very valuable newspaper clipping of an interview with Tarasov:

"What did you like in the young goaltender?" the reporter asked.

"First of all," replied Tarasov, "his diligence and fanatical loyalty to hockey. His ability to work hard. His strong intelligence. Vladik can analyze his actions, and make the right conclusions."

"What is the difference in Tretiak's style, as compared to other goaltenders?"

"Tactics. Vladislav maneuvers boldly in all directions. All his actions are thought out in advance."

"Could he really become an outstanding goalkeeper?"

"Right now, everyone is counting on him. But the boy is just seventeen years old. He has to grow up a bit. Then Vladik will be able to solve all his minor problems, and manage his success. Personally, I think he can do it. I believe in Tretiak."

Of course I was very lucky that Tarasov had noticed me as a boy, that he had started to teach me, and that he had patiently made me a goaltender, day by day.

"Always learn — every hour, every minute; be hard on yourself; don't deceive yourself with your success; find the root of your failures. March forward step by step!" Since then these words of Anatoly Tarasov have served as the personal rule for all of my activities in life.

DAVID LEVINE

Way Ahead of the Game

HE IS, AT TWENTY-THREE, A FOLK HERO. Stories circulate around him as they would a legend, and the truth tends toward fiction, as it does with all legends. Wayne Gretzky's feats do seem fictional, unreal, but we who can see him perform, as those ten years hence will not, should pause and reflect rationally and soberly on his irrational, intoxicating achievements. This is an attempt to analyze Gretzky's game, to take it apart, to determine *how* he does what he does.

This, of course, is not the first such attempt. Others have tried, but the answer has usually been a resounding, "Who knows?" The problem is Gretzky's skills are subtle. Bobby Hull had his ferocious shot; Bobby Orr had his dazzling speed; Maurice Richard had his frightening drive; but Gretzky seems to possess none of the unusual physical skills that set other stars apart from the common. He is not bigger or stronger or faster. His greatness, in fact, is mostly subconscious. It is, as others have said, genius. It is also art. Both are beautiful to see, but both are difficult to describe.

Gretzky does possess certain technical skills that he has honed, and we can address those skills as we would Orr's speed or Hull's power. But his artistic skills, if you will, are what truly define his essence. Though more passive, this artistry is what makes Wayne Gretzky great.

Let's start with technique. Let's also start with the myths: Gretzky is a lousy skater; Gretzky's shot couldn't cut through fog; Gretzky's a wimp who, in the old days, would've been body-checked out of the league; Gretzky can't even the spell the word "defence." Now, let's take them one at a time. What we find is that some of these knocks may be true, but all of them are irrelevant.

Gretzky is not an ice-melter on skates. Several of his own teammates can beat him in a straight sprint. Nor is he an effortless skating beauty; in fact, he is an ugly skater — bent over awkwardly, he resembles Quasimodo on double runners. But he is fast enough. In the intricate, weaving style of Edmonton's play, how often is he required to skate in a straight sprint? And try to remember him being caught from behind on a breakaway.

He is an efficient skater, getting from point A to point B without wasted effort. He also has a more important bonus. "Gretzky is great coming down the middle of the ice because he has great lateral speed," says New Jersey goalie Ron Low, who was Gretzky's teammate in Edmonton for three years. "He gets to the blueline and the defencemen have to back off. He has eight million moves to either side, so they have to give him room." Then, he just drifts to either side, and with his speedy wingers flying past him "he's more dangerous than ever."

Gretzky's shot, like his speed, is fast enough. But again, there is a more important factor: accuracy. He is always among the top in shooting percentage, which couldn't be said about scorers such as Hull or Esposito. "It's his release more than anything," says Low. "He can open up the blade of his stick and make the puck drop, or close it and make it dive, and he doesn't give any inclination what he'll do." Other players make the puck dive or knuckle occasionally, but mostly accidentally. Gretzky does it intentionally. He controls his stick like a golfer controls his club, hooking and slicing at will. "He does things in practice that are scary."

Gretzky has also exploited an area left unattended for years — the top corners of the net. Ken Dryden, the ex-Montreal great and hockey analyst, notes that in the Seventies, as shooting speed outdistanced goalies' protection (masks were still primitive), players were admonished to "keep the puck down" in practice, and that habit filtered into the games. "Gretzky rediscovered the top of the net," says Dryden, "which effectively gave him another foot of target to work with. He's very good at hitting the top corners."

The charge against Gretkzy's defensive skills is, on examination, largely unfounded. With Edmonton's system, Gretzky is usually the deep man in the offensive zone. When play comes back toward Edmonton's zone, Gretzky is the last man back; his job therefore is to pick up the opponent's defenceman or trailing winger. Thus, if Gretzky were, in the words of Islander goalie Billy Smith, "taken by the hand and introduced to his own goalie," he would really be out of position.

Physically, Gretzky *is* a wimp, but only muscularly. He's skinny, hollow-chested, thin-armed. When tested for physical strength a few years ago, he finished last on the Oiler team. (When he saw the results, it's been reported, he asked, "Am I stronger than my mother?") A good hit could wipe him out, but he rarely takes a good hit. "He goes with every check," says Low. "He doesn't try to withstand it or stop it. Hitting him is like hitting a pillow. He just goes away."

But beyond his physical strength (or lack of it) is his stamina. The same tests that showed Gretzky to be a weakling proved him a recuperative wonder. When he played, Gordie Howe's resting heart rate was around 40 beats per minute; he never tired, even at the age of 52. Gretzky is similar. He logs 25–30 minutes of ice time per game (a high amount for a forward), and his stats show he often scores many of his points late in the game, when others are tiring.

What all this means is that Gretzky may not possess the "normal" skills of past greats, but he has something else. His technique and physique seem ideally suited to his particular style: quick, patient, pliable, emphemeral. Artistic.

Understanding Wayne Gretzky's technical skills and physical attributes helps, but it doesn't help enough. Explaining the rest is where it gets tricky.

Gretzky's greatest skill falls into an area of sports philosophy, the concept that great performers can in effect "stop time." The usual examples are of the batter who waits that split second longer on a pitch, or the basketball star who seems to hang suspended in mid-air while others fall around him, or the running back who can wait, wait, wait for the hole that no one else sees, then burst through. "We all recognize the feeling in various things we do," explains Dryden, "that given a set of circumstances, there is a certain moment at which we react and do what we feel is right. If we don't respond at that moment, there's an element of panic that creeps in, and we end up responding less well than we could. Those who seem to suspend time have that split second extra to set up and prepare themselves to respond properly, while others around them are panicking. That's the way Gretzky is when he plays hockey.

"For instance, when a player comes in on goal, there is a moment when the goalie and the player can sense when it's all going to happen. You sense the moment, and when it arrives you both make your play. It is the very unusual player who doesn't play to that rhythm. He will hold the puck a bit longer and throw the goalie's rhythm, and the rhythm of the game, all off. And when you disrupt the rhythm of the game, you throw everyone else into a panic."

Picture Gretzky in one of his favourite spots, camped behind the opponent's net, the puck firmly on his stick. You can sense that panic paralyzing the other team as they scramble, dash for position while Gretzky, in control, unharassed, waits for *his* moment. This one picture, which anyone who has watched Gretzky has seen, is the essence of his art.

It goes further, though. Others have "stopped time," disrupted the flow and rhythm of a game and then worked their magic. But Gretzky's magic spreads among the entire team; Edmonton has set team scoring records three straight years, and is on course for a Stanley Cup, largely because of Gretzky. Without him this year, they were 1–5. His teammates conform to his rhythm, so that Gretzky doesn't merely stand out, he in effect melds in. It's been said that Gretzky is most conspicuous in that he is so *in*conspicuous. You don't notice him until it's too late.

"Gretzky is the first of our great scorers who essentially plays with the other four skaters," Dryden says. "The Hulls, the Espositos, the Mahovliches were the driving force of the unit, and the others were support players to them, in many ways put with them for that purpose. Esposito, for example, had his cornermen to get him the puck. Gretzky is different in that he combines effectively and mutually with the others. They are not just support players to him. Gretzky gives up the puck to someone in better position, to move in turn into better position to get the puck back, to give it up, to get it back. It creates all sorts of interesting and ambitious schemes which all function as a distraction. In many ways, that's why he is as hard to stop as he is."

This helps explain Gretzky's astounding assist totals. Hockey assists, by their nature, are misleading; a puck hits Player A in the head, bounces to Player B, who scores, and Player A gets an assist. But Gretzky's numbers are different. He gets few cheapies. "Most of his assists are like those in basketball, where there is a direct and close relationship between the assist and the goal," says Dryden. "His statistical achievements aren't misleading like they are for many other players. He really has that big an impact on the game."

As ethereal as all this sounds, what Gretzky does is not instinctual. It is learned. Great athletes "see" the game differently, it's been said, but what that really means is they have seen it all before. Just as great chess players remember entire chess games, Gretzky remembers hockey games. "I've studied hockey," Gretzky has said, "like doctors study medicine." And to know a game, really *know* it, allows for creativity. It presents possibilites others don't see, and reactions others don't expect. Gretzky sees these possibilities, and reacts to his own rhythm. He appears, the red light flashes, Edmonton scores. Opponents shake their heads. Fans sit dumbfounded. How did he do that?

Genius leave a wake, an altered sense of what came before and a new set of possibilities unthought of previously. Bobby Orr had genius, and he left a trail of offensive defencemen trying to refine his art. Bill Russell had genius, and the NBA discovered the art of defence. Muhammad Ali's genius changed the art of boxing. What will Gretzky leave, besides his records? If his skills can't easily be described or copied, will he leave anything? Or is he a freak, a cipher, a chimera that is here, and then is gone?

Dryden thinks not. Gretzky's legacy could be profound. "Any great player suggests the kinds of ways in which a game can be played. What Orr did was put into the mind of the game a model to aspire to, and although Gretkzy has special skills that can't be copied, his sense of the game is what he'll leave behind. In a game I saw the other night, he scored a short-handed goal, and what he did, very few others would have done before. Even though they were a man down, he saw a moment where there was a good chance for a change of possession, and so he left his normal defensive penalty-killing position and headed toward centre ice. Most people would think, 'You can't do that, it just turns a five-on-four into a five-on-three.' But, sure enough, the other team lost possession, his defenceman pick it up, passed it to him at centre ice, and he had a breakaway. Now, few would have thought you could kill a penalty that way.

"Gretzky will have a large effect on the understanding of the game," Dryden continues, "in the sense of how the game may be played. He will provide a model for others, and the thing that's great is that it's fun to play his way. It's not the grinding, uncreative game. You don't need much encouragement to play his way.

"His legacy will be the sense of movement, of speed, of just breaking into the openings wherever they happen, whenever they happen. He'll leave behind his terrific sense of this combination game, that any individual star, no matter how great, is fairly easy to stop, but is much harder to stop if he works with the others to their advantage and to his advantage."

If Dryden is right, Gretzky may be the cutting edge toward a new game. It's a game hockey can be proud of — fast, clean, creative — and may even push the sport over the edge to mass acceptance in the U.S. Those who say that Gretzky is simply the best scorer in an age of scoring may be missing the point. "If anything, Gretzky is the driving force toward a different game," Dryden concludes. "He is not the product of a changing game. He is Gretzky."

Part 3

MOVING IN ALONE

One of the things that this sport can and should do for a person is to make him into a cultivated sportsman, some-one who can mix with other people, who can analyze a situation, who is self-critical and self-disciplined — someone who is a human being *in other words.*
                                        — Anatoly Tarasov

Success is not the result of spontaneous combustion. You must set yourself on fire.
                                        — Fred Shero

I have nothing to regret. What's done is done; I have no excuses. Some days were good days, some days were bad days. But I cannot recall any day that I did not try my best — so how can I regret even the bad days.
                                        — Rocket Richard

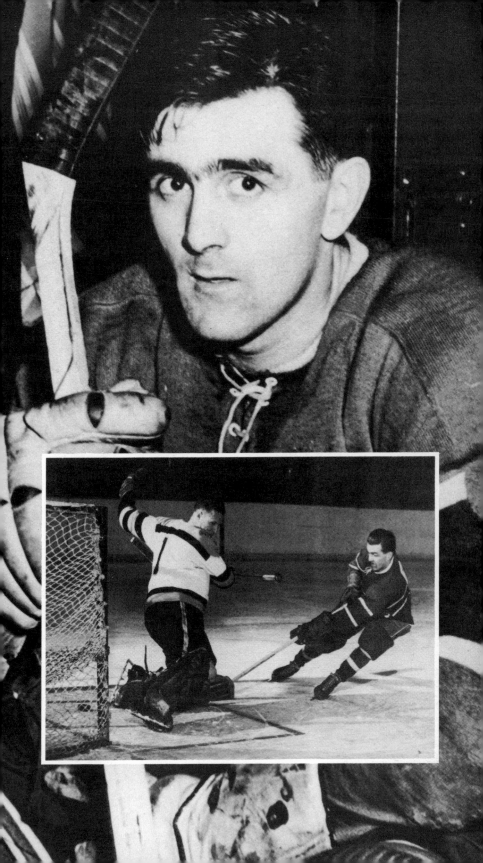

PETER GZOWSKI

The Night the Rocket Came Back

PHOTOGRAPHS OF MAURICE RICHARD, taken during his great days in the 1940s and 1950s, have captured the physical characteristic that those us who saw him play remember best: the fiery intensity of his eyes. In a hundred pictures of Richard embracing the Stanley Cup, of Richard holding a record-setting puck, of Richard — Joseph Henri Maurice "Rocket" Richard, the machinist's son from east-end Montreal — being presented to the Queen — in all these pictures his eyes burn defiantly through the lens and out from the printed page. Even in some of the characteristic action shots, when the camera shows Richard swooping in on goal, the student who looks closely can see the fire flickering in his eyes.

The eyes summed him up. In terms of over-all efficiency, perhaps, Richard wasn't the greatest hockey player of all time — perhaps not even the greatest of modern times — but he was the man the customers paid to watch. The Rocket, the most exciting player in the game, the most exciting athlete of any kind that many of us have ever seen.

The excitement of his play, say the men who knew him best, sprang directly from his complete dedication to the game, to scoring goals. Hockey was his whole life in a way that it is not the whole life of, for instance, Bobby Hull. Hull is the heir to Richard's mantle as the greatest scoring threat in the National Hockey League, and a deserving one. But he is also a prosperous cattle-breeder and a swashbuckling man about town. Richard was a hockey player — which is as under an understatement as you are likely to read today — and that was all. After losing a game, Hull has been known to sign autographs cheerfully. When the Canadiens lost, Richard, who could take a team defeat as a personal responsibility, would simply glower, and his eyes would burn more deeply. It was the depth of his involvement, too, that explained the violence of his rages, the raw, naked ugliness of his anger in a dozen explosive battles on the ice.

Today, six years later after his last game as a Canadien, Richard has increased the dimensions — as who has not? — of his jowls and his equator. But his eyes seem scarcely to have changed at all. The fire may be less noticeable, but it has not yet burned out. It is only banked. On at least two occasions since his retirement it has roared forth with all its old energy: once, in 1961, when he bopped a fan who had been needling him in the stands during a playoff series between Montreal and Chicago, and once, last season, when he took an overhead sock at the Toronto defenceman Kent Douglas, when Douglas was leaving the ice after a stick-swinging incident.

At 44, Richard is the vice-president in charge of sales for a Montreal fuel-oil company, and a part-time ambassador of goodwill for the Canadiens, but he is also still The Rocket, and this year, when it was announced he would play in an old-timers' game at the Forum, 15,653 people — the largest crowd of the hockey season to that point in Montreal — turned out to welcome him back. Most, we can suppose, were there for sentimental reasons: to get one last look at and give one last cheer for Richard and some of the other stars who had given them so many pleasant and exciting evenings in the past. But many made it into a kind of educational evening, too, taking along sons or even daughters to show them what a *real* superstar looked like.

Whatever his reason for going there, no fan went home disappointed. Richard scored two goals for the Quebec Oldtimers, including one that tied the game with just two minutes, seventeen seconds left to play, and helped his team beat the Detroit Red Wings Oldtimers 6–5.

There were, in truth, better players on the ice. One of them, not unnaturally, was Gordie Howe, whom the Detroit club was using apparently on the grounds that any man who started in the NHL twenty years ago is an old-timer, whether he's still playing hockey or not. Another was Ted Lindsay who, though he'd already come out of retirement after four years to play for Detroit last season and then retired again, still can't stop working out with the Red Wings every day. And, among Richard's own teammates, Ken Mosdell, who also got two goals, Ken Reardon, Buddy O'Connor, Dickie Moore and Dollard St. Laurent were all skating faster than The Rocket.

But once again the one the fans had come to see was obviously the old-timer of them all, The Rocket.

His return to the Forum was stage-managed to perfection. After a few minutes' skating to warm up their aging muscles, the old-timers of both teams retired to their dressing rooms while the fans filed in. The Quebec team — three or four of its members never made it past the Montreal Royals or the Quebec Aces — used the accomodations of the Junior A Canadiens and there, on a bench, Richard sat in quiet concentration. "I was nervous all day before that game," he said later, "just as nervous as before any game when I was playing at the Forum all the time. Maybe more nervous — like in a Stanley Cup." Then, his face white so that the oases of scars stood out like birthmarks, his eyes staring straight ahead as if in terror, he joined the parade of his teammates clump-clumping down the corridor toward the ice.

On the PA system the line-ups were introduced numerically. First, the Detroit goalies: Normie Smith who, since his retirement, had had a serious throat operation; Lefty Wilson, the Red Wings' trainer; and, to the loudest applause, Harry Lumley, old Applecheeks himself. Lumley had faced Richard a few times earlier, like the night in Montreal in 1944 when The Rocket scored five times on him and assisted on three other goals; and the night in Toronto when Richard finally tied Nels Stewart's lifetime record of 324 goals.

Then the Quebec goalie, Denis Brodeur, one of the Quebec Old-timers who had never played in the big time. (In previous games the Oldtimers had used Jacques Plante, but Plante, never the most emotionally simple man in hockey, had failed to show up for an exhibition in Sudbury this winter, and he and the team agreed to part.)

And the defencemen: first a Red Wing, then a Quebecker. And the memories came flooding back. From Detroit, Stu Evans, oldest man on the ice. Evans played his first NHL game in 1930. His hair is now ice white, and he is one of the biggest Lincoln-Mercury dealers in Detroit, but down there on the Forum blueline he had obviously, as they say, come to play. And Hal Jackson and Jimmy Orlando, the NHL's badman of the 1940's, now the owner of a Montreal nightclub where girls take their clothes off on stage and hustle drinks off stage; and Red Doran — who should be called White Doran now — and Scotty Bowman and Leo Reise. A lot of Stanley Cups bear those names.

From Montreal, Emil "Butch" Bouchard got the biggest hand to date, probably one of the loudest rounds of applause given to a tavernkeeper in Canada this year; and the Marcel Bonin, Harry Hoy, and the coach of the current Canadiens, the most successful coach in the league, Toe Blake, wearing his old number 6, and Floyd Curry, number 7.

Detroit's number 7, Ted Lindsay, drew the first mixed reaction of the night: part cheering, part booing, but prolonged, and even the booing seemed good-natured, just for old time's sake, one last rap at one of the best and chippiest left wings ever. From Detroit, number 8, Scotty Bowman. From Montreal, Glen Harmon.

Then Gordie Howe, Detroit's number 9, drawing the loudest ovation since Bouchard and Blake. Montreal fans are as partisan as they come, but they know a great hockey player when they see one.

And then Richard, wearing the number that had been retired with him in 1960, the *original* number 9, and the applause rolled out like thunder. For forty-five seconds, Richard skated in small circles in front of the Montreal line, his face grim, his eyes staring, just as he used to circle centre-ice, looking up only at the clock, after scoring one of his 544 goals in regular season's play. Forty-five seconds and then back into the line, until Harmon, the Quebec Oldtimers' manager, sensing that the crowd still wanted to prolong its tribute, patted him once gently with his stick and sent him out for just one more circle.

And on and on rolled names that so many of us remembered. Syd Howe, whose stick Gordie Howe had carried as a boy in Saskatoon, and George Gee, and Don Grosso — "The Count" — and Jim Peters, whose son has been playing in the NHL, and Marty Pavelich, and Carl Liscombe, and Bep Guidoilin, and Joe Carveth, and, from Montreal, intact, the old Razzle-Dazzle Line of Gerry Heffernan, Buddy O'Connor and Pete Morin...on and on, the winners of, in all, twelve Hart trophies for the League's most valuable player, twelve scoring championships, and even two Lady Byngs for gentlemanliness. How many all-star teams? The mind boggles. Richard alone made fourteen.

Following the introduction of the players, the PA announcer drew still another lusty cheer from the crowd by bringing out the evening's referee, Red Storey, the man who quit hockey in disgust when Clarence Campbell, the NHL's president (and never too popular a figure in the Forum), questioned his courage.

A night when even the *referee* gets an ovation, I couldn't help thinking, is a rare occasion in hockey.

The opening face-off was a rare occasion in itself, with two of the greatest forward lines in history — probably *the* two greatest of modern hockey — facing each other once again. For Montreal, united for the first time since January, 1948, when Toe Blake broke his leg and retired from play, the Punch Line: Blake, Richard, and Elmer Lach. For

Detroit, the Production Line: Lindsay, Howe and the current Detroit coach, Sid Abel.

Play started...well, to be truthful, slowly. Old legs wouldn't quite respond the way they used to, and some of the passing reflexes seemed to be missing. The first couple of minutes looked pretty slow and scraggly. When, after three minutes without a whistle, the two great lines went to the bench, they were pretty obviously out of puff. Even Howe, who was suffering from a bout of flu, seemed to be taking it fairly easy. He had played an NHL game the evening before and had two coming up on the next two nights.

But the fans, still basking in the glow of nostalgia, cheered nearly every move and, gradually, two things began to happen. First, those of us in the stands or press box, accustomed to the fast, wide-open play of today's NHL, began to adjust our viewing to the rhythm of the old-timers. Speed on the ice is, after all, only relative and, while there was no one out there that night who would be able to stay with Bobby Hull for more than a stride, they were still playing the fastest game on earth. And second, they were playing it pretty well. When all those car salesmen and publicans and vice-presidents got into their hockey suits again and skated out before 15,000 fans and realized how much those fans were *with* them, they responded like professionals. Beer-bellies they might have, but they began to play their hearts out anyway.

About half-way through the first period, Ken Reardon picked up a rebound near his own net and began to skate in a smooth arc toward the blueline. Reardon was once one of the finest rushing defencemen in hockey and he is still in marvelous physical condition. In the dressing room he had looked like a young Floyd Patterson.

At centre, Reardon hit full speed, still pushing the puck in front of him. The Detroit defence, moving backward, gave him some space through the middle. He lunged, broke clear, cut to his right and, from the face-off circle in the Detroit end, whistled a perfect backhand past Normie Smith.

The applause was a roar but it was to get even louder. After two shifts on his old leftwing, Toe Blake went to the bench and Marcel Bonin, a forward of more recent vintage, took his spot. Just past the fifteen-minute mark of the first period, the Toe-less Punch Line broke into the Detroit zone. Elmer Lach, playing as elegantly as ever, if a little more slowly, carried the puck to within fifteen feet of the net, a little off to his left. Suddenly, Richard broke from his right wing position across the front of the net, leaving his opposing wingman far behind and moving into and across the Detroit defencemen standing in front. Unlike nearly every other right winger in hockey, The Rocket has always shot left-handed, so that when he cuts across from his own wing he is offering his forehand to the goal. Lach saw Richard move and fed the puck out to the front. 2–0. Richard had just flicked it while it was still in motion, spinning it through the short side into an opening that couldn't have been even six inches wide. Around the net there has never been anyone like him, and the fans showed their appreciation of his art.

"Even now," Ken Reardon said after the game, "any team in the league could just use him on the power-play, and he'd still get them 20 or 22 goals a year." For The Rocket himself, a return is out of the question. When he played, he was the best — Mr. Hockey — and there is no way to imagine him as anything else.

In the second period, Leo Reise belted Richard in full flight, shoulder to shoulder, and, since bodychecking had been outlawed in deference to the old-timers' age, Reise drew a penalty. He also seemed to draw a little of the stuffing out of Richard, who appeared on the ice for only two shifts all period. In the third, though, as Detroit came from behind to lead 4–2, Richard summoned new energy. After Ken Mosdell, the outstanding player on the ice, had brought the Canadiens back to within one goal, it seemed inevitable that Richard would score again. Three times, Lumley robbed him outrageously; three times Richard seemed to come back even harder, bursting around defencemen, hurtling recklessly toward the puck. Then, with less than three minutes left to go, he drew the puck out of a scramble in front of the net, faked once and rammed home a mighty backhand.

As the crowd roared, he skated once again in a small circle, out around centre-ice, eyes blazing, looking only occasionally up at the clock.

JACK BATTEN

The Gentle Farmer from Delisle

IN 1902 a quirky old Anglican named the Reverend Isaac Barr, from Halton County, Ontario, had a vision. He would persuade some hardy and willing Englishmen to enlist with him and establish a unique colony, English and religious, in the Saskatchewan Valley on the nearly empty Canadian prairies. He spread his word throughout England. "Let us take possession of Canada!" his promotion literature read. "Let our cry be, 'Canada for the British!'" So on March 31, 1903, two thousand men, women, and children sailed from Liverpool on the S.S. *Lake Manitoba*. The crossing was disastrous, full of sickness and mutiny, and the trip across Canada by train and covered wagon was more defeating yet. The Reverend Barr turned out to be a careless organizer (he was also part con-man), and his brave English pioneers suffered from consumption, confusion, blizzards, and a bizarre diet. Perhaps most of all they suffered from the Reverend Barr; eventually, the light dawning, they dismissed him as their leader. The Reverend Barr's vision ended as a nightmare.

But most of his prospective colonists stayed on in the West. Many settled on a plot of land two hundred miles west of Saskatoon which they named Lloydminster after another man of God, the Reverend George Sexton Lloyd, who was the original chaplain for the Barr expedition. Other Barr colonists scattered over the prairie, and among these was William Bentley, born in 1874 in Yorkshire. Willam Bentley dropped out of Isaac Barr's group with four other men, all brothers, at a point twenty-five miles or so southwest of Saskatoon, which was then a tent city of two thousand people. The brothers whom Bentley kept company with were named Delisles, and the odds, four Delisle to one Bentley, settled the name on the spot they stopped at — Delisle, Saskatchewan, as it is still called to this day.

Bentley prospered in Delisle. He opened a general store, he farmed, and he sold real estate. He married a woman from North Dakota and lived until 1963, eighty-nine years old at the end, leaving behind him six sons and seven daughters. His two youngest sons, Doug, born in 1916, and Max, born in 1920, brought fame to the Bentley name and to Delisle — they grew up to become two of the very best players in the National Hockey League in the 1940s and '50s.

"All the boys could've made it in the pros," Max Bentley told me when I visited him in Delisle. "But with Roy and Jack, my dad didn't want 'em to leave home, and they never did more than be real good senior-league players out here. Then Scoop — his name's Wyatt but everybody's called him Scoop for as long as we can remember — was the guy my dad wanted to look after the horses, so he was too busy to go to the pros. But he was real, real good. And Reg played for Chicago a few games when me and Doug were there. Reg liked his fun. He'd rather shoot pool the afternoon of the game when he should've been resting. He'd be ready to sleep by the time the game was starting. He didn't last. My dad was just as glad to have him home. He didn't want any of us to go, not even me and Doug."

Despite his years with National League teams — five with Chicago, six with Toronto, one with New York — Max Bentley never has left Delisle. He lived in hotel rooms and rented houses in the big cities — then hurried west as soon as the last goal had been scored in each season. Once, in the middle of a year with the Leafs, when an injured back was keeping him in excruciating pain, he climbed into his father-in-law's new car and, without a word to Conn Smythe, drove through three days of blizzards until he reached home. He'd be back, he told Smythe on the phone later, as soon as Delisle had soothed his aches. The town, it's clear, has meant familiarity and security to Bentley, and they rate at the top of his priorities.

"I like to stick close to home," he said when I asked about his life in Delisle, shrugging as if he were puzzled that I should wonder. "I know everybody. I'm with my friends."

He and his wife Betty live in the one small apartment building in town, and in the summers he raises wheat on land near by. He has two spreads: one, of 240 acres, reaches to the edge of Delisle, and the other, 640 acres, is nine miles away. In the winters, "just for something to keep busy", he looks after the curling ice at the Delisle Centennial Arena.

The arena was where I tracked Bentley down when I phoned Delisle one day early in March. He said I was welcome to come out, but that the curlers in town were so active he hardly ever got away from the rink for long. A few days later I took a plane to Saskatoon, rented a car at the airport, and drove southwest on Highway 7. It was the flattest landscape I'd ever looked across. As I drove along the empty highway, my view to forever was interrupted only by occasional clumps of bare trees and clusters of snow-covered farm buildings. Overhead the sky seemed higher than it did in the city, farther away, as if it had stepped back to accommodate the vastness down there on the winter prairie.

I spotted Delisle a couple of miles before I reached it. Grain elevators aimed into the sky on the left side of the highway where the railroad passed, and on the right, past the sign "Welcome to Delisle. Population 700" and beyond the Esso station, the town's buildings, none more than two storeys high, teetered on the edge of the prairie's oblivion. I drove down the wide main street, past the IGA, Jim's Sportswear, Orchard Farm Equipment, the hotel and the bank on either side of the largest intersection, and I recognized the shapes of the buildings from a movie I'd seen a couple of months before my trip. *Paperback Hero* was all about a young guy name Dillon (Keir Dullea played the part) who played hockey, chased women (one of whom was Elizabeth Ashley), generally ran wild, and ended up shooting it out with the Mounted Police, and it had been filmed in Delisle two years earlier. The corner where the hotel and the bank stood, I realized, feeling giddy over my tiny perception, was exactly where Dillon had made his stand when he got it from the Mounties at the climax of the movie. I drove through the intersection, turned left at the next street, and pulled into the Centennial Arena's parking lot.

It was just past noon and Bentley was alone in the arena lobby. We shook hands and he gave me a smile that was a beam of generosity and kindness. Smiles, I came to understand over the next day or so, are Bentley's gift to everyone. At the back of his cheeks there are deep lines that look like brackets for the rest of his features — they're laugh lines and they've been worn to grooves over a lifetime of offering his friendship.

He's a short man, about five-eight, and has the beginnings of a paunch. His hair is black, his eyes are small (and vanish into slits when he laughs), his skin is burned brown leather, and his nose is a trademark. When Doug and Max Bentley played in the NHL, two characteristics marked them off from the rest — their skills with the puck and their noses. The noses were large, straight, and as obvious as the prow of a ship. Max Bentley's nose is still large and obvious, but hockey collisions have left it no longer straight. It has the ridged seam of an old scar running down its centre, and the tip is bent and gouged as if some mad sculptor had handled it like silly putty.

Bentley said that the ladies wouldn't be along for their afternoon curling until two o'clock, and we sat down to talk in a row of seats that looked through a long glass panel at the rink he'd just finished sweeping. I asked him about stickhandling. It was a natural first question — any hockey fan who watched Bentley in his best years remembers him as a master of puck control. Phil Samis had described Bentley to me as the Nureyev of hockey. I think of him as the Fred Astaire. He had the moves that were the on-ice equivalent of tap dancing. He zigged and zagged and hardly ever took two strides in the same direction. He did stutter steps, feints, and shifts, and all the while, through every intricate manoeuvre, he kept the puck on the end of his stick. He had remarkable balance. And he elevated stickhandling into a skill more advanced than anyone else could match, into something close to magic.

"I learned stickhandling right outside of where we're sitting now," Bentley said. "You noticed the house beside the parking lot, big two-storey white place?"

I nodded.

"That's where we grew up, my dad's old place. Doug and I used to play road hockey out front of it. Just sticks and a tennis ball. We'd be there hours every day, chasing the ball around, deking each other, all that stuff. The old rink where we played on skates when it got cold enough was up the street from here. It was real narrow, not like in the NHL, and probably that helped the stickhandling."

"Later on," I said, "I guess you played on the junior team in town."

Bentley straightened up in his seat, jabbed his finger at my chest, and laughed. "I *never* played junior." He let out a happy whoop. "Nope. I was sixteen and I went straight into the seniors. One year I was with a team my brother Roy coached down the highway from here in Rosetown, then I was two years over at Drumheller and one year with Saskatoon Quakers. Doug had gone up to the pros by then, up to Chicago, and I come along the year after, 1940 it was. I never saw a big city like that before. Chicago opened my eyes, I tell you honest."

With the Black Hawks, Doug played on left wing and Max at centre, with Bill Mosienko on right wing, and they made up a line that may

have been the most colourful and popular in the NHL through the early
1940s. It was called the Pony Line because each member was small,
quick, and frisky.

"I don't know who give us the name. But it felt nice and it stuck. We
had so much fun playing together, us three. Doug and Mosie, well . . ."
Bentley's eyes floated away from mine, out to the empty curling rink.
His face had no talent for hiding emotion, and now it was registering a
fond reaching-back for the most satisfying of times. "In my heart,
those two were the best I ever saw, the fastest. They had different
styles, y'know. Like, when we were coming up to the other team's
blueline, Mosie liked me to pass him the puck before he hit the defence
and he'd carry it around them. With Doug, he wanted me to dump the
puck between the two defencemen and he'd swoop around and pick it
up. We used to talk about ideas like that — Mosie was very conscien-
tious for talking — and I had to keep all the ideas in my head. But I
always knew those two were the best and I'd be all right."

I asked Bentley if the Pony Line's small size made them victims for
the league's heavy body-checkers.

"That's where the speed comes in. We had to keep moving fast all
the time. We had to have our legs in shape. It was hard in Chicago
because there was never any ice to practise on." Bentley's voice
quickened in indignation. "The Black Hawks had nice teams in those
days, but most of our guys couldn't get in that good condition. We'd be
ahead at the end of the first period or the second period, then we'd fade
out of the picture and lose. The only guys who were okay for condition
were me and Doug and Mosie. That's because we played at least half of
every game all by ourselves."

"Chicago," I said, "sounds like a funny place to play hockey."

Bentley broke into another of his wide grins. "Sunday night games,
we used to go into the Stadium at noon for an hour or so to have a team
meeting, and the balcony would be already filled up with fans. They'd
let people in, and these fellas'd play cards and drink beer till the game
started at eight o'clock. By then they'd be looped. They'd go wild,
throw things on the ice, paper planes, like that. Once somebody threw
a fish. Talk about drunks — that's practically all there was up in the
balcony."

The arena door opened behind us and shut with a bang that
ricocheted like a gun shot. Four or five women, all laughs and flutters,
dressed in ski pants and bulky sweaters, stretch pants and quilted

jackets, ambled into the lobby, as at home as in their own kitchens. The hour for the Delisle Ladies' Curling Club had arrived, and soon high-pitched chatter from a couple of dozen women echoed around the lobby's walls. Bentley welcomed all with his smile, helped some find their curling brooms, and assured others that the ice was silky smooth. His manner, and the women's, was easy and close, and made me, for a moment, envy small-town intimacy.

"See the girl there in the white sweater," Bentley said to me, pointing through the glass. "That's Gloria, my boy Lynn's wife. Isn't she cute? Just like a bug in a rug."

Gloria was a short, amply shaped woman in her late twenties. She had a round face and even features. She reminded me, when I saw her laughing on the ice, of a Happy Face button come to life.

"Lynn could've made a success in the pros," Bentley said, looking melancholy. "Chicago had him to training camp when he was young, and one night he phoned us up, his mother and me, and he said they wanted him to sign a contract. Next night he phoned and said he was coming home. He said he was gonna get married to Gloria. She was only about sixteen, and they had three kids right away, bang, bang, bang. So he stayed home — we helped them out with money — and he never turned pro. Broke my heart."

Out on the ice, Delisle's women threw the rocks and swept the ice, and behind the glass, some of Delisle's men drifted in to watch and kibitz. Everyone kidded with Bentley. He tossed back his own jokes and asides. And somewhere in the multi-level conversation, I learned that Bentley had played on a Delisle team that represented Saskatchewan in the Canadian Senior Curling Championships the year before and finished runner-up to the winners.

"You must be a good curler," I said to him.

He gave me a quick look. "Ah, go on," he said. "That tournament's just for old men."

The women finished their matches and the crowd slowly broke up. Bentley swept the rink and sprinkled water over it to give the surface a proper pebbly texture. When he finished, he suggested we go downtown for a beer.

"Downtown" in Delisle is the pub in the hotel at the main intersection. It's a long, plain room. It has dark panelling, a pool table, a jukebox, and a crowded, almost claustrophobic, atmosphere. It may also be the last bar in Canada that still sells a bottle of beer for fifty cents.

Bentley chose a table close to the centre of the room, sat down, then turned and pointed out another table in the corner. "Me and Doug sat over there in the movie they made in town. They did a whole lot of filming in here, and you can see us two drinking beer in the crowd. We sat there for hours. Doug didn't drink much that time. He wasn't well, y'know. He had terrible pain from the cancer, and he died two years ago now, a little after they finished the movie. Isn't that something? Doug died."

Bentley was silent for a few moments, his head down, his hand brushing absently at cigarette ash on the table. He looked up when a waiter welcomed him and unloaded two bottles of beer and a glass of tomato juice from the tray he was carrying.

"See the boy that brought the beer?" Bentley said in a low voice, leaning across the table. I looked around at the waiter, a tall, good-looking, blonde young man, no older than twenty. "He's my brother Jack's grandson. Heckuva good goalie. He oughta be playing for the Delisle juniors, but he had some kind of run-in with the coach. Know who the coach is? My brother Roy. Don't know what the trouble is there. None of my business. I told the boy I'd find him a job in another town for next year where he can play goal."

Bentley mixed beer and tomato juice in his glass, half and half. I stuck to straight beer, and as I lifted my drink, I noticed a row of photographs of hockey players on the wall facing me. One showed Doug and Max shaking hands — Doug in a Black Hawk uniform, Max in a Leaf outfit. The picture had been taken just after the trade that broke up the Pony Line, and the two brothers are wearing bittersweet expressions.

The trade was made in November 1947 when Max was approaching his peak. He'd won the league scoring championship in the two previous seasons, and he'd been voted to the First All-Star Team in 1946 — the year he was also given the Hart Trophy as the most valuable player in the league — and to the Second All-Stars in 1947. Doug's record was almost as grand; he led the league in scoring in 1943 and he was the All-Star left-winger in three seasons — 1943, '44, and '47. Then came the trade, the most sensational in the NHL for many years: five first-line Leafs — Gaye Stewart, Gus Bodnar, Bud Poile, Bob Goldham, and Ernie Dickens — for Bentley and a minor-leaguer named Cy Thomas who played only a handful of games for the Leafs.

"I didn't have to go to Toronto if I didn't want," Bentley said, sipping his scarlet drink. "Mr. Tobin, the Chicago president, called me and Doug into his office for a talk this one day. I'd heard rumours about a trade but I never dreamed it'd be me. Mr. Tobin said it was up to myself whether I went or not. He said it'd help Chicago a lot, getting five top players like that. So I thought, well, I'll go. One person was very disappointed when he learned about the trade — my dad. He heard it on the radio. He wanted me and Doug to stay together. Maybe I should've phoned him right away so he wouldn't've heard it on the radio."

"I was at the first game you played for the Leafs in Toronto," I said, "and I remember when you came out we gave you a terrific cheer."

"Yeah, yeah." Bentley smiled, then looked serious. "But I felt pretty lonesome in Toronto. Didn't know a soul and it took me a couple of months to get going. Turk Broda was the guy — my place in the dressing room was beside him and he made me feel at home."

"Broda had the reputation as the happy man on the team," I said.

"This one night Turk took me to a Chinese restaurant. In the middle of the place there were some very steep stairs. Turk'd had a lot to drink and, my gosh, he fell all the way down the stairs. He hurt himself something bad. Next day at practice, he went up to Hap Day.

" 'Boy, do my bones ache,' Turk told him. 'I got a really bad case of the flu.'

"All week he kept that up. 'Boy, I wish this flu'd go away.'

"I don't know if Hap ever caught on. The thing was, you couldn't ever get mad at Turk. I was always grateful to him. Poor fella, dead now y'know."

Bentley ordered another round of beer and tomato juice. "Bring this man some peanuts and potato chips," he told the young blond waiter, nodding at me. "I don't think he's had enough to eat today." I pulled some bills from my pocket. "No you don't," Bentley said. "Your money's no good long's you're in town." He paid.

The bar was beginning to fill up. Almost everyone who came in had a few words for Bentley. "Going to the game tonight, Max?" some asked. "Better believe," he'd answer.

When the socializing fell into a brief lull, I mentioned to Bentley something Howie Meeker had told me.

"The sad thing about Max," Meeker said, "is he had to lose twenty points a year under the system in Toronto. The son of a gun never had any wingers with the Leafs who complemented him, nobody in his class. He couldn't be the superstar at Toronto that he would have been with a free-wheeling team."

"Twenty points?" Bentley said. "I guess so. Mr. Smythe told me he was gonna give me a bunch of rookies for wingers but he said I shouldn't worry. You'll get your goals, he said, you'll get 'em on the power play. That was about right. I played the point on the power play and I scored my share that way."

"But how about your wingers?"

"Well, I had Joe Klukay on right wing for most of the time, a real hard-working player, and I had umpteen rookies for left wing. It wasn't like playing with Doug and Mosie. But listen" — Bentley leaned forward, his elbows on the table — "I'm not gonna say anything bad about anybody. They were all nice fellas, everybody on the Leafs."

We finished our drinks and drove back to the arena. High school kids were on the curling rink, near the end of their matches. Bentley shot the breeze with the teacher in charge, fooled around with a couple of boys who'd come off the ice, and had a few words with a big, slow man in rubber boots and overalls who'd wandered in out of the cold.

"Listen," Bentley said to me, suddenly breaking away from the others. "Remember I said I had a hard time starting out with the Leafs? I didn't score two points in the first six weeks. What I was worried about was Mr. Tobin promised me a new Cadillac if I won the scoring title. That would've been three of them in a row. Nobody'd ever done that up till then. But I got too far behind at the beginning in Toronto. Elmer Lach won it. Doug was about third and I was a couple points behind him. Gee, I wanted that Caddie. I'll never forget — I wanted it so bad."

When the kids were done, Bentley once again swept and pebbled the rink, tidied up, returned to the lobby, and, hands on hips, let out a long sigh.

"Y'know," he said, staring back at the rink, "if I get a good price for my wheat this year, I think Betty and me'll go to Phoenix next winter. Only reason I do this job is because I think I oughta. When they built the curling rink five or six years ago, everybody pitched in, everybody in town, but I was away and when I come back and there was nobody to look after the ice, I figured I'd be doing my share by taking the job. But it's getting to be too much."

He turned and looked at me.

"Not as if I get paid a fortune," he said in his most matter-of-fact tone.

He put away the sweeping and pebbling equipment and led the way out of the arena.

"Come on," he said briskly. "Gloria's invited us for supper. My wife's away — did I tell you that? — up at her sister's. Gloria now, she puts on a fine supper."

Bentley's son and daughter-in-law and their children live in a small development of new houses, done in one-storey suburban style, on the north edge of Delisle. It was easy to recognize Lynn Bentley as his father's son. Even if he wore a drooping moustache and modishly long hair, he was still a Bentley in his smile and his welcoming nature. He opened bottles of beer for the men and he talked a little hockey. At six o'clock we sat down in the small dining-alcove to a meal of minute steaks, baked potatoes, peas, salad, and lemon meringue pie. There were seven of us — Max, Lynn, Gloria, a teen-aged Bentley nephew, me, and the three kids, two girls and a boy, aged nine to thirteen, all of them blond and lively. Gloria was shy, the kids giggled, and Lynn, the genial host, guided the conversation. Talk got around to violence in hockey.

"Fights?" Max said. "I couldn't lick my lips. I was in three fights my whole time in the pros. That big defenceman at Boston, Bob Armstrong, he practically strangled me. The second fight, another Boston guy, Ed Harrison, hit me such a punch I thought I was gonna die. The last fight was right near the end when I was with the Rangers. Glen Skov speared me in the neck. I was so mad I grabbed him round the neck and held on for all I was worth. If I'd let go, he'd've killed me. Fights made no sense to me. I didn't care what anybody else did — I wanted to take the puck and go. Never mind the violence."

Max hurried away after the meal to make sure the rink was ready for the night's curling. Gloria washed the dishes, the kids watched Cher on the big colour television set in the living room, Lynn and I shot pool in the basement. Lynn, the shark, won every game. As he played, he talked in a bright anxious-to-please voice about his job (he worked in the nearby potash mines and on his holidays helped Max on the farms), about his hockey (he was player-coach for the Delisle seniors), and about his father.

"Quit his job at the curling rink?" he smiled. "He won't do that. He

has to keep busy. Y'know what happens in the mornings? He'll phone
here at six o'clock and ask if I'm up for work. If that doesn't do the job,
he walks over and taps on our bedroom window till we come out."
Lynn laughed, sounding exactly like his father, and shook his head.
"He can't sit still a minute."

Lynn ran a string of six balls to win another game, just as Max
arrived to drive me to the hockey game, the Delisle juniors against a
team from Saskatoon in a playoff series. The hockey rink was in
another section of the Centennial Arena, on the opposite side of the
lobby from the curling ice and beyond the hot-dog stand. It was a
dowdy place, old and ramshackle, but large enough to seat the population of Delisle twice over. It was about half full for this game. Many of
the spectators, as it turned out, were Bentleys.

"Here, you gotta meet Doug's wife," Bentley said to me after he'd
paid for our tickets. "And there's my brother Jack. Come on. You want a
coffee or anything?"

Inside the arena, another brother, Roy, the junior team's coach,
paced behind the Delisle bench. He was seventy-two but looked and
acted twenty-five years younger. I sat beside a couple of female
Bentleys, two women in their early fifties who kept up a din of insults
at the referee and the Saskatoon team.

"Look at their number seven," one woman said over and over.
"He's got a face like a retard. HEY, YOU RETARD!"

The game was fast and rough, and it was clear that Delisle, efficient
and strong on positional play, had a fairly easy win on its hands.
Bentley watched the game, looking intent, saying nothing, until the
end of the first period. "Let's go on home and talk," he said. "Our
team's okay, but not as sharp as they oughta be."

I'd planned to stay in the local hotel, over the pub. Bentley refused to
hear of such an idea, and we drove to his apartment. The rooms were
crowded and cheerful. Knick-knacks overflowed the shelves and
tables, and a life-sized blowup of Bentley in a Leaf uniform decorated
the main hall. I had a bottle of Scotch in my case and poured two
drinks. Bentley turned on the colour television set in the corner, the
sound kept low, and his eyes were on the screen as he tasted his drink
and talked. He seemed a little tired, a little down.

"What I wanted to do, my real ambition," he said, "was last twenty
years in the NHL. I was going great in the eleventh year, '52–'53. I had
the two best wingers I ever played with on Toronto, George Armstrong

on one side, young Hannigan on the other. They were kids, single guys, full of vim and vigour. They protected me. Anybody looked sideways at me, they'd smack the guy."

"Was that the year you scored a lot of goals right off the bat?" I asked.

"That's the one." Bentley nodded. "I got twelve goals my first twelve games. The thirteenth game of the year, everything came apart. Paul Masnick from the Canadiens hit me in the back. We were playing in Montreal and I never even had the puck at the time. Masnick was really flying and he drove me right into the ice from behind. I don't want there to be any hard feelings by my saying this, but, y'know, maybe he was sent out on purpose to get me."

"I don't remember you playing very much the rest of that year," I said.

"It was my back," Bentley said, his face as morose as Buster Keaton's. "Right when Masnick hit me, I felt the cord in the centre of my back go pop. I couldn't get up off the ice. In hospital, they put me in traction, and when I got out, I had to walk funny."

He stood up from his chair and waddled across the floor like a hunch-backed ape. "Isn't that awful?" He sat down again. "Worst thing I did was come back and play a game against Detroit before I was ready. I took a shot and I felt my back go snap again. I was never any good after that."

"But you played the season after that with the Rangers."

"It was Mr. Boucher's idea, the Rangers' coach." Bentley took timid sips at his Scotch — he was, I decided, a beer drinker. "Mr. Boucher talked me and Doug into playing for him. Doug had been retired a couple of years, but he played real good for New York. And Mr. Boucher worked out a deal for me with Mr. Smythe. I told them I wasn't any good no more. I had no speed, I had no shot. But I still got around fifteen goals for them. It was nice being together with Doug again. But . . ." Bentley stopped for a moment.

"Know what the matter was?" he said finally.

"What was that?"

"I wasn't earning my pay. I didn't feel I was. Everybody was nice to me, but I wasn't happy. I wasn't playing good. And another thing, I didn't want to get booed. The fans in New York got on some guys and booed them. They drove those guys right off the team. I was sick when that happened."

We sat silently and watched "Front Page Challenge" on television. I poured myself another Scotch. Bentley worked on his first.

"Does that sound like an alibi?" he said. "About my back?"

"Not at all."

"It hurt so much I'd go home at night and practically climb the walls with the pain."

"That doesn't sound like an alibi."

"Betty used to rub it with liniment every night," Bentley said. "I never told anybody in New York it hurt me all the time."

"How is it today?"

"Well, I can't sweep too hard when I curl." Bentley looked away from the television program and broke into one of his smiles. "Tell you the truth, I never felt better in my life. A million dollars."

We finished our drinks and Bentley showed me into the guest bedroom. "I wake pretty early," he said. "But I'll let you sleep till you want." He closed the door and I got into bed. I looked through the copy of *The Complete Encyclopedia of Ice Hockey* I'd brought with me. Bentley, I read, finished his NHL career with 245 goals and 299 assists, 544 total points. His brother Doug was a point behind — 219 goals, 324 assists, 543 points. I remembered how they looked on the ice when they were scoring all the goals, how small and vulnerable they seemed, how clever and how . . . enchanting. I closed my book and switched off the light.

Next morning I could hear Bentley moving quietly around the apartment before he called me. I dressed and we drove two or three blocks to a restaurant — "*the* restaurant", Bentley called it — that was attached to the Esso station on the highway. He introduced me to the station owner and to the restaurant proprietor, a Chinese, and he ordered a cup of coffee.

"That's my breakfast these days," he said. "I was 150 pounds when I started the pros. A while ago I went up to 200. Now I'm moving the other way — 185."

The proprietor's wife brought me bacon and eggs and toast, and while I ate, Bentley talked about his good times.

"The best I remember," he said, "the biggest thrill, was when we won the Stanley Cup in 1951. We were ahead of Montreal three games to one and the fifth game was at the Gardens and we were behind in it by a goal with around half a minute left. I had the puck in the Montreal end and I could see two of our guys beside the net, Sid Smith on one side,

Tod Sloan on the other. All the Montreal guys were behind me and those two. I don't know how that come about. Anyhow, Butch Bouchard, their defenceman, rushed at me, and I flipped the puck over his stick to Smitty. The goalie — Gerry McNeil, wasn't it? — he turned toward Smitty and Smitty slid the puck to Sloanie. The net was wide open for him to tap it in. Tie game. The fans hollered so much I think the noise lasted fifteen minutes. I never heard anything like it. Seemed it must've kept up right through the intermission before the overtime, that loud crowd noise, and then Barilko scored right away to win the Cup. That was the best."

"How about the night you got the horse?" I asked between mouthfuls of bacon and toast.

"The horse!" Bentley shouted loud enough to bring the Chinese restaurateur from behind his cash register to investigate the excitement. "*Two* horses. I got two on the same night."

"One was from a man named Hemstead, right?" I said, as the proprietor listened in.

"Right." Bentley nodded his head vigorously. "And the other was from George McCullagh, the man that owned the Toronto *Globe and Mail*. Hemstead's horse came first. We were losing a game 2–1 against Detroit at the Gardens somewhere in 1951, '52, around then, and there was a delay in the game because their goalie got hurt, Terry Sawchuk. Well, Mr. Hemstead started talking to me in the delay. I didn't know his name, but I used to see him all the time. He subscribed to the two seats at the end of the Leaf bench and I had the habit of sitting at that end a lot of the time. So he spoke to me.

" 'Max,' he said, 'if you score a goal on the next shift, tie the game up, I'll give you a race horse.'

" 'Go on,' I said.

" 'I will so,' he said.

"Like I say, I didn't know Mr. Hemstead. Later on I stayed at his hotel, the St. Charles, around the corner from the Gardens. He gave me a good deal on a room. He owned the hotel and he had some race horses and other things, a very well-to-do fella.

"Well, I guess you know what happened next. I scored right away, and Mr. Hemstead came jumping up at the boards. 'You got the horse!' he hollered, and he shook my hand and I was dancing around."

"But that didn't end it?" I asked, as anxious to hear the climax to the story as the eavesdropping proprietor was.

"Mr. McCullagh was a director of the team or something," Bentley said, "and he always used to bring his little boy into the dressing room after the games. He came in with the boy this time and he heard all the excitement about the horse.

" 'Well,' he said, 'if Charlie Hemstead can give you a horse, I can give you a better one.' "

Bentley paused, turning over the last line in his mind. "And he *did*, a heckuva horse!" Bentley sent a radiant smile at me and at the proprietor, whose joy was silent and immense.

"What happened to the horses?" I asked.

"Both of them got claimed on me." Bentley held up his cup for more coffee. "I ran them out here on different tracks, Winnipeg, Calgary, and other owners took them both in claiming races. I got good enough money from them to make it all right."

We sat over our coffee for another half-hour. Bentley chatted, touching on old games he remembered with pleasure, on incidents that made him laugh. From time to time, men coming into the restaurant stopped for a few words with him, local talk and gossip. One of the talkers was a rotund man named Dickie Butler who played briefly with the Black Hawks in the late 1940s. "Dick could've been real good," Bentley whispered, "if he'd watched his weight." He ordered a last cup of coffee.

"I haven't been east for a while now," Bentley said in a low voice. "I used to go around and play in lots of old-timers' games, but I stopped since Doug died." He leaned forward. "I'll probably go down to Toronto sometime in a year or so." He hesitated for a moment. "Something I'm doing — I'm going in to Saskatoon next month and get my nose fixed. Nobody except my wife knows. I saw a plastic surgeon and he says he can fix it up good as it was before I got it broke and cracked. Five times it was one thing or the other in hockey games, broke or cracked." His voice dropped to a hush. "I was too embarrassed to go back to Toronto with it looking the way it is."

It was time for Bentley to check the curling rink, time for me to drive to the airport in Saskatoon. Bentley promised we'd have some beers when he came to Toronto. I turned my car out of the Esso station onto the highway, watching Bentley wave to me in the rear-view mirror, and headed across the flat, white landscape.

As I drove, a few words that someone had said to me the afternoon before came into my head. I suppose they came naggingly to mind because I'd forgotten to write them in my notebook. My journalist's memory was jogging me. It was one of Bentley's nephews who'd spoken, a dark, handsome man about forty-five. We talked while Bentley was on the curling ice giving it one of his endless sweeps, and he sounded as if he meant me to understand something very clearly.

"About Max," the nephew said. "He's a fine man. We're very proud of him, all of us in town."

I knew what he meant.

HUGH HOOD

The Sportive Centre of Saint Vincent de Paul

Snow. Moist, heavy, fat flakes melting as they hit, down your coat collar, in your boots, underfoot, piling up in eaves-troughs and on outdoors Christmas trees, shorting their ice-blue, silver, yellow and red strands of light. Snow everywhere this mid-December, not a heavy fall this time — we haven't had much yet — but irksome on Friday night at six-fifteen because of the traffic. If snow, then snow-removal equipment and crews, the salt trucks lug-ging slowly up the hill on Van Horne, growling in low gear. Whish...whish...whoosh...the salt tumbles out behind in crystals, melts, and electrolizes the body metal of fifty thousand cars.

When we got into the car that Friday night, the windows clouded over immediately, and we both began to swear as we threw the goalie equipment and my kitbag and skates into the back, conscious of the half-hour drive ahead, and wondering how long it would take to traverse the level-crossing on Rockland. I spun the wheels backing away from the garage, which made Seymour, the goalie, turn and stare at me.

"Gotta do it in second."

We sunfished up the driveway. After two minutes in the car, our breath made it impossible to see out. I hate cold weather, even moder-ate cold, so I usually keep the windows shut, but a little cold air on the glass works wonders, so I nodded when Seymour glanced at me.

"All right, open the damn things." We went down the street, around the corner, and hit bad traffic as soon as we tried to get onto Rockland; we were a couple of hundred yards short of the level-crossing, just by the park, and the bells were ringing, the red lights swinging, the combined efforts of two wealthy suburban municipalities, Outremont and the Town of Mount Royal, having succeeded for years in denying the plain public interest of the rest of Montreal. They don't want anything done to the level-crossing that will increase heavy traffic on Rockland, so to the detriment of the needs of the citizenry in general, they have put off from one year to the next the creation of an overpass or underpass, from planning council to engineering study, until the issue has evolved from scandal to joke to folklore.

They claim they're going to do something about it next summer, but I'll believe that when I see it.

Only ten minutes to get across this time, though, and from Rockland to L'Acadie, where we turned north towards the Metropolitan, was another five minutes. Half the time for the ride out of town spent on the first half-mile, such is the obduracy of the flourishing suburbanite.

Sometimes, working my way along beside the park towards the level-crossing in winter twilight or blackness, I used to have an infernal vision of the place as an immense and horrid ash-pit. There are piles of ashes and discarded rubbers, old tires, dead cats, at the back of the park where the snow-removal men heap tumuli of gray slush to await the coming of spring. It seemed ashy, gray to black, infinite, that stretch of obscurity along the railroad right-of-way, where now and then a truck might be seen, its body tilted at a dangerous angle. Spectral muffled figures prodded at lumps of packed snow and ordure as one came by; it was always mysteriously saddening to observe their dauntless activity.

Not too bad on L'Acadie, a bit of a tie-up trying to get into the far right lane for the Metropolitan turnoff, but after fifty cars had passed on my right somebody finally slowed and waved me on. I don't think he saw my grateful salute because my car, a degraded Volkswagen bus, allows of little visibility in or out from abaft the beam. We pulled up to the green arrow and headed east, neither of us with much to say, concentrating on the coming game.

Seymour won't eat before a game. He takes a light lunch about two-thirty and dines afterwards, natural in a goalkeeper, I suppose, whose tensions are great. I play defence, and Seymour makes me look good or bad depending, so I can perhaps afford to do as I do and eat around five-thirty. After the game we have drinks and sandwiches. We don't talk much on the way out; that comes later.

"You left the front of the net on their second goal."

"I did, hell. Polsky should have been there; the play came in on my side."

"Anyway don't keep doing it."

We play in an informal two-team league, the Sportsman's League, organized a dozen years ago by some men who had played hockey all their lives and wanted to keep up with it as they got into their late twenties and early thirties. There is one strict rule: no board checking. There's a seasonal series of twenty-five games, and scoring records are kept; we have an elaborate and convivial end-of-the-season dinner.

"Shibley has taken up curling Friday nights," mumbled Seymour. "Curling!"

I eased up the ramp onto the Metropolitan and at once began to drive as fast as possible, which isn't all that fast. We crept up to fifty-five and the bus began to shudder a bit in the wind, always strong on the elevated highway. I couldn't get over fifty-six or seven, but that speed will heat the car slightly, and I got much better vision as our breath stopped condensing on the windows.

Past Place Crémazie, spic and span in black and white and gray brick, all lit up for the Friday night shoppers. Past a parish church of daringly advanced design, its big front window radiating pale yellow and apple-green bars of light over the snow. Over and past myriads of streaking lights. Then a wide sweeping turn coming down towards Saint-Hubert and Christophe-Colomb, whizzing on towards D'Iberville and at last Pie-IX, pronounced 'peanoof'. I looked at my watch as we came down off the Metro.

"Quarter to seven."

"I've got my equipment anyway," said Seymour. "I can dress in plenty of time." It takes him around twenty minutes to get it all on; he has pads for very unusual parts of the body, and rightly so. His face-mask, a strange plastic structure of his own design, closely remembles the death mask of Keats. He said, "We'll be there before seven," as we took a right onto Pie-IX.

Here the prospect of the city changes as you go north, heading off the island. The lights of the Metropolitan recede, a pale stippled line away behind to the west. On your left there's nothing but dark space belonging to Saint-Michel de Laval, half-developed industrial park, I think, with spur lines jutting off into fields, and here and there an occasional abandoned boxcar, and a taxi park or gas station. Pie-IX was just a ribbon development a few years ago, but now there is begining to be a bit of a spread eastwards towards Ville de Saint-Léonard. There are Dairy Queens, closed for the winter, on our right, and used-car lots, small restaurants and raw new shopping centres all the way to Rivière des Prairies.

The name Pie-IX always makes me think of the first Vatican Council of 1870–71, and the promulgation of the dogma of Papal Infallibility. It isn't very long since the tone of Catholicism in the city was much in the spirit of the lamented Pius the Ninth. What he would have said about contemporary Montreal church architecture, or about *aggiornamento* or the opening to the left, or Vatican Two, confounds me as I think of it. I don't believe anyone would name a *ruelle*, let alone a six-lane main artery, after Pius the Ninth, at this time. John, yes: Pius, no. Things are moving fast.

We cross the bridge fast because it has only two lanes and there's always a press of traffic behind, the river wide and black and very cold beneath. Swing to the right, right again along the north shore to Saint Vincent de Paul, left here, stop at the grocery store for a dozen Black Horse which will be drunk in the dressing room after the game, win or lose, and on to the edge of town to the *Centre Sportif* where, according to local legend, the Rocket and some of his life-long friends have played pickup hockey on Sunday afternoons since he retired five years ago. He still has his shot, they say around the arena, and from the blueline in, his legs.

The arena is shaped in what seems to my ungeometrical eye to be the arc of a parabola described by beautifully curving, powerful steel beams covered by crimped steel roofing and terminated by brick walls. It's about the size of a dirigible hangar and is surely the most useful building in the community, churches and schools apart. There's a parking lot at the main entrance, accommodating maybe fifty cars, and just past the building a flat expanse of ground which might be a soccer or football field. I've never seen it in daylight. Away off to your right, a very dim shape in this darkest week of the year, looms a building of unmistakably institutional shape, a college or an orphanage, evidently not a convent school because of the heavy predominance of males in the neighbourhood. Its presence probably explains those lurking gray-headed Christian Brothers with their collars like divided spades, who pace in the runway around the ice-surface at all times, keeping an eye on their students' development.

"*Il a quitté son aile, l'idiot.*"

"*Jeu de position là-bas. Position!*"

Strictly speaking, this is the Laval Community Arena, but since Laval

is so expansive and sprawling a collection of suburbs, I prefer to
associate it with the small township where it lies, named for a Saint of
very charitable reputation.

LIGUE DES FRANCS COPAINS

	W	L	T	P
GARS:	5	1	2	12
CHUMS:	3	3	2	8
AMIS:	2	2	4	8
COPAINS:	1	5	2	4

I'm sorry but amused to note that the Guys, the Chums and the Pals
are still beating hell out of the Comrades. I'd have preferred it otherwise — this is a local French league, much like ours, but on a grander
scale. They play a devastatingly good brand of hockey and have no
prohibition on board checking and other impolitenesses. One time a
couple of seasons back a disgruntled forward in their league, objecting
to a bad call, struck the referee — his close friend — in the eye with
his stick. He got carried away, I suppose, and so in another sense did
the official, who lost the sight of the eye permanently. *Les Francs
Copains*. There's a big sign hanging inside the main entrance giving the
current standings in their league, the Comrades securely in the cellar.
In the foyer are hung dozens of photographs: the blessing and opening
of the arena fifteen years ago, this year's local Junior B team, a
championship Pee-Wee team ranked behind an enormous trophy as tall
as anyone on the club, the Rocket in a referee's striped shirt kneeling in
the middle of a crowd of autograph seekers.

There are arenas like this all over Montreal and the suburbs, with a
foyer much used for ping-pong, for meeting your girl friend, for
loitering. In this one anyway I've never seen any rough stuff, no
rowdyism, no delinquents. Often a lad of thirteen will hold the door
open for you if you're carrying kitbag, sticks, skates. Plenty of long
hair, and some remarkably chic girls of twelve or thirteen, but nothing
even close to criminal.

We pass one of the gangways as we go to the dressing room. Two
Pee-Wee teams are on the ice, working out at either end. Their hour,
six-thirty to seven-thirty, seems to be devoted to shooting and playmaking practice, not to league games which are likely played through
the week or on Sunday afternoon. The players don't look at all like little

boys dressed in outsized equipment. They look like hockey players, having played the game for seven or eight years, since they could stand up on skates. They have moves that I, who never played the game seriously growing up in Toronto, will never acquire: they shoot better than I do, feed a pass better, head-man the puck. They have the game in their legs and arms and hearts from the cradle.

Waiting for our league prexy to unlock the dressing rooms, I watch what the kids are doing. Tonight they're working on faking the goalie out, a line of fowards at the blueline carrying the puck in, one after the other, with a spindly defenceman rapping it out to the next man after the goalie has moved on the play. They don't shoot from the blueline on this exercise, but skate in close, perhaps take a head fake or a stick fake, move to the right or left to persuade the goalie to commit himself, so they can swing with the puck and shoot behind him as he goes the wrong way. At the west end of the rink, the team is dressed in green, apple-green sweaters with yellow trim, which makes me think of the church we passed coming out, a broad band of yellow around the mid-section, and pants in a darker green; most wear headgear. Two defencemen, not taking shooting drill, are skating backwards from side to side of the ice, practising passing the puck forward while moving back, necessary for a defenceman and not as easy as it looks when done right.

Groaning behind me. Carpenter. The dressing rooms must be open now, time to dress so as to be on the ice the moment it's been reflooded at seven-thirty. We only have an hour's ice-time this year, but hope for an hour and a half next season.

Carpenter was taking a drink as I came past, filling himself with ice-cold water, glugging, not a good idea before the game. He straightened.

"Sixty minutes tonight, kid?"

"Sure," I said, "I'm in shape, Fred." I shouldn't have said that. He looked ashen. He could have been a good player too, lots better than me. He said, "I play, vomit, play. You know."

"No you don't. Not in this league." We went on down to dressing room Four to get ready. Paul Bowsfield had a dozen sticks he'd picked up in a job lot, good ones, and some of us took a look at them. Brian Tansey, an insurance man of twenty-nine, our best defenceman, who more or less keeps an eye on Carpenter, had a small dig for me.

"You were using a Number Seven last week."

"So what? I'm getting the puck into the air."

"Yeah, but you're missing passes, and the puck keeps hopping over your stick, damn you. Try a Five."

He had a point. I bought two Fives from Bowsfield, cost me four bucks, and I didn't notice any improvement. I missed passes just the same.

In this city hockey is the chief social cement. The sportsman's League plays pretty poor hockey because most of us are in there once a week for fun. But there are five or six really good players, all of whom play in other, better leagues. Seymour plays in the town of Mount Royal Senior. One week he was complaining to me about the play there.

"I'm getting beat where I shouldn't get beat. There's this guy Gary Paxton, he had three goals on me last night."

"Yeah?"

"He's pretty good. He played a couple seasons out west."

That got my ear. "Where out west?"

"In the Western League. Where else?"

I thought somebody might be kidding somebody, because the WHL is a very fast minor league, full of guys like Charlie Burns who had three seasons with the Bruins, or Andy Hebenton who holds the NHL ironman record, around seven hundred consecutive games with New York and Boston. One season he had over thirty goals, which means that at that time he was one of the best hockey players alive. So if Paxton played in the WHL he was bound to be damned good. When I got home that night I checked him out in the record book (I have record books going back a good long way) and there he was, PAXTON, GARY. Born 1940, and the rest, and he really did play for Los Angeles, 1963–64, 1964–65, and he had fifteen goals last year, which means that he wasn't just hanging on.

He probably realized that he was twenty-five and about at his peak. If you haven't made it at least to the American League by then, you likely won't ever make it to the NHL. I suppose he figured he'd gone about as far as he could and decided to come back to Montreal to settle into some kind of career, playing amateur hockey on the side. This happens in all sports; the phenomenon is familiar in sandlot baseball. You go out to throw the ball around and some guy is cruising back of second in that unmistakable way. Or get up a weekly game of touch football among friends in a park, and one fine summer Saturday somebody shows up who suddenly fires the ball seventy yards with a nice easy arm motion, and it turns out that he played for NDG and had a tryout with the Alouettes, that he might have had a football scholarship to Arizona State but chose to stay home and look after his mother.

Seymour could have signed with the Rangers' organization when he was seventeen, but his parents didn't want him to turn into a hockey bum. "If they'd only known how I'd turn out," he says, "they'd have signed, they'd have signed."

"My son, the painter," I say, and we laugh. But he keeps wondering how things would have worked out if he'd turned pro. I tell him he'd never have made it; they had Worsley and Marcel Paillé, and some other guys, but he keeps wondering.

"You're better off where you are."

"Yeah, but I'm not playing well. It's the quality of the competition."

He's quite right. Playing behind me isn't doing him any good. He gets a lot of shots but all from the wrong places, because I'm not good enough to jockey the forwards over to where they should be. Still, I'm playing with Seymour who was wanted by the Ranger chain, and he's playing with Gary Paxton who had fifteen goals in the WHL last year, see what I mean? And Paxton was playing with Hebenton and Burns who once upon a time played with Andy Bathgate and Johnny Bucyk. I feel as though I belonged to the club in a small way, and it's relations like these that give society its meaning. Me and Andy!

There's a dining and conversation group in the city called the Veterans. *Not* an ex-service club, which can be awfully tedious, but a collection of types who have been associated with hockey as player or coach or even as owner. Every year they give a big dinner with speakers, newspaper coverage and awards. Elmer Ferguson always comes, and gives the function a fine advance write-up; they tape some of the speeches for the sports shows. This year their big award went to Claude Provost who beat out Gordie Howe for first all-star last season; everybody was there. Newsy Lalonde was there, who used to live a block away from me back of Maplewood. King Clancy was there, sitting with a lot of hockey men from Ottawa. Hooley Smith is dead now, but some of the old Maroons got to the dinner, Jimmy Ward, whose son has made it in major-league ball. Men like these have associations going back before 1910, the Arenas, the Wanderers, the Silver Seven, Montreal A.A.A.

In the Forum Tavern after the game, talking to Léon the waiter, we ask him to tell us who is the greatest player he ever saw, and he tells us the story of the time Maurice scored five.

"Gordie Howe is a better hockey player," he says generously, "and Bill looked better than anybody. But the Rocket...there was never anybody like him. There *will* never be anybody like him. One time the Rangers hired this boxer, this heavyweight, Dill. The Rocket flattened him with one punch. If it hadn't been for injuries, he could have played three or four more seasons."

"He cut a tendon," somebody says, "and he was putting on weight. They were calling him *pépère*."

"He's still playing. He plays every Sunday out in Saint-Vincent. They say he can still score."

"Sure he can score."

"He could score," says Léon, "on the Devil himself. If Maurice was dying and the goalie gave him the angle, he'd get up and score. I saw him carry Earl Seibert in from the blueline on his shoulders and score with one hand. I saw him...."

He goes off for more beer talking happily to himself.

Before our game Fred Carpenter was babbling loosely and happily about a set of irons he'd picked up, a steal. I didn't follow what he said because I was concentrating on dressing and taping my sticks, and thinking about the game, wondering which line I'd be on against, Leo's line, or Kenny, Eric and Eddie? A lot of the quality of your play depends on your checks. I'd sooner be on against Leo's line because the forward coming in against me will be either Pierre or Chaloub, depending on how we line up and which side I'm playing. I turn best to the right and should play on that side, but as we often have somebody missing we shuffle our alignment every time out.

Playing against their other line, I'm too slow. All I can do is try to jam the wing on the boards, while avoiding the appearance of sin. Tactics, tactics, and ritual; hockey isn't a game but a complex set of rituals. That night Carpenter violated them all. He wandered up and down, smoking, which you never do before a game, and he was talking too much, in a disconnected way. Once or twice I saw Paul Bowsfield, who more or less captains our side, give him a strange evaluating look. Seymour seemed upset about something too.

The silent lines of communication that develop in a dressing room before a game are subtle, tight and unsmiling. They don't vary. Years ago some individual pencilled the single word 'Boisvert' over the hook where I hang my clothes. Boisvert, if that was his name, may long ago have died or moved away, but nobody will remove the name, and that's simply where I sit, facing Seymour. Tommy sits on my left by the door to the showers and George sits next to Seymour facing me. George and I take turns bringing the beer, twelve cans, one for each player and one over for the man who brings it. Watch how the Leafs come on the ice behind Johnny Bower. Shack is always the first man out. When the Canadiens take their warm-up, Terry Harper is almost always the last man to go off. At the start of the game, you skate back and say something to the goalie, whacking his pads. After the game, if you've won, you meet the goalie coming to the bench and congratulate him, whether he had a good game and kept you in there or was just lucky, or even if he was lousy and you had to outscore the other team eight to seven. You just do this.

When Carpenter kept on horsing around, getting up, sitting down, smoking, getting in people's way, he was violating many silent agreements.

That night I was first out of the dressing room as usual. When I'd been on the ice, which was very fast, fresh and new, for a couple of minutes, the others came on, we took the goalie's warm-up and then Paul gave us the line-up for the night and the game started. We only had three defencemen out. Polsky hadn't turned out, so the arrangement was that Tansey and Carpenter would start and I would spell them off alternately; each of us would get some short shifts and some doubles. Brian was playing a strong rushing game, as he always does, and we kept the puck in their end for the first minutes. Soon Carpenter hollered, and I hopped over the boards and took him off, and things were all right for another three minutes.

Then the roof fell in. Brian had played around six or seven minutes, which he can do because he skates strongly and knows how to pace himself. But when Carpenter came on with me, and I had to change over to the left side where I'm uncomfortable, we gave up three goals, bang, bang, bang, with the game still young. The first was my fault. I got beat on the play but good and told Seymour so, as he fished the puck out of the net. But on the second I was nowhere near the play, and I was glad, because Seymour was pretty red-faced over it. After the goal he said something to Carpenter which was evidently fairly blunt. It was a funny play — the last thing I saw was somebody's glove deflecting the flying puck. The third goal was a clean play, a two-on-one situation where I had to play the puck carrier or anticipate a pass, and I made a wrong guess.

When you get down three in the early part of a game, two things can happen. Either you play stronger, hold them and come on when they tire towards the end, or you fall apart, lose your cohesion and stop skating. This night we fell apart. Oh, we got one goal to bring it up to three to one, and it looked for a second as if we might pick up, then they got it right back and led at the end of the first period, four to one. We only have ice-time for two periods, and the second was worse than the first. Nothing rolled right for us, the forwards weren't skating, and they weren't coming back. I took to falling all over the place out of haste and lack of confidence. Midway through the second period, Carpenter went off and could be heard some distance back of the bench vomiting into a fountain. We got bombed, seven to one. Trooping into the dressing room after the game, we saw the clogged fountain loaded with expelled matter; it was a dismal sight, but appropriate.

Silence, oh, boy, like you could spread it on pumpernickel, thick, heavy. I put the dozen Black Horse in the middle of the floor, and nobody dived for it, very unusual, that. Finally I popped it open, took one myself, handed out a few. Somebody took off a jersey; somebody fiddled with his skates. Tommy looked soberly at a cracked stick.

You could hear singing from the next dressing room.

After a couple of minutes of this Seymour rose and addressed the meeting: "I don't mind losing," he started off, gathering steam as he proceeded. "I think I can say that. I've lost a lot of games in my time. I've had my off nights, but this wasn't one of them, and I don't want to lose any more like that one. If there are guys here who don't care enough about the league to turn up sober — I'm not naming any names and I'm not talking about any one person — I don't want to play behind them. It's dangerous. You can get hurt on a goal-post or in the corners, playing like that, and you can injure somebody else permanently, and you might just as well take the game and hand it to the other team. A beer in the dressing room afterwards, that's fine, everybody likes that, but nobody but a fool, and I mean a fool, drinks before the game. That's all." He sat down and started taking off his pads.

Carpenter looked up from his skates — he'd had his head down while Seymour was talking — and said briefly, "I quit." He got the rest of his things off, didn't bother about a shower, and went out, shutting the door quietly.

Bowsfield said, "I was going to talk to him about it."

"Does anybody think I'm wrong?" Seymour said. "He could hurt any of us. He put their second goal in the net himself, just batted it in with his glove. I suppose he was trying to clear it, but what the hell, a goalie has no protection against that."

"He'll be back," somebody said.

"I think he'll be back," I said.

"Sure, after Christmas," We have to take a break at Christmas.

"Did he come up with you, Brian?"

"Naw, not tonight; he got away from the office early. I think he caught a ride with Yvan."

"Does he drink in the office?"

"Not in the office, no. Right after."

"I didn't think he looked so bad," I said.

"You could smell it."

"Ah."

I collected quarters from the few who had taken a beer, picked up the remaining cans and my equipment and hustled out to stick them in the car. Carpenter was standing at the coffee counter under the *Ligue des Francs Copains* sign. I joined him; he looked bereft.

"See you after New Year's," I said cheerfully.

He said nothing, just drank his coffee, shivered and went outside. I don't know who drove him home; he certainly didn't come with us. After he left there was the usual kidding around at the coffee counter.

"Tonight you couldn't make a wrong move," Seymour said jovially to Leo, "the way you hang around that red line."

Leo grinned at me. "You want to play with more confidence," he said. "Try charging the forwards. I don't mean so as to hurt anybody."

There were exchanges of holiday greetings, kind of a line-up in which we all shook hands and wished each other a good Christmas. Tansey looked around, wondering where Carpenter was.

"He's gone," Seymour said glumly. "I didn't catch him. I meant to."

"After Christmas," I said.

"That's it."

When we went out to the cars, it had stopped snowing; there were solid wet cakes of white on every car, oozing water down windows. It was growing colder. The sky had cleared, and you could see the clouds moving and the stars back of them. Car doors slammed. People joked about the lopsided score, gradually the parking lot cleared. When Seymour had had his weekly argument with the league president, about who should trans-ship his equipment to the Town of Mount Royal Arena, we drove away.

"Ron is taking care of it?"

"What?"

"Your pads."

"Oh, that." He lit a cigar Ron had given him, and a rich vapour filled the car. I coughed critically. "That's all right, now," said Seymour, "this is a good cigar. I wish I had Ron's dough."

"You will when you're dead."

"I suppose so." We drove in silence through Saint Vincent to the highway, through the underpass, up the ramp, onto the approach to the bridge. Coming back into town, the approach slopes sharply down and there is a fine wide view of the river and the lights along the dark shore. You almost seem to swoop down like a plane, and the lights of the town rush to meet you and the dark water somehow draws your eyes. You have to take care, coming off the bridge, as the traffic divides into streams headed for various suburbs across the northern part of the city.

Tonight, perhaps because of the snow, there was much bright reflection from the river, white on dark, with faint moving pin-pricks of red and green here and there. I felt cold, and the cigar smoke was oppressive. Down Pie-IX in the centre lane southbound, we were bowling along pretty good, catching the lights in sequence, heading for the Metropolitan West, and a few beers and some sandwiches in a tavern on the Main called *Le Gobelet*, where we always go. By the time we were across town, the cold had become intense and we were glad to get out of the car and into the clatter and warmth of *Le Gobelet* where we sat watching colour TV, going over the game, eating, till it was time to go home.

Three weeks later the shoe was on the other foot; we got off to a grand start, got the right roll from the puck every time. I played my first decent game of the season and the rest of the club was hustling too. We won it, three to one, which started us off on a winning streak that lasted quite a time.

Tansey, Polsky and I played defence; the other fellow never came back, although we hear of him sometimes through Brian. Once, after a game we won really big, Seymour and I stood around the foyer for a while watching the kids come and go around the ping-pong tables. Just by the entrance there's a little door which might lead to the building superintendent's office, and over it stands a big gray plaster statue of the Blessed Virgin with the Child in her arms; the statue has a circular electric halo. It all fits in.

Seymour took me by the arm for a second. "We have a lot in common, you know."

I agreed with him silently.

He said, "We take a pretty high moral line, don't we?"

I said I thought we did.

"You know," he said slowly, "if the position has a defect — I'm not sure it has — it would be self-righteousness, wouldn't it?"

I thought he was right, and said so.

Howe Incredible

CLEARLY, HE COMES FROM GOOD STOCK. Interviewed on Canadian television last year, his eighty-seven-year-old father was asked, "How do you feel?"

"I feel fine."

"At what time in life does a man lose his sexual desires?"

"You'll have to ask somebody older than I am."

His son was only five when he acquired his first pair of skates. He repeated the third grade, more intent on his wrist shot than on reading, developing it out there in the sub-zero wheat fields, shooting frozen horse buns against the barn door. A mere fourteen-year-old, working in summer on a Saskatoon construction site with his father's crew, both his strength and determination were already celebrated. He could pick up ninety-pound cement bags in either hand, heaving them easily. Preparing for what he knew lay ahead, he sat at the kitchen table night after night, practicing his autograph.

I'm talking about Gordie Howe, born in Floral, Saskatchewan, in 1928, a child of prairie penury, his hockey career spanning thirty-two active seasons in five decades. The stuff of legend.

Gordie.

For almost as long as I have been a hockey fan, Mr. Elbows has been out there, skating, his stride seemingly effortless. The big guy with the ginger ale bottle shoulders. To come clean, I didn't always admire him. But as I grew older and hockey players apparently younger, many of them even younger than my eldest son, he became an especial pleasure to me. Even more, an inspiration. My God, only three years older than me, and still out there, chasing pucks. For middle-aged Canadians, there was hope. In a world of constant and often bewildering change, there was also one shining certitude. Come October, the man for whom time had stopped would be out there, not taking any dirt from anybody. Gordie, Gordie. He became our champion.

Gordie Howe's amazing career is festooned with records, illuminated by anecdote. Looked at properly, within the third-grade repeater there was a hockey pedagogue longing to leap out.

Item: In 1963, when the traditionally stylish but corner-shy Montreal Canadiens brought up a young behemoth from the minors to police the traffic, he had the audacity to go into a corner with Mr. Elbows. He yanked off his gloves, foolishly threatening to mix it up with Howe.

"In this league, son," Howe cautioned him, "we don't really fight. All we do is tug at each other's sweaters."

"Certainly, Mr. Howe," the rookie agreed.

But no sooner did he drop his fists than the old educator creamed him.

Toe Blake, another Canadien who played against Howe, once said, "He was primarily a defensive player when he started, and he'd take your ankles off if you stood in front of the net."

That was in 1946. Harry Truman was ensconced in the White House. In Ottawa, Prime Minister Mackenzie King, our very own wee Willie, consulted his most trusted advisor nightly — a crystal ball. Everybody was reading *Forever Amber.* The hot stuff. Bob Feller was back from the war; so were Hank Greenberg and Ted Williams. Jackie Robinson, a black, broke into the line-up of the Montreal Royals. On June 19, Joe Louis knocked out Billy Conn in the eighth round at Yankee Stadium. Eighteen-year-old Gordie Howe, in his first season with the Detroit Red Wings, scored all of seven goals and fifteen assists. Thirty-four years later Steve Shutt, who wasn't even born when Howe was a rookie, reported a different problem in playing against the now silvery-haired legend. "Sure we give him room out there. If you take him into the boards the crowd boos, but they also boo if you let him get around you."

Which is to say, there were the glory years (more of them than any other athlete in a major sport can count) and the last sad ceremonial season when even the fifty-two-year-old grandfather allowed that he had become poetry in slow motion. But still a fierce advocate for his two hockey-playing sons, Marty and Mark.

"Playing on the same line as your sons," Maurice Richard once observed, "that's really something."

Yes, but when I finally got to interview Howe I asked him if, considering his own legendary abilities, it might have been kinder to encourage his sons to do anything but play hockey.

"Well, once somebody said to Marty, hey, kid, you're not as good as your father. Who is? he replied."

Consider the records, familiar but formidable. Gordie Howe has scored the most assists (1,383) and, of course, played in the most games (2,186). He won the NHL scoring title six times, a record, and was named the most valuable player six times in the NHL and once in the WHA. He has scored more goals than anybody (975 — 801 in the NHL). His 100th goal, incidentally, was scored on February 17, 1951, against Gerry McNeil of Montreal as the Red Wings beat the Canadiens 2–1 on Maurice Richard Night.

Obloquy.

And a feat charged with significance, because if some of you cut your ideological baby teeth on such trivial questions as whether Stalin was justified in signing a pact with Hitler in 1939, or if FDR threatened the very structure of the republic by running for a precedent-shattering fourth term, or whether Truman needed to drop that bomb on Hiroshima, my Canadian generation came to adolescence fiercely debating who was really *numero uno,* Gordie Howe or the other No. 9, Maurice "The Rocket" Richard of the Montreal Canadiens.

Out west, where the clapboard main street, adrift in snow, often consisted of no more than a legion hall, a curling club and a Chinese restaurant, the men in their lumberjack jackets — deprived of an NHL team themselves, dependent on radio's *Hockey Night In Canada* for the big Saturday night game — rooted for Gordie. One of their own, shoving it to the condescending east. Gordie, who wouldn't take dirt from anybody, educating the fancy-pants frogs with his elbows. Giving them pause, making them throw up snow in the corners.

But in Montreal, elegant Montreal, with its beautiful young women, clean old money and some of the finest restaurants on the continent, we valued élan (that is to say, Richard) above all. For durable Gordie, it appeared the game was a job at which he had undoubtedly learned to excel, but the exploding Rocket, whether he appreciated it or not, was an artist. Moving in over the blueline, he was incomparable. "What I remember most about The Rocket were his eyes," goalie Glenn Hall once said. "When he came flying toward you with the puck on his stick, his eyes were all lit up, flashing and gleaming like a pinball machine. It was terrifying."

Seven years older than Howe, Richard played 18 seasons, retiring in 1960. Astonishingly, he never won a scoring championship, coming second to Howe twice and failing two more times by a maddening point. He was voted most valuable player only once. But the one shining record he does hold is a touchstone in the game: Maurice Richard was the first player to score 50 goals in 50 games. That was in 1944–45, in the old six-team league, when anybody scoring twenty goals in a season was considered a star. Toe Blake, once a linemate of the Rocket and a partisan to this day, maintains, "There's only one thing that counts in this game and that's the Stanley Cup. How many did Jack Adams win with Gordie and how many did we take with the Rocket?"

The answer to that one is Detroit took four Cups with Gordie and the Canadiens won eight propelled by the Rocket. However, Richard's supporting cast included, at one time or another, Elmer Lach, Blake, Richard's brother Henri, Jean Beliveau, Boom-Boom Geoffrion, Dickie Moore, Doug Harvey, Butch Bouchard and Jacques Plante. Howe had Sid Abel and Terrible Ted Lindsay playing alongside him and there also was Alex Delvecchio. He was backed up by Red Kelly on defense, either Glenn Hall or Terry Sawchuk in the nets and, for the rest mostly a number of journeymen. Even so, the Red Wings, led by Gordie Howe, finished first in regular-season play seven times in a row, from 1949 to 1955. They beat the Canadiens in the 1954 Stanley Cup final and again in 1955, although that year the issue was clouded, a seething Richard having been suspended for the series.

"Gordie Howe is the best hockey player I have ever seen," Beliveau has said. Even Maurice Richard allows, "He was a better all-around player than I was."

Yes, certainly, but there's a kicker. A big one.

The Rocket's younger brother, former Canadien centre Henri Richard, has said, "There is no doubt that Gordie was better than Maurice. But build two rinks across from one another. Then put Gordie in one and Maurice in the other, and see which one would be filled."

Unlike the Rocket, Bobby Hull, Bobby Orr and Guy Lafleur, Howe always lacked one dimension. He couldn't lift fans out of their seats, hearts thumping, charged with expectation, merely by taking a pass and streaking down the ice. The most capable all-around player the game may ever have known was possibly deficient in only one thing — star quality. But my, oh my, he certainly could get things done. In the one-time rivalry between Detroit and Montreal, two games linger in the mind, but first a few words from Mr. Elbows himself on just how bright that rivalry burned during those halcyon years.

"Hockey's different today, isn't it? The animosity is gone. *I mean we didn't play golf with referees and linesmen.* Why, in the old days with the Red Wings, I remember once we and the Canadiens were traveling to a game in Detroit on the same train. We were starving, but their car was between ours and the diner, and there was no way we were going to walk through there. We waited until the train stopped in London [Ontario] and we walked around the Canadiens' car to eat."

Going into a game in Detroit, against the Canadiens, on October 27, 1963, Howe had 543 goals, one short of the retired Rocket's then record total of 544. The aroused Canadiens, determined not to allow Howe to score a landmark goal against them, designated Henri Richard his brother's record keeper, setting his line against Howe's again and again. But in the third period Howe, who had failed to score in three previous games, made his second shot of the night a good one. He deflected a goalmouth pass past Gump Worsley to tie the record. Howe, then thirty-five, did not score again for two weeks and, lo and behold, the Canadiens came to town once more. And again they put everything into stopping Howe. But, in the second period, *with Montreal on the power play,* Detroit's Billy McNeill sailed down the ice with the puck, Howe trailing. As they swept in on the Canadien net, Howe took the puck and flipped a fifteen-foot shot past Charlie Hodge, breaking the Rocket's record, one he was to improve on by 257 NHL goals.

Item: In 1960 there was a reporter sufficiently brash to ask Howe when he planned to retire. Blinking, as is his habit, he replied, "I don't want to retire, because you stay retired for an awfully long time."

Twenty years later, on June 4, 1980, Howe stepped up to the podium at the Hartford Hilton and reluctantly announced his retirement. "I think I have another half-year in me, but it's always nice to keep something in reserve." The one record he was terribly proud of, he added, "is the longevity record."

Thirty-two years.

And possibly, just possibly, we were unfair to him for most of those years. True, he's now an institution. Certainly, he won all the glittering prizes. And for years he was recognized wherever he went in Canada. But true veneration always eluded Howe. Even in his glory days he generated more respect, sometimes even grudging at that, than real excitement. Outside of the West, where he ruled supreme, he was generally regarded as the ultimate pro (say, like his good friend of the Detroit years, Al Kaline), but not a player possessed. Like the Rocket.

In good writing, Hemingway once ventured, only the tip of the iceberg shows. Put another way, authentic art doesn't advertise. Possibly, that was the trouble with Gordie on ice. During his vintage years you seldom noticed the flash of elbows, only the debris they left behind. He never seemed *that* fast, but somehow he got there first. He didn't wind up to shoot, like so many of today's golfers, but next time the goalie dared to peek, the puck was behind him.

With hindsight, I'm prepared to allow that Gordie may not only have been a better all-around player than the Rocket, by maybe the more complete artist as well. The problem could have been the fans, myself included, who not only wanted art to be done, but wanted to see it being done. We also required it to look hard, not just all in a day's work.

A career of such magnitude as Gordie Howe's has certain natural perimeters, obligatory tales that demand to be repeated here. The signing. The injury that all but killed him in his fourth season. The rivalry with the Rocket, already dealt with. The disenchantment with Detroit. Born again Gordie, playing in the WHA with two of his sons. The return to the NHL with the Hartford Whalers. The last ceremonial season, culminating in the great one's final goal.

History is riddled with might-have-beens. Caesar, anticipating unfavourable winds, could have remained in bed on the 15th of March. That most disgruntled of stringers, Karl Marx, might have gone from contributor to editor of the New York *Tribune.* Bobby Thomson could have struck out. Similarly, Gordie Howe might have been a New York Ranger. When he was fifteen, he was invited to the Rangers' tryout camp in Winnipeg, but they wanted to ship him to Regina, and he didn't sign because he knew nobody from Saskatoon would be playing there. The Red Wings asked him to join their team in Windsor, Ontario. "They told me there would be a carload of kids I knew, so I signed. I didn't want to be alone."

The following season, the Red Wings handed Gordie a $500 bonus and a $1,700 salary to play with their Omaha farm club. ("Twenty-two hundred dollars," Gordie says. "I earn that much per diem now.") A year later he was with the Red Wings, signed for a starting salary of $6,000. "After we signed him," coach Jack Adams said, "he left the office. Later, when I went into the hall, he was still there, looking glum. 'All right, Gordie, what's bothering you?' "

"Well you promised me a Red Wing jacket, but I don't have it yet.' "

He got the jacket, he scored a goal in his first game with the Wings, and he was soon playing three, even four-minute shifts on right wing. A fast, effortless skater with a wrist shot said to travel at 110 miles per hour. Then, in a 1950 playoff game with the Toronto Maple Leafs, Howe collided with Leaf captain Teeder Kennedy and fell unconscious to the ice. Howe was rushed to a hospital for emergency surgery. "In the hospital," Sid Abel recalled, "they opened up Gordie's skull to relieve the pressure on his brain and the blood shot to the ceiling like a geyser."

The injury left Howe with a permanent facial tic, and on his return the following season, his teammates dubbed him "Blinky," a nickname that stuck. Other injuries, over the years, have called for some 400 stitches, mostly in his face. Howe can no longer count how many times his nose has been broken. There also have been broken ribs, a broken wrist, a detached retina and operations on both knees. He retires with seven fewer teeth than he started with.

The glory years with Detroit came to an end in 1971, Howe hanging up his skates after twenty-five seasons. Once a contender, the team had gone sour. Howe's arthritic wrist meant that he was playing in constant pain. Hockey, he allowed, was no longer fun. But, alas, the position he took in the Red Wings' front office ("A pasture job," his wife Colleen said) proved frustrating, even though it was his first $100,000 job. "They paid me to sit in that office, but they didn't give me anything to do."

Then, after two years of retirement, the now forty-five-year-old Howe bounced back. In 1973 he found true happiness, realizing what he said was a life-long dream, a chance to play with two of his sons for something called the Houston Aeros of the WHA. The dream was sweetened by a $1-million contract, which called for Howe to play for one season followed by three in management. Furthermore, nineteen-year-old Marty and eighteen-year-old Mark were signed for a reputed $400,000 each for four years. A package put together by the formidable Colleen, business manager of the Howe family enterprises.

Howe led the Aeros to the WHA championship; he scored one-hundred points and was named the league's most valuable player. Mark was voted rookie of the year. A third son, Murray, later shunned hockey to enter pre-med school at the University of Michigan. Murray, now twenty, also writes:

So you eat, and you sleep.
So you walk, and you run.
So you touch, and you hear.
You lead, and you follow.
You mate with the chosen.
But do you live?

Gordie went on to play three more seasons with the Aeros and two with the Whalers, finishing his WHA career with 174 goals and 334 assists. With the demise of that league and the acceptance of the Whalers by the NHL in 1979, Howe decided to play one more year so that the father-and-sons combination could make it into the NHL record books.

It almost didn't happen, what with Marty being sent down to Springfield. But they finally did play together March 9 in Boston. And then three nights later, out there in Detroit, *his* Detroit, Gordie finally got to take a shift in the NHL on a line with his two sons, Marty moving up from his natural position on defense. "After that game Gordie could have just walked off," Colleen said. 'I've done all I ever wanted,' he told me."

I caught up with Gordie toward the end of the season, on March 22nd, when the Whalers came to the Montreal Forum for their last regular-season appearance. Before the game, Gordie Howe jokes abounded among the younger writers in the press box. Scanning the Hartford lineup, noting the presence of Bobby Hull and Dave Keon, both in their forties, one wag ventured, "If only they put them together on the ice with Howe, we could call it the Geritol Line."

"When is he going to stop embarrassing himself out there and announce his retirement?"

"If he's that bad," a Hartford writer cut in, "why do they allow him so much room out there?"

"Because nobody wants to go into the record books as the kid who crippled old Gordie."

Going into the game, Hartford's 72nd of the season, Howe had fourteen goals and twenty-three assists, and there he sat on the bench, blinking away, one of only six Whalers without a helmet. The only one on the bench old enough to remember an NHL wherein salaries were so meagre that the goys of winter had to drive beer trucks or work on road construction in the summer.

There were lots of empty seats in the Forum. It was not the usual Saturday night crowd. Many a season ticket holder had yielded his coveted place in the reds to a country cousin, a secretary or an unlucky nephew. Kids were everywhere. Howe, who had scored his 800th NHL goal a long twenty-three days earlier, jumped over the board for his shift at 1:27 of the first period, the Forum erupting in sentimental cheers. He did not come on again for another five minutes, this time joining a Hartford power play. Howe took to the ice again with four-and-a-half minutes left in the period, kicking the puck to Jordy Douglas from behind the Montreal net, earning an assist on Douglas' goal. Not the only listless forward out there, often trailing the play, pacing himself, but his passing still notably crisp, right on target each time, Howe came out six more times in the second period. On his very first shift in the third period, he threw a check a Rejean Houle, sending him flying. Hello, hello, I'm still here. But his second time out, Howe drew a tripping penalty, and the Canadiens scored on their power play. The game, a clinker, ended in a 5–5 tie.

In the locker room, microphones were thrust at a weary Gordie. He was confronted by notebooks. Somebody asked, "Do you plan to retire at the end of the season, Gordie?"

"Not that f ——— question again," Gordie replied.

So somebody else said, "No, certainly not. But could you please tell me what your plans are for next year?"

Gordie grinned, appreciative.

A little more than two weeks later, on April 8, the Whalers were back, it having been ordained that these upstarts would be fed to the Canadiens in their first NHL playoff series. This time the Canadiens, in no mood to fiddle, beat the Whalers 6–1. Howe, who didn't play until the first period was seven minutes old, took his first shift alongside his son Mark. He only appeared twice more in the first period, but in the second he came on again, filling in for the injured Blaine Stoughton on the Whalers' big line. He was, alas, ineffectual, on for two goals against and hardly touching the puck during a Hartford power play. Consequently, in the third period, he was allowed but four brief shifts. There must have been some satisfaction for him, however, in the fact that Mark Howe was easily the best Whaler on ice, scoring the goal that cost Denis Herron his shutout.

The next night, with Montreal leading 8–3 midway in the third period, the only thing the crowd was still waiting for finally happened. Gordie Howe flipped in a backhander. It was his sixty-eighth NHL playoff goal — but his first in a decade. It wasn't a pretty goal. Neither did it matter much. But it was slipped in there by a fifty-two-year-old grandfather who had scored his first NHL goal in Toronto thirty-four years earlier when Carl Yastrzemski was seven years old, pot was something you cooked the stew in and Ronald Reagan was just another actor with pretentions. (For the record, that first goal was scored against Turk Broda on October 16, 1946.) "Hartford goal by Gordie Howe," Michel Lacroix announced over the PA system. "Assist, Mark Howe." The crowd gave Gordie a standing ovation.

Later, in the Whalers' dressing room, coach Don Blackburn was asked what his team might do differently in Hartford for the third game. "Show up," he said.

Though the Whalers played their best hockey of the series, they lost in the twenty-ninth second of overtime, Yvon Lambert banging in the winning goal for Montreal. In the locker room, everybody wanted to know if this had been Gordie's last game. "I haven't made up my mind about when I'm going to retire yet," he said.

But earlier, in the press box, a Hartford reporter had assured everybody that this was a night in hockey history. April 11, 1980. Gordie Howe's last game. Whaler director of hockey operations Jack Kelley had told him. "They've got a kid they want to bring up. Gordie's holding them back. The problem is they don't know what to do with him. I mean, shit, you can't have Gordie Howe running the goddamn gift shop."

The triumphant Canadiens stayed overnight in Hartford, and I joined their poker game. Claude Mouton, Claude Ruel, the trainers, the team doctor, Floyd "Busher" Currie, Toe Blake. "Jack Adams always used him too much during the regular season," Toe said, "so he had nothing left when the playoffs came round."

"Do you think he was really a dirtier player than most?" I asked.

"Well, you saw the big man yesterday. What did he tell you?"

"He said his elbows had never put anybody in the hospital, but he was there five times."

Suddenly, everybody was laughing at me. Speak to Donnie Marshall, they said. Or John Ferguson. Still better, ask Lou Fontinato.

When Donnie Marshall was with the Rangers, he was asked what it was like to play against Howe. In reply, he lifted his shirt to reveal a foot-long angry welt across his rib cage. "Second period," he said.

One night, when Winnipeg Jet general manager John Ferguson was playing with the Canadiens, a frustrated Howe stuck the blade of his stick into his mouth and hooked his tongue for nine stitches.

But Howe's most notorious altercation was with Ranger defenceman Lou Fontinato in Madison Square Garden in 1959. Frank Udvari, who was the referee, recalled, "The puck had gone into the corner. Howe had collided with Eddie Shack behind the net and lost his balance. He was just getting to his feet when here's Fontinato at my elbow, trying to get at him.

"'I want him,' he said.

"'Leave him alone, use your head,' I said.

"'I want him.'

"'Be my guest.'"

Fontinato charged. Shedding his gloves, Howe seized Fontinato's jersey at the neck and drove his right fist into his face. "Never in my life had I heard anything like it, except maybe the sound of someone chopping wood," Udvari said. "THWACK! And all of a sudden Louie's breathing out of his cheekbone."

Howe broke Fontinato's nose, he fractured his cheekbone and knocked out several teeth. Plastic surgeons had to reconstruct his face.

The afternoon before what was to be Howe's last game, I took a taxi to his house in the suburbs of Hartford. "You can't be a pauper living out here." the driver said. "I'll bet he's got race horses and everything. There's only money out here."

Appropriately enough, the venerable Howe, hockey's very own King Arthur, lives down a secluded side road in a town called Glastonbury. Outside the large house, set on fifteen acres of land, a sign reads HOWES'S CORNER. Inside, a secretary ushered me through the office of Howe Enterprises, a burgeoning concern that holds personal-service contracts with Anheuser-Busch, Chrysler and Colonial Bank. A bespectacled, wary Howe was waiting for me in the sun-filled living room. Prominently displayed on the coffee table was an enormous volume of Ben Shahn reproductions.

"I had no idea," I said, "that you were an admirer of Ben Shahn."

"Oh, that. The book. I spoke at a dinner. They presented it to me."

After all his years in the United States, Howe remains a Canadian citizen. "I can pay taxes here and all the other good things, but I can't vote." One of nine children, he added, the family is now spread out like manure. "It would be nice to get together again without having to go to another funeral."

Sitting with Howe, our dialogue stilted, not really getting anywhere, I remembered how one of the greatest journalists of our time, A.J. Liebling, was once sent a batch of how-to-write books for review by a literary editor, and promptly bounced them back with a curt note: "The only way to write is well and how you do it is your own damn business." Without being able to put it so succinctly, Howe, possibly, felt the same way about hockey. Furthermore, over the years he had also heard all the questions before and now greeted them with a neat flick of the conversational elbow. So we didn't get far. But, for the record, Howe said that in his opinion today's hockey talent is bigger and better than ever. Wayne Gretzky reminds him of Sid Abel. "He's sneaky clever, the puck always seems to be coming back to him. Lafleur is something else. He stays on for two shifts. I don't mind that, but he doesn't even breathe heavy." Sawchuk was the best goalie he ever saw and he never knew a line to compare with Boston's Kraut Line: Milt Schmidt, Woody Dumart, Bobby Bauer. Howe is still bitter about how his years in Detroit came to an end with that meaningless front-office job. "Hell, you've been on the ice for twenty-five years, there's little else you learn. I was a pro at seventeen. Colleen used to answer my fan mail for me, I didn't have the words. Now it's better for the kids. They get their basic twelve years of school and then pick a college."

Trying to surface with a fresh question, I asked him when he planned to retire.

"I can't say just yet exactly when I'm going to retire, but I'm the one who will make that decision."

But the next morning, in the Whaler offices, Jack Kelley asked me, "Did he say that?"

"Yes."

Kelley ruminated. "When's your deadline?"

"Not until the autumn."

"He's retiring at the end of the season."

Almost two months later, on June 4, Howe made it official. "It's not easy to retire," he told reporters in Hartford. "No one teaches you how. I found that out when I tried it the first time. I'm not a quitter. But I will now quit the game of hockey."

Howe had kept everybody waiting for half an hour after the scheduled start of his 10 a.m. press conference. "As it got close to 10:30, I had the funny suspicion that he had changed his mind again," Kelley said.

But this time Howe left no doubt in anybody's mind. " My last retirement was an unhappy one, because I knew I still had some years in me. This is a happy one, because I know it's time."

This winter, then, Gordie is not going to be out there, skating. He will be the Whalers' director of player development. His No. 9 has joined Maurice Richard's No. 9 in retirement. An ice age has come to an end.

"They ought to bottle Gordie Howe's sweat," King Clancy of the Maple Leafs once said. "It would make a great liniment to rub on hockey players."

Yes. Certainly. But I remember my afternoon at Howe's Corner with a certain sadness. He knew what was coming, and before I left he insisted that I scan the awards mounted on a hall wall. The Victors Award. The American Academy of Achievement Golden Plate Award. The American Captain of Achievement Award. "I played in all eighty games this year and I got my fifteenth goal in the last game of the season. Last year I suffered from dizzy spells. My doctor wanted me to quit. But I was determined to play with my boys in the NHL. I don't think I have the temperament for coaching. I tried it a couple of times and I got so excited, watching the play, I forgot all about line changes."

But that afternoon only one thing really seemed to animate him. The large Amway flow chart that hung from a stand, dominating the living room. Gordie Howe — one of the greatest players the game has ever known, a Canadian institution at last — Blinky, the third-grade repeater who became a millionaire — today distributes health care, cosmetics, jewlery and gardening materials for Amway.

Offering me a lift back to my hotel in Hartford, Howe led into his garage. There were cartons, cartons, everywhere, ready for delivery. Cosmetics. Gardening materials. It looked like the back room of a prairie general store.

"I understand you write novels," he said.

"Yes."

"There must be a very good market for them. You see them on racks in all the supermarkets now."

"Right. Tell me, Gordie, do you deliver this stuff yourself?"

"You can earn a lot of money with Amway," he said, "working out of your own home."

Say it ain't so, Gordie.

My Career with the Leafs

I'LL EXPLAIN HOW I CAME to play hockey for the Toronto Maple Leafs. It was surprisingly easy, and other people with similar ambitions to play in the Big Leagues might be able to pick up some valuable tips. I'm a poet, you see, and one of the things we do as part of our job is an occasional public reading. I had a reading to do in Toronto, and one of the first things I did when I got there was to drop down to Maple Leaf Gardens. The day I went, the Leafs happened to be practicing.

As I sat in the stands watching the Leafs skate around the rink I got an idea. I walked down to the equipment room, and politely asked a man who turned out to be the trainer if it would be okay if I joined the practice.

"Sure thing," he told me, just like that.

I asked if I could have a uniform to wear.

"Sure," he said. "What number would you like?"

"How about number 15?" I said innocently.

The number belonged to Pat Boutette at the time, but he was injured and I knew he wouldn't be around. I felt a surge of ambition — maybe I could beat him out of the job! Minutes later I was out on the ice with the Toronto Maple Leafs.

I skated around for a while, carefully declining any involvement in the passing and shooting drills while I tried to get my floppy ankles to co-operate. Instead of co-operating they were beginning to hurt, so I drifted in the direction of the coach, Red Kelly, who was yelling instructions at the players. I leaned casually on my stick the way I'd seen Ken Dryden do on television, and looked down at my skates. I watched the drills for two or three minutes until the ache in my ankles started to fade, then edged closer to Kelly.

"Mind if I take a turn?" I asked as evenly as I could.

"Not at all," he replied. "Let's see what you can do."

Somebody pushed a puck in front of me and as I reached for it I tripped on the tip of my left skate and fell flat on my face. What to that point had almost been a dream turned abruptly into a nightmare. I lay on the ice for a second, peering at the puck as if it had tripped me, and wondered why I couldn't wake up. I thought about quitting right then and there.

I had nothing to lose, so I didn't quit. I got up, picked up my stick, and looked Red Kelly in the eye. He didn't move a muscle — didn't laugh or anything. I pushed the puck forward and skated after it in the direction of the goalie — it was Gord McRae I think — slowly gathering speed. About fifteen feet from the net I deked to my left without the customary deke to the right. The deke took McRae with it, and I cut to the right. The net was wide open and I shovelled the puck into it on my backhand.

All of this is incredibly difficult for a left-shooting skater to do. In fact, the whole manoeuvre is an impossible one, and everyone who saw it knew it, including Kelly, who was staring at me with his mouth open. For my part, I had no idea how I'd done it, except that it had been awful easy.

"Not bad," Kelly shouted. "Not bad at all."

If scoring that first goal had been easy, the rest of the practice wasn't. I'm not a great skater at the best of times, and I wasn't in shape. I seemed able to score goals almost at will, but I had difficulty with the defensive drills, particularly the ones that involved things like skating backward. I fell several times, and one time I went into the boards so hard that Kelly skated over and told me to take it easy.

As the practice ended, he asked me if I could drop by his office after I showered. I told him I'd be pleased to, and after a shower I can't remember at all, I was sitting in a stuffed red Naugahyde chair staring across a big desk at Red Kelly and Jim Gregory, the General Manager of the Leafs.

Kelly was writing something on a pad of yellow foolscap. Gregory did the talking.

"You've got some interesting moves out there," he said. "I caught the whole thing from up in the box. Where'd you learn your hockey?"

I decided to tell them the truth.

"Well," I replied, "I really haven't played organized hockey since I was about twelve. I watch Hockey Night in Canada, of course, and I guess I've learned a lot from that."

"Where do you come from?" he asked.

"That's kind of a hard question," I replied, trying to figure out what the truth was. "I'm from the West Coast. Well, not the coast, actually. I'm from up north."

"What brings you to Toronto?"

"I'm a poet," I said, "here on business, doing a public reading."

"No kidding," he said, looking reasonably satisfied with my answer.

"I guess you know Rota. He's from up there."

I was stumped. I didn't know any writer from up north named Rota. Kelly saw my confusion.

"New kid," he said. "Plays for Chicago."

"I've heard of him," I shrugged. "But I never played with him. He's a bit younger than I am."

There was a silence, as if the two of them were trying to decide which of them should speak. Finally, Gregory stood up and cleared his throat.

"How would you like to play hockey for the Toronto Maple Leafs?" he said.

"I'd really like that," I said quickly. "I'd prefer to play just the home games, though. I hate travelling."

Gregory seemed puzzled by my request, but he agreed to it, probably because I didn't ask for anything else.

"We play Boston on Monday night," he said. "We'll see you at the rink at 6 p.m." He paused. "Make that 5:30, and you can get in an extra half hour of skating."

I stood up. "I can probably use it," I smiled.

Kelly grunted, and then grinned, and I followed him out of the office and down the long concrete corridors of Maple Leaf Gardens to the players' entrance. He shook my hand.

"Good to have you with us," he said, with a lot of sincerity.

"It's good to be part of an organization that takes chances," I said, with even more sincerity. "Toronto treats its visitors well."

Kelly smiled and waved goodbye as I stepped through the open door into a fine early winter blizzard.

The next thing I knew I was sitting in the Leafs' dressing room beside George Ferguson, suiting up for the game. Kelly came in and announced the player assignments.

"Fawcett here is going to be playing home games for us," he shouted, pointing vaguely in my direction. "He'll play on the wing with Ferguson, and Hammerstrom for a while, and we'll see how things go. Any questions?''

To my surprise, a fair number of the players knew who I was, and it turned out that some of them had even read my work. Out of the corner of my eye I saw the two Swedes, Hammerstrom and Salming, exchange glances. Maybe they thought having a poet on the team might take some of the heat off them. They were still relatively new in the league, and they were taking a lot of physical and verbal abuse from the rednecks and goons who were worried about foreigners changing the game and taking their jobs. The rap on the Swedes was that they were chicken, particularly Hammerstrom, who the papers were saying was allergic to the boards. Personally, I thought his skating more than made up for those faults.

I wondered a little at Kelly putting me on a line with him, but decided that he was trying to compensate for my poor skating. Every team in the league would stick their goons on our line, that was certain. Kelly probably figured Hammerstrom would skate his way out of trouble, and I would talk my way out.

We'd see soon enough. It was nice to be able to play with Ferguson, who I thought was one of the smarter centres to come into the league in a while. I planned to do what any rookie should — keep my head up and my mouth shut. It would be a new way of working, that was for sure.

The first period of that game was nothing to remember. My check, predictably, was Wayne Cashman, probably the dirtiest player in the league. I went up and down my wing without incident, partly because Cashman wasn't much of a skater either. He cut me with his stick several times, but I didn't bleed much, and I ignored it when he got me with the butt end just as the period ended. I waited until I could breathe again and skated off to the dressing room with the rest of the team.

Early in the second period Lanny McDonald and Don Marcotte were sent off for trying to remove one another's vital organs, and Kelly sent me out with Hammerstrom on a five-on-five. The Bruins sent out Greg Sheppard and Cashman. The face-off was in our end, and Hammerstrom won it, got the puck back to Ian Turnbull, and he banked it around on the boards to where I was waiting. I circled once, almost lost my balance, and headed up the ice. As I crossed the red line, I saw Cashman skating toward me with a gleam in his eye. I kept going toward Orr at the blueline, did the deke to my left as if to move between Orr and the boards, and then cut sharply right. Orr went for the first deke and so did Cashman, who by this time was right behind me prodding at my liver with his stick. When I deked to the right, Cashman ran into Orr and both of them went heavily to the ice. I had a two on one with Hammerstrom, and I slid the puck over to him. He drew Al Simms over, passed back, and I had only Cheevers to beat. I did it again; deked left, cut right, and plunked the puck over the bewildered netminder into the upper right corner of the net.

I stuck my stick up in the air the way I'd seen it done on television, and was trying to honk my leg when I ran into Hammerstrom and we both fell down. Turnbull came over to congratulate me and Salming skated over to dig the puck out of the net. He handed it to me, grinned, and said something in Swedish I didn't understand. Hammerstrom grinned at me the same way and pointed to Cashman, who was skating in small circles at centre ice with his head down.

It was a tight-checking game, and the score was still 1–0 halfway through the third period. That was as far as I got that night. I skated into the corner for a Ferguson pass, Cashman went in behind me, and only Cashman came out.

Eventually I came *to*, but that was well after the game was over. The Leafs had won it 2–0. Cashman got a penalty for hammering me, and Sittler scored on the ensuing power play. That's what they told me, anyway.

I made it to the practice the next afternoon, none the worse for having spent the night in the hospital to make sure I didn't have concussion. I didn't get much sleep because the interns kept coming in every half hour to see if I was going to go into a coma.

"Are you there?" they asked, and lifted my eyelids with one finger to flash their penlights at my pupils. About 4 a.m. a very young intern came in. He was a hockey fan.

"You're the new guy with the Leafs, eh?" he asked.

"Yeah," I croaked.

"Nice move you made on that goal you scored," he said. "Where'd you learn that?"

"Watching television," I answered, telling the truth.

"I hear you write poetry too," he said.

My head hurt, so I just grimaced.

"Pretty strange," he said. "Watch out for Cashman."

He checked my eyes so carefully I thought he was looking for poems, but he said I'd probably be able to leave in the morning.

At the practice the next day, Ferguson told me to watch out for Cashman too.

"You were lucky," he said. "Cashman spent two periods setting you up. We all knew it was coming, but I guess you had to pass the test like anyone else."

"Some test," I complained. "All I can remember about it is my bell ringing when it was over."

I played the three games in that home stand, scoring again in the last one against the Rangers, and setting up a goal by Ferguson. The team was away for the next three games, and then back for three more. While they were away I worked on my skating, circling the rink again and again until my ankles were too sore for me to move anymore. I tried skating without a stick, but found, as I had when I was a kid, that skating that way was beyond me. I needed the stick for balance and without it I could barely stand.

When the team came back, I confided to Ferguson that I couldn't skate without a stick.

"You're kidding," he said.

"No," I told him, "It's true. I only got skates every three years, and the first year they were too big and the third year they were too small."

Ferguson had a good eye for details. "What about the second year?" he asked.

"I had weak ankles back then."

"You still have weak ankles," he said.

"I use the stick for balance," I said, as we went on circling the rink.

Ferguson was skating backward to tease me. "Skating is easy," he laughed. "For me it's like breathing."

"I feel that way about some other things," I replied, "but not about skating."

"You don't look as if breathing is very easy right now," he pointed out.

While we unlaced our skates after practice, he asked me cautiously what it was like to be a writer.

"It's my way of breathing," I said.

"How'd you get into it?" he asked with genuine curiosity.

"I guess I was about thirteen," I said. "Right after I quit playing minor league hockey."

Ferguson and I became friends. He taught me a lot of the basics of pro hockey and I gave him books to read in return. I was interested in Rilke and an American poet named Jack Spicer at the time, and he pored through everything I lent him. I always had books in my equipment bag, and he dug through it regularly to see what was there. He asked me if Canadian writers were as good as Americans.

"The old guys are pretty tame," I said, "but there's a few writers under forty who might turn out to be interesting."

"Jeez," he said, "how long does it take to get good at it?"

"Usually about fifteen years of hard work," I said. "A few get good earlier than that because they have special attentions or come from environments that encourage them," I went on. "But that's rare. Most of us have to learn pretty well everything about the culture twice, and that takes time. After that, there's the job of keeping on top of it as it changes. A lot of writers get one good review of their work and they have to please their public, or worse, they decide that they're geniuses, and don't have to listen to anything. So they imitate themselves until they lose their ability to learn. After that they just get drunk, or academic, or spend all their time trying to please the reviewers and filling out grant applications."

He wanted to know about the grants, so I explained to him the economics of trying to be a serious artist in a country that wants to have serious art without having to put up with the inconvenience and cost of paying the artists.

He looked skeptical. "Except for that, hockey is pretty much the same," he said after a moment's thought. "Only hockey players get screwed up more easily and a lot faster."

"That's because there's more people paying attention," I said, "and there's more money involved."

That home stand was a good one. I scored my third goal, drew assists on one of Ferguson's, and another on the power play, passing from behind the net to Sittler in the slot. Only four goals had been scored while I was on the ice, and after seven games I was plus five. Then the Leafs were off again on a five-game road trip and I went back to my solitary skating, circling the ice over and over again until slowly, very slowly, my skating began to improve. I skated clockwise first, and then counter-clockwise. Going counter-clockwise was easier, maybe because on the corners my stick was closer to the ice. But I couldn't quite master skating backward, and stopping remained a problem unless I was close to the boards. But I developed reasonable speed skating straight ahead, and during games I combined my lack of stopping skill with my speed to provide the team with some excellent bodychecking.

Ferguson and I went out on the town the night after the team flew in from Los Angeles. He showed me the important sights of Toronto, like Rochdale and Don Mills, and later that night we walked down to Lake Ontario and threw rocks at all the empty cartons floating in the water. There had been a thaw, and it was like spring — dirty snow was piled up everywhere, abandoned cars were being towed off the street, and the curious sensation I'd had of being in Middle Earth began to dissipate. There were lovers everywhere, discussing Parliament, and kissing and fist-fighting as the fog rolled in from the lake to meld with the darkness coming up from the East.

We played our only other home date of the season with the Bruins several weeks later. As the game approached, I got a lot of good-natured ribbing from the guys about what to do with Cashman.

"Check him into the boards with a powerful metaphor," advised Sittler.

"And then slash him with an internal rhyme," someone else chimed in.

I laughed at the gags, but deeper down I was worried. The press had picked it up and were amusing themselves, mostly at my expense. Allen Abel in *The Globe & Mail* wrote something about it being a test of whether the stick is mightier than the pen, and in an interview Cashman noised it around that he not only disliked my style, he detested poetry. Anybody who wrote poetry, he said, had to have something wrong with their hormones. That wasn't all he said, either. He told the interviewer he was going to show the fans that there was something fishy about me, promising to make fillets out of me *and* my poetry.

As I skated out for the pre-game warm-up, Cashman gave me the evil eye, so I gave the fans a demonstration of how fast I could skate through the centre-ice zone. Kelly, out of kindness I guess, kept our line away from Cashman's as the game began, but on the second shift, I saw the Bruin right-winger head for the bench right after the face-off, and Cashman came over the boards. Somebody froze the puck, and as we lined up for the face-off deep in Bruin territory, Cashman skated up to the circle, and around me once with his stick about a quarter of an inch from my nose.

"I hope you got a nice burial poem written for yourself," he sneered. "You skinned my behind and I'm gonna carve yours off and throw it to the crowd."

I looked him right in the eye and mustered up all my powers of language.

"Suck eggs," I said.

On the face-off Ferguson drew the puck back to Salming and I skated to the corner to wait for a pass. Cashman ignored the puck and followed me. I ducked an elbow. It missed me, but the ref didn't miss it, because I slid down the boards as if I'd been pole-axed. Cashman got whistled for an elbowing penalty, and then got a misconduct penalty when he tried to chase me into the stands. I skated away from him, and three of my teammates stayed between us to make sure I stayed alive. Kelly kept me on for the power play and I banged Sittler's rebound past Gilles Gilbert to make it 1–0.

When I got to the bench, Kelly told me Howie Meeker wanted to interview me after the first period. It was Saturday, and the game was being televised nationally.

I'd forgotten it was Hockey Night in Canada. You get like that in the pro's — you forget everything that makes the world tick for real people. You also pay a price. The price I was going to have to pay for my forgetfulness was an awful one. I hadn't brought any poems in my equipment bag. I was being handed the largest audience any poet in this country ever dreamed of and I wouldn't have a thing to read.

A few minutes later I was sitting in front of several television cameras with the customary towel over my shoulder, watching Howie Meeker introduce me to the nation and thinking that the dream was going to turn into a nightmare if I couldn't think of something quickly. My mind was a blank.

"We've got Toronto left-winger Brian Fawcett here in the Hockey Night in Canada studios at Maple Leaf Gardens," Meeker announced in a voice that sounded more nasal in real life than on television.

He was hunched toward the cameras and I noticed he sat closer to them than I did. I hadn't seen a brush cut for years or, for that matter, as much make-up as he had on his face, and I was sorting through all that novelty without listening to what he was saying. Luckily, he was babbling as inanely as usual at the camera and ignoring me completely:

"...nice to see a young player come up to the NHL with a good grasp of hockey fundamentals and play sound, heads-up positional hockey the way you've been doing. Gee whiz, but I just get thrilled when I see a young kid with his mind on the game skate away from a player like Wayne Cashman. And it pays off, don't you see? It must have been less than a minute before you scored that beautiful goal like you were born with a stick in your hand and skates on your feet."

He hadn't actually asked me a question, but he seemed to have finished.

"Actually, Howie," I said, too nervous to do anything but tell the truth, "I haven't played much hockey since I was twelve or thirteen years old, and I'm thirty, so I'm not much of a kid any more. I've been mainly concerned with language, and more specifically with disjunction in poetry, for the last few years. You might say I've been learning the tools of an extremely complex trade."

Meeker appeared not to have understood. Maybe he thought I was speaking French. He ignored everything I said, and went off an another rant.

"Well, Brian, how do you like being with a team like the Leafs, eh, with their tradition of ruggedness and hard work?"

"Well, Howie," I said, still not sure if he realized that I understood English, and pretty sure he didn't know I was a poet, "I find the ruggedness something of a problem. Northrop Frye and Margaret Atwood created a problem a few years ago by writing some books about the importance of Nature and the frontier, and a lot of similarly empty glamour nonsense about rugged Canadian pioneers, and as a result a lot of the writers in this country now go around wearing logging boots and punching people for no reason. I used to do it myself, actually."

Meeker was staring at me, his jaw somewhere down around his navel. I took this as a signal to continue.

"I mean, violence may be natural, but Nature isn't a very good model for behaviour. It's really been overestimated."

I knew I was gesticulating too much, and starting to yap. I'd forgotten about the cameras — it was Howie Meeker I wanted to convince. I couldn't stop.

"Art is really about civilization," I said, "not about Nature. All

Nature does is overproduce, then waste most of it, and then resort to violence when the garbage starts to stink. When human beings follow Nature, you get guys like Hitler."

I was really flying, so I went to Meeker's question about hard work next.

"Hard work, like you say, is really important, Howie. The more I know about this game, the more I begin to realize that the real secret is hard work. I guess that goes for hockey as well."

Meeker, for some reason, seemed to have lost his voice, so I went right on.

"If you'd given me a little more notice, I could have brought some work here to read, but I guess these interviews are a bit too short to give the folks at home any real idea of what's going on, let alone a sense of the breadth and skill and variety of good writing going on in this country today."

Meeker stuttered back to life.

"Ah, ahhh. . . . Yes, well. . . . Well, Brian, I wish you and the Leafs the best of luck in the upcoming second period," he said, regaining a measure of control that didn't show in his face.

"Back to you, Dave Hodge!" he said hoarsely.

I smiled politely at the camera until fade-out. I'd seen a few guys start to pick their noses when they thought they were off-camera, and I wanted people to remember what I'd said.

Meeker turned on me. "What was that all about, you crazy sonofabitch?"

I began to explain, but he walked out of the studio without listening to my answer.

The dressing room was oddly silent when I returned. I sat down next to Ferguson and pulled the towel from around my neck. He was sitting with his head between his knees, as if he were air-sick.

"Didn't you know about Meeker?" he asked incredulously.

"Know what?" I said, stuffing the towel into my equipment bag as a souvenir. "He seemed kind of ticked off when I talked about writing, but then he did ask those dumb questions, and he didn't stop me from answering them the way I wanted to."

"Geez, man, that's the unwritten law of hockey," Ferguson said. "You're supposed to pretend you're really dumb."

It was my turn to be incredulous.

"Darryl thinks there's some kind of agreement between the owners about it," he said. "When you get out of Junior Hockey, you're given a sheet of things you can say to the press. You talk dumb, talk about teamwork, and all that crap."

My head was reeling. When I was a kid I believed that the world was full of secret rules and conspiracies, but this was real life — the Big Leagues. I couldn't believe what I was hearing.

"I mean, a few years ago," he continued, "when Kenny Dryden started getting interviewed, he used all kinds of literate words like 'tempo' and so on, pronounced all the words properly, and there was a terrific uproar. But he was in law school and they had to accept it. I dunno. They may get him yet — force him to retire."

Ferguson shrugged, and a note of hopelessness entered his voice. "Rumour is," he said, "that this whole business about us being stupid and inarticulate is an explicit policy of the Feds — right from the top."

I looked around me to see if he was kidding. A couple of guys just nodded and looked the other way, but most of them were glaring at me. Kelly looked really angry.

"Aw, come on, you guys," I said to no one in particular. "Why put up with this? I've seen what's really true. Look at the books lying around the dressing room."

Several players slipped large hardbound books into their equipment bags. Sittler, everyone knew, was a big Henry James fan — said it helped his passing game. And Tiger Williams had come up from Junior already heavily into Artaud. The league had its share of jerks, it was true, but unless you noised it around, you were left alone if you had intellectual interests. I guessed they were mad at me because they thought I might have let the cat out of the bag. Hockey, Kelly told me later, was in enough trouble.

There was a TV set in the dressing room, and we watched as Meeker came on the screen to do the highlights of the period. My goal wasn't one of them. A few of the guys exchanged significant looks, but everybody remained seated, as if they were watching something very sad.

When a commercial came on, I asked Ferguson who'd died.

"You did, dummy," he said.

"Aw, come on," I said. "Why? Is it that bad? All I did was to get Howie Meeker mad at me."

"It's a lot worse than you think. You'll be blacked out," he said, grimly. "No radio perks, no television interviews, and as little newspaper coverage as they can give you. What you *will* see will all be bad."

"That's okay," I said, philosophically. "I'm pretty used to that."

I scored the winning goal in the third period by going around the defence in the usual way, and I didn't even get third star. I went up and down my wing against Cashman, took his checks, many of which were flagrantly vicious and should have drawn penalties, and I threw a couple of my own in his direction. Cashman was given third star, actually, and Meeker said he was the one Bruin on the ice who had dominated his opponent.

Ferguson and I had a few beers after the game. I invited the rest of the guys, but nobody seemed interested.

"You're really a goof," Ferguson said cheerfully, "Do you know that?"

"How was I supposed to know?" I said, irritably. It seemed like everybody knew the rules but me.

"Look," I said, "I didn't go through the system like you guys did. For me it was all watching the tube, and thinking about it. How was I supposed to know — I mean, I've never believed much of what I've seen on television, but I did think Hockey Night in Canada at least was for real."

Ferguson grunted. "Rules are rules," he said. "Nobody but you believes they're supposed to be just."

"I'd settle for knowing what they are," I said bitterly.

"Would you really?"

"I'm not sure," I admitted. "I guess I really want to know who the big shots are who make them."

I didn't find out who the big shots were, that night or on any of the ensuing nights that season. I played my hockey as well as I could, and I played it in more or less the kind of obscurity I had been warned to expect. I scored nine goals and built twelve assists in twenty-seven games, and I was invited back for training camp the following season even though I played increasingly less often toward the close of the season.

As I was packing up to go home, the two Swedes came over and mentioned how much they'd enjoyed my presence during the home games, and asked if I'd be able to visit them in Sweden during the summer.

"I've got a lot of writing to catch up on," I told them. "My season's really just starting now."

Salming grinned that same grin I'd seen in my first game.

"I understand this," he said. "No fun to go to Sweden if you're interested in the Pros in English language."

"Something close to that," I admitted.

He and Hammerstrom left the dressing room laughing. They sure weren't like the Scandinavians I knew from watching Ingmar Bergman movies. I wandered over to where Ferguson was packing his equipment, and said goodbye. His bag was full of books, and he was having a hard time getting them all in. Finally, he had to give up, and he left with a pile of them under one arm. He turned at the door.

"I'm going to try to write some stuff myself this summer," he said. "Mind if I send you some of it?"

"Do," I replied. "You've got my address?"

"Sure have," he smiled, "Well, see you. Stay in shape."

"You too," I said. But I was talking to his shadow. He'd disappeared.

That summer passed in a flash, and by mid-September I was back skating and shooting again with the Leafs. The season started, and by December I had four goals and as many assists and, I thought, I was doing okay.

But the team wasn't doing well at all. We were fourth in our division, and Ballard could be heard snorting and snuffling all the way to Buffalo.

Then, before a practice right after a road trip that had gone badly, King Clancy walked into the dressing room, announced that Kelly had been fired, and that John McLellan was the new coach. Two days later Ferguson was traded to Pittsburgh. The day after that, McLellan called me into his office.

"Brian," he said, "I talked things over with Jim, and we, uhh...."

He seemed to be stumbling for the right words.

"We don't think your heart is really in this game. You're not skating...."

"I can't skate," I cut in, but he ignored that and went on.

"We want you to retire."

"I'm practically a rookie!" I sputtered.

"You're thirty-one," he said, "and you're not going to get any better. Meeker is still after your behind, and you're a target for every goon in the league. Both Jim and I spent some time over the summer reading your work. You're a better poet than a hockey player. You've got to go for that."

I fussed and fumed, but I ended up agreeing with him. I had two, maybe three years of good hockey in me. With poetry I had maybe forty years, and I would only get better. I'd miss the crowds and the attentiveness of the critics, even though they'd done a good job of ignoring me. But I wouldn't miss Toronto and its bars, and I wouldn't miss the poetics, which, try as I did to ignore them, are as venal and profit-oriented at Maple Leaf Gardens as they are in the English departments of the nation's universities. If more poets were to play pro hockey instead of pretending flowers or vacant lots are really interesting things might get better. But I wasn't going to hold my breath.

"You're right," I told McLellan. "I'll retire right now."

And I did. I walked out the way I had come in, gave back the blue on white and the number 15, and stepped out into the dull Toronto streets as if it were the next morning and not the next year I'd awakened to.

Three weeks later I got a letter from Ferguson, postmarked Atlanta. In it was this poem:

It's cold in Pittsburgh, colder still
in Philly. The north wind blows all night
from Canada, and these raucous crowds
that hoot and holler for our blood, Hey!
They're the coldest thing of all.
Skate and shoot, the coaches tell us
Skate and shoot. But masked men block the goals
and I am checked at every turn.

Each year more miles to go
More senseless contests of the will.
My heart is like the puck; often frozen
too often out of play, too often

stolen by the strangers
in the crowd.

RICK SALUTIN

Preface to Les Canadiens

IT WAS GUY SPRUNG who suggested doing a play about the Montreal Canadiens. When I heard about it, it didn't occur to me that I might be the writer. I was a life-long Maple Leafs fan. You need an emotional investment to write well about something, and I didn't even *hate* the Canadiens. In the aftermath, I did become a Canadiens fan, but long before, I'd found a way around the problem: make a play not just about the Canadiens, but about Quebec. It was well known that the Canadiens were "more than just a team" — were the virtual embodiment of Quebec — and Quebec was a topic I felt strongly about.

Yet, regardless of the outcome, I was delighted. Delighted to be the Canadian playwright someone would go to for a play not about love, or history, or the meaning of life — but about hockey.

Hockey is probably our only universal cultural symbol. It is universal not because every Canadian has played the game — everyone hasn't. But even those who haven't played hockey (most women, for example) nevertheless relate to the game. They know what it is, connect it to some context, and have some *feelings* about it. The point is not whether hockey is the world's best, fastest or most barbaric game; nor whether we are the best in the world at playing it. The point is — as Margaret Atwood has said in a similar context about Canadian literature — it is *ours*.

Some aspects of our involvement with hockey may be questionable: the hysterical identification with Canadian teams in international competition, for example. What does it show — that a country loses control over a hockey team? I would say it shows that we have so little we feel is clearly ours that we develop a — to say the least — very intense relationship with whatever is unequivocally Canadian.

Yet this was to be a play about hockey not in Canada, but in Quebec.

In English-speaking Canada, hockey sometimes seem to be the sole assurance that we *have* a culture. That is something never in question in Quebec. Quebec may be ambivalent about its culture and its identity.

It may be stiff-necked and proud or, at times, self-hating. But it knows it is. Its problem in not *whether* it is, but how it feels about *what* it is. Accordingly, hockey as a cultural fact in Quebec differs from what it means to *nous autres*.

The point was put eloquently on the banks of the Bow River in Alberta by Red Fisher, sports editor of *The Montreal Star* and visiting lecturer at the Glen Sather Hockey School of Banff.

"What you have to understand," said Red, "is that ever since the Plains of Abraham the French people have been number two, *but on the ice they're number one.*"

He went back to *the* crucial event in the history of the French-speaking people of Canada: the conquest of their land by the British Empire over two hundred years ago. Not that they were a free people before then; they were a colony of France. But that was, as it were, *en famille*; it did not have the character of a conquest and subjugation by a foreign power. Since Wolfe's victory, though, that sense of being a conquered people ruled by a foreign power has remained in Quebec.

This may seem strange to many people outside Quebec (and to some within). Yet, in spite of elections, the trappings of modern democracy, etc., that sense of a continuing conquest has not left Quebec. It has been sustained by the experience of real and/or felt oppressions — economic, cultural and political. In 1970, with the proclamation of the War Measures Act and the dispatch of the Canadian Army into Quebec, kids in the streets said to each other, *"Regardez les soldats d'Ottawa."* They felt they'd been (re-)invaded. A popular show in support of the prisoners held without rights under the Act cast a glance over the entire Quebec past and introduced each scene with the phrase, *"Québec, territoire occupé,"* and then the date, up to the present. In this kind of thinking, the actual rule of the British was simply replaced or joined by that of English-speaking Canada (Ottawa) under Confederation, and in recent years America too has joined the "forces of occupation".

How do people deal with the sense of being perpetually conquered and "occupied"? How do they deal with the humiliation, frustration, anger and defeat? One way taken in Quebec was proclaimed by the Church. Worldly, political power was unimportant to the people of Quebec since they were a uniquely "spiritual" race. Their "vocation" was not to rule, even themselves, but to cultivate religious and intellectual activities. All this was excellent from the viewpoint of the British, or whoever was in charge in Quebec, and it reflects an accommodation reached between the Church hierarchy and those ruling authorities.

Another route was to refuse to accept subjugation, to fight back. This has happened throughout the history of Quebec. In fact, the entire history of French-English relations since the conquest can be seen as an interrupted history of resistance: the revolutionary movement of 1837–38; the Riel rebellions and the support they received in Quebec; the anti-conscription movements of World War I and II; and a host of nationalist and *indépendantiste* political movements. A continuing resistance but, at the same time, never a victory. They fight but they do not win.

Here is where Red Fisher's insight comes in. If you fight but don't win the real battle against the real rulers, then you may try to win elsewhere, in another form. It is not the same, but at least for the moment you experience victory over your opponents. Enter *les Canadiens.*

Years ago, at a bar in Quebec City, I watched a hockey game on television and marveled at the frenzied involvements of the patrons. I put to my drinking partner the same question I was later to ask Red Fisher, "How come?" She said, "The Canadiens — they're *us.* Every winter they go south and in the spring they come home conquerors!"

Winners. No team in the history of professional sports, including the New York Yankees, has such a record of winning as do the Montreal Canadiens. The pennants connoting years of Stanley Cup victories are strung like an enormous tapestry the length of the Montreal Forum.

That tradition reached its height with the great Canadien teams of the fifties that won five consecutive Stanley Cups. They were led by Maurice "Rocket" Richard, the embodiment of that spirit in a way no one will ever be again.

His career was contemporaneous with that of Quebec Premier Maurice Duplessis, under whose rule all forces of political opposition in Quebec were ruthlessly suppressed. Just before the start of the Duplessis era, the spirit of Quebec resistance expressed itself in the great anti-conscription campaign of the Second World War. Almost immediately after Duplessis's death began the incredible series of street demonstrations and mass protest movements that extended right through the sixties and into the seventies. Yet, in the entire intermediary period, there was only one event of mass protest: the night in March 1955 when Canadien fans abandoned the Forum and took to the streets to protest the suspension of Maurice Richard by that walking symbol of Anglo-Canadian authority, NHL president Clarence Campbell. As Tim Burke of the Montreal *Gazette* says, "It was the opening shot of the Quiet Revolution."

The Campbell-Richard riot represents the height of the identification of the cause of Quebec with *le club de hockey Canadien*. Yet it also represents a sort of going beyond the symbol. By spilling out of the Forum and into the streets, the fans seemed to say, "This hockey arena will no longer contain the feelings we have been expressing within it." Such a change is explored in Act Two of *Les Canadiens*.

Today, even though things have changed in Quebec, the past remains sufficiently present that *winning* is still what the Canadiens are about:

> I went into the Canadiens' dressing room one Saturday night in 1976 after a game with Boston. The Canadiens had lost. It was the most depressed atmosphere I have ever encountered. I felt like one of those writers who have described being among the first Allied soldiers into a concentration camp. And yet it was the *only game in forty* that the Canadiens lost at home all season.

> Ken Dryden: "If the Canadiens lost a lot at home, I don't know what the fans would do. It's unthinkable."

> Dickie Moore: "When you don't win the Cup, it's an awfully long summer in Montreal. Most of the players live here and *everyone* asks, 'What happened?'"

> Many teams give players bonuses for a high team finish in the standings. I've been told players on relatively good teams start receiving increments for every point their team gets over 65. The Canadiens' bonuses don't *start* until 115 points.

But Red Fisher put it best.

The Centaur Theatre of Montreal commissioned *Les Canadiens* for their 1976–77 season. Maurice Podbrey, Artistic Director of the Centaur, suggested that Canadiens' goaltender Ken Dryden, a sometime subscriber and frequent audience member at the theatre, might be willing to help with the preparation of the play. This turned out to be an enormous understatement. Ken became a very real collaborator at all stages of development of the script.

I spoke regularly with Ken about what I was learning, what opinions I was forming, what notions for the play were taking shape. Of the many things I came upon, I'd like to mention two.

First, for those who play it, hockey is still a game. I had felt, until this point, that professional hockey must have become something like a business for those on the ice. There were such large sums involved, so many games in a season; they were, after all, professionals; surely they simply did their jobs more or less consistently, regardless of other, especially emotional, factors. I was wrong. Players, at least on the Canadiens, feel good when they win, depressed when they lose — in spite of how many dollars they are making per game. It is much more of a game than a business, and much closer to the games we used to play on natural ice after school than to the kind of cool corporate experience I'd anticipated.

The other matter concerns the Rocket, Maurice Richard. He is the only figure who appears in the play whom I probably could have talked to but did not. I intended to meet him, yet as my research went along, a strange thing began to happen. Everyone else talked about the Rocket, and in a unique (though not uniform) way. "It's gotta be Rocket," said Dickie Moore, when I asked him what he would write the play about. "Maurice Richard might be difficult," cautioned someone else. "Ach, Maurice," shrugged his brother, Henri Richard.

I had thought Rocket would be one of the line of Canadien greats in the play: Vezina, Lalonde, Morenz, Richard, Beliveau, Lafleur. But it became clear that the Rocket was *sui generis*. He *was* the Canadiens, in some unique way, and the play had to reflect that. I felt that speaking with him would be superfluous. I knew clearly, through others, what he represented for the team and the people of Quebec, and for the purposes of the play that was sufficient.

I returned to Toronto and started to write.

Then came November 15, 1976. I was well along, somewhere in Act Two, and I'm not sure what I was planning to do with the rest of the play, had the election victory of the Parti Québécois not occurred.

The following night I spoke on the phone with Ken. He said the game at the Forum the previous night, election night, had been a very strange experience. He went on to describe it in the acute manner to which I'd become accustomed. I took notes furiously.

The crowd, he said, was dead. Deader than he'd ever seen at the Forum. They seem uninterested in the game. So, for that matter, did most of the Canadiens. In fact, the only people in the place who seemed concerned with hockey that night were the hapless St. Louis Blues, who, in spite of the inattention of the Canadiens, still lost the game, 4–2.

But each time an election result flashed across the message board, everything changed. The crowd awoke. Their excitement mounted with each result, from the early PQ lead in Montreal, to the final declaration that there was a *"nouveau gouvernement"* in Quebec. The surer the success of the PQ, the more the crowd's ecstasy grew — and the less they cared about the game taking place before them.

As for the players, they had a hard time keeping one eye on the puck and the other on the latest election standings. Moreover, their reaction was opposite to that of the fans. The team — French and English — were known to be overwhelmingly federalist. Former captain Henri Richard had even written a newspaper editorial several days earlier urging people to vote Liberal. The impending victory of the independence party sent them down as much as it lifted the fans up, and yet the Canadiens had for so long been the embodiment of that very nationalism now swamping the polls. Even stranger, in the odd emotional mix that was the Forum that night, was the fact that the team was being *ignored,* by their *fans,* in the middle of a *game*, because of an *election*. One thing hockey players in Montreal are not used to is low visibility. They reacted with surprise, dismay, anger, gallows humour ("Take Dryden out and put in Laroque." "Got your passport for the game in Toronto?" "Call me Jean-Pierre Mahovlich."); above all, it was, as Ken said, very *confusing* for the young avatars on the ice.

My first thought was: there goes the play. That game meant the cancellation of all I had been building (à la Red Fisher) as the symbolism of *les Canadiens.* But reflection proved that hasty. For the game of November 15 could be taken as a very natural culmination, fulfilment, transformation and perhaps new beginning for that symbolism.

Since the days of the Rocket, Quebec had been changing. Starting with the Quiet Revolution of the early sixties, Quebeckers began to express their sense of national pride and desire for self-assertion in ever more direct ways. It was summed up in the slogan, *"Maîtres chez nous"* — masters in our own house. Movements arose demanding greater opportunity for Francophones in the economy, and for French language rights. The trade union movements became far more self-confident and, at the same time, both more radical and more nationalistic. Provincial government activity expanded. Francophone cultural activity — novels, theatre, movies, television, music — exploded. And political parties dedicated to the independence of Quebec appeared.

As for the Canadiens, their meaning was changing as the society changed. In the late sixties, Robert Charlebois wore a Canadiens sweater when he performed, but he was a rock singer, not a hockey player. And the more Quebec expressed its national feelings in these *many* ways, the less it had to channel so much of its feeling through its hockey team. This whole process — the repoliticization of a society — culminated on November 15.

It was as though, on that night in the Forum, the people of Quebec finally transferred their need of victory from the shoulders of the hockey team onto their own backs. The Canadiens no longer bore the weight of national yearning; they had become, primarily, "another hockey team". A good team, perhaps the best, and one their fans would never cease to adore, but in essence a hockey team and no longer an "army on ice".

This is not to say that the Canadiens teams of the past *considered* themselves standard bearers. It is their fans and their society who assigned them the symbolic role. They considered themselves to be hockey players, and that was all. Nothing would be more implausible than a conscious symbol carrying a puck up the ice. This is especially true of the Rocket, who had always maintained he was only playing hockey in spite of many interpretations, recent and ancient, to the contrary. When he attended the opening of *Les Canadiens* in Toronto, he commented that he preferred Act One to Act Two because he "didn't like politics in a play about hockey".

The whole Act Two became The Day of the Game — that very game played at the end of election day. This gave the play an extraordinary timeliness when it was first performed. Within three months of the most dramatic political event in the history of modern Quebec (and perhaps Canada as well) we had a full-length play onstage which incorporated the event as a central structural element. I doubt I will ever again be as timely with a work.

It also gave the play a structure. It would open on the Plains of Abraham with the battlefield turning into a hockey arena, and it would end on November 15, 1976, when a hockey rink was transformed into the site of a great political victory, a sort of conquest of Quebec in reverse.

Act One would be myth: the myth of *les Canadiens,* standard-bearers of the Quebec spirit; and Act Two would be the demythologization of *les Canadiens,* their replacement by the reality of "just a hockey team".

Yet it is neither sad nor tragic because the loss (of the myth) is a gain. Heroic myths of the "Canadiens" ilk serve a purpose because they keep alive the spirit of a people in dark times. But in the end they are poor solutions to real problems. If the problem is political, then the solution must be political, not symbolic. Nor have people really "lost" the Canadiens. On the contrary, they are now free to be what they actually are: not national saviours, but a great team and beloved institution.

Brecht said, "Unhappy the land that has no heroes." This could well stand as the motto for Act One. But then he added, "No. Unhappy the land that *needs* heroes." This could be the motto for Act Two, expressing the strength to divest oneself of myths, face reality and seek out real rather than symbolic solutions.

The structure (from myth to reality) was also the theme.

During the second production of *Les Canadiens,* at Toronto Workshop Productions in 1977, the play found its audience.

The Montreal audiences at the Centaur had responded very warmly to the play, because of the love of all Montrealers for their hockey team. Still, there was something in the point of view of the play not directly useful to them. The scattering of Francophones who came each night appreciated the sympathy of the play towards Quebec nationalism, particularly since it was coming from an Anglophone source — yet in the end, it was nothing new to them. Their own writers have taken this point of view for years.

The Montreal Anglophones — the vast majority of our audience there — had varied reactions, but I think it would be right to say that the play did not really address their particular problem, which is: becoming a minority. For years the Anglophones of Quebec have identified with the rest of Canada and assumed thereby the sense of being a majority. Now, whether independence actually comes to Quebec or not, they are faced with the need of making the transition from majority to minority.

But English-speaking Canadians outside of Quebec are not faced with any such drastic alteration in their circumstances as a result of recent events. Their problem regarding Quebec is simpler: what to make of it all — of the election, and the entire train of events in Quebec over the last seventeen years.

In high-school history class, I recall that Quebec always seemed to be a trouble-maker. Those French Canadians were fractious, destructive — the fly in the ointment of Canadian history (or as a McGill University professor put it less quaintly during World War II, "cockroaches in the kitchen of Canada"). Much of the initial commentary in English-speaking Canada after the PQ victory was an extension of that approach: a bunch of agitators up there in the Parti Québécois were duping their own people and messing things up for the rest of us. It was a mean-spirited response, and not very historically relevant.

I hope *Les Canadiens* achieves a different, non-hysterical response to those events. To begin with, no one should be *surprised*. The election of the PQ is one more in a long chain of national self-assertions by the people of Quebec that extends through the length of their history. Beyond that, one can be heartened at the sight of a people standing up for their dignity and asserting themselves. (I hope it is clear that the hopefulness of the play hangs not on the PQ nor on the new government of Quebec, much less on any particular policies of that government, past or future: it is a hopefulness based on the act of self-respect by the *people of Quebec* which the election represented.) And, beyond that, I think one can even draw some inspiration: if the people of Quebec can stand up for themselves, then perhaps the rest of us in Canada can do the same for ourselves.

There was great confusion in English-speaking Canada in the wake of the November 15 election. It was not unlike the confusion of the players on the ice at the Forum that night. Many who cared about the future of the country felt it was being broken apart. Yet it was hard not to admire the concern for *their* country of those very people who seemed to be breaking Canada apart. And those politicians who previously seemed content to preside over the disintegration of Canada by selling it off or letting it drift, those very politicians, suddenly proclaimed themselves the *saviours* of Canada.

In the aftermath, some clarity started to emerge. What at first seemed a threat could be taken as a challenge. Not only a challenge, but possibly an opportunity. An opportunity for those of us outside Quebec

to rethink what kind of country *we* want, with or without Quebec —
and, in the urgency of crisis, to reshape what is obsolete or undesirable. I hope *Les Canadiens* can aid in that process of clarification for
those in audiences outside Quebec, not insofar as they are theatre-
goers, but insofar as they are Canadians.

What a season! Montreal won the Stanley Cup; the people of Quebec
reversed a historical verdict and, on another level to be sure, we made
Les Canadiens. What a hell of a season it was!

Alma's Night Out

As the audience enters, RINK RAT *is skating around in a miniature hockey rink, shooting pucks into the empty nets. He is wearing a Montreal Canadiens jersey, and listening to a personal portable radio. In the middle of his little rink, there is a huge bassinet. When the house has settled, he finally notices them. He is amazed to see them. Pause.*

RAT: Hi. If you don't mind me asking, what are all of you doing in my rumpus room? Shhh! The baby's asleep.

[He checks the crib.]

Sorry about the mess. I get busy and never get anything done. Can I offer you a beer? How many would like one?

[He counts.]

How many for a "light?"

[He counts, then, speaks to a specific audience member — a woman.]

You don't look like you need to drink light. [*To others*]: She doesn't look like she needs a diet, does she?

[They agree, she doesn't. He points at a fat guy in the audience.]

I'll give the "light" to him.

So ... that's a hundred and twenty regular beers, twenty-eight lights. [*Starts out, then*]: Anybody want hi-test? [*Counts*]: Eighteen hi-test ... Well, make up your mind, for crissakes. Some guys ...

[He goes out. From offstage, a crash.]

Jesus Christ!

[Comes back on, carrying a child's push-car. Goes to baby carriage, speaks into it.]

There's a name for that. It's called "patricide." [*To audience*]: I looked it up last week, eh, after falling over that thing twice in one night. I think I'm going senile.

[He starts to go out again. Stops.]

Alma's out for the night, so I'm here with the kid. TV's broken, eh, or I'd be watching the game. Goddamn guy up at the shop where I bought it . . . : "Any time you have a problem, day or night, just give us a call." And right before the puck is dropped in the seventh game, BINGO, it cuts out. So I phone the shop. [*Plugging his nose*]: "I'm sorry, there's no one in the office at this time. Please leave your message after the tone." You know where they all are, eh? Out at the pub, watching the game.

[*He starts out, stops.*]

I guess you folks aren't hockey fans, or you'd be someplace where there's a TV. You want to hear the score? I only ask because there's a lot of guys — I guess I should say people, but it's really mostly guys — who videotape the games these days and play it back later. I used to work with this guy who did that all the time. He'd threaten everybody that if they told him the score during the game, he'd piss in their thermos.

Okay, it's 2–2, second period just ended. Same pattern as in game six, Calgary scored two unanswered goals, then the Oilers finally showed up for the game in the second and scored on two great plays, Anderson on a three-way feed from Gretzky and Coffey, then Messier sent in alone by Kurri to tie it up. Sounds as if the Oilers would have scored another two if the second period had lasted five minutes longer.

Jeez, I hope Alma shows up soon . . . She said she'd try to get home in time for me to go to the pub for the third period . . . Those Oilers, eh? Totally irresponsible. They always have to give the opponents a two-goal spot before they really start playing. This whole series has been like that. But there's no way they're not going to win this one. They're going for their third straight Cup for sure. Oh ya, that reminds me . . .

[RAT *goes out, comes back on with a cardboard box. He opens it and takes out an Oilers hockey jersey. He strips off his Canadiens jersey, puts on the Oilers jersey, then, looking around for something to do with the Canadiens jersey, tucks it into the baby's bassinet.*]

There. Wear that honourably, little sweetie-pie.

[*To audience*]:

I'm an old Montreal fan from when I was a kid, eh? All those Flying Frenchmen. But at the same time, Edmonton's my home town. And besides, those Oilers, they're the ones who're playing like the real old Canadiens. Like when they were really *les Canadiens, calice.*

I'll bet any money they come out in the third and blow the Flames away. Anybody in this room take that bet? [*If somebody will*] . . . guy's probably from Calgary. Okay, buddy, I'll bet you a hundred bucks the Oilers score the winning goal in the next period. They were obviously flying in the second. The Flames were just hanging in there by their teeth. It's a matter of pride, eh? I mean, if the Oilers lost this one, they'd probably all go out and start doing drugs or something. Oh, ya, drugs! The beer!

    [*He goes out. From offstage*]:
Shit!

    [*He returns carrying a bottle of champagne.*]

I drank it all! I was going to go out and get some but then I figured, what the hell, if I'm gonna watch the game at the bar anyway . . . and I never bought any. Damn. This is all I got. Listen, do you mind if I don't offer this? This is special: I'm saving it for when the Oilers win the Cup. Maybe when Alma gets home, we could all go out for a beer and watch the third period.

Alma's taking a course in computers. She bought one of those Commodore 64s at Woolco. They had a sale after they became obsolete. About seven months after they came out, y'know? I play games on it now and then, but Alma is actually learning how to talk to the damn thing. My wife. Me, I just like to play. I get a lot higher scores on Space Invaders than she does. Remember Space Invaders? That was back in the old days. Before 1983, I mean.

    [RAT *stops, listening to his headphones. Something really disgusts him.*]
What!!? That's ridiculous!

    [*He goes out, comes back onstage with a phone book. Mutters*]:
Fucking idiot, wouldn't know his ass from a hole in the ground. . . . [*Picks up phone, dials number, waits, then*]: Hello, is this . . . ? Ya, I'll wait . . . I just want to talk to whatzizname. You know who I mean. The fat guy who doesn't shave very well who writes for the *Journal*. Ya, the guy with all the opinions. Well, of course I won't swear over the air, what kind of an asshole do you take me for? So what if he's broadcasting, he's s'pose to run a talk-show, isn't he . . . ? Well can I leave a message? Good. Tell him, "John, the world is full of guys whose mother used to come out to the rink and tell the other guys not to pick on their son because he was too *sensitive*. Most of these guys ended up as *critics* . . . " Hello . . . ?

[He slams down the phone, laughing.]

I just hate guys that sit in their goddamn armchair and criticize. Okay, so the Oilers aren't playing top form, it's only the quarter-finals for god's sake. And those Flames, talk about pesky. But big. The only Oilers who don't look like midgets playing them are Gregg and Semenko.

Jesus, the third period is going to start in a few minutes. She promised she'd be home in time for me to get out to the pub to watch it . . .

[He begins to dismantle his nets.]

But tonight I'm babysititng. And Alma's learning computers. Jesus, I wish she'd show up! It must be after nine.

Listen to me. "After nine." When I was a bachelor, I used to drink every night, go to work on four hours' sleep, take off to Vancouver on a whim. Glen and me — he's my buddy, eh — well his old man had a cabin on an acreage out near Wabamun. Nothing special, just a little place tucked away in the woods, beside the Stoney Indian reserve.

God, the times we had. There was this old girlfriend of mine, you know. Linda. This was B.A., you know, Before Alma. Well, she was a wonderful, mad girl. One night we were out there, it was about February. She was standing in front of the wood stove, and all of a sudden, she started peeling off all her clothes. "Feel like it . . . ?" she says. "If you put it that way," I says. "Okay, peel 'em." I did, and the next thing you know, she grabs my clothes and stuffs them into the stove. I chased her about half a mile through the snow, both of us in the buff, laughing our heads off. . . .

And the nights with the boys. We used to get drunk and race around on Glen's dad's skidoo. Carl broke his arm. I ran the thing smack into a hill, windshield bounced up and broke my nose. I staggered back into the cabin, blood all over my face, the rest of the guys thought I'd been shot. *[He laughs]*. Great times. Remember the Alberta overhand?

[He mimes tossing a beer bottle over a car roof.]

God, we were incredibly stupid. Glen's family still has that cabin, but not the skidoo. Glen's a very enthusiastic cross-country skier now. Married. *[Proudly, referring to the baby]*: But he hasn't got one of these.

As I say, this was before Alma. Alma and I have had some crazy, companionship moments like that, but we've also got this deeper thing. Being married is like a religion. Because Alma, all Almas, are goddesses.

Alma says that she doesn't want to be a goddess any more. She says that her mother and her grandmother used to be thought of as goddesses, put up on a pedestal, and treated like shit.

Alma may not want to be a goddess, but I'm always going to believe in her, no matter what she says. I've worshipped her in every one of her incarnations, which includes Linda. (I'm talking about Alma now in her generic role as a goddess, All-ma). When I was this age [*indicates*], she was King Kong. I was terrified of her. I needed her, but she could destroy cities if she got mad.

Later, when we were both about thirteen, I became obsessed with trying to touch her body, particularly those breasts. I pursued them religiously, and mastered the two-fingered-brassiere-unbuttoning technique. Which she always pretended she didn't want me to do. Good thing I never believed her.

Because she's always been a shameless liar about it. I mean, about me touching her. When I first started touching her she lied about not wanting me to. And I lied about how much I wanted to. But she kept letting me. You know what I mean.

I mean, once *it* actually happened, we kept on lying to each other shamelessly. I kept telling her that I could control myself. I mean, it was a white lie, because I *thought* I could. She in turn kept on consenting even though she knew I was lying. She knew whose fault it would be: *mine*, of course.

This was in a different world than kids grow up into nowadays. We weren't protected against procreation. Nature's little computers, programmed for input.

And Alma and I inputted as often as we could. We inputted in the river valley, in the back of my dad's Ford Galaxy and in her mother's Nash Metropolitan. Remember the Nash Metropolitan? Stupidest looking car ever built, but the front seat folded down.

We even inputted across the front seat of her mother's Nash Metropolitan. And by some accident of fate, we didn't have any output.

Alma and me have come a long way since then. We finally got around to the business of procreation.

[*He looks into the crib, wistfully.*]

Another little goddess. Whose name, of course, is Alma.

[RAT *puts his radio headphones back on and adjusts the volume.*]

Okay, the players are coming out on the ice for the third period.

Fuhr, eh? Hasn't he been fantastic this series? Jesus, the way he stood on his head in Game four. . . .

[*The telephone rings.* RAT *answers without removing head-phones.*]

Hello. Oh, hi, Alma, you coming home soon? The third period's about to start. A *what?* They can't make you write an exam just like that. . . . The hockey game's on, for chrissake! The third period's starting. This is the biggest game of the season, this is the goddamn *Stanley Cup Playoffs*, has this teacher never heard of hockey or WHAT?

[*He covers the transmitter of the phone.*]

Jesus!

[*The baby starts crying. Over the next paragraph, the cries become louder and louder.*]

What? Ya, that's little Alma. She's just bawling. No, she's been quiet. Of course I'll look after her, but are you coming home? You absolutely can't. No, fine, it's wonderful, I'm just missing the best goddamn period of hockey since the Canada Cup, that's all. No, write your exam. Look, I gotta go, I gotta look after the baby. *Thanks.*

[RAT *slams down the receiver. Baby cries louder.*]

God damn it. An exam. Nobody gives exams when the goddamn playoffs are on. She's probably going out to the pub for a drink. With some fucking computer wizard. [*To the baby*]: That's it, she's absolutely staying at home when the Oilers play in the final series. Okay, okay, calm down. Okay, take it easy, I didn't mean it about the old lady.

It's okay, little munchkin, daddy's happy now.

[*He demonstrates this by smiling.*]

Aren't we happy? [*Beat*] No, we're not.

Look, sweetheart, the third period is just starting, they just dropped the puck. . . . How about a nice bottle? Would you like a bottle? I'll get you one. Hang on.

[RAT *exits. The baby cries louder. From offstage*]:

Okay, little one, daddy's coming. Now where did she put the goddamn . . . oh . . . Coming!

[RAT *reappears, with a bottle.*]

Here, sweetheart, here's your ba-ba. Come on, have a suck. Please, just suck the bottle. Nice nipple, just like mama's, except it's made of Playtex. Whatever that is. Look, I'd let you suck mine, but it wouldn't do you any good.

[Something happens in the game. RAT tries to listen, but it's impossible with the baby crying.]

You don't want all these nice people to see you having a tantrum, do you? Don't you want to be a nice little girl?

[Baby hollers really loudly.]

Listen, sweetheart, your mommy's not home right now, but when she gets here, you can have a nice long suck. Would you like that?

Now see here, young lady. . . . Jesus, I sound like my grade-two teacher. Miss Johnstone. *[Queen-Mom voice]*: "No, see here. I am Miss Johnstone. Not Johnson, but John*stone!*"

[Baby cries a little more quietly:]

Oh, you like the Miss Johnstone voice. *[Same voice]*: "Now see here. We will have no babycrying, babysucking, babypuking, or babypooping in this crib!" *Diapers!* Jesus, why didn't I think of that before?

[He feels the diapers. Withdraws finger, smells it.]

Yup. Solid evidence.

[RAT takes the baby out of the crib and puts it on his chest. It immediately stops crying. He stands there, feeling very paternal indeed. Pause. He takes off the earphones, hums quietly.]

I used to sing all the time. When I was younger. *[Sniffs the baby's bottom.]* Whew. I better change her. Excuse me a minute.

[He goes out. From offstage]:

Jesus, all these little snaps. The guy who invented these is making a mint. . . . There we are, my little one. All washed off and clean. Bit o' bum cream. There. *[Loudly, to audience]*: I love to touch this baby's bum. You know the expression, soft as a baby's bum? Well, nothing is as soft as a baby's bum.

Shit! Where's the diaper? Okay, you just stay there. Don't roll off, daddy's got to get your diaper. . . .

[RAT runs on, trying to keep eyes on baby offstage. Finds diaper, grabs it, exits.]

That wasn't so hard, was it? You know, when you first came back from the hospital I thought you were weird-looking? Your mother, she looked at you and went all ga-ga. But you were so wrinkly, and you had this little pink face. You looked like a boiled cabbage.

[RAT re-enters with babe in arms. To audience]:

You know what I felt like when she came back from the hospital? Have you ever seen *Eraserhead*? I felt like that guy in *Eraserhead*, whose wife gives birth to this sort of alien. Except that the thing is not really an alien, because it has this intelligence, and this . . . need. Like it needs him so much that he just has to take care of it. Well, when I saw that film, I thought it was depressing, ugly. But when Little Alma was born, I was just like that guy. She would cry and cry, and I'd be feeling, what is this crying animal, but I'd have to pick her up. And that's when I started feeling like a father.

I used to sing all the time. When I was courting your mother. Courting. Jesus, that sounds so old-fashioned. Well, I guess I am pretty old-fashioned. Anyhow, she used to love it when I sang, because my granny — she's dead now — used to sing all these old Irish and Scots songs. Alma couldn't believe it, eh, because they never did that in her family. She thought it was so hokey. But she liked it. I wonder if she really has that exam? No, that's stupid. [*Pause*] Getting tired?

[*He lays the baby down in her cradle. On an impulse, he plays with the baby's toes.*]

This little piggy went to market,
This little piggy stayed home,
This little piggy had roast beef
This little piggy had none.
And this little piggy went WEE WEE WEE
All the way home!"

God, my granny would have adored you. She came out here in a Red River cart, you know. Before there was anything out here, just two little communities on the north and south banks of the North Saskatchewan River. Came out from stiff old Southern Ontario, where the Irish Catholics and Protestants were still killing each other now and then. Out to the prairies, to marry her man. Who died when she was forty. Left her in a big old house in Garneau, so she turned it into a boarding house and survived the depression and the war. "Sunny Alberta," she used to say. "I'm so glad we live in Sunny Alberta." My granny. God, I can remember her playing "this little piggy went to market" with my toes.

[*Short pause.* RAT *is almost crying.*]

I wonder if when you become a father you begin to secrete a hormone that makes you do this weird stuff: talk about your dead grandmother and stuff. And put on weight. And stop caring about things you used to care about; the beer with the boys, the poker games, the booze, the little vanities . . . the booze . . . Christ, the game!

[*Grabs headphones, puts them on, listens.*]

Nope. Nobody's scored yet. I guess they're just feeling each other out.

Hold on, the Oilers are on a power play. This is it, they're gonna tuck this one away now. Christ, they keep going off-side. Calgary's just standing up at their blueline, same as they did in the other games. Four guys. The Oilers try to dipsy-doodle around them and just get stood up. . . . Calgary on a two-on-one . . . how can this happen, for crissake? C'mon, you guys, let's have a little gusto. Wait a minute . . . Gretz has it, he's crossing their blueline, spins . . . they tripped him . . . no call, I don't be*lieve* the refing in this series, it's like the league has decided to give Edmonton a handicap. Calgary dumps it again, Jesus!

I find it pretty ironic that Calgary, who have been coached to play like the Russians did when they finally learned how to beat us, has been grinding down the Oilers, who play like the Russians did when *we* first started watching *them*.

Oh-oh. Loob's got the puck again . . . that guy is dangerous, eh? Whenever he makes one of those rushes it's "watch out Oilers." No, Calgary's just dumping it, no threat. Fuhr's just playing it behind the nets. Smith's back. Now watch out: the Oilers are going to make an end-to-end rush and . . . WHAT? . . . I don't believe this. . . .

[*Pause*]

Smith just scored on his own net. Banked it in off the back of Fuhr's pads. The whole building is completely in awe, nobody can believe this. *I* can't believe this. Maybe they'll disallow it or something. . . . No, they're gonna face off again. Crediting the goal to Perry Berezan. Who was a mile from the play. Jesus. As I understand it, Smith was coming out like this and was intending to pass the puck up-ice to somebody. Just a silly little misjudgement. And now he's got to sit on the bench beside all the other guys. Poor bastard.

Oh, well, what the hell, the Oilers can come back. They always do. Never fails . . . like clockwork . . . Jesus, to score on your own net in the last period of the seventh game of a semi-final. What if that goal stood up? Smith would have to live with that forever. Those mistakes, those missed opportunities, those goals we failed to score come back to haunt us. You relive them again and again, like a criminal being punished in hell. Like the time when I was ten.

Playing Pee wees. The coaches had stuck me on defence, which in Pee wees is no position of honour. I remember this kid skating in on

me, one-on-one, just me between him and our goalie, and I was so
terrified that I'd blow it that it seemed as though the world just froze
up, like it does on the TV replays. I could see my coach and my
teammates on the bench, their faces full of anxiety, could feel the
sweat under my chin-strap, and the opposing player seeming to fill my
view, like a body coming too close to a camera, and in that instant, the
blade of my skate caught a crack in the ice and I fell backwards onto the
ice, like a fish being landed in a boat, doomed. Guy skated around me
and scored. That was twenty years ago, and I can feel the humiliation
burning in me still. God, how Smith must feel. . . .

Then there are the ones that aren't memories at all, but dreams and
fantasies. The one that got away. What *was* her name, anyway?

[*Pause. He is lost in a memory.*]

Ya, the good memories, too. That same year, stripping the puck
from one of their centres, going in alone, and turning their goalie
upside down before tucking it away in the upper left-hand corner. . . .
How many of these does Gretzky have? Guy Lafleur? And how many of
the other kind?

I read a book about Greek mythology once, and I remember the
story about these guys sailing past this island where these women
sang, and all the sailors who didn't have their ears plugged would row
their boat towards these women, and end up crashing against the rocks
and drowning. Well, I don't think that's a story about women. I think
that's a story about memories. . . .

[RAT *listens to his radio.*]

Edmonton doesn't seem to be mounting much of an offensive. The
Oilers had better win this one, or Pocklington's going to need money
for the new players next year. He's gonna have to grind a few more
bucks out of that Gainers plant. Maybe he should get the Oilers working
out there. Y'know, like Rocky, with those meat carcasses [*sings*]
"gonna fly now" [*as he mimes punching a carcass of meat*].

That Stallone, he kills me. Only in America could a guy I wouldn't
trust my daughter with get paid millions of dollars for acting out
fantasies that most people wouldn't even admit to.

Anyway, I'm trying to lose a little weight, get my form back, take the
flab off. It's like a never-ending cycle: I do my sit-ups in the morning,
so to reward myself, I drink a couple of beer at night. So many things
changed since little Alma was born. You do stuff you never thought

you'd do, or be able to do. Stick your finger in a diaper, pat somebody on the back till they throw up on you. . . .

Jesus, when are they gonna score? Sounds like Calgary is really bottling them up, just getting the puck and dumping it . . . wait a minute . . . Calgary's got a three-on-one, Christ almighty a three-on . . . Jesus, Fuhr's got it, another brilliant save. If the Oilers wouldn't play like they were playing shinny, maybe he wouldn't have to be so brilliant.

Smith's still sitting there on the bench, having to watch the whole thing go down. . . . What's Sather thinking of? It can't be good for morale. Sather's gotta stick to his game plan. Smith's a good defenceman, he just made a mistake. If Sather would just have a bit of faith. He must have a plan. I'll bet I know what he does. I'll bet he's gonna keep Smith on the bench till the last minute, *then* play him. Smith will just smoke!

Christ, Calgary's buzzing the Oiler net again. Why can't the Oilers get anything going? . . . *Another* goal-line save.

[RAT *tears off his headphones in disgust.*] Jesus, I wish Alma would get here. I wish the goddamn television was working!

[*He kicks the television.*]

Alma wonders why I have to watch the games on TV. She doesn't understand the ritual, for crissake. It's like church. Saturday night: Hockey Night in Canada. If you haven't got a date, or a show, or a girl, or your friends are all working up north . . . you sit down with a couple of beers and watch the Maple Leafs lose another one. I mean this is Canada, after all, so the old CBC has to give us some tradition: those exciting games from Toronto. And Howie Meeker . . . [*In Meeker voice*]: *"You kids, now, you watch the way that guy fell over. I see something like that, and I say to myself, hey!"*

And the interviews with Dave Hodge. [RAT *enacts both roles alternately.*]

(*Hodge*): Well, John, it was a hard second period out there. Your down 7–0. There must be some way for your team to get back into this game.

(*Player*): Ya. Score eight unanswered goals.

(*Hodge*): Well, thanks a lot, and good luck in the third period.

(*Player*): I'm not gonna play in the third period.

[RAT'S *attention is drawn to the radio; he has the headphones; half on.*]

Whoops, a bit of a scrap. . . . No, guess not. I guess after the first game, they pretty well figured it was a stand-off for fighting though. Fotiu and Semenko, Sheehy and Jackson, Peplinski and Messier. What about that Peplinski, eh? Mess rearranges his face for him in Game One, and he comes right back out there and plays like he won the fight. He scored one tonight. Skated right *through* Coffey. You gotta give a guy like that credit.

That first game, the way they fought . . . Alma was just livid. "That's not hockey," she shouted. "Why do they have to do that?" "Well," I explained to her, "the Oilers have to prove they're as tough as the Flames." "Fine," she says, "they should score a few goals to prove that." "They will," I said. That was in Game One. Which they lost 4–1. I wish to Christ they'd score a few goals right now. Only got a few minutes left. . . .

[RAT *begins to put his skates back on.*]

It wouldn't be the worst thing in the world if the Oilers lost this series. I mean, they've been playing it like guys who didn't believe they could lose. "Pride goeth before a fall." My granny used to say that sometimes. It wouldn't be all that bad. There's always next year.

[*He gets up and skates around, pained about what he hears.*]

Come on, you guys, *move* the *puck*! . . . Jesus.

[RINK RAT *grabs the bottle of champagne and begins to uncork it.*]

Ya, I know, I was saving this for when the Oilers won their third straight Stanley Cup. [*He pops the cork. The baby frets.*] It's okay, sweetheart. It's just Daddy being a sentimental idiot. [*The baby cries louder.*]

I know how you feel. You wet? Nope. Bottle empty? Nope. I know, you want that breast. It's a feeling we all have to get over.

[*He drinks from the bottle. Looking just slightly guilty, he gives the baby some. The baby stops fretting.*]

I notice Randy Gregg, when the Oilers won their second Cup, he had his kid in the dressing room, and they were covering him with champagne and everything. Alma thought that was a bit crazy, but I thought it was great. I mean, Gretzky drank from one before he needed his first shave. That kid can say the same before he needed his first haircut.

When she arrived, the doctor said, "It's a girl." "No hockey player for you," said Alma. "How is she going to support us?" I asked. "Get her into sports medicine", said the obstetrician. Who was a woman.

I take my daughter out to the park, and there's this girls' soccer match on. These twelve- or thirteen-year-olds, and they're playing not badly, heading the ball properly, and playing their positions okay. . . . and I'm thinking, hell, these kids are doing fine, I mean, remembering our soccer team when I was that age. And I thought, jeez, when I was a kid, nobody ever thought of getting a girls' team together. And then I thought, jeez, when I was a kid, did a dad go out to the park with his daughter? A dad wheeling a baby carriage . . . I guess some guys still feel that way.

Time is running out. Jesus, sounds like the Oilers are just being frustrated to death out there. Those Flames will do anything to keep the puck out of their own net. They're dropping down in front of slapshots, stopping them with their teeth. It's like playing the goddamn Russians all over again. They've just cleared it again. How do you like that, they've got McDonald out there, that old warhorse. Good for him. The only guy on the ice as old as I am.

[*Almost pleading*]:

Look, you have to understand. . . . When I was a kid, the professional team here in Edmonton was the Flyers. A kid growing up on the prairies, he wanted to play for the Flyers, because they were the Canadian farm team that provided all the great players for the Detroit Red Wings. But you knew that the Stanley Cup, our Cup, could never come home to Canada except through Toronto or Montreal. You see, when the Oilers won that first Cup that first year, that's why everybody went crazy. Because we finally grew up, we . . . belonged.

Wait a minute . . . Gretzky's got it . . . over to Kurri . . . Kurri's alone in front of the net! He . . . he . . . he didn't shoot! Kurri didn't shoot! Son of a goddamn bitch!

[*The baby starts crying. Over the next paragraph, it will cry louder and louder.*]

The Oilers can't get anywhere, they're being strangled . . . Calgary clears it again. The Oilers just can't seem to . . . wait a minute, they're making a line change. Anderson and Kurri are coming off, replaced by Napier and . . . Smith. Sather has finally put Smith back on. Coffey has it at the blueline. Coffey crosses the blueline, dodges a check, he's in the corner . . . everybody's in front of the net. Coffey gets it to Mactavish in the other corner. Mactavish is battling with Tonelli . . . they're killing each other . . . Napier has it . . . he kicks it over to Gretz . . . Gretz dodges a check, spinarama . . . thirteen seconds left, this is

incredible . . . Gretz still has it, he's looking for someone to pass to . . .
he feathers one to . . . Smith. Smith winds up at the blueline, fakes,
dekes around McDonald . . . nobody can get the puck from him.
Vernon sprawls . . . He lifts it over Vernon's pads! *It's in!* Smith has tied
the game with four seconds left! Incredible!

> [*The baby is screaming like a banshee now. He goes over to the
> bassinet, picks up the baby.*]

They're dropping the puck again. It's Messier, he takes it straight
from the face-off circle, he skates right through the Calgary defence
. . . He shoots . . . HE SCORES! They win the game with a second left!
The Oilers are on their way to a third straight Cup! It's true!

> [RAT *has been skating around carrying the baby, relating
> these events. He trips over the child's push-car he carried on at
> the beginning of the play. He falls over with a shout, protecting
> the baby's head from being dashed against the ground by
> landing awkwardly. He lies there, shocked. Pause.*]

Don't cry, little sweetheart. You don't have to cry . . . [*He tries to
get up.*] Ow, ow, ow, ow, ow! Dammit, I think I jammed my shoulder.

> [*He cradles the baby.*]

Come on, little Alma. Come to daddy. Mom isn't home, but your
daddy's here. It's a special night. Our night out. Little Alma's night out.

> [*To the audience*]:

The game ended five minutes ago. The Oilers are on summer
vacation, so this year the Cup belongs to somebody else. [*Sings*]:

> Oh, the summer time is comin'
> And the leaves are sweetly bloomin'
> And the wild mountain thyme
> Grows along the blooming heather
> Will you go, lassie, go?

> [ALMA *enters: she is ready to fight if she has to.* RAT *doesn't
> notice her, as he keeps singing.*]

> I will build my love a tow'r
> Near yon clear and crystal fountain
> And on it I will pile
> All the flowers of the mountain
> Will you go, lassie, go?

And we'll all go together
To pluck wild mountain thyme
All along the blooming heather
Will you go, lassie, go?

[*Pause.* RAT *is holding the baby quietly. He is now aware that she is there. They begin delicately.*]

ALMA: Hi.

RAT: Hi.

ALMA: It's nice to hear you singing. You haven't sung much lately.

RAT: No , I guess I haven't, have I.

ALMA: Is she asleep?

RAT: Yeah.

ALMA: That's good. Did you hear about the hockey game?

RAT: What? Oh yah.

ALMA: Too bad about it. Poor Steve Smith.

RAT: Yeah, well, the game wouldn't be worth winning, if you didn't have to lose sometimes. [*Beats*]: How was your exam?

ALMA: I aced it.

RAT: That's good.

ALMA: Thanks.

[*This ritual of reconciliation finished,* ALMA *comes over to the bassinet, stands over it.*]

ALMA: Thank god she's starting to go to sleep without breast-feeding. My nipples are getting callouses.

RAT: Ya. [*With overdone self-pity*]: Poor me.

ALMA: Poor you. [*Pause.*] She's beautiful, isn't she?

RAT: Yeah. [*Short pause.*] Alma, you know that goal, the Bossy goal, that won the 1984 semi-final Canada Cup game against the Russians? Well, I scored that goal.

ALMA: [*Without irony*]: Sure. And Guy Lafleur wants you to play on his team.

[RAT *doesn't speak. He goes over to the bottle of champagne.*]

RAT: You want some?

ALMA: Champagne? What's it for?

RAT: For us.

ALMA: Bring it upstairs when you come. I really need to have a bath. Okay?

RAT: Fine. I'll see you in a minute.

> [ALMA *smiles and goes out.* RAT *takes off his Edmonton Oilers jersey. He turns to the audience.*]

Look, I'm gonna go upstairs. Listen, anybody who took my bet about the outcome of this game, it's okay. You don't need to pay me. Even if the Oilers did score the winning goal. Maybe you can buy me a beer if you see me on the street.

> [RAT *goes over to the bassinet, pulls a Canadiens' jersey out of it, and puts it on.*]

Besides, it's always a good practice to be able to make adjustments, isn't it?

You can find your own way out, eh, if I turn the lights down in here?

ALMA: [*from offstage*]: Rat? Who you talking to?

RAT: [*tiny pause*]: The baby.

> [*He goes to the cradle, takes the baby, kisses her.*]

Sweet dreams, my little one.

> [*He goes to the door.*]

Sweet dreams.

Everyone.

> [RAT *turns out the light. To the baby*]:

Next year, I'm gonna teach you how to skate.

> [*He goes out.*]

THE END

Hockey Player:
Eric Nesterenko

HE HAS BEEN A PROFESSIONAL *hockey player for twenty years, as a member of the Toronto Maple Leafs and the Chicago Black Hawks. He is thirty-eight. He has a wife and three small children.*

"I lived in a small mining town in Canada, a God-forsaken place called Flin Flon. In the middle of nowhere, four hundred miles north of Winnipeg. It was a good life, beautiful winters. I remember the northern lights. Dark would come around three o'clock. Thirty below zero, but dry and clean.

"I lived across the street from the rink. That's how I got started, when I was four of five. We never had any gear. I used to wrap Life magazines around my legs. We didn't have organized hockey like they have now. All our games were pickup, a never-ending game. Maybe there would be three kids to a team, then there would be fifteen, and the game would go on. Nobody would keep score. It was a pure kind of play. The play you see here, outside the stadium, outside at the edge of the ghetto. I see 'em in the schoolyards. It's that same kind of play around the basket. Pure play.

"My father bought me a pair of skates, but that was it. He never took part. I played the game for my own sake, not for him. He wasn't even really around to watch. I was playing for the joy of it, with my own peers. Very few adults around. We organized everything.

"I see parents at kids' sporting events. It's all highly organized. It's very formal. They have referees and so on. The parents are spectators. The kids are playing for their parents. The old man rewards him for playing well and doesn't reward him for not doing so well. (Laughs.) The father puts too much pressure on the kid. A boy then is soft material. If you want a kid to do something, it's got to be fun.

"I was a skinny, ratty kid with a terrible case of acne. I could move pretty well, but I never really looked like much. (Laughs.) Nobody ever really noticed me. But I could play the game. In Canada it is part of the *culture. If you can play the game, you are recognized. I was good almost from the beginning. The game became a passion with me. I was looking to be somebody and the game was my way. It was my life."*

(At sixteen, while in high school, he was playing with semi-pro teams, earning two hundred dollars a week. At eighteen, he joined the Toronto Maple Leafs.)

There's an irony that one gets paid for playing, that play should bring in money. When you sell play, that makes it hard for pure, recreational play, for play as an art, to exist. It's corrupted, it's made harder, perhaps it's brutalized, but it's still there. Once you learn how to play and are accepted in the group, there is a rapport. All you are as an athlete is honed and made sharper. You learn to survive in a very tough world. It has its own rewards.

The pro game is a kind of a stage. People can see who we are. Our personalities come through in our bodies. It's exciting. I can remember games with twenty thousand people and the place going crazy with sound and action and colour. The enormous energy the crowd produces all coming in on the ice, all focusing in on you. It's pretty hard to resist that. (Laughs.)

I was really recognized then. I remember one game: it was in the semi-finals, the year we won the Stanley Cup. I was with Chicago. It was the sixth game against Montreal. They were the big club and we were the Cinderella team. It was three to nothing, for us, with five minutes left to go. As a spontaneous gesture twenty thousand people stood up. I was on the ice. I remember seeing that whole stadium, just solid, row on row, from the balcony to the boxes, standing up. These people were turned on by us. (Sighs.) We came off, three feet off the ice...(Softly) Spring of '61.

When Toronto dropped me I said, "I'm a failure." Twenty-two, what the hell does one know? You're the boy of the moment or nothing. What we show is energy and young bodies. We know our time is fleeting. If we don't get a chance to go, it makes us antsy. Our values are instant, it's really hard to bide your time.

Violence is taken to a greater degree. There is always the spectre of being hurt. A good player, just come into his prime, cracks a skull, breaks a leg, he's finished. If you get hit, you get hit — with impersonal force. The guy'll hit you as hard as he can. If you get hurt, the other players switch off. Nobody's sympathetic. When you get hurt they don't look at you, even players on your own team. The curtain comes down — 'cause it could have been me. One is afraid of being hurt himself. You don't want to think too much about it. I saw my teammate lying there — I knew him pretty well — they put forty stitches in his face. I saw him lying on the table and the doctors working on him. I said, "Better him than me." (Laughs.) We conditioned ourselves to think like that. I think it's a defence mechanism and it's brutalizing.

The professional recognizes this and risks himself less and less, so the percentage is in his favour. This takes a bit of experience. Invariably it's the younger player who gets hurt. Veterans learn to be calculating about their vulnerability. (Laughs.) This takes a little bit away from the play. When I was young, I used to take all sorts of chances just for the hell of it. Today, instead of trying to push through it, I ease up. It takes something off the risk. The older professional often plays a waiting game, waits for the other person to commit himself in the arena.

The younger player, with great natural skill, say Bobby Orr, will actually force the play. He'll push. Sometimes they're good enough to get away with it. Orr got hurt pretty badly the first couple of years he played. He had operations on both knees; now he's a little smarter, a little more careful, and a little more cynical. (Laughs.)

Cynicism is a tool for survival. I began to grow up quickly. I became disillusioned with the game for not being the pure thing it was earlier in my life. I began to see the exploitation of the players by the owner. You realize owners don't really care for you; you're a piece of property. They try to get as much out of you as they can. I remember once I had a torn shoulder. It was well in the process of healing, but I knew it wasn't right yet. They brought their doctor in. He said, "You can play." I played and ripped it completely. I was laid up. So I look at the owners. He shrugs his shoulders, walks away. He doesn't really hate me. He's impersonal.

Among players, while we're playing we're very close. Some of the best clubs I've played with have this intimacy — an intimacy modern man hardly ever achieves. We can see each other naked, emotionally, physically. We're plugged into each other, because we need each other. There have been times when I knew what the other guy was thinking without him ever talking to me. When that happens, we can do anything together.

It can't be just a job. It's not worth playing just for money — it's a way of life. When we were kids there was the release in playing, the sweetness in being able to move and control your body. This is what play is. Beating somebody is secondary. When I was a kid, to really *move* was my delight. I felt released because I could move around anybody. I was free.

That exists on the pro level, but there's the money aspect. You know they're making an awful lot of money off you. You know you're just a piece of property. When an older player's gone, it's not just his body. With modern training methods you can play a long time. But you just get fed up with the whole business. It becomes a job, just a shitty job. (Laughs.)

I'm not wild about living in hotels, coming in late at night, and having to spend time in a room waiting for a game. You've got a day to kill and the game's in back of your mind. It's hard to relax. It's hard to read a good book. I'll read an easy book or go to a movie to kill the time. I didn't mind killing time when I was younger, but I resent killing time now. (Laughs.) I don't want to *kill* time. I want to *do* something with my time.

Travelling in the big jets and going to and from hotels is very tough. We're in New York on a Wednesday, Philadelphia on a Thursday, Buffalo on a Saturday, Pittsburgh on a Sunday, and Detroit on a Tuesday. That's just a terrible way to live. (Laughs.) After the game on Sunday, I am tired — not only with my body, which is not a bad kind of tiredness, I'm tired emotionally, tired mentally. I'm not a very good companion after those games.

It's a lot tougher when things are going badly. It's more gritty and you don't feel very good about yourself. The whole object of a pro game is to win. That is what we sell. We sell it to a lot of people who don't win at all in their regular lives. They involve themselves with *their* team, a winning team. I'm not cynical about this. When we win, there's also a carry-over in us. Life is a little easier. But in the last two or three years fatigue has been there. I'm sucked out. But that's okay. I'd sooner live like that than be bored. If I get a decent sleep, a bit of food that's good and strong, I'm revived. I'm alive again.

The fans touch us, particularly when we've won. You can feel the pat of hands all over. On the back, on the shoulder, they want to shake your hand. When I'm feeling good about myself, I really respond to this. But if I don't feel so good, I play out the role. You have to act it out. It has nothing to do with pure joy. It has nothing to do with the feeling I had when I was a kid.

'Cause hell, nobody recognized me. I didn't have a role to play. Many of us are looking for some kind of role to play. The role of the professional athlete is one that I've learned to play very well. Laughing with strangers. It doesn't take much. It has its built-in moves, responses. There is status for the fans, but there's not a whole lot of status for me. (Laughs.) Not now. I know it doesn't mean very much. I shy away from it more and more. When I'm not feeling good and somebody comes up — "Hello, Eric" — I'm at times a bit cold and abrupt. I can see them withdrawing from me, hurt. They want to be plugged into something and they're not. They may make a slurring remark. I can't do anything about it.

I'm fighting the cynicism. What I'd like to do is find an after-life and play a little more. I don't have another vocation. I have a feeling unless I find one, my life might be a big anticlimax. I could get a job, but I don't want a job. I never had a job in the sense that I had to earn a living just for the sake of earning a living. I may have to do that, but I sure hope I don't.

I have doubts about what I do. I'm not that sure of myself. I doesn't seem clear to me at times. I'm a man playing a boy's game. Is this a valid reason for making money? Then I turn around and think of a job. I've tried to be a stockbroker. I say to a guy, "I got a good stock, you want to buy it?" He says, "No." I say, "Okay." You don't want to buy, don't buy. (Laughs.) I'm not good at persuading people to buy things they don't want to buy. I'm just not interested in the power of money — I found that out. That's the way one keeps score — the amount of money you earned. I found myself bored with that.

I've worked on construction and I liked that best of all. (Laughs.) I'd been working as a stockbroker and I couldn't stand it any more. I got drunk one Friday night and while I was careening around town I ran into this guy I knew from the past. He said for the hell of it, "Why don't you come and work on the Hancock Building with me?" He was a super on the job. The next Monday I showed up. I stayed for a week. I was interested in seeing how a big building goes up — and working with my hands.

A stockbroker has more status. He surrounds himself with things of status. But the stockbroker comes to see me play, I don't go to see him be a stockbroker. (Laughs.)

The real status is what my peers think of me and what I think of myself. The players have careful self-doubts at times. We talk about our sagging egos: Are we really that famous? Are we really that good? We have terrible doubts. (Laughs.) Actors may have something of this. Did I do well? Am I worth this applause? (Laughs.) When I'm not pushing that puck well, how come the fans don't like me? (Laughs.) Then there's the reverse reaction — a real brashness. They're always rationalizing to each other. That's probably necessary. It's not a bad way to handle things when you have no control over them. Players who are really put together, who have few doubts, are usually much more in control. If you're recognized by your peers, you're all right.

I still like the physicality, the sensuality of life. I still like to use my body. But the things I like now are more soft. I don't want to beat people; I don't want to prove anything. I have a friend who used to play pro football, but who shares my philosophy. We get into the country that is stark and cold and harsh, but there's a great aesthetic feedback. It's soft and comforting and sweet. We come out of there with such enormous energy and so fit. We often go into town like a couple of fools and get mildly drunk and laugh a lot.

Being a physical man in the modern world is becoming obsolete. The machines have taken the place of that. We work in offices, we fight rules and corporations, but we hardly ever hit anybody. Not that hitting anybody is a solution. But to survive in the world at one time, one had to stand up and fight — fight the weather, fight the land, or fight the rocks. I think there is a real desire for man to do that. Today he has evolved into being more passive, conforming. . .

I think that is why the professional game, with its terrific physicality — men getting together on a cooperative basis — this is appealing to the middle-class man. He's the one who supports professional sports.

I think it's a reflection of the North American way of life. This is one of the ways you are somebody — you beat somebody. (Laughs.) You're better than they are. Somebody has to be less than you in order for you to be somebody. I don't know if that's right any more. I don't have that drive any more. If I function hard, it's against a hard environment. That's preferable to knocking somebody down.

I come up against a hard young stud now, and he wants the puck very badly, I'm inclined to give it to him. (Laughs.) When you start thinking like that you're in trouble, as far as being a pro athlete is involved. But I don't want to be anybody any more in those terms. I've had some money, I've had some big fat times, I've been on the stage.

It's been a good life. Maybe I could have done better, have a better record or something like that. But I've really had very few regrets over the past twenty years. I can enjoy some of the arts that I had shut myself off from as a kid. Perhaps that is my only regret. The passion for the game was so all-consuming when I was a kid that I blocked myself from music. I cut myself off from a certain broadness of experience. Maybe one has to do that to fully explore what they want to do the most passionately.

I know a lot of pro athletes who have a capacity for a wider experience. But they wanted to become champions. They had to focus themselves on their one thing completely. His primary force when he becomes champion is his ego trip, his desire to excel, to be somebody special. To some degree, he must dehumanize himself. I look forward to a lower key way of living. But it must be physical. I'm sure I would die without it, become a drunk or something.

I still like to skate. One day last year on a cold, clear, crisp afternoon, I saw this huge sheet of ice in the street. Goddamn, if I didn't drive out there and put on my skates. I took off my camel-hair coat. I was just in a sort of jacket, on my skates. And I flew. Nobody was there. I was free as a bird. I was really happy. That goes back to when I was a kid. I'll do that until I die, I hope. Oh, I was free!

The wind was blowing from the north. With the wind behind you, you're in motion, you can wheel and dive and turn, you can lay yourself into impossible angles that you never could walking or running. You lay yourself at a forty-five degree angle, your elbows virtually touching the ice as you're in a turn. Incredible! It's beautiful! You're breaking the bonds of gravity. I have a feeling this is the innate desire of man.

(His eyes are glowing.) I haven't kept many photographs of myself, but I found one where I'm in full flight. I'm leaning into a turn. You pick up the centrifugal forces and you lay in it. For a few seconds, like a gyroscope, they support you. I'm in full flight and my head is turned. I'm concentrating on something and I'm grinning. That's the way I like to picture myself. I'm something else there. I'm on another level of existence, just being in pure motion. Going wherever I want to go, whenever I want to go. That's nice, you know. (Laughs softly.)

Credits

The author wishes to thank the following individuals and publishers for permission to reproduce articles as listed. All rights reserved.

"**Fury on Ice**" by Hugh MacLennan, first published in *Holiday Magazine*, 1954.

"**The Game That Makes a Nation**" by Morley Callaghan, from *New World*, February 1943.

"**The Sheer Joy of Shinny**" by Doug Beardsley, from *Country on Ice*, Polestar Press.

"**The Greatest Game Ever Played**" by Eric Whitehead, from *The Patricks*, Doubleday Canada.

"**Building the Gardens**", excerpts from *If You Can't Beat 'em In the Alley* by Scott Young and Conn Smythe. Used by permission of the Canadian Publishers, McClelland and Stewart, Toronto.

"**Foster Hewitt from the Detroit Olympia**", excerpts from radio broadcast "Hockey Night in Canada", April 16, 1942. Used with permission of Frederick Dixon.

"**The Siberia of Hockey**", Parts I and II, by Don Cherry with Stan Fischler, from *Grapes*, Prentice-Hall Canada, Inc.

"**The Time of Your Life**" by Al Purdy, from *The Collected Poems of Al Purdy*. Used by permission of the Canadian Publishers, McClelland and Stewart, Toronto.

"**The Style is the Man**" by Hugh Hood, from *Strength Down Center*, Prentice-Hall Canada, Inc.

"**Saturday**" (Part I) by Ken Dryden, from *The Game*. Reprinted by permission of Macmillan of Canada, a Division of Canada Publishing Corporation.

"**Hockey Players**" by Al Purdy, from *The Collected Poems of Al Purdy*. Used by permission of the Canadian Publishers, McClelland and Stewart, Toronto.

"**Incognito at the London Gardens**" by Stan Dragland, from *Journeys Through Bookland*, The Coach House Press, Toronto.

"**The Flyers' Bible**" by Fred Shero, from *Total Hockey*, a presentation to the 1976 International Hockey Coaches Symposium, Research Institute for the Study of Sport, by permission of Dr. Richard Lonetto.

"**Why the Rangers Will Never Finish on Top**", adapted from "Hockey Fan-Antics, or...Why the Rangers Will Never Finish on Top or Win the Cup!", by Jeff Greenfield, from *Hockey Action*, Henry Regnery Company.

"**The Enforcer**" by Martin O'Malley, from *Globe Magazine*. Adapted as part of *Gross Misconduct: The Life of Spinner Spencer*, Penguin, 1988.

"**We Have Only One Person to Blame, and That's Each Other**" by Jeffrey Klein and Karl-Eric Reif, from *The Hockey Compendium*. Used by permission of the Canadian Publishers, McClelland and Stewart, Toronto.

"**Playing Against Orr**" by Roy McGregor, adapted from "September 2, 1963 — Sudbury, Ontario", in *The Last Season*. Reprinted by permission of the author and of Macmillan of Canada, a Division of Canada Publishing Corporation.

"**Hanging Together, Falling Apart**" by Scott Young, adapted from *War on Ice* (pp. 196-219). Used by permission of the Canadian Publishers, McClelland and Stewart, Toronto.

"The Man Tarasov" by Vladislav Tretiak, from *Tretiak: The Legend*, Plains Publishing Inc.

"Way Ahead of the Game" by David Levine, from *Sport Magazine*, May 1984.

"The Night the Rocket Came Back" by Peter Gzowski, from *Weekend Magazine*, March 12, 1966.

"The Sportive Centre of Saint Vincent de Paul" by Hugh Hood, from *Around the Mountain*, Oberon Press.

"Howe Incredible" by Mordecai Richler, from *Inside Sports* magazine, November 30, 1980.

"My Career With the Leafs" by Brian Fawcett, from *My Career With the Leafs and Other Stories*, © Brian Fawcett, Talon Books Ltd., Vancouver, Canada, 1982.

"The Gentle Farmer from Delisle" by Jack Batten, from *The Leafs in Autumn*. Reprinted by permission of Macmillan of Canada, a Division of Canada Publishing Corporation.

"Preface to *Les Canadiens*" by Rick Salutin, from *Les Canadiens*, © Rick Salutin, Talon Books Ltd., Vancouver, Canada, 1977.

"Alma's Night Out, A Play in One Act", by Ken Brown, © Kenneth Brown, 1986. First produced by Theatrepublic Theatre Society, Edmonton, Alberta.

"Hockey Player: Eric Nesterenko" by Studs Terkel, from *Working*, Pantheon Books.

Epigraphs

Marshall McLuhan quotation from *Understanding Media: The Extensions Of Man*, McGraw-Hill, New York; Bruce Kidd from *The Death of Hockey*, New Press, Toronto; Jim Dorey from *Slashing!* by Stan Fischler, Thomas Y. Crowell Company, New York; Anatoly Tarasov from *Tarasov's Hockey Technique*, Holt, Rinehart and Winston, Toronto; Bobby Orr from *Bobby Orr: My Game*, Little Brown and Company, Toronto. Excerpts in "Cooler Heads: Suggestions for Cleaning up the Game" are from Gary Ronberg, *The Violent Game*, Prentice-Hall, New York; and Edmund Vaz, *The Professionalization of Young Hockey Players*, University of Nebraska Press.

Photo Credits

Page ii: Bobby Orr scores in overtime as the Boston Bruins beat the St. Louis Blues to win their first Stanley Cup in 29 years. UPI/Bettman Newspapers, BHP 1668894. *Page iii*: The same goal, a split-second later. © Ray Lussier, *Boston Herald-Examiner*. *Page 2*: Hockey in Dawson City, Yukon, circa 1904. Public Archives of Canada, PA 16329. *Page 3*: Hockey in Victoria Rink, Montreal, 1905. Hockey Hall of Fame. *Page 84*: Gordie Howe with Wayne Gretzky at Kiwanis Sports Dinner, 1972. *The Brantford Expositor*. (Inset) Gordie Howe vs. Montreal, 1967. Scott Kilpatrick, *Detroit News*. *Page 85*: Wayne Gretzky. © Wen Roberts/Photography Ink, Inglewood, CA. (Inset) Gretzky at seven. Hockey Hall of Fame. *Page 226*: The young Maurice Richard, circa 1942. AP/Wide World Photos. *Page 227*: Maurice "Rocket" Richard. Hockey Hall of Fame. (Inset) Rocket Richard vs. Red Henry, Stanley Cup playoffs, 1953. © David Bier Photo Inc.